Praise for Bertrice Small, "THE REIGNING QUEEN OF THE HISTORICAL GENRE"* and her novels

"With its proud, stubborn, beautiful heroine and richly detailed plot, packed with history, adventure, and sexy, passionate romance, *A Dangerous Love* is classic Small."
—*Booklist*

"[An] action-packed erotic tale set in the English and Scottish borderlands. . . . Small again delivers what her fans have come to expect—a strong heroine and steamy romance—in what promises to be a popular series."—*Publishers Weekly*

"Small's fans . . . know what to expect . . . a good story."
—*Library Journal*

"The name Bertrice Small is synonymous with passionate historical romance. [She] doesn't just push the limits—she reinvents them."   —*The Literary Times*

"Ms. Small delights and thrills."   —*Rendezvous*

"An insatiable delight for the senses. [Small's] amazing historical detail . . . will captivate the reader. . . . Potent sensuality."   —*Romance Junkies

"[Her novels] tell an intriguing story, they are rich in detail, and they are all so very hard to put down."
—The Best Reviews

"Intriguing . . . fascinating."   —*Affaire de Coeur*

"[A] captivating blend of sensuality and rich historical drama."   —Rosemary Rogers

"A fabulous late-fifteenth-century tale filled with intrigue and treachery. . . . Bertrice Small provides a great read."
—Genre Go Round Reviews

BOOKS BY BERTRICE SMALL

BERTRICE SMALL

THE BORDER LORD'S BRIDE

A SIGNET ECLIPSE BOOK

SIGNET ECLIPSE
Published by New American Library, a division of
Penguin Group (USA) Inc., 375 Hudson Street,
New York, New York 10014, USA
Penguin Group (Canada), 90 Eglinton Avenue East, Suite 700, Toronto,
Ontario M4P 2Y3, Canada (a division of Pearson Penguin Canada Inc.)
Penguin Books Ltd., 80 Strand, London WC2R 0RL, England
Penguin Ireland, 25 St. Stephen's Green, Dublin 2,
Ireland (a division of Penguin Books Ltd.)
Penguin Group (Australia), 250 Camberwell Road, Camberwell, Victoria 3124,
Australia (a division of Pearson Australia Group Pty. Ltd.)
Penguin Books India Pvt. Ltd., 11 Community Centre, Panchsheel Park,
New Delhi - 110 017, India
Penguin Group (NZ), 67 Apollo Drive, Rosedale, North Shore 0632,
New Zealand (a division of Pearson New Zealand Ltd.)
Penguin Books (South Africa) (Pty.) Ltd., 24 Sturdee Avenue,
Rosebank, Johannesburg 2196, South Africa

Penguin Books Ltd., Registered Offices:
80 Strand, London WC2R 0RL, England

Published by Signet Eclipse, an imprint of New American Library, a division of
Penguin Group (USA) Inc. Previously published in an NAL trade paperback
edition.

First Signet Eclipse Printing, June 2009
10 9 8 7 6 5 4 3 2 1

THE
BORDER LORD'S
BRIDE

Prologue

"Ye'll nae hae my lands nor my lass," old Ewan Mac-Arthur, laird of Lochearn, told his cousin Gavin. "My sister's grandson will inherit, and he's a better husband for my granddaughter, Ellen, than any of yer wild lads."

"Yer proposed heir is a MacNab," Gavin Mac-Arthur said angrily. "Will ye gie MacArthur lands to a MacNab?"

"What the hell would ye know about my lands?" the laird demanded. "Ye live miles from here on Skye. This is but the first time in my life that I've ever laid eyes on ye. Has yer vaunted master nae given ye lands?"

"I hae four sons," Gavin MacArthur said. "One will inherit my small holding. Another will hae my position as one of the lord's pipers, which will gie him a home. The third is a scholar, and hae gone to the Church. 'Tis the youngest for whom I seek Lochearn. His name is Balgair, and he is a fair strong lad, cousin. He would do the MacArthurs proud. Tell me you will at least consider it."

"I hae made my choice," the laird replied stubbornly. "Donald MacNab will take my place, and he will wed wi' my sweet Ellen."

"Ye're a damned obdurate old man!" Gavin said.

"Now, my lords, dinna quarrel," Ellen MacArthur said from her place by the fire, where she had been listening to the two men. She was a very pretty girl of sixteen with thick red-gold hair and lovely gray eyes with just the faintest hint of blue in them. "You are going to live forever, Grandsire." She smiled at Gavin MacArthur. "Please understand, my lord, that my grandfather made his decision several years ago. We are well acquainted with my cousin Donald MacNab. And our people know him, and are content to have him follow in my grandfather's footsteps. We did not know the MacArthurs on the island of Skye were kin to the MacArthurs of Lochearn. Until you rode into our keep today we knew ye not. Ye are a stranger to us."

"I may be a stranger, lady, but I am yer blood kin," Gavin said. "Ye canna deny blood. Yer grandfather's lands and chiefdom belong to the MacArthurs, nae to a MacNab. I hope when I am gone ye will convince him to face the truth of this. Should ye nae hae some small decision in the choosing of a husband?" He smiled back at her, but it was an icy smile that did not reach his dark, fathomless eyes. "Highland women are outspoken in all manner of matters. Certainly this is the most important decision ye'll ever make, lady. Will ye just accept the man placed before ye? Would ye nae prefer a choice? My son is a man grown, and 'tis said he is fair to look upon, and a lusty lover. Ye would make pretty bairns together for this family."

Ellen colored at his words, making the faint sprinkle of freckles upon her face stand out in bold relief. "I know my cousin Donald, and he is a gentle, kind man, my lord. We are very well suited to each other. I am content wi' my grandfather's decision."

"I am pleased to see ye are an obedient lass," Gavin MacArthur said.

"Why should it matter to ye that my granddaughter

is obedient?" the old laird demanded. "She is naught to ye, nor will she be."

"We will see," Gavin MacArthur said, smiling toothily.

"Get out!" Ewan MacArthur roared. "Get out of my house."

"Grandsire, 'tis night already, and the laws of hospitality demand that we treat our guest with courtesy. He will depart on the morrow. Now dinna distress yerself." She got up and moved to draw his woolen shawl about his hunched shoulders. Though it was midsummer, the evenings were chill near the western sea. "I will get ye both a nice goblet of ale, and then we will hae our supper at the board."

Gavin MacArthur left early the next morning, but not before once more telling Ellen to convince her grandfather to change his plans. "Ye're a good lass; I can see it. Ye'll make my Balgair a fine wife."

When he had gone, Ellen told her grandfather what his cousin had said to her.

"They mean to steal ye," Ewan MacArthur said. "I'll nae hae it! I canna protect ye here, lassie. I must send ye south to King Jamie for yer own protection. We canna waste time about it either. I hae nae doubt that once back on his damned island that cousin of mine will arrange to kidnap ye and take ye to Skye. He'll see ye wed to his son in order to force my hand to disinherit young Donald. I'll nae hae it! Tell Anice to pack yer things, for the pair of ye will go tomorrow. And ye'll nae come back until I sense I am close to death. But when ye do ye'll marry Donald MacNab, and I will rest easy knowing that ye're safe. Now run along, lassie, and tell Birk I wish to write a letter."

Ewan MacArthur watched as his granddaughter hurried from his hall. He did not want to lose his Ellen in his last years, but there was no other choice. In King James's custody she would be safe, and the king would follow the laird's wishes should Ewan die before she returned home to Lochearn. He knew the island branch of the family by reputation. They were wild people. He sighed. Sending Ellen away was not the happiest solution for him, but now it seemed the only solution if she was to be kept safe.

Chapter 1

"But I dinna want to leave Lochearn," Ellen Mac-Arthur's servant and companion wailed, and she began to cry.

"There is nae choice in the matter, Anice," Ellen told the weeping girl. "Grandsire is convinced that once his cousin returns to Skye he will mount a raiding party and come to steal me away. He doesn't want me to be kidnapped, and I dinna want to be stolen. We'll be safe at court. I ne'er thought I would go to court."

"I dinna want to go to court." Anice sniffled. "Why must I go? Nae one will bridenap me, Ellen. Do I have to go wi' ye?"

"I canna go wi'out a serving woman, and ye're the one who serves me, Anice. Ever since I grew too big for my nursemaid, Peigi, ye hae been my servant and friend," Ellen said quietly.

"I'll go wi' ye, lassie. Ye need nae put up wi' the likes of *her*," Peigi, who had been helping the two younger women pack, said sharply. "She dinna know the meaning of loyalty or clan, as she hae none."

"Peigi, 'tis cruel, ye are!" Ellen scolded. "Ye know very well that Grandsire considers Anice a MacArthur."

"The old laird's heart is a good one," Peigi replied.

"It isn't my fault I was found on the hillside," Anice said, and her lower lip trembled. "It isn't my fault that me mam dinna want me."

"Born in shame, ye were, and that's for certain, else ye would nae hae ended up naked in the heather. Yer mam was probably little better than ye are, and God only knows the seed from which ye sprouted. Yer mam probably dinna know either. The wild beasts would hae made a meal of ye had the old laird not found ye himself and taken ye in, ye ungrateful lass. Ye would hae nothing wi'out him. He gave ye a home, food, garments to cover yer nakedness, and a purpose in life. If ye let the lady Ellen go south alone, what would ye hae or do? Now cease yer caterwauling, and hurry wi' the packing. The lady must be safe away before the MacArthurs of Skye come calling."

"I thought ye wanted to go in my place," Anice said slyly.

"I'm too old to travel," Peigi snapped.

Ellen hid a smile. Peigi had resented Anice from the moment her grandfather had assigned the young woman to serve her. Peigi did not trust Anice. But when she had protested, the old laird had told Peigi that Ellen needed a younger companion; and Ellen had promised her nursemaid that she would care for Ellen's bairns one day after she and Donald MacNab were wed. Now, however, it appeared that the wedding, which was to have taken place in another year, would be postponed further. Ellen sighed. She didn't want to leave Lochearn either, but her grandfather's instincts were still sharp, and there seemed to be no other solution at hand.

A rider was dispatched that same day to King James with instructions to ride as quickly as he could and find the king. He carried a letter from the laird of Lochearn explaining in full the situation that Ewan and his granddaughter faced. Ewan MacArthur begged the king to take charge of Ellen MacArthur's care, and keep her safe until he sent for her, which would not be until he sensed his death. She was a good and obedient girl, a virgin, the laird wrote. If the king would be so kind as to put Ellen MacArthur in the household of some respectable lady, the lass would earn her keep, as would the serving wench who traveled with her.

Upon receiving the missive from this unfamiliar Highland laird, the king turned to his aunt Margaret for advice. "What the devil am I supposed to do with a good and obedient virgin, Aunt?" he said. And then he grinned wickedly. When he had been a little younger, the king had been terrified of Margaret Stewart, but as a bachelor king, James had needed a respectable older woman to oversee the females at his court. He had called upon his late father's younger sister, now in her mid-thirties. And she had come from her house on Castle Hill in Edinburgh to give him her loyalty and her help.

Margaret Stewart barked a sharp laugh. "I'd tell you to behave yourself, Jamie, but I know how difficult that might prove," she said. She was a very tall, bony woman with the long, straight Stewart nose, fine amber eyes, and auburn hair that was pulled into an untidy bun at the back of her head. When she walked, the princess thrust her chin forward as if to meet all of life's obstacles without fear. She had been convent educated, and was highly intelligent and very well-read. The king had come to both respect and adore her. They were oddly much alike.

"However, this laird of Lochearn has a difficult problem to solve," the princess continued. "But it will be solved one way or another. In the meantime I will take this little Highland flower into my household. She'll be uneducated, have no sense of fashion, and speak in a Highland cant, but we will keep her safe for her grandfather. When I have her civilized, Jamie, I will present her to you once so she may return to her Highlands able to say she met and spoke with the king. *And you will not tamper with the lass, nephew.*"

The king grinned again. "I promise," he said to his esteemed relation.

"I mean it, Jamie. The girl's life is well planned, as it should be. She's promised to the laird's heir, Donald MacNab, the laird's letter said. He's her cousin, and the old man's inheritor. Marrying this lass will permit the MacArthurs of Lochearn to accept a MacNab laird, and that is important. There is already enough trouble in the Highlands for you to contend with, and you don't need any more."

"Many a marriage is planned, but is not celebrated," the king said slyly to his aunt. "How is my cousin, Maggie?"

"Your father, in a well-meaning political gesture, tried to send me from Scotland into England to marry Queen Elizabeth Woodville's brother, Earl Rivers. I had no intention of being a sacrificial lamb upon the altar of futility. The English cannot be trusted, as we well know. I tried to convince your father otherwise," Margaret Stewart said, "but he would not listen."

"So you had an affair?" the king chuckled.

"I looked about the court—I still had the advantage of youth then, Jamie—and chose the man I decided I would enjoy giving my virginity to, and then I let him fuck me well for several months so that he got me with bairn. Oh, your father was so angry to have all his fine plans spoiled, but I told him I would not leave Scotland. It was not my fault he didn't listen." And now it was the princess who chuckled. "My daughter is frail but well."

"Ye're a wicked woman, Aunt," the king told her.

"Nonsense!" Margaret Stewart replied. "I've had no man since Will Crichton, nor none before him. Until you asked me to come back to court, dear Jamie, I was most content living in my house on Castle Hill and reading my books. And your cousin is content in her convent. She will soon take her vows, and it's a good fate for a lass born on the wrong side of the blanket. God bless my brother for dowering her."

"Did you love him, Aunt?" the king asked her. "Lord Crichton."

"Love is a fool's game, Jamie. And you are already proving to be a great fool," she teased him. "But, by God, the people love you, and your lords for the most part love you. You are Scotland's most perfect king, with your charm, your fecund mistress, and your healthy little bastards. But you should begin to consider taking a wife, Jamie."

James Stewart laughed aloud. "Aye," he admitted. "I am indeed a fool where love is concerned, Aunt. I can no longer casually bed a woman. I must care for her, for if I sheathe myself in her she is certain to give me bairns, for my seed is strong. A man should like the mother of his bairns." Then he grew serious again. "You will take in this lass from Lochearn, then, and watch over her? When do you think she will arrive?"

"Sooner than later, unless I miss my guess," Margaret Stewart said tartly. "The old laird's cousin, having been refused, would have hurried home to Skye, gathered a raiding party, and returned with all due haste to take the girl. He will be mightily surprised to learn his quarry has eluded him. If she rode swiftly enough she would not be worth going after at this time. If these MacArthurs of Skye are determined enough, they will wait for their prey to eventually return home. I wonder if Ewan MacArthur's strategy is as clever as he believes it to be. I hope young MacNab is capable of defending himself, for he may have to fight for his betrothed bride."

Gavin MacArthur, being predictable, did indeed return to Lochearn several weeks after his first visit. His son Balgair rode with him. Ewan MacArthur was not surprised to see them. And the moment he set eyes on Balgair MacArthur he knew he was right in refusing his cousin's request. The younger man was rough and coarse. Stocky and of medium height, he had dirty blond hair and light blue eyes. He could neither read nor write his name. Such skills, he told the laird, were a waste of time when all a man needed was a knowledge of how to fight well, hold his ale, and fuck a woman.

"Ye've met my granddaughter," the laird said to his cousin Gavin. "Do ye really think this ignorant bear of a lad of yers is fit to be her husband?"

"He's strong enough to hold Lochearn, and lusty enough to put a bairn in her belly, cousin. What more could she want in a husband and protector? And ye would hae the protection of my lord, the MacDonald of the isles."

"I dinna need his protection, unless it would be from ye and yer kin," Ewan MacArthur snapped.

"Where is the lady Ellen?" Gavin MacArthur asked.

"On her way, two weeks now, to King James. I hae put her under his protection," the laird said. "I told ye that she will wed Donald MacNab and nae other."

"Search the keep," Gavin MacArthur said to his son and his men.

"Go ahead." The laird chortled. "She's gone. Did ye think I dinna divine yer purpose when ye left here? But ye'll nae steal this bride!"

The MacArthurs of Skye departed Lochearn an hour later, Ewan MacArthur's laughter ringing in their ears.

"One day I'll kill that old man," Balgair told his father.

"Not until ye hae the lass in hand," Gavin replied.

"Could we nae send to the king and demand her return?" Balgair asked his father.

" 'Twould do us nae good, for my cousin hae got to Jamie first, and besides, we hae nae legal rights to Lochearn. The girl will come back in time, and we will be waiting. The priest, Father Birk, comes from the isles. I hae asked him to let me know when the young mistress returns. And I gae him a silver penny. He's old and a bit confused in his mind. We'll know when Ellen Mac-

Arthur is coming home to Lochearn, Balgair, for he will let me know. He thinks I am in the laird's favor, for I hae spoken most kindly of Ewan MacArthur. And you will be there awaiting her when she does return."

"But when will that be?" Balgair demanded to know.

"We hae time, my lad," Gavin MacArthur replied. "Now look about ye and see what ye'll inherit one day. Lochearn is a fair land to look upon."

"Why can we not simply slay the old man and take it then?" Balgair said. "I am a MacArthur born. Are Mac-Arthurs not entitled to MacArthur lands?"

"Ye need the lass to make yer claim a legitimate one. If yer clansmen rebel ye hae no power, lad. With Ellen MacArthur for a wife yer claim on Lochearn is a valid one."

"Then I'll wait for her to return, Da," Balgair said.

"When can we return home to Lochearn?" Anice asked for what surely was the hundredth time, Ellen thought.

"When Grandsire sends for us, and not before," she said.

"What if he doesn't send for us? What if he dies, and no one knows where we hae gone?" Anice whined. "I dinna like it here in the south. I dinna like that high and mighty Lady Margaret either. She treats me like a servant."

"You are a servant," Ellen said. "A very spoiled one, it would seem."

"They say yer da fathered me before he wed yer mam. They say the old laird knew it. They say when I was found he recognized me, and that is why he took me in."

"*They* seem to say a great deal," Ellen responded. "But it means little."

"This chamber is a wee one. There is scarce room for the bed and my trundle," Anice remarked meanly.

"Dinna you realize how fortunate we are to hae this

wee chamber?" Ellen asked her serving woman. "We might hae been put in wi' the other women of the princess's household. She was most gracious to us. Now stop complaining and unpack what ye can. I am going to join the lady Margaret in her little hall." Ellen hurried from the room. Anice had done nothing but fuss and wail since they had departed Lochearn. Ellen almost wished they had left her behind and brought Peigi instead. She made her way to the private hall where Lady Margaret spent her afternoons.

Seeing her enter, the princess waved the girl to her.

Ellen came forward and curtsied politely.

"You are settling yourself, lassie?" Margaret Stewart asked.

"I am, ma'am. Yer kindness is appreciated. I dinna nae what to expect here at the king's court. I hae ne'er seen such a grand place as this Sterling."

The girls sitting about the princess giggled at Ellen's Highland accent, and the girl flushed, knowing the reason for their hilarity.

The princess, however, addressed them all sharply. "Ellen is from the western Highlands, and of course she speaks differently than we do. What do you think the English would think of your accents, my lasses? They would consider you barbaric."

"Surely not, madam!" one girl, Katherine Gordon, cried.

"Indeed they would," Margaret Stewart said. "Now apologize to Ellen MacArthur, and offer her your friendship. She will, I expect, be with us for some time."

"We're sorry!" the girls surrounding the princess chorused.

Ellen smiled brightly at them. "Thank you," she said. "And ye must correct me when I speak so that my speech is as fine as yers."

"You, not ye," one girl answered. "And yours, not yers."

Ellen nodded. "I'll remember," she told them.

Margaret Stewart smiled to herself. The girl would fit in nicely with the other lasses in her charge. And she was certainly a pretty creature with her bright hair and pale skin. She was just the sort of lass the king would favor. Petite. Soft-spoken. Round. *I shall have to keep her very close,* the princess thought to herself. The laird of Lochearn would not be pleased to have his granddaughter returned to him carrying a bastard in her arms. Even a royal bastard. *Damn! I should rather be back in my own house reading than overseeing all these women. Why do they bother to come to court?*

The princess was surprised to find that Ellen Mac-Arthur was not the ill-educated bumpkin she had thought she would be. The girl spoke French and English, as well as her Highland language. She had a small knowledge of mathematics and history. She had been taught, she said, by an old scholar who had somehow ended up spending his last days at Lochearn.

"Grandsire was not certain I should waste my time in learning, but he liked the old wise man. He kept the hall well entertained in the evenings with his tales," Ellen explained. "It gae ... gave Bothan pleasure to teach me, and as long as I dinna ... did not neglect my duties my grandsire allowed it."

"How long was he with you?" the princess asked.

"Until he died last year," Ellen said.

"What of your parents?" Margaret Stewart wanted to know.

"They died in a winter epidemic when I was two," the girl answered. "I hae ... have no memories of them at all. My grandsire is all the family I have ever known."

"And the lad you are to wed?" the king's aunt persisted.

"Donald? We are cousins. Grandsire and his grandmother are brother and sister. I've met him several times in my life. He is a good man."

"Is he handsome?" Margaret Stewart asked with a small smile.

"Oh, aye, he is. He hae . . . has fiery hair like I do, and the loveliest blue eyes," Ellen replied with an audible sigh.

The other girls giggled at this.

"Has he ever kissed you?" one girl asked mischievously.

"Nay! I am no light-skirt!" Ellen answered indignantly.

"What harm would there be in a kiss?" the girl said. "You are going to be wed."

"But we are nae . . . not wed yet. My old nursemaid says a man will not buy the cow if he can have the cream for free."

A burst of giggles greeted this observation, but Margaret Stewart held up her hand to silence them all. "Ellen's nursemaid is correct, my lasses. If you expect to make good marriages you should be mindful of your reputations. A man will not wed a lass whose character is besmirched. A road too well traveled holds no surprises."

It was, Ellen realized, an entirely different world at court from the one she was used to living in at Lochearn. A clever girl, she adapted quickly. Her speech grew less rough and countrified. While she was not well-read—few girls her age were—she could speak passable French with the ambassador from that land, and her good manners distinguished her from many of the other young women in Margaret Stewart's household. She was cheerful, and others frankly enjoyed being in her company.

Anice, however, did not adjust to life at court. She was forever complaining; she grew lazy and neglectful in her duties. When Ellen caught her in a compromising situation with a serving man, she had no other choice but to go to the princess for advice. Anice would not listen to her mistress and was even openly rude.

"You will send her home immediately before she gets a big belly, if she does not already have one," Margaret

Stewart said. "I'll send a messenger to your grandfather telling him that Anice is to be returned home, and asking him to send you another lass to serve you. You must have a serving woman, but this girl who came with you is sly and disobedient, Ellen. She causes strife among my servants. The man you caught her with is promised to another, and Anice flaunts her wickedness."

"I am sorry, madam, that my servant has caused dissent in your house," Ellen apologized, and her gray-blue eyes filled with tears. "Anice's life has not been easy."

"Nonsense!" Margaret Stewart said sharply. "Your grandfather took her in when she was found, you have told me, and she has been well treated."

The messenger was dispatched that same day, and several days later Anice, weeping copiously now because she was being sent home, was returned north. Ellen had assured the princess that she was perfectly capable of caring for herself until her grandfather sent another servant for her. And when he did it was, to her delight, her old nursemaid, Peigi, which suited Ellen very well.

The king had decided to keep Christmas at Sterling. Walking into the magnificent great hall for the first time, Ellen was both astounded and awed. Its walls were painted in a rich lime-gold color known as King's Gold. She gazed openmouthed at the roof of the chamber, which had been built in the style called hammer-beamed. The tall windows lining the hall were of colored glass. Stained glass, Princess Margaret explained to Ellen. There were five enormous fireplaces with huge metal andirons holding great logs that burned high and bright. Behind the high board hung the king's cloth of estate, a magnificent tapestry embroidered in gold and silver. The hall smelled of sweet herbs, and there were no rushes upon its floor.

"Wonderful, isn't it?" Margaret Stewart murmured to the obviously astonished young girl with her. She had already found Ellen more intelligent and observant than most of the lasses she chaperoned. "My brother built it.

James had a flair for decor and other artistic pursuits that came from our mother. Alas, he was more like her, and less like a king of Scotland, and hence his sad end. That distinction was not lost upon his son, now our king. But come, Lady Ellen of Lochearn. It is time for you to meet your liege lord."

The crowd in the hall opened before Margaret Stewart as she moved across it, her maidens in her wake, to where her royal nephew sat upon the dais speaking with Lord Grey. Ellen had seen the king before, of course, but only from a distance. Now, up close, she could see he was a very handsome young man, with reddish gold hair and blue eyes. Near him on a stool sat a pretty young woman with dark hair. Ellen immediately recognized Marion Boyd, who was the king's current mistress. She was the niece of Archibald Douglas, the Earl of Angus, and the mother of the king's firstborn son, Alexander Stewart. Two rumors currently surrounded Marion Boyd. The first claimed she was again with child. The second suggested that the king was growing tired of her.

Overhearing her ladies gossiping about this possibility, Margaret Stewart had sharply put an end to their speculations. "Marion Boyd," she said, "disturbs the Church, which would prefer to see the king take a wife and get his children on her. But Marion will not suffer by her liaison with my nephew."

And Marion Boyd still sat in her place of honor near the handsome young king, Ellen noted as the princess brought her forward to meet James IV. He had concluded his conversation with Lord Grey, his head swiveling about, his eyes lighting up with pleasure upon seeing his aunt. She quickly kissed his hand as Ellen curtsied deeply.

"And who is this pretty lass, Aunt?" James Stewart asked.

"May I introduce to Your Majesty his ward, Ellen MacArthur of Lochearn," Margaret Stewart replied.

"Welcome to my court, Ellen MacArthur," the king said pleasantly. *What a lovely lass,* he thought to himself. He thought her green velvet gown flattering.

"Thank you, Your Majesty," Ellen murmured softly.

"Do not look so awed, lass," the king addressed her in the Highland Celtic tongue. "And speak to me in this same language so we may converse freely."

"But I have been working so hard to smooth away my rough edges, my lord," Ellen told him. "Your da did not speak our language. How is it you do?"

"Because I am king of *all* of Scotland," James Stewart said with a small smile. "My aunt tells me you are not the ignorant lass she expected. She says you speak French to King Louis's ambassador."

"I try to set a good example of Scots womanhood, my lord, for the ambassador thinks our women forward, and he says we give our kisses too freely," Ellen replied.

"Does he?" The king was fascinated by this seemingly trivial bit of information. "Do you give your kisses freely, Ellen MacArthur?" the king asked her mischievously.

"Unlike many of the ladies of your court, I do not give them at all, my lord," she told him pertly. "I am betrothed, and I am no light-skirt. When I return to Lochearn, I will return in the same condition as I left it, else I shame my grandfather."

The king smiled a genuine smile at her. "I am pleased to learn that, Ellen MacArthur. I have trouble enough with the lord of the isles. I do not need the laird of Lochearn angry with me. Still, you are a very pretty lass," he said, and chuckled when she blushed.

"My lord, you are too bold!" Ellen scolded him, finding herself comfortable with this king who spoke her Highland tongue and teased her as an older brother might have.

"A man who would be king and remain king must be bold," he told her.

"Aye, my lord, and that I know to be a truth," Ellen agreed.

"Do you play chess, Ellen MacArthur?" James Stewart asked her.

"I do!" she responded. "But none of your aunt's ladies seem to possess that skill."

Again he chuckled. "My poor aunt, 'tis her reluctant fate until I take a wife to shepherd the little featherheads who come to court hunting husbands. She would far rather be in her untidy house on Castle Hill in Edinburgh reading the days and nights away. She does play chess. Tell her I would have you play with her, and if she thinks you are good enough you shall play the game with me," James Stewart said.

"My lord, the question is not am I good enough to play with you; 'tis are you good enough to play with me?" Ellen surprised him by saying.

James Stewart burst out laughing, to the astonishment of those near him. Even Marion Boyd looked sharply at the red-haired girl who had been engaging the king in conversation in that barbaric Highland tongue. The king now spoke in the more common language of his court. "This little wench thinks she can best me in chess," he said. "Well, I should not make her cry. Play a few games with her, Aunt, and then tell me if she is up to keeping me amused for a game or two." He grinned at Ellen, and then turned to his mistress, who was now tugging at his sleeve.

Margaret Stewart ushered Ellen from her nephew's presence. "He spoke to you in the Celtic tongue. I do not speak it. What did you converse about?" she asked Ellen.

Ellen told her, and the king's aunt smiled. It was unlikely she would have to worry about James's intentions toward Ellen. The lass had wisely made her own position quite clear, and the king was respectful of women. He never pursued one who did not evince an interest in his attentions. But he had turned on his considerable charm with Ellen, and quite put her at her ease by speaking the Highland tongue. "Are you a good chess player, Ellen?"

she asked the girl. "My nephew does love a hard-fought game."

"You shall test me, madam, and then judge for yourself," Ellen responded.

And the king's aunt did, discovering in the process that the quiet Highland girl was an excellent chess player. She told her nephew just that, and from then on Ellen became the king's chess partner. She did not disappoint him, now and again beating him, to James Stewart's delight. And suddenly Ellen MacArthur of Lochearn was no longer just a little girl from the northwest. She began to be noticed by the gentlemen of the royal court, but Ellen, while quick-witted and sweet, would not encourage any man. She made it plain to all that she was betrothed and true to Donald MacNab. Oddly she found herself respected for it by both men and women.

Marion Boyd, the king's mistress, befriended her. Aye, she admitted to Ellen, she was indeed again with child.

"Why doesn't the king wed you?" Ellen asked Marion as they sat one afternoon in the private apartments of Linlithgow Palace, the king's favorite home.

"Och, Ellen," Marion replied, "I am hardly grand enough to be Scotland's queen. Nay, Jamie must wed a princess of the blood royal one day, and he will. When I have been delivered of this child I now carry he has promised me a fine dowry and a husband of my choosing. I will have no lack of suitors, and when my bairns are past their infancy they will be raised in their father's house at no cost or trouble to my husband."

" 'Tis a strange way of doing things," Ellen remarked. "When my parents died and there were none but me, Grandsire looked about his family and chose his sister's grandson to follow him at Lochearn. I was betrothed to him so that even though Donald is a MacNab, the MacArthur blood would be represented. And, of course, my virginity belongs to Donald MacNab, as my husband-to-be."

Marion smoothed a wrinkle from her burgundy velvet gown. "Aye, 'tis the way for most women, but when a king beckons you cannot really refuse. At least, I couldn't," she concluded with a small smile.

"He is a bonny lad," Ellen agreed with a smile of her own. "Do you love him? Won't you be sad when you leave him?"

A quick shadow touched Marion Boyd's face, and then it was gone. "I care for Jamie, aye, but I also know my place. I never had any illusions. My uncle, old Bell the Cat, made certain of that, Ellen."

"Why do they call the Earl of Angus that?" Ellen asked.

"Once when this king's father reigned, his nobles had met secretly to murmur against the old king's policies, but none dared to speak to the king directly of their complaints. Finally my uncle Archibald, who does not suffer fools easily, jumped up and said, 'I'll bell the cat!' And he did, though it did little good in the end. After that he has always been known as Bell the Cat Douglas."

Ellen giggled.

"Now I have a question," Marion said. "Why did you come to court if you already had a husband chosen for you?"

Ellen explained her situation.

Marion nodded. "The MacDonald lord of the isles thinks he is every bit as good as James Stewart. He thinks the Highlands are his alone. He will eventually learn to his detriment that they are not."

Ellen listened and said nothing. You learned a great deal at court by just listening. She wondered if Marion understood how powerful the MacDonald family really was.

The months passed, and she had been at court a full year. There was no word from her grandfather, and so she had to assume he was well. Marion Boyd was delivered of a daughter who was baptized Catherine. She did not return to court, and after a time the king fell desperately in love with sweet Margaret Drummond, known as Meg.

Finally in midautumn a messenger came from Lochearn, and Ellen was called with Margaret Stewart into the king's privy chamber. She dressed carefully, as she always did when she was called into the king's presence. "My few gowns are growing worn," she said to Peigi. "And I have no coin to spare for material to make new. I hope Grandsire has sent a purse for us."

"I hope 'tis a request for us to come home," Peigi replied. "I miss our loch, and I miss the hills." She coughed, and her body shook with the sound.

"Oh, do not wish it!" Ellen cried. "He said that when he called for me he would be near death. I have so wanted to go home, but I cannot bear the thought of his dying. And now you are ill with this terrible ague and cough."

"There, there, my bairn," Peigi soothed. "Near death is nae dead, and you'll hae time to bid him a proper farewell. And while I am sick, lass, I will recover. I am nowhere near death." She swore softly as the lace she was tying broke.

Ellen giggled, her spirits suddenly restored. "Take a lace from my other gown," she said. "Perhaps it would be a good thing for us to go home before I am disgraced with these tinker's garments. Then get back into bed, Peigi." She walked over to the little hearth in the small chamber they shared and added more wood. Then, returning to her serving woman, she finished dressing.

Her few gowns were really close to rags now, although Peigi had worked hard to keep them in good repair, and remake them to conform more to the fashions here at the court. But one could do only so much with the fabric, Ellen knew. Her grandsire had sent her with only a small purse of silver pennies, and Margaret Stewart—while watching carefully over her charges' spiritual welfare and trying to teach them something—rarely concerned herself with their clothing. And most of the girls seeking husbands were not of a mind to share what little they had.

The gown Ellen had chosen was of faded yellow velvet. It fit closely with a long waist and sleeves. Ellen knew the new fashion worn by some of the wealthier girls like Katherine Gordon was far more practical, for the skirt and bodice were separate garments. A single skirt might have several bodices, which allowed a girl to look as if she possessed more clothing than she actually did. Ellen sighed as she brushed her hair. She knew she would never have anything as fashionable.

"Ye look as fair as any here at court," Peigi said from her bed.

Ellen smiled. "You love me," she replied. "I'll come back as quickly as I can with the news." And she hurried from the chamber.

Ellen moved through the corridors of the palace. The young guardsmen along her route always looked favorably upon her, and the two at the door to the king's privy chamber smiled as they allowed her to pass. One of them even winked at her. She smiled back and entered into the chamber where James Stewart, his aunt, and another man were waiting. The king and his aunt were seated. The stranger stood. She curtsied deeply.

"You are to go home, my bonny," the king said to Ellen. "I have had a message from Father Birk, who transcribes for your grandfather. He is failing, and wants to see you wed before he dies. You will leave tomorrow and be escorted by my friend Duncan Armstrong, the laird of Duffdour, he who stands by my side now."

"Tomorrow?" Ellen was surprised. She had thought to have a few days to pack when the call came to return. And Peigi certainly wasn't well enough to go yet.

"I know it is short notice, but I am told your serving woman is too ill to travel now. Pack only what you will need, my bonny, and when your servant is well again she will follow with the rest. The reason I am sending you off so quickly is that it is certain that word of your grandfather's health will also reach his cousin on Skye. It is possible he may attempt to intercept you and have his way in this matter after all. I must do what I can to help you carry out your grandfather's wishes, my bonny." He used his pet name for her.

"By coincidence, my old friend Duncan Armstrong has just come to court. He does not visit often, and is not known by my lords from the north. Therefore your little party will attract little if any attention as you travel. And the MacDonald's spies here at my court will not realize you have gone until it is too late. And they will not know with whom you travel. I believe I can assure your safe passage home," the king concluded with a small smile.

"I shall miss our chess games, Your Majesty," Ellen said. "You have been a most worthy opponent for me." Her gray-blue eyes twinkled mischievously.

"Beware this wench, Duncan," the king warned his friend. "She is a most devious lass. I am not certain she has not cheated me on several occasions."

Ellen laughed aloud at this remark. "I do not have to cheat with you, my lord," she taunted him wickedly.

Now James Stewart laughed. "Oho, 'tis unfortunate we shall not have time for another game, my bonny."

"Indeed it is," Ellen agreed.

"Ellen must be presented to Duffdour, Jamie," Margaret Stewart reminded the king. She beckoned the laird forward from his place behind the king's chair.

"Aye, you are correct, Aunt. Ellen, my bonny, this is Duncan Armstrong, the laird of Duffdour, a holding in the borders. And this, Duncan, is Ellen MacArthur, the heiress to the laird of Lochearn in the Highlands."

Ellen curtsied prettily as Duncan Armstrong bowed politely.

"There, Aunt, 'tis done."

"I will see you safely home, mistress," the laird said to Ellen. He was a very tall man, with black hair and blue eyes.

"I thank you, sir, for your escort," Ellen replied. *My*,

she thought, *how handsome he is*. It was unusual for her
to take note of any man, being a betrothed maiden.

"I would like to leave before sunrise on the morrow,"
Duncan Armstrong said. "We are less likely to be noticed by any at that early hour."

Ellen nodded. "I can be ready," she said.

"Come to the stables then, one hour before dawn,
mistress," he told her.

"With Your Majesty's permission," Ellen said quietly, "I will go and do what needs be done." She curtsied
again at the king's nod of dismissal, and hurried from
James Stewart's privy chamber.

"She is a sensible and practical girl," Margaret Stewart remarked when Ellen had gone. "She will travel well.
I shall miss her, for few among my charges possess her
good traits and her intelligence."

"My aunt means Ellen reads well, and discusses her
books with her," the king responded with a small smile.

"Why has she been here?" the laird of Duffdour
wanted to know. "I would have thought a lass like that
would have married several years back."

The king briefly explained Ellen's plight. "That is why
it is so important that she be returned home safely to
marry her betrothed," he said. "The MacDonald is loyal
to those who are faithful to him. If this MacArthur piper
of his wants Lochearn for his son, and by marrying Ellen
he can gain it, the lord of the isles will help his man. But
the old laird has chosen his successor and made his own
plans. Lochearn is his, and he has a right to choose his
granddaughter's husband and dispose of his lands in the
way he wants. Get the lass home as quickly as you can,
Duncan."

"Are you sure you can keep her going a secret?" the
laird of Duffdour asked.

"Ellen MacArthur isn't important; nor is she well-
known here at court. The only people who might be interested in her departure would be those the MacDonald
has here spying for him. Ellen will say nothing to anyone

of her going. My aunt will leave here on the morrow with a party of her ladies to prepare Falklands for my arrival. By the time we reach Falklands in another week or so, anyone watching for Ellen MacArthur, and not finding her, will have no time to send to the MacDonald," the king told his friend.

The laird nodded. "I'll travel as quickly as she can," he promised.

"She rides well," Margaret Stewart said. "She's no pampered lass. But 'tis fortunate her servant is too ill right now to travel, for poor Peigi and horses do not mix well at all. When she can travel, we will send her in a cart. Ellen can manage without her old servant, but how well Peigi can manage without her is another matter." She chuckled.

And indeed, Peigi was not pleased to learn her mistress would depart on the morrow without her. "Ye canna go wi'out me. It isn't decent," she complained.

"You cannot travel now, Peigi," Ellen said. "When you are fit again the princess has said she will send you home. There is no time now to pack all my garments. I intend taking next to nothing in my saddlebag. And we will ride hard to reach Lochearn as quickly as possible. You know how you hate riding. I'm sure the princess will see that you come north in a cart with all my possessions." She sat on the edge of the bed next to Peigi and patted her hand comfortingly.

"I willna see ye wed," Peigi said, starting to weep.

"There is no help for it," Ellen answered her. "Grandsire is failing, Father Birk writes, and he would see me wed before he dies. I'm almost eighteen now, and it is past time I had a husband. I just want you to get well again."

Peigi sneezed several times. Then she admitted, "As much as it distresses me, I really am nae able to accompany ye, my chick. Now tell me who will escort ye."

"The king has chosen a border lord of his acquaintance who has just arrived at court. His name is Duncan

Armstrong, and he is the laird of Duffdour. He's very big, and very handsome," Ellen said with a small smile. "I suspect I will be safe with him."

"Young, then, he is?" Peigi noted.

"Not so young," Ellen replied.

"That's better, then," Peigi said. "A respectful older gentleman. My mind is more at ease knowing that. I wouldna want ye in danger of seduction by some stranger."

Ellen laughed. "He is handsome, but he did not appear to be foolish," she said. "And I am certain that the king would not put my safety into the hands of a rogue." She stood up. "I had best decide what I am to take with me tomorrow."

"Dress warmly," Peigi advised. "It is October, and each new day grows a bit colder, and the nights will be quite chilly now."

Ellen opened her trunk and dug down into its bottom, where she had placed her leather saddlebag when she had arrived at court. Drawing it out, she laid it on the foot of the bed, and then paused to consider. She would wear breeks, a shirt over a chemise, and her leather jerkin with the staghorn buttons. She took out a second chemise and shirt and two pair of knit hose, which she stuffed in the bag along with a hairbrush. She would wear her heavy woolen cape, which would serve as a coverlet at night wherever they slept. Digging deep into the trunk, she drew out last a small blue velvet cap with an eagle's feather in it. Pinned to the cap was her late father's silver clan badge with the MacArthur clan's motto, *Fide et opera*, which meant "By Fidelity and Work." Ellen always wore this cap when she rode out. She set it atop her saddlebag.

"Ye're nae taking much," Peigi noted.

"I don't want to burden the horse. I have what I need: a change of garments and warm socks, a hairbrush. I took the ashwood one. The carved oak one Grandsire gave me when I turned sixteen you will bring with you

when you come home. Now I'm going to go and fetch
you some soup. And I want to speak with the princess to
make certain you are remembered when she leaves for
Falklands tomorrow."

"Go along then," Peigi told her mistress.

Ellen hurried to the princess's apartments. They were
an untidy jumble of books and garments and small musical instruments. It was, to Ellen's mind, the coziest place
in the palace. There was no pretension in any room the
king's aunt inhabited, and, oddly, James, a man who
prized order, seemed to enjoy visiting his aunt in her
own quarters, despite the disorder, no matter the castle
or palace that he was inhabiting.

Seeing her enter, Margaret Stewart beckoned her
forward and then, linking her arm through Ellen's, said,
"We will walk." She directed their steps into her privy
chamber, leaving the door open, but keeping her voice
low. "You are ready?"

"I am, madam, but one boon I would beg. Until my
Peigi can leave her bed—and I believe that will not be
for a few more days—can you make arrangements to
see she is cared for and fed? I know you leave for Falklands tomorrow."

"I will have one of my own women remain behind,"
the princess promised.

"This laird with whom the king sends me north—do
you know him well?" Ellen wanted to know.

"He was one of the border lords who supported my
nephew in the last troubles with my late brother. He is a
good man, Ellen. Set your mind at ease. Jamie would not
put you in his care if he could not trust him."

"Thank you, madam," Ellen responded.

"Go and get some rest, lass. The morning will come
quickly. Farewell, and Godspeed," Margaret Stewart
said, taking Ellen by the shoulders and kissing her on
the forehead. "Tell your grandfather that I said you were
a good lass, and did the MacArthurs proud. I want him
to know that before his end."

"Thank you, madam," Ellen replied, taking up the princess's big hand and kissing it. "It has been an honor to serve in your household." Then she backed from the room and hurried from the princess's apartments toward the kitchens to gather a supper for the bedridden Peigi and for herself.

Chapter 2

It was dark when the little party led by the laird of Duffdour rode out from Linlithgow Palace. The air was raw and chill. A light wind blew across the loch. The riders hunched down into their cloaks, still half-asleep with the predawn hour. And when the day came it was a gray one, although there was no rain until late afternoon, when the darkness arrived early because of the time of year. They sheltered in a small dry cave on the side of a hill, which allowed them a little campfire, over which they cooked the three rabbits they had trapped as they traveled. They ate them with the bread the laird had been given before they left the court. The cold salted meat that had also been included they saved for a day when they could not trap their meal; the hardboiled eggs they had been given they would eat in the morning with the last of the bread.

The cave and its fire gave them refuge from the cold, rainy night outside. Ellen was glad she had worn her heavy woolen cloak. It was not elegant, like the beautiful velvet ones some of the girls at the court had possessed, but it kept out the bitter chill. They had ridden silently the day long but for a word now and again.

When the laird offered her a bit of whiskey from the flask he carried, Ellen seized the opportunity to initiate a conversation.

"Have you known the king long?" she asked him. "How did you meet him?"

"My half brother, the laird of Cleit, is wed to a distant English cousin of the king's. I first met him several years ago when he came to Cleit. I was living there then, for 'twas my oldest brother, Ian Armstrong, who was Duffdour's laird after our father died. Our mother married the Bruce of Cleit and gave him two sons, Conal, the eldest, and young Murdoc. Actually I was raised at Cleit. I barely remembered Duffdour."

"What happened to your brother?" Ellen asked him.

"He was killed at Sauchieburn," Duncan said. "As he had no wife or child the lands and laird's bonnet came to me."

"And have you a wife and child?" Ellen asked him, smiling.

"Nay, there has been no time for me to go courting since King James arrived on his throne," the laird said with an answering smile. "There is still much trouble in the borders, and keeping order isn't easy. And too, Duffdour needed my attention. My brother, Ian, God assoil his soul, had been its laird since he had been breeked, but he was not a man who thought ahead, being more like our father. The house was falling down and needed to be rebuilt. My cotters were living badly in crumbling cottages. I had not a penny, not even one of old King James's black ones, to my name."

"You seem to have survived nonetheless," Ellen noted.

Duncan Armstrong smiled at her remark. "Aye, I have, thanks to the king. He gave me a portion of the revenues he gains from the sale of livestock in the borders. It has allowed me to rebuild my home, and to rebuild my cotters' homes. We even built a church and have a priest. Duffdour is a prosperous place now, which is why I am forever having to defend it from the English." He chuckled. "They seem to think my cattle and sheep are there for the taking. I came to court this time to request royal permission to fortify my village and my house. They will be easier to defend, and suffer less damage from the English raiders that way."

"I hope the king agreed to your request before you were given the privilege of taking me back to Lochearn," Ellen said, laughing softly.

He grinned back at her. "He did. I'm an easy man to bargain with, provided I get what I want, Ellen MacArthur." The laird chuckled.

"Now you must take a wife," she told him.

"Ah, but there is the problem. My sister-in-law taught my brother of Cleit a valuable lesson, and I learned from it. I'll only wed a woman I can love, and I haven't found one yet. But now you need to get some rest, for we will leave again just before dawn. Sleep near the fire, and I will rest on the other side of you. We should be able to keep somewhat warm, and from freezing that way," he told her.

She did as he bade her, pulling her hood up to cover her head and wrapping the cloak about herself tightly. Between the fire, which was kept burning the night long, and the bulk of the man lying by her side she was able to sleep. When the sound of the camp stirring awoke her the following morning, Ellen slipped deeper into the cave to relieve herself. Then, coming back to the fire she discovered a pot of water warming.

"I thought you might like to wash," the laird said to her as he lifted the small vessel from the coals. "We have no basin or cloth, I fear."

"I have a handkerchief," Ellen replied as she dipped it into the water and, wringing it out, washed her face. Then she washed her hands. The heat seeping into her fingers and palms felt wonderful. "Thank you, my lord. 'Twas most thoughtful." He handed her a small stick, and she cleaned her teeth with it. Then she accepted a hard-boiled egg and a chunk of bread from him, noticing that the six Armstrong clansmen and the messenger who had come to court and now returned with them were eating too.

The fire was carefully put out. The horses were saddled, and they ventured out into the dark morning. When the dawn finally came it was a bright one without wind, and they were able to ride comfortably the day long. The second night they stopped beneath a rock outcropping, but no cave was to be found to harbor them. They did not light a fire for fear of attracting robbers, and so their dinner was of cold meat and oatcakes that the clansmen carried. They traveled in this fashion for several days, some of those days and nights being more comfortable than others.

Ellen now rode by Duncan Armstrong's side, and he apologized for the rough mode of their journey. "The king has explained to me how important it is that I get you to your home safely," he said. "I am not a man to shirk my duty. By traveling in the manner we have, we have avoided most travelers, and the farther northwest we go the less likely we are to see anyone at all, as there are no real roads to take. Tomorrow I'll send your clansman on to Lochearn to let your grandfather know you are almost home."

"He is no one I recognize," Ellen said. "I was surprised that my grandsire did not send someone familiar to me, but I cannot know all the MacArthurs of Lochearn."

Immediately the laird of Duffdour was concerned. "You do not recognize the man as one of yours, lady?"

"Nay, my lord, I do not," Ellen said.

The laird signaled one of his men to come forward to ride with Ellen, and then he dropped his horse back until he was riding next to the messenger. "My lady says she does not recognize you as one of her own," he said quietly. "Are you a MacArthur of Lochearn?" His hand had moved slowly to his sword as he spoke.

"Nay, my lord," the messenger answered him. "I am

nae MacArthur. I am a MacNab. 'Tis my master, Lord Donald, who sent me."

"You wear no plaid or badge," the laird of Duffdour noted quietly.

"I could take nae chance of being identified by the MacDonald's spies, my lord," the man answered him calmly. "Ye ne'er know who is watching."

"I had to ask," the laird replied.

The man nodded. "Aye," he said laconically.

"Tomorrow you will ride on ahead of us to let the lady's grandsire know she will be with him in another day or two," Duncan Armstrong instructed the messenger.

"Aye, my lord. If the good weather continues ye should reach Lochearn by midmorning of the day after tomorrow," the man told the laird.

The following day before they were ready to depart the messenger left them.

"Tell Donald MacNab that I am looking forward to our marriage," Ellen said to the messenger. "And tell my grandsire that I have missed him terribly."

"Aye, my lady," the messenger responded.

"I'm sorry we cannot reach Lochearn today," Ellen said with a sigh.

"The way is harder now," the laird noted. "The messenger will be fortunate to reach the keep before dark the second day, but alone he can travel faster than our small party can. Just another two nights on the trail, Ellen MacArthur."

"A few more meals of oatcakes and dried meat," she replied with a small smile. "How I long for a hot bath and a hot supper! I am relieved that my poor Peigi did not travel with us. It would have been very difficult for her."

"I can see you are eager to be home again," the laird remarked.

"I have missed Lochearn," Ellen admitted. "I have missed my grandsire. He is all the close blood family I have left. Donald and I are cousins, but it is not like my grandsire. I can't even remember my parents. Grandsire is all the family I have ever known. I wish he could live long enough to see my bairns and know the warmth of a family gathering once again. The realization that he will soon be gone is painful, and I cannot forgive the MacArthurs of Skye for forcing me from him these last months. He has had no one to look after him but the servants. He has been alone when he need not have been alone." Tears sprang to her eyes, and she brushed them quickly away.

"Family is all-important," Duncan Armstrong agreed. "My brothers and I stayed together after our mam died, but it was Adair, Conal's wife, who brought back the true meaning of family for us. I miss Cleit yet, although I have lived several years at Duffdour. I visit them as often as I can. They have several bairns: Jamie, Andrew, John, and Janet."

"Now you must find a lass to marry and have your own bairns, my lord. I am so happy to be coming home to wed with Donald," Ellen said.

"Do you love him?" the laird asked, curious.

"I am not certain what exactly love is," Ellen admitted. "The king, they say, is in love with Lord Drummond's daughter, Meg. He is not the same man when she is not with him, but when she is he seems happiest. I am not sure I would want someone else to be responsible for my moods, if that is what love does to one."

Duncan Armstrong smiled at this observation. "My brother Conal fell in love with Adair, but he could not say the words to her, and she would not wed him until he did. When I love a woman I shall tell her, so there is no misunderstanding between us."

They camped that night in a dry cave, and the next night on the edge of a wood. Ellen was restless. She could sense her home just over the horizon, but she could also sense that something was wrong. What, she was not certain, but she was overwhelmed with a feeling of foreboding. Her grandfather always said that she had the sight, but she hoped it wasn't so. She had seemed to lose those odd feelings when she was at court, but now within a few hours' ride of her home she was experiencing them again.

She was eager to depart that last morning. They crossed the meadow where they had camped before first light. The horses moved through several copses of wood, up some low hills, and down again, finally coming to the shores of a small, very blue loch. On its far side was Lochearn Keep, two dark stone towers connected by a hall and surrounded by a high stone wall. The horses slowly picked their way around the barely discernible trail edging the loch, finally arriving at the keep's barred gates.

They stopped, and riding forward the laird called out, "I am Duncan Armstrong, and I have brought the lady Ellen MacArthur home to Lochearn. King James sends all here his greetings."

The heavy wooden gates slowly creaked open after a short span, and they rode into the courtyard before the keep. Looking about her Ellen did not recognize many familiar faces, and she was surprised that her grandfather was not there to greet her. He was obviously sicker than she had been told.

Then Father Birk came from the keep. "Welcome home, my lady," he said, but he was not smiling, and she could see the concern in his rheumy eyes.

"What has happened?" Ellen wanted to know. "Where is Grandsire?"

"Come into the hall, my lady," the priest said, beckoning them. "You also, sir."

The laird moved next to Ellen. "What is wrong?" he murmured as they walked.

"I am not certain, but something is not right here," she answered him.

They followed the priest into one of the towers, and then turned toward the hall. It was a small, cozy chamber with a beamed ceiling and a large fireplace on one side of the room. The other side had tall windows that looked out into the court. At the far end from which they had entered was a high board, and at that board sat two men.

"Grandsire! Donald!" Ellen ran forward, but when she reached the foot of the high board she stopped short. She stared hard, and then she screamed a terrible scream.

It was at that moment that Balgair MacArthur stepped from behind her grandfather's chair, where he had hidden himself in the shadows. "Welcome home, Ellen MacArthur," he said, and he smiled at her.

"What have you done?" Ellen cried out. "What have you done, Balgair MacArthur?" Her legs began to shake.

Duncan Armstrong reached Ellen and put a firm hand beneath her elbow to steady her. He gazed briefly at the two seated men. They were newly dead, their blood still draining slowly, but already congealing from and about the wounds on their throats. "I am Duncan Armstrong, the laird of Duffdour, the king's representative," he said quietly. "What has happened here, my lord?"

"The old laird and Donald MacNab hae both met an unfortunate end," Balgair MacArthur said as he came down from the high board. "Before he died Ewan MacArthur changed his will. I am now the laird of Lochearn. And at yer grandsire's request, mistress, ye will be my wife."

"*Never!*" Ellen hissed at him. "*You murdered them!* And now you think to steal Lochearn and to wed with me to make your claim legitimate? *Never!*"

Balgair came and stood before her. " 'Twas yer grandsire's wish that I wed ye, Ellen, my hinny. Ye canna deny me, or the old man's last wishes." He smiled a slow smile at her, reaching out to take her hand.

Ellen leaped back as if she had been scalded. "Get away from me, you murderer," she told him. "I shall return to King James and tell him what you have done! Do you think you will go unpunished? Even your father's master, the lord of the isles, will not condone these murders. And you will bring Clan MacNab down on us, having murdered its lord's youngest brother, you great fool!"

Balgair MacArthur laughed. "Ye're a hot-blooded lass, I can see. I will enjoy bedding ye when we are wed. And wed me ye will this same day, wi' the king's own representative here to witness it." He turned to the laird. "Ye will stay?"

Before Duncan might answer Ellen shouted, "I'll not wed you or anyone until my grandsire and betrothed are properly buried, and then I will have my year's mourning, Balgair MacArthur. If afterward the king orders me to take you as my husband I will have no other choice, but I will beg him to give me to another. Any other man would be preferable to you! Could you not have allowed my grandsire the dignity of a natural death? He was old. He wrote that his end was near." Her eyes were now filled with tears, and her voice was raw with her emotion.

"The old man sent ye no message, my hinny. I sent it. He was going to live forever. It was time for me to take matters into my own hands, and I did. Ye'll be eighteen come spring, and 'tis past time ye were wedded and bedded and wi' a bairn in yer belly. *My* bairn. The next heir to Lochearn. My father tried to reason wi' old Ewan MacArthur. The MacDonald even sent his own representative to treat wi' yer grandsire, but he was a stubborn old devil. He was determined to gie MacArthur lands to a MacNab. We decided nae to wait any longer. A messenger was sent to court to call ye back to Lochearn. And then I came wi' the documents the old man needed to sign, making me his heir and ye my wife. He wouldn't sign them, of course, but then Donald MacNab arrived, for it seems he too received a message from your grandsire telling him to come to Lochearn to wed ye, for ye were coming home at long last." Balgair MacArthur laughed.

"It seems yer grandsire actually believed me when I

told him I would spare the young MacNab if he would
sign my documents. He rattled on about the honor of
the MacArthurs. He apologized to his great-nephew for
what he must do to save his life, and then he put pen to
parchment. It was nae more than an hour ago, my hinny.
As I could nae hae the blood of my kin on my hands I
had two of my men slit their throats. It was quick. Neither suffered."

Ellen had listened to this recitation with horror. "If
I could kill you I would," she said softly. "No one could
love a murderer such as you."

"Ye dinna hae to love me, Ellen MacArthur. As my
wife ye legitimize my claim to these MacArthur lands,
and our children will carry the blood of Ewan Mac-
Arthur. What hae happened here today will eventually
be forgotten. The MacArthur clansmen of Lochearn will
be more content knowing a MacArthur still leads them,
and nae a MacNab. But I am a fair man. We will post-
pone the wedding. First ye will bury old Ewan and Donald. Then ye will hae a month in which to grieve. But
ye'll wed me before the solstice, my hinny, and by this
time next year ye'll hae my son suckling at yer tit."

"I will never wed you," Ellen said implacably.

Balgair MacArthur laughed. "Aye, ye will," he said.
Then he turned to Duncan Armstrong. " 'Tis nae yet
noon, my lord. Ye and yer men are free to go."

"Will you give me your word before God, and in the
presence of this priest," Duncan said, motioning to Father Birk, "that you will give the lady Ellen her month
to mourn? And will you give me your word that my men
and I may depart in peace, and not be followed with
murder in mind? I have done what I was requested to do
by my *friend* the king. I have returned Ellen MacArthur
to Lochearn. I will inform him so when I return to court.
I am expected to return." He smiled coldly.

"I hae no quarrel wi' ye, Armstrong, and I dinna want
the king coming to look for a missing friend here. Are ye
truly his friend?"

The laird nodded. "I was with him on many occasions before he took his throne, and I fought by his side at Sauchieburn."

Balgair MacArthur nodded. "The MacDonald told me to do what I must to gain Lochearn and the lady Ellen, but he would punish my family severely if I brought the king north and down on his head. Go! I gie ye my word no harm will befall ye."

"And your word regarding the lady Ellen too," the laird pressed.

Balgair laughed. "Aye, I swear before God that I shall nae harm ye or yers, and that I shall gie Ellen MacArthur a full month to mourn her family before I wed her."

"Father?" the laird said quietly.

"Aye, I have heard and accepted his oath," the priest replied.

The laird of Duffdour turned to Ellen. "Lady, I have done what scant little I could to protect you. God comfort you in your mourning." He bowed politely. Then he turned again to face Balgair MacArthur, giving him a scant bow, but saying nothing more.

"With your permission," Ellen said, looking at the man she now considered her enemy, "I will escort our guest from the hall."

"Go," he said with a wave of his hand, pleased by what he considered her public show of respect toward him. Like all women, he decided, she could be brought around.

As they exited the hall the laird looked quickly around to see if there was anyone to hear him. There was no one. "I will tell the king of what has happened here today," he said. "Try to hold your kinsman off as long as possible. I will attempt to convince the king to interfere in this matter. But if you cannot prevent this marriage, and there comes a time that you need my help, you have but to send to me, Ellen MacArthur. I am sorry there is naught I can do this day to aid you. My men and I will ride as quickly as we can, for I do not trust Balgair

MacArthur's promise to let us go freely. Keep him with you as long as you can to prevent him from giving the order to follow after us. If he has not already done so." Duncan caught Ellen's hand up in his and kissed it. It was such a small hand, he thought. What could such a dainty lass do to prevent a man like Balgair MacArthur from having his way?

"I understand your position, Duncan Armstrong. Thank you for all you have done—have tried to do for me. God keep you safe, my lord," Ellen said, feeling the warmth in her cheeks when his lips touched the back of her hand.

"Be brave, lass," he replied, and then turned quickly away before he succumbed to the urge to carry her off with them before Balgair MacArthur could harm her. But he knew such a gesture would be a futile one under the current circumstances. He had done what he could for her. Signaling to his men in the courtyard to mount up, he led them back through the wooden gates, which shut firmly behind them, and they rode away from Lochearn Keep as quickly as he could.

With a sigh Ellen returned to the hall, where her captor was waiting for her. "You have arranged for the gravediggers?" she asked him.

"Aye, but there is nae time for coffins. They'll hae to be interred in their shrouds, my hinny."

"Not before the women and I have washed the bodies properly, and re-dressed them," Ellen replied in a firm voice. "My grandsire was laird here. His passing will be treated with the honor and the dignity he was due, as will my cousin's, Donald MacNab."

Balgair did not argue the point. She was right, and he knew any misstep on his part could cost him the loyalty he needed from the clansmen of Lochearn. That point had been drilled very firmly into his head by his father. "I'll play the pipes for them myself," he suggested to her.

"Nay," Ellen said quietly. " 'Twould not be fitting, Balgair. You are now laird here. You have your own piper to play the lament for my grandsire, which is as it should be. You must remember your position here. Now I will find the women and attend to the bodies of the dead." She curtsied politely to him, thinking as she did how very much she would enjoy plunging the dirk she always carried into his black heart. That would wipe the self-satisfied smirk he wore off his too-pretty face. Some, she suspected, would have thought him handsome. Ellen did not.

In the kitchens she found all the women servants hovering nervously, many of them weeping. She had no time to weep. "Lasses," she said in a quiet, gentle voice, "we must prepare my grandsire and poor Donald MacNab properly for their burial. We will save our sorrow for the graveside."

" 'Tis a poor welcome home for ye, mistress," the cook said. Her normally red face was pale. "What is to happen to us all now?"

"Balgair MacArthur will be the new laird of Lochearn—" Ellen began.

"The murderer!" an unseen voice said bitterly. Ellen recognized it as the voice of the woman who personally cared for her grandsire in his old age.

"Aye," she answered calmly. "The murderer. But I must wed him, I fear."

A collective groan arose from the women.

"When did he come?" Ellen asked them, curious to know, trying to extract what information she might, although to what purpose she wasn't certain.

"They rode into the keep about two months ago," the cook said. "This foreign island-born MacArthur and his great troop of about fifty men."

"Yer grandsire knew then he hae been caught unawares," Sorcha, her grandfather's serving woman, said. " 'I hae been caught in my own trap, Sorcha,' he told me, 'and I am too old to defend us all.' He knew then his end was certain. Then Father Birk was forced to write the letter to the king. At first he refused, but this foreign

MacArthur said he had nae qualms about killing a recalcitrant priest. If he would nae write the letter someone else would. They sent a false message to poor young
MacNab. From the moment he arrived he was used to
threaten yer grandsire into cooperating. They kept the
lad in the dungeon beneath the north tower."

"Poor Donald!" Ellen cried.

"But the foreign MacArthur promised to let him go
once ye were home again," the cook said. "Yer grandsire
hoped it was the truth, but 'twas nae. They were killed
this morning as they sat at the high board awaiting yer
arrival. The little whore saw it all, and could nae wait to
come into the kitchens to tell us."

"The little whore?" Ellen looked confused.

"The tinker's bastard yer grandsire took from the
hillside those many years ago," Sorcha answered her.

"*Anice?*" Ellen exclaimed, surprised.

"Aye. From the moment the foreign MacArthur arrived she flirted wi' him. It took only a few days for her
to get into his bed, lady. She flaunts her position as his
mistress, and has now begun to hint she is wi' bairn, the
shameless hussy!" Sorcha said.

Now, here was something to consider. Duncan Armstrong had told her to try to delay her marriage as long
as she could. If Anice was Balgair's mistress, then, knowing her as well as she did, Ellen suspected Anice would
not be happy about his upcoming marriage, although the
girl would realize sooner or later that her lover would
wed. Still, she would be jealous. If Ellen could stoke that
jealousy it might prove to be to her advantage, Ellen
thought. "You have given me much to consider, my
lasses," Ellen told the women. "Now, however, we must
prepare the bodies of the dead for burial. They must be
in the ground before the sun sets this sad day."

The group of women servants, Ellen leading them, repaired to the hall carrying buckets of hot water and rags.
Sorcha hurried to the old laird's chamber to find his finest garment, in which he would be buried. The young

MacNab's clothing was yet in the chamber he had never occupied on this visit. Sorcha looked carefully through it and found what she suspected were the lad's wedding garments. She brought the fresh clothing for each man to the hall, where the others now worked sponging away the dried blood. The woman who made the clothing for the keep took her needle and thread from the deep pockets of her gown and sewed up the wounds as best she could. The laird was bathed and then dressed in a long dark velvet gown trimmed with marten, a length of the green MacArthur plaid across his chest, the clan badge of the laird holding it. His worn leather boots were pulled onto his big, narrow feet.

Ellen gently brushed her grandfather's long white hair back from his brow and, bending, kissed his cheek for the last time. "Farewell, Grandsire," she whispered in his ear. Then, looking up, she nodded to the women to sew him into his shroud, the tears slipping silently down her cheeks.

A titter of laughter broke the solemnity of the early afternoon. It was Anice, who had come into the hall and now stared at the naked body of young Donald MacNab.

"What a wee manhood he hae." She giggled, pointing rudely as she flounced about the board where the body lay. "Now, my lord Balgair is built like the bull in the meadow. That poor thing would hae gi'en ye no pleasure, Ellen. Yer fortunate that Balgair will be yer husband. He's a real man, and wields his weapon with skill."

"I would sooner die than wed him," Ellen said through gritted teeth. "Now get out of the hall, Anice, and go back from wherever you came. If you have no respect for the dead, others do."

"Oh, ye'll wed him, and more is the pity, for ye're not at all the wife for him. He only wants what ye can do for him. But I am the wife for him. At least I'll hae the privilege of gieing him his first son." She patted her belly with a smirk.

"If he is indeed the man you claim he is, he'll already have had his share of bastards," Ellen replied sharply. "Yours will be nothing special."

"Mine will carry my MacArthur blood," Anice spat.

"Ye've nae a drop of MacArthur blood in yer veins," the old cook snapped. "Ye're naught but a tinker's bastard left on the hillside to die."

"Then why did the old laird gie me his name?" Anice demanded of them. "I'll tell ye why! Because he knew I was his son's get on some clansman's wife. I was left out by that woman's husband to die to cover his shame, but God led the old laird to find me."

"Who ever told ye such nonsense?" Sorcha sneered. "That poor good fool who raised ye? My master's son loved only one woman in all his life. From the time he was ten and laid eyes on the lass he would make his wife, he loved her. The old laird worried that his son would not take a woman for his pleasure, but the young master was adamant, and saved himself for that lass. They were wed less than six months when ye were found. 'Tis a pity it wasn't the winter, else ye would hae already been eaten by the wolves."

"That's a horrible thing for ye to say to me," Anice shrieked, outraged.

"Ye're no better than ye ought to be," the cook added scathingly. "Ye're just a nameless bastard, but ye shame the man who gae ye his name by yer wanton behavior. And yer disrespect to the mistress of this keep hae been duly noted, and will be remembered by all who serve here. Now get ye gone, ye worthless piece of baggage!"

"Don't ye dare speak to me that way! Any of ye! I'll hae the new laird turn ye all out, I will," Anice threatened them.

"He'll not turn me out," Ellen said softly. "Now, I have asked you to leave the hall once. I'll not ask again, and believe me, Balgair MacArthur wants nothing more than to please me right now. If I should ask him to give you a good beating, Anice, he will."

The defiant girl actually blanched at Ellen's hard words. Turning on her heel, without another word she stalked out of the hall. The women turned back to the body of Donald MacNab, finished bathing him, and dressed him in his wedding finery, adding his red-and-green MacNab plaid. Cleaned, his red hair still damp, he almost looked asleep. What kind of a man had he really been? Ellen wondered. Well, she'd not know now. What she would remember was that he had been a kind boy when they were children. "Sew him into his shroud," Ellen told the women with a sigh. "I'll fetch the priest."

At afternoon's end on that late autumn day Ellen MacArthur, her plaid tied across her chest, followed the bodies of her grandfather and her betrothed husband from the hall of Lochearn Keep to a nearby hillside, where the two graves were opened and ready. Father Birk led the way, preceded by the family piper. Behind the girl a procession of servants, clansmen, and women followed to pay their last respects to Ewan MacArthur and the young MacNab.

At the grave site the bodies were carefully lowered into the ground. Father Birk said the words of burial. Each clansman and -woman filed past the graves in a gesture of respect as the graves were being filled in. Each spoke a word of comfort or kindness to Ellen. Balgair MacArthur was nowhere in sight; nor was Anice. Finally the two graves were filled in, and Ellen stood alone. Everyone had gone, even the piper. She stood upon the hillside, the sky blazing red behind her with the early sunset. To the east a single bright star had risen in the darkening firmament above her.

Alone. She was alone. She had no one now. Grandsire was gone. Donald MacNab was gone. Duncan Armstrong was gone. Now why, she wondered, had she thought of the laird of Duffdour? Because he was kindness in a world gone suddenly cold for her, Ellen realized. And then she knew with a certainty such as she had never before known: There was nothing left for her here at Lochearn.

The life she had anticipated, looked forward to, had been stolen from her by the MacArthurs of Skye, even as they had stolen those last months with Grandsire from her. She loved Lochearn. She had grown up here, but her months at court had shown her that as long as she was happy it didn't matter where she was. Her memories of her childhood would always be hers. Unless she allowed Balgair MacArthur to take those from her too.

"Fare thee well, Grandsire, and Godspeed to both ye and my Donald," Ellen said quietly in their Highland tongue. "I will nae pass this way again." Then, turning away from the fresh graves, Ellen made her way down the hill in the fast-falling night and entered the keep. She made her way to the hall, where Balgair sat before the fire, Anice in his lap, his hand in her gown fondling a breast. Ellen raised an amused eyebrow at Anice's smug little face as she cuddled with her lover.

Balgair gave her a slow smile, but his hand remained in Anice's bodice. "Ye've buried them then," he said. It was not a query.

Ellen nodded. "I have, my lord," she addressed him formally and politely. "With your permission I would retire to my own chamber. This has been a long and difficult day for me after so many days of travel. I am very weary, and I would be alone to mourn my family. There is much new here to which I must accustom myself."

He nodded. "Aye, ye look tired," he admitted. "Go along then, Ellen."

"Good night then, my lord." She curtsied to him.

"Will ye nae bid me a good night?" Anice whined.

"No, I will not. You are his whore, and it does not behoove me even to acknowledge you, Anice. I will not address you again." Then Ellen turned and walked from the hall.

"Will ye let her speak to me that way?" Anice raged at her lover.

"She's right," Balgair MacArthur said, and then he laughed heartily. "She hae spirit, does Ellen MacArthur." And he laughed again.

Ellen made her way from the hall, his laughter echoing in her ears. At least he had not chastised or scolded her for her speech to Anice. She climbed the narrow stone staircase to the second floor, where her chamber was located. The room was dusty. There was no fire in the small hearth. But before she might return downstairs to fetch a servant to aid her, the door to the chamber opened and several entered, led by Sorcha.

"Come wi' me, lassie, to the kitchens. Cook and I will see ye fed while yer chamber is put in order," Sorcha said, leading her back out into the hall. "It hae been a bad day for us, and I'm sorry ye were greeted with cold and darkness here."

In the kitchens Ellen was seated at the long wooden table that was the heart of the place. Cook placed a full trencher before her and ladled rabbit stew into it. A slab of buttered bread was set next to the trencher, along with a polished wooden cup of watered wine. Ellen ate greedily, realizing that she hadn't eaten since morning on the trail. Her last meal of oatcakes and dried meat, she had thought. She spooned the hot stew into her mouth, almost burning her tongue in her eagerness. She drank several swallows of wine to save herself. When she had finished she thanked the cook, asking her, "May I take a bit of bread for the night? The rations were scant on our travels, and I'm still hungry, but I fear to eat more right now lest I be sick."

The cook looked at the girl curiously, and then nodded. "Here, lassie," she said, handing her a round, freshly baked loaf.

"Thank you," Ellen replied, and, quickly tucking the bread beneath her skirts, she hurried from the kitchens.

Behind her the cook nodded to herself, and wiped a tear from her eye.

Upstairs Ellen found her room now in a most welcoming condition. A hot fire burned in the hearth. There was a basin on the table, and a large jug in the coals of the fire that would be filled with water. Her bed had been made, the heavy curtains now free of dust. Everything smelled fresh. And her saddlebag lay on a chair. Ellen poured some hot water into the basin and bathed herself as best as she could. What she really wanted was a tub, but that would have to come tomorrow. She needed a good night's rest, and she needed to think about how she was going to make her escape from Lochearn. There was no way she would ever marry Balgair MacArthur. There was no way she would ever wed the man who had so callously slain her grandsire and her betrothed husband.

Ellen climbed into her bed. Thank heavens Peigi hadn't traveled with them. Suddenly she was sleepy. The bed was comfortable and familiar, the room warm with the fire. She sighed, and her eyes closed as she fell into an exhausted sleep. It was the sound of her bedchamber door creaking open that awakened her again with a start.

"Who is there?" she called out, and a shadow loomed up next to her bed.

" 'Tis me, my hinny," Balgair MacArthur said. His words were slurred slightly, for he was quite drunk, and he stumbled as he came toward her.

"You have entered the wrong bedchamber, my lord," Ellen said warily.

"Nay, I hae nae entered the wrong chamber, my hinny," he replied.

"We are not wed, Balgair, and I am not your whore, Anice," Ellen told him.

He half fell, half sat upon her bed and grabbed at her hand. "Do ye think that I am a fool, Ellen MacArthur? I saw it in yer eyes tonight when ye returned from the hillside. Ye mean to run, but I'll nae let ye. I promised before God that I would gie ye yer month to mourn before I wed ye, and I will. But I dinna say I would nae bed ye, did I?" He grinned slyly at her. "Ye'll nae run wi' my bairn in yer belly."

"To where would I run, Balgair?" Ellen asked him in what she hoped was a strong voice. "I have no family. No real connections at court." These were questions she had asked herself. But she would return to court, if for no other reason than to fetch her Peigi. And perhaps the king's aunt would take pity on them. *Perhaps*. And Balgair MacArthur didn't have to know it. "Please, my lord," Ellen said, already feeling her throat closing with her fear. "Please leave me be. At least for tonight."

"Ye're a pretty lass," he said softly. "Prettier than yer sister, Anice."

"Anice is not my sister!" Ellen exclaimed. "Has she been telling you that tale her foster mother told her? That she was sired by my father? Well, she wasn't! She's some tinker's get, and nothing more. Grandsire gave her the MacArthur name so she would have a clan, but we share no blood, Balgair."

He ignored her words, saying, "She says ye sent her from court when she caught ye futtering some serving man." He grinned at her. "Do ye like futtering, then?" He moved to pull down the coverlet she clutched to her breast.

Ellen slapped his hand away. "It was Anice who was sent home for her wanton behavior, my lord. I am a virgin. I kept myself for Donald MacNab!"

For a moment he looked befuddled, and then his brow cleared. "She's known other men? Then how can I be certain the wench carries my bairn?" His look was now one of perfect outrage, and Ellen almost laughed aloud.

"If she says she does you may be certain the bairn is yours," Ellen replied dryly. "Anice is no fool, and it would appear she is very ambitious."

"She's my whore," he responded, "but ye're to be my wee wife, Ellen, my hinny."

"Aye, Balgair, I am to be your wife," Ellen soothed

him. "Now go and find your own bed, my lord. It is past late."

"Nay," he growled. "I want to fuck ye so ye willna run away from me. Ye won't run if I fuck ye. Ye're too proud a lass to run to another wi'out yer virginity."

"There is no place for me to run," Ellen insisted.

"I saw the way that laird of Duffdour looked at ye, my hinny," Balgair told her.

"Duncan Armstrong is a decent man, Balgair. He was concerned by what he saw when he entered the hall. Do you think he shouldn't have been?"

"Did he kiss ye?" Balgair demanded. "Did he fondle yer titties?" Reaching out swiftly, he yanked her into his embrace. "Answer me, lass! Did he hae ye?"

"I never met the laird until the day the king told me he was to be my escort," Ellen said, fighting back her fear. "I told you I am a virgin, and I was saving myself for Donald. There was—is—nothing between me and the laird of Duffdour."

"But ye wish there were, don't ye?" Balgair persisted. Putting his hand into the neck of her chemise, he ripped it open and grasped one of her breasts.

"Nay, I do not!" Ellen insisted. This was ridiculous. Balgair was jealous of something that never existed, never happened. What had put such a thought into his head? And then she knew. *Anice!* Anice was attempting to cause trouble between Ellen and Balgair, to fuel the man's jealousies, because she had discovered he was a possessive man who would defend what was his. "Balgair, let me be, I beg you!"

"Ye're going to be fucked, lass. Well fucked before this night is ended. Ye'll ne'er run from me, Ellen, my hinny. Ye belong to me, and I mean to hae ye!"

His mouth found hers in a hard kiss. Her first kiss, and it was horrible! His tongue pushed into her mouth, and she tasted sour wine and rotting teeth. She was pushed back into the pillows as he struggled to climb all the way onto the bed. He was kneading her breast with one hand,

and seeking to get beneath her chemise with the other. Ellen struggled against him with all her might, shrieking with both terror and outrage when that second hand slid up her leg and a finger pushed between her nether lips.

"Now we'll see if ye're telling me the truth," he growled, his fetid breath assailing her nostrils. And his finger pushed into her a short way before he crowed with delight as she squealed. "Ye dinna lie to me, my hinny. Ye're a virgin, and tight as any I've known before. My cock is more than ready for ye!" He shifted his body to straddle her, licking his lips in anticipation of what was to come as she twisted and struggled beneath him.

Ellen hit him with a balled-up fist while her other hand reached beneath her pillow, where she had put her dirk. Yanking it out, she stabbed him with it, almost laughing at the look of total surprise upon his face. "You will not have me, you rutting pig! You will not have me! You won't!" she told him as her anger at all that had happened to her, to her grandsire, to Donald MacNab, was finally unleashed. She could barely see through the red haze before her eyes. Her heart was pounding with her fury. Her arm fell again and again, the dirk plunging into his thick flesh as it found its mark. She didn't know how many times her knife fell, cutting him, but suddenly he collapsed with a loud groan, rolling from atop her and onto the floor.

Ellen lay upon her bed for how long she did not know. There was no sound from Balgair MacArthur at all. Had she killed him? Finally she sat up as the anger drained away. She was covered in blood. Ellen shuddered at its wetness and its smell. Quickly she arose from the bed, keeping to the far side, away from her victim. She tore her chemise off, letting it lie where it dropped. She fetched the basin and washed her hands, and then her body where his blood had splattered. She was shaking now, and struggled to gain mastery over herself. This was no time to go to pieces.

Slowly she drew on clean clothing, realizing as she

did that she was dressing herself for flight. Aye! She had to run. There was nothing else to do. When Balgair's men discovered their master dead, she would be killed. There were not enough Lochearn men to protect her, and frankly she had noted that there was no resistance to Balgair MacArthur from them at all. She suspected that they really would prefer a MacArthur, even a foreign MacArthur, as their laird rather than a MacNab, and the death of her grandfather had allowed them to express their preference—a preference they would have never voiced when Ewan MacArthur was alive.

Where could she go? Ellen considered. The laird of Duffdour was about twelve hours ahead of her on the road south. She would endeavor to catch up with him, beg his protection, and plead for his escort back to the king. If she left Lochearn now and rode the rest of the night, she might find him sooner than later. There was certain to be initial confusion when Balgair's body was discovered, and then a messenger would probably be sent to Skye for instructions. That she was missing would certainly confirm her guilt, but she knew that the men in the keep, and even Anice, would consider that she couldn't escape them forever. They would believe she had fled into the woods, and that they could catch her.

Ellen went to the door and, opening it, peeped out into the hall. There wasn't a sound to be heard. Taking up her heavy woolen cloak—and as an afterthought the round cottage loaf—she slipped from the chamber, quietly closing the door behind her. She turned the key in the door's lock, and then put it in her pocket. Tiptoeing down the narrow stone stairs she peeped into the hall. It was empty of all life but for an old dog that snored by the fire. Ellen followed the stairs down into the kitchens, for she knew the door there was less likely to be barred, and she found she was right. The smell of baking bread assailed her nostrils as she slipped through the kitchens.

The cook appeared to be sleeping at the table, her

head upon her folded arms. She did not stir as Ellen crept past her, but she was awake. Her loyalties had not yet been turned, and so she remained where she was, silent and motionless as she heard the door into the yard open and click shut. "Godspeed, lass," she whispered softly, and then dozed again until her bread would be finished.

Outside Ellen kept to the shadows as she hurried to the stables. She could see that the main gate was guarded, but she knew it was unlikely that the postern gate would be. Once inside the stables she moved cautiously, for she could not be certain where the stable lads would be, but hearing giggles from the hayloft she smiled. Finding her own horse, she quickly saddled the beast and led it from the building across the courtyard, keeping again to the shadows as she moved toward the postern gate. She could hear her own heart hammering as she slowly walked the short distance. And then she gained the gate, and to her relief the key was where it had always been, and the gate hinges made no sound as she opened it and led her horse through. She locked the gate from the outside and pocketed its key with the other. Mounting the beast, she guided it carefully along the edge of the loch until she reached the narrow trail that would lead her south. She stopped a moment before urging her horse onto the trail, looking back across the water at the grim, dark outline of Lochearn Keep. Then, digging into her pocket, Ellen took the keys out and threw them one by one as far as she could out into the loch.

With the postern gate locked, and seemingly without a key, no one would think she had exited the keep that way. They would at first believe she was either still in the keep or had been helped by someone on the main gate. Few, if any, had ever used the postern gate, and fewer knew it had a key. It didn't matter if they finally figured it out or not. She would be long gone. As for her bedchamber, it would first be believed that Balgair MacArthur had locked the door from the inside and was enjoying his victory over the young heiress of Lochearn. But eventually sometime during the day Anice would become suspicious. She would demand that the door be opened, and when knocking produced no results, when no sound was heard from within the bedchamber, the door would finally be broken down. Balgair Mac-Arthur's body would be discovered, and all hell would break loose. But Ellen MacArthur would be long gone.

She urged her mount up onto the trail. A late waning moon had now risen, and the track was just barely visible as the horse picked its way up the hill. The night was cold but still. Above her the stars blazed in the black heavens. Ellen rested the animal a few moments when they had completed the steep climb. She gazed down through the trees, half-bare of their leaves with the coming winter. The keep stood out in stark relief against the night. *Lochearn*. Her home. Her home no more. Ellen knew with a deep certainty that she would never see it again. There was nothing left for her there. It was both frightening and exciting to realize that she had absolutely no idea of what the future would hold for her. If indeed she even had a future. The peaceful, settled life that she had always known would be hers was gone, and she could not imagine what would arise in its place. For now, however, her future entailed getting far away from Lochearn, and as quickly as she could. Balgair's men would not be kind if they caught her. She kicked her horse gently, urging it onward, hoping she could find Duncan Armstrong quickly.

Chapter 3

Ellen MacArthur rode slowly through the chill, dark night, the scant light from the waning moon just barely illuminating the path through the forest. Just before dawn, when the sky had lightened to a pale gray, she crossed the meadow where they had camped the night before she reached Lochearn. She was gratified to have made such progress despite her slow pace. She stopped by the stream on the border of the meadow to water her horse and let it crop some of the green grass, while she tore off chunks of her loaf and slowly ate the bread. Then, relieving herself behind a bush, she mounted up again.

She rode the day long, never seeing a soul. Now and again she would see a deer, or a rabbit would dash from the underbrush into the deeper wood. There was sun, but it was a cold sun. Ellen could already feel the Highland winter coming, and there was snow on the tops of the far, high bens. She did not relish spending the night alone, but as the autumn day began to wane she considered that she had best seek shelter. Ahead of her she saw a fox on the hunt, a sure sign of day's end. The light breeze that had teased at her hair all day disappeared, and above, in the blue sky, a hawk skreeked.

Then ahead of her Ellen heard voices. Her first instinct was to increase her horse's gait, but she realized that while she might have finally caught up to the laird and his men, she might not have. Dismounting, she led her animal forward, keeping to the wood on the edge of the track so she would not be easily detected. There was a clearing, a stone overhang, a fire, a group of travelers. She counted the horses tied to the trees. Seven. Aye, that was right. The laird and his six men. And then she saw him. He stood three inches over six feet, and when he turned Ellen saw his face—his handsome, familiar face.

She stumbled forward with a glad cry, dragging her horse behind her. At once the party of clansmen was on the alert, but the laird recognized her. He hurried forward to greet her.

"Mistress Ellen, what has happened? Are you all right?" And then he saw the bruise on her cheek. His blue eyes darkened with anger.

"Help me!" Ellen managed to gasp out the two words, and then she collapsed.

He caught her as she fell, gathering her up in his strong arms. "There, lass, there. Tell me what has happened." His face showed his concern as his arms tightened about her. "Give me some of your whiskey, Jock," he said to one of his men.

"I have killed Balgair MacArthur," Ellen said, and then she began to cry.

The laird nodded. "Are you sure?" he asked her. "Here, take a sip of this," he said, holding his clansman's flask to her lips. "You looked chilled through."

Still sobbing, Ellen swallowed twice, and then coughed hard. "He wasn't moving when I left him," she said. "Nor was he making any sound."

"Start from the beginning and tell me everything," Duncan Armstrong said. He set her down on her feet and helped her to sit on one of the large stones about the fire.

"After you left, the women and I prepared Grand-

sire and Donald for burial. Father Birk said the words
just before the sunset. When I went back into the hall I
found Balgair with Anice, a foundling raised in our village who had been my servant. I had to send her home
from court for her wanton behavior. He has made her
his mistress, and she is already with child. I asked Balgair
if I might retire, as my day—the last few days—had been
difficult. He agreed. The servants fed me, and I went to
my chamber, where I washed and then went to bed. I
had probably been sleeping no more than an hour or
two when I was awakened by Balgair entering my chamber. I asked him to leave, and he laughed. He said he had
promised not to wed me for my month of mourning, but
he had not promised not to bed me. And then . . ." Ellen
faltered. "I killed him," she finally managed to say, and
then she began to cry.

He had to ask it. It wasn't the gentlemanly thing to
do, but he had to ask. "Did he rape you, Ellen?"

She looked up at him, startled. "He tried," she finally
replied. "But I have always kept my dirk beneath my
pillow, my lord. While he fumbled and groped at me, I
took it out, and I stabbed him. I don't know how many
times my blade pierced his flesh, but when he fell to the
floor with a single groan he made no further cry; nor did
he move. I killed him." She began to cry again. "God and
his Blessed Mother forgive me, for I have killed a man!
How will I ever atone for such a sin?"

"The man was a murderer," Duncan Armstrong
said. "And he was a low cur to attempt to assault you,
Ellen."

"He said he could see in my eyes that I wanted to flee.
He said that with a bairn in my belly I would not run, for
I would be too ashamed." Ellen sobbed.

"It's all right, lass," the laird soothed her. "You were
but defending yourself from an attack. I will take you
back to the king, Ellen MacArthur, and we will tell him
what has happened. Jamie is a just man."

"But the MacDonald tries the king greatly, I know.

And Balgair's family is in the MacDonald's service," Ellen said. "Will not the king want to assuage their anger?"

"James is a just man," the laird repeated. "He will not give you over to certain death. You were protecting yourself, avenging your grandsire, as was your right. Now, do you think you were followed? Or that anyone will divine where you have fled?"

"I was careful, and no one saw me leave," Ellen said. "And I locked my bedchamber door and threw the key in the loch. I suspect it was midday before anyone thought to seek out Balgair in my chamber. And they will not at first consider that I have fled farther than the woods about the keep. They will attend to Balgair first, and then perhaps tomorrow they will spend a day seeking me. After that I do not know."

The laird nodded. "Then we will be at least three days ahead of anyone seeking for you, if they are clever enough even to consider that you have fled to the king. They may believe you have perished in the forest, and your home will be taken as a forfeit by either the MacArthurs of Skye or the MacNabs. They will undoubtedly fight it out for Lochearn. It is unlikely you can ever return."

"I know," Ellen said. "I knew before Balgair came into my chamber that I must leave it for good, my lord." Several tears rolled down her cheeks. "How could I ever eat or dance in our hall again after seeing the bodies of my grandfather and poor Donald murdered in their chairs as they sat at the high board?" She brushed her tears away.

Jock brought Ellen an oatcake, and a small haunch of rabbit he had placed upon a large leaf. "Mistress, you must eat."

Ellen gave him a tremulous smile. "Thank you," she said. "If you will seek in my saddlebag you will find almost an entire cottage loaf I took with me. It's still fresh. Portion it out among yourselves, Jock, and thank you for the whiskey. I feel warmer now." She began to eat the food she had been given.

"Will you be all right if I leave you for a few moments?" the laird asked her, and when she nodded he got up and joined his men. "We must keep a sharp eye out, lads. It's unlikely we'll be followed, but tomorrow we will make all haste to find the king and bring Mistress Ellen to safety. She has killed the man who murdered her grandfather and betrothed husband. We should have a few days' lead, but we cannot be certain they won't follow after the lass for revenge. It is our duty to get her to the refuge of the king's protection. Post a guard, and we will keep watch the night at three-hour intervals."

Ellen slept exhausted that night, realizing only as her eyes closed that but for a brief nap she had not slept in two days. She forced herself to remain awake the next day as they rode south at a far quicker pace than she had anticipated. After several days they came out of the western Highlands and down into the hills about Falklands Palace, where the king was now ensconced. Ellen had never been wearier in all of her life, but she was anxious to beg the king's protection, and to reassure Peigi that they would somehow survive this unfortunate turn in their fortunes now that they were homeless.

Falkland Palace was one of James IV's favorite palaces for hunting and relaxation. It had been built some two hundred years back, and while the king was now considering a new palace nearby, he still used the old one, which consisted of three rectangular wings set about a central courtyard. Its style was considered Scottish Gothic. They rode into the courtyard, and stablemen hurried to take their horses. Ellen could hardly walk at this point, for she was so tired. Duncan Armstrong had his arm about her shoulders as they walked.

"Where is Princess Margaret?" he asked a servant as they entered the palace, and when he was told, the laird directed his steps in the correct direction. The guardsmen at the door to the princess's apartments flung the doors open for them, and they passed through into Margaret Stewart's quarters.

The king's aunt was seated with some of her ladies, discussing a book of poetry, when they entered. Her eyes widened as she saw Ellen, and she immediately stood up. "What has happened, my lord?" she demanded of the laird.

"Please, madam, could a bed be found for this lady before she collapses?" Duncan said. "I will be glad to explain then."

"Peigi," Ellen said weakly.

"And could a messenger be sent to Linlithgow to Mistress Ellen's serving woman? She must not travel north to Lochearn," the laird said.

The princess directed two of her women to help Ellen to the women's dormitory, where she might rest. Then she sent a male servant to Linlithgow to prevent Peigi from leaving, and if possible to bring her back to Falkland. "Tell her that her mistress has returned and is with me." Now Margaret Stewart turned to Duncan Armstrong. "Come, sir, into my privy chamber, where you will tell me what is going on. Should I send for my brother first?"

"If you would, madam. It would be simpler to tell the tale but once," the laird responded with a small smile.

Margaret Stewart nodded. "Katherine Gordon, go and fetch the king to me. Tell him I do not care what he is doing; he is to come with all possible haste."

The girl curtsied and hurried off. She was stunningly beautiful, the laird noted. Gordon. Perhaps Huntley's daughter? Curious, considering the Earl of Huntley's opposition to the young king, but hardly his business. Right now all he wanted to do was go home to Duffdour and begin fortifying it, now that he had permission. He had taken Ellen MacArthur to Lochearn, and he had brought her back when she sought his help. He had been away from home long enough. He would tell the king what had happened, and then he was finished. He wanted to go home.

James Stewart had been with Margaret Drummond when the Earl of Huntley's daughter had come to fetch him. He had not wanted to leave his mistress's side, but Lord Drummond's daughter was no fool. She sent him off with a smile and a kiss to discover whatever it was his aunt had to tell him. The king was surprised to see the laird of Duffdour. He had assumed that Duncan Armstrong would return directly to his own home in the borders after delivering Ellen MacArthur to her grandfather. If he was here, however, then something was wrong.

"What has happened?" the king asked his border lord.

"There has been murder done at Lochearn. I arrived with the lass to discover that the MacArthurs of Skye had taken the keep. The old laird and his heir were tied to their chairs at the high board, where they had both been brutally slain. Then Balgair MacArthur produced a document he claimed was signed by the old laird. It made Balgair his heir, and instructed him to wed with his granddaughter, Ellen. I asked the lass if it were truly her grandsire's hand, and she said it was. I had no choice but to leave her there."

The king nodded. "Is that all?" he asked.

"Nay, my liege, it is not. We departed Lochearn with the new laird's promise to give the girl a month to mourn, for he would have wed her that same day had the priest been there; and he gave his promise not to follow us. We rode for half a day, and then another full day. That second night as the sun was setting Ellen MacArthur came into our camp. She was exhausted and frightened. She says she has killed Balgair MacArthur. He attempted to rape her; she protected herself and fled. She begged us to bring her back to your protection, my lord, and so I have. She is in the Lady Margaret's household now," Duncan Armstrong said.

"The lass is worn out with her travels and her grief," Margaret Stewart said. "But she should not remain here, Jamie. She needs to be in a safe place. A place where she will be no cause for controversy between your troublesome lords. You will remember that the MacArthurs of Skye are greatly in the MacDonald's favor. I believe Ellen once told me that this Balgair is a son of the MacDonald's piper. The father will go to his master, and the master will call upon the king for justice—and for revenge."

"What of the poor MacArthurs of Lochearn, and the MacNab lad, who were murdered?" the laird of Duffdour said. "Is there no justice for them?"

"Nay," Margaret Stewart replied sanguinely. "Lochearn has no influence or power. It is a simple Highland holding. It is not right, but there is the truth of it."

"The lass has had her revenge, and it is fair," the king said. "She took the life of the man who murdered her grandfather and betrothed husband. There is no disputing those facts. When the MacDonald sends to me with his own tale I must render some form of kingly justice to satisfy him and his piper. Mistress Ellen is not likely ever to be safe again at Lochearn. Since the MacArthurs of Skye coveted the holding, I will give it to them as a forfeit for their kinsman's life."

"And the girl?" Margaret Stewart asked. "What is to become of Ellen MacArthur?"

"As you have said, Aunt, she cannot remain here at court. This unimportant little lass could nonetheless prove a flash point for partisan squabbles. We must find a safe haven for her," the king said. And then his blue eyes grew bright, and he looked directly at the laird of Duffdour. "Take her home with you, Duncan," he said, and James Stewart grinned wickedly. "You have already made yourself the lass's champion. It is the perfect solution. And she will be safe. Would any at Lochearn remember the man who brought Mistress Ellen home? It's quite doubtful. Until the MacDonald sends to me, and I may settle this unfortunate matter, the lass can be hidden at Duffdour."

"My lord, mine is a man's house. I have no women in it—not even servants, for I saw the trouble women servants brought to my brother before his marriage. I cannot take an innocent lass like Ellen MacArthur into my home. Her reputation must be considered. One day she will certainly wed, and what would any man think of a wife who spent time in another man's household alone? You must find another place for her."

Margaret Stewart leaned over and murmured something in her nephew's ear.

"You have a sister, my aunt informs me, who bears my aunt's name," the king said.

"Maggie? She's a nun at the convent of St. Mary near Duffdour," the laird acknowledged. "They are an almost cloistered order, and I haven't seen her in years," he said. "Aye, you could put Mistress Ellen at St. Mary's, my lord. She would be quite safe."

"Nay," the king replied. "I will send to the mother superior of this convent, asking her to release Sister Margaret in order that she may chaperone a young ward of mine who will be sheltering with the laird of Duffdour."

"But wouldn't the convent be a better place for Mistress Ellen?" the laird protested nervously. What was he to do with the lass?

"There is always the possibility that the MacDonald could learn where Ellen is, and you are in a far better position to protect the lass than is a convent of almost cloistered nuns," the king responded with a chuckle. "Nay, Duncan, I am putting the lass in your charge. I will see that she has a small purse to pay for any expenses she may incur, for I know you are not a rich man." He looked to his aunt. "When can the lass travel?"

"She must have several days of rest, Jamie," Margaret Stewart said. "And I have already sent to fetch her servant and possessions from Linlithgow. They should both be ready to travel within a week's time, my lord."

The king nodded. "Excellent," he said. "I know you'll do a fine job of caring for Mistress Ellen, Duncan. She'll find the borders far different from her Highlands."

"But every bit as hostile, my lord," the laird said. "The English grow more bellicose every day. I wish we might put an end to it. I had hoped for peace between you and King Henry, but he is as bad as his predecessors."

"I wonder if there will ever be a real peace between Scotland and England," came the king's observation. "This Tudor thinks highly of himself, but 'tis only his wife's blood that gives him legitimacy. There are yet those alive with stronger claims to England's throne than Henry Tudor. I have heard it said that King Edward's youngest son, Richard, still lives. Would his not be the stronger claim?"

"My lord, my brother's wife has told us that her brothers were murdered at Middlesham Castle after King Richard's defeat," Duncan said.

"Her tale was secondhand," James Stewart murmured thoughtfully. Then he brought himself back again. "Give Ellen MacArthur time to rest, and then take her home with you. I will send a message to St. Mary's convent tomorrow. You may expect to find your sister awaiting you when you get home."

The laird of Duffdour bowed and backed from Margaret Stewart's privy chamber. This afternoon's turn of events had surprised him. He would have to send one of his men home to Duffdour with instructions to his household steward to prepare bedchambers for both his sister and Ellen. His cook would have to be ready to create daintier meals. And what the hell was the lass supposed to do to amuse herself in his house? He had a small library. Perhaps that would be of interest to her.

And his sister! Margaret had been the oldest of them. He barely remembered her. He had been five when his father died. Six when his mother married the Bruce of Cleit and taken him with her. Ian had been left behind, as at the age of ten he had become the new laird. Maggie, at thirteen, had shown a distinct preference for the church, and so went to St. Mary's with her small dower portion. The last time he had seen her was after Ian was killed. He had gone to her convent to tell her and ask her prayers for their brother's soul, and for his. Prior to that he had seen her when their mother had died. And before that he could not even remember, it had been so long. How did one entertain a nun? He expected he was going to find out soon enough.

Duncan did not seek Ellen MacArthur for several days. He knew she needed time to rest and recover from her shock. He wondered if anyone had bothered to tell her that she would be going to Duffdour for her safety. After three days he sought out the princess's old tiring woman, and asked after Ellen.

"You'll find her in the great hall with the other lasses, my lord," he was told.

He went to the great hall of Falkland Palace, and stood watching for several minutes as Ellen played a game of tag with the other young lasses. She wore a green gown. They were all flushed, laughing, and he saw they had attracted the attention of some young men, who seemed to head directly for Ellen, whose red-gold hair was like a beacon. He felt a stab of irritation. He knew what the young men at court were about: a rowdy bunch of seducers, and nothing more despite their fine pedigrees.

He walked directly across the hall to her. "I am pleased to find you well after all our travails and travels," he said as he bowed politely to her. "Has the princess told you of the king's decision regarding your care?" He was pleased to see the young men who had been preparing to approach Ellen fade into the background again.

"Why, no, my lord. I have been told naught. Do you know what is to happen to me? I am certain the MacArthurs of Skye will not rest until they have found me." Her pretty face showed her worry, and her gray-blue eyes were sad.

"Which is precisely why the king has entrusted you to my care, mistress," he told her. "You and your servant are to come home with me to Duffdour. My sister, who is a nun, has been sent for to chaperone you while you are in my house." He looked closely at her, wondering just what her reaction would be to this news.

"I cannot remain with the princess's household?" Ellen asked him.

"Come and walk with me," the laird said to her, and he slipped her little hand through his sinewy arm. When he spoke again his voice was low and intimate, for her ears alone. "The king does not wish for your troubles to become a flash point among his lords. They are less apt to if you are not here, not seen. There may be gossip, but gossip dies, especially if there is nothing to be seen."

"But I killed a man," Ellen said in equally low tones.

"The king understands you were but defending yourself from your attacker," the laird told her. Her face was like a small flower, and her lips looked sweet. He swallowed hard, and continued. "The king will wait for word to come from the north, and it will. When it does you will be forced to forfeit Lochearn in payment for the life you took."

"What of the lives Balgair took?" Ellen asked spiritedly.

"That must be decided among the MacArthurs of Skye and the MacNabs," the laird told her. "The Mac-Donald is a fair overlord. When the manner in which Balgair MacArthur obtained your grandfather's lands and his consent to marry you is made public, the Mac-Donald will do the right thing."

Her head drooped a moment, but then she looked up into his face. "When are we to leave?" she inquired of him.

"Is your Peigi here, and is she able to travel now?" he queried.

"She is here, and we can leave on the morrow if you wish it. You have been gone well over a month in the king's service on my behalf. You will want to get home as soon as possible and begin building up your defenses against your neighbors on the other side of the border," Ellen said with utmost seriousness. "We will need a cart, however, for my belongings. But we can be ready on the morrow, my lord."

He nodded. "If we ride hard I can be home in two days. The cart will be but a day behind us."

"Peigi is not good with horses. She must ride with the cart," Ellen said.

"I sent to Duffdour when we returned here. A goodly party of my men arrived this afternoon. We will be protected, and the cart will be protected," he told her.

"Poor man," she said to him with a small twinkle. "You came to court to gain a simple permission from the king, and you have paid dearly for it, haven't you, my lord?"

"A man of good sense knows he cannot beg a favor from any man, especially a king, without giving one, mistress," he told her with a small smile. "I might have been put to a far harder task in exchange for my right to fortify Duffdour than just the care of a pretty lass," Duncan said softly. "You are aware of how pretty you are, Ellen MacArthur, aren't you? I believe I am taking you from court just in time. The king is surrounded by seducers and rakes."

She blushed, but then she surprised him by saying, "The king is a seducer, and the young men but emulate him, my lord."

"And outspoken too." He chuckled.

"What time are we to leave on the morrow?" she asked, changing the subject.

"Just before dawn. The days are so short now it will be dark by midafternoon," he told her. "I would not prolong our journey."

"We will be ready, my lord," Ellen said. Then she curtsied and left him.

He watched her go, and realized he was glad that

the king had put her into his care. He wondered what
James Stewart would do with her once the matter of
Balgair MacArthur's death was solved. The king would
probably find her a husband if he could, but a lass with
no lands and no dower would be hard to place. *Poor
lass.* But at least for the interim she would be safe at
Duffdour.

Their journey into the borders was a swift one. True to
his word the laird set out the following morning even before the sunrise. The skies were grayish with the coming
day. Peigi was mounted upon the cart next to the driver,
with whom she was already chattering. Duncan's party
quickly left the cart behind as they pushed their horses
into a canter and then a gallop, which they sustained for
several hours. When the sun had reached the zenith of
its day's journey, they stopped to rest the horses for a
brief time and refresh themselves. They spent the night
at an abbey guesthouse along their way, and were off
again the following morning at the same early hour. It
was at dusk on that second day when they reached Duffdour Keep.

   It was a dark stone house with a single tower topped
by a slate roof. It sat on the crest of a hill, which gave it a
fine view of the lands around it. There was a small village
below the hill. The cottages were of stone, like the house
above, but their roofs were of sod. Still, Ellen could see
they were well kept, and there was a small stone church
at one end of the village. She could just see the smoke
rising from the cottages as they rode through the village
and up the hill.

   "I can see why you need to fortify," she said.

   "Aye," he said. " 'Tis a fine house, but it stands out
like a wart on the end of a nose, and is a tempting target.
Only because I am known to have a strong force of men
at arms have I managed to keep most of the English
borderers at bay. But there is always some damned fool
who tries to make a reputation by attacking me. We've

been fortunate so far, but come the spring, the raids will begin again in earnest."

"You will build a wall?" she asked as they rode up to the house.

"Aye. We've been quarrying the stone for it over the last several months. Now that I have royal permission we will begin to build, and we will continue as long as it does not snow. I'm starting with a wall ten feet high." He dismounted and helped her down from her horse. "Welcome to Duffdour, Ellen MacArthur."

"Thank you, Duncan Armstrong," she replied, looking up into his face and giving him a little smile. "You may call me simply Ellen, if I may call you Duncan."

"Agreed!" he told her, and then led her into his house.

"Welcome, my lord!" An older man came forward to greet them. "You will find your sister in the hall awaiting your arrival."

"Ellen, this is Sim, my steward. Sim, this is the king's ward, Mistress Ellen MacArthur, who has been put into my care. We will speak on this matter, and I will have instructions for you after I have met with my sister." Reaching out, the laird took Ellen's hand. "Come, and we'll go into the hall." He led her off down a short hall that opened into the house's main hall.

A woman seated by the fire arose when she saw them. She was tall and slender. Her face was enclosed by a snow-white wimple, and her robes were as black as night. "Duncan," she said, "I am happy to see you looking so well. And this will be Ellen MacArthur, I expect. You have had a difficult time, I am told. Well, no matter. You will be safe here at Duffdour." She smiled warmly, and her whole face was suddenly changed from a severe demeanor into a friendly one.

"Maggie," the laird greeted the nun, and he kissed her cheeks. "You grow more like our mother despite your vocation. How much do you know?"

The three settled themselves before the hall's great

hearth, which was filled with huge logs that burned bright
orange and with a crackling noise as golden sparks flew
up the chimney. A servant immediately brought a tray
with three goblets that were filled with wine. He offered
them around.

"In answer to your query, little brother," the nun said,
"the king sent a most careful and fully detailed letter to
Mother Mary Andrew, which he instructed her to give
to me after she had read it herself. I have been told I am
to remain with Ellen until the matter between her and
the MacArthurs of Skye is settled and the king chooses
a husband for her."

Duncan nodded. "Aye," he said.

"I shall be no trouble," Ellen told the nun. "And my
servant, Peigi, should arrive tomorrow to care for me."

"My child, you hardly look as if you would cause anyone trouble," the nun said. "I am astounded you were
quick enough to kill your attacker, may the lecher's soul
burn for eternity. How did you do it?"

"Maggie!" The laird looked shocked at his sister's
question.

The nun looked at her brother, amused. "I have devoted my life to God, brother, but I am not entirely un-
mindful of the world outside of my convent."

"My grandsire gave me a dirk when I was seven,"
Ellen said. "And he taught me to use it properly. He said
I should wear it during the day, and keep it beneath my
pillow at night. He said that he hoped I would never
have to use it in defense of myself, but if that need arose
I should know what to do." She slipped the small weapon
from its sheath, which was attached to the leather girdle
she wore, and showed the nun.

The older woman took the dirk and admired its small
carved bone handle. She tested the blade with her finger,
noting that both it and the tip were well sharpened. "It's
a fine weapon, and it served you well," she told Ellen as
she handed the dirk back to the girl. Then, reaching into
her robes, she drew forth her own dirk. "My father gave

it to me," she said, "with very much the same advice as your grandfather gave to you."

"God's bones!" the laird swore. "You're a nun, Maggie!"

"Oh, come now, Duncan; do you think my vocation and my robes will protect me from violence?" She reached out and patted his cheek. "You are really such a dear laddie, little brother. Every woman—even a nun—should be prepared to protect herself."

Ellen could not refrain from giggling. The look on the laird's face was of pure astonishment. "Sister Margaret Mary is correct, Duncan," she told him. "We are not all entirely helpless creatures."

"Please call me Maggie, Ellen," the nun said.

"Women are the frailer sex," the laird replied. "It is God's law. Man was created first, and then woman from Adam's rib."

"I am pleased to see you know that fact," Maggie said with a mischievous wink at Ellen. "I am not certain that God gave women the task of carrying and bearing new life because they are weaker than men, little brother. But for now it is the supper hour, and I see the servants carrying in the meal to the high board as we sit chattering." She arose. "Come along now, and let us eat. I imagine you are both starving after your long, cold ride from Falkland. We've a fine haunch of roasted venison tonight."

They adjourned to the table, where there was not only roasted venison, but a capon in a sweet sauce, and ham as well. There was a pottage of vegetables, fresh bread, sweet butter, and roasted apples cooked with cinnamon in heavy cream. There was a pitcher of rather excellent October ale to drink, and Ellen found herself eating more heartily than she had in the last few weeks. When the meal was over the two women returned to their chairs by the fire to chat while the laird disappeared in the company of his steward.

"Have you prayed for the black soul of your attacker?" the nun asked the girl.

"I have, every day," Ellen admitted. She had told her companion the entire story while they sat together.

"Would you have wed him if he had not approached you during the month of your mourning?" Maggie wanted to know.

Ellen shook her head. "Nay. He was right. I was considering how to run. How could I live in Lochearn's hall again? The memory of my grandsire and poor Donald, tied into their chairs and murdered, would have made it impossible. And while I know it is a duty to marry the man chosen for you, the truth is that I did not like Balgair MacArthur. He was ignorant, and rough and crude. And I could not have tolerated his flaunting his mistress before me. Poor Anice. She is a fool."

"You know the wench?" Maggie asked.

"Aye," Ellen said, and explained, concluding, "and she told me she was with child already. The clansmen in the north are not so scrupulous about their children. If she births a son he might inherit Lochearn, unless, of course, the MacNabs claim it as a forfeit for poor Donald's death."

"You are well out of it," the nun said.

"But what is to happen to me now?" Ellen said. "I have no land; I have no coin, no dower of any kind. What man will have me to wife? I have gone from being my grandfather's heiress and a betrothed wife to a pauper. I suppose I could ask the king's aunt to take Peigi and me into her service. She is a kind woman."

"You are thinking too far into the future, my child. You must trust in God to direct you. He will. For now— for the next several months—you are safe here at Duff-dour. It is unlikely we shall hear anything from the king before the spring. There will already be snow in the Highlands, which means most travel will cease."

Comforted by the nun's kind words, Ellen settled into the keep. She was given a spacious room on the floor above the hall. It had a large fireplace, which kept it warm. The double window faced southwest, and it was rare in winter for the winds to come from that direction. It had interior wooden shutters and heavy brocade draperies of natural-colored linen and green velvet. The great oak bedstead had matching curtains that could be drawn above the bed for extra protection from the cold. A small table had been placed on one side of the bed. It held a taperstick. There was an oak table near the window, and by the hearth a single chair of oak with a high tapestried back and seat. The floors of her chamber were wood, and a large sheepskin had been placed before the fireplace, a smaller one on one side of the bedstead. To her surprise Ellen found a small interior room just big enough for a single bed, with a tiny nightstand and a taperstick.

Peigi would have her own little nest, although Ellen knew her old nursemaid would not be pleased. But Ellen was. She was long past sleeping with her serving woman, and the little chamber offered Peigi far more comfort than a trundle bed would have given her. The accommodation was really quite good, considering that Duffdour was only a border keep. She considered that perhaps she had been given the finest room. She would ask Sim. She did not want to put anyone out.

Peigi arrived just before the early sunset the next day. She was exhausted with her travels, but pleased with the keep. "It's a civilized place," she said to Ellen. "When I heard we were being sent to the borders I feared for our safety and comfort." Her brown eyes were taking in everything, and to Ellen's surprise she was delighted with her tiny chamber. "I'm too old and too fat to share a bed with anyone now," she said bluntly. "And I like me comfort, my baby."

The November days dwindled away. December brought the shortest days of all. It was cold, and the landscape about them bleak. Their days took on a comfortable routine. Maggie insisted that her brother's priest, Father Iver, say the Mass each morning in the hall before they

broke their fast. Duncan would not gainsay his sister's
wish. And each day they prayed for the black soul of
Balgair MacArthur. God, Maggie had told Ellen most
firmly, had already forgiven her the sin of killing the mis-
begotten mongrel.

After the Mass they would break their fast with a
hearty meal of oat stirabout in bread trenchers, fresh
bread, butter, and cheese. Then Duncan went off to
manage the affairs of Duffdour. Ellen spent her days in
the keep's small, cozy hall, sewing while Peigi knitted
and Maggie worked at her tapestry frame, explaining
that the tapestries now hanging had been worked by her
mother and her grandmother. Twice a week the cotters
came to the hall to have their miseries and sicknesses
tended to by the three women. As Ellen was well acquainted with the making of salves, ointments, potions,
and pills, Maggie encouraged her to replenish the keep's
apothecary. One day each week, accompanied by six
men at arms, Maggie and Ellen would ride out to the
most distant cottages to see to the infirm. On the other
days they checked to make certain that the miller was
grinding the grain in a timely manner, and distributing
the flour fairly so the Duffdour folk might make their
bread; or they saw that there was enough salt available
for the villagers to preserve the meat and fish they were
given. Once the larder in the keep was filled they saw
to the fair distribution of the hunt. For the first time in
many years Duffdour had women managing the domestic needs of its people.

Ellen found she was every bit as busy as if she had
been managing her own home in the Highlands. And
Duncan Armstrong noticed. Noticed that his hall was
cleaner than usual. That there was a bowl of small
branches laden with orange berries on the high board.
That the sheets on his bed were changed with more fre-
quency, and smelled of fresh lavender. The meals put on
the table now offered more variety. The three women
had brought comfort and peace to his house.

One evening his sister asked him if he would ride out the following day with Ellen to the far cottages. "I am no longer a girl, and my bones ache with the damp and the coming winter. I cannot ride tomorrow, Duncan, but Ellen needs to go. There's a clansman's young wife who will drop her first bairn in the winter around the time the ewes are lambing. Ellen has made a special tonic for her. The lass is frail, I fear."

"Aye, I'll ride with her," the laird answered. He was actually glad to have the opportunity, for since their arrival at Duffdour he had been kept busy. The only time he saw her was at Mass and at meals. And he had had no time at all to speak with her. Was she happy? Was there something he might do for her? How could he know if he couldn't speak with her?

Maggie smiled to herself. She had already come to the conclusion that Ellen MacArthur would make an excellent wife for her youngest brother. The fact that it had not occurred to Duncan didn't surprise her. Like most men, he wouldn't wed until he was backed into a corner and the arrangement made for him. He was so far past his boyhood she doubted he could remember it. He was closer to forty than thirty. But he was a good man, and he needed an heir, which would necessitate his taking a wife. As for Ellen, her impoverished state put her in a very difficult position, and she could hardly be considered at her peak when she was almost nineteen. Yet she was still young enough to have children, and Ellen MacArthur was a good lass.

Maggie Armstrong might be a nun, but she had eyes in her head. She could see her brother was attracted to Ellen, even if he didn't realize it yet. Ellen, however, still thought of Donald MacNab and the life they might have had. Had she loved this man to whom her grandfather had betrothed her? Maggie didn't think so. But her life had been laid out for her, and she had accepted what was put before her. She had loved her grandfather, and if old Ewan MacArthur said Donald MacNab was the man for her, then Ellen would have followed her grandfather's decision without question. Love, however, would not have necessarily entered into it.

Most people would have wondered what a nun knew about love, but Maggie knew. She had fallen in love at the age of ten with the son of one of her father's cotters. They had known each other since infancy, for the lad's mother had been Maggie's nursemaid. They romped and played together, and then one day when he was fourteen and Maggie twelve, they had kissed. And they had known in that instant that they loved each other.

But they had also known that the laird of Duffdour would not sanction his daughter's marriage to the son of a lowly cotter. Her friend had been married to his cousin, a match that had long ago been approved by the laird. And her father had decided the dower he had for his daughter was too small to bring her a good husband. So Maggie Armstrong had been sent to St. Mary's to become a nun. She had accepted her father's decision, as Ellen had accepted her grandfather's decision. But she had been resentful of it, even though she realized that without a husband she had no place in the world.

Now she saw a young lass in a similar position. And Ellen was a girl who should have a husband and family. Maggie had discovered over the years that she was not. She was too independent a female. She had worked her way into her convent's hierarchy and now stood in line to become the mother superior one day. Maggie knew when to yield a point. But she loved making things right, and she was going to make this come out right for her brother and for Ellen MacArthur.

She watched them ride out the next day, a smile of satisfaction upon her face.

"Ye're a sly boots," she heard Peigi say as she turned back to the keep.

"Do you disagree?" she coolly asked the old servant.

"Nay," Peigi replied shortly, and she cackled. "You

would hae yer brother safe wi' a good wife, and I would have my mistress safe wi' a good man."

Unaware of the plotting about them, Duncan and Ellen rode some distance with the men at arms until they reached the far cottage they sought. The clansman, coming from the cottage, greeted them. His wife, he told Ellen, thought the child inside her too active, and was frightened. Ellen dismounted and entered the cottage.

"Here I am, Annie, with the tonic I promised you," she said cheerfully. "Laren tells me the bairn is stretching his wee legs." Ellen plunked herself down on the bench by the fire, smiling at the young woman. "Come, lass, and sit with me. Tell me what troubles you, and I will see if I can help you. But first get a spoon, and take a sip of my tonic."

Annie did as she was bidden. "It tastes of peppermint, my lady," she said.

"It will strengthen you for the birth in a few months," Ellen told her. "The king's own aunt gave me the recipe, Annie. Now speak with me."

"The child is so active, my lady, I fear he will come before it is time," the girl said. "And I am all alone here out on the moor. What if the English come raiding?"

"Is yer mam in the village?" Ellen asked her.

"Aye, she is," Annie said.

"That the child moves strongly tells you that he is a healthy bairn, and will live. I am told that as your time draws near the bairn will rest in preparation for his birth. You are fine, lass, but I think Laren should take you home to your mother until the bairn is born, and I will tell him so. And I will speak with your mother. It is better you be in the village near the midwife, your mam, and your female relations. Your fears will subside with the other women about you to comfort you. As for the English, the laird tells me they will probably not raid once the snows come. Another reason for you to go quickly."

The laird and the clansman entered the cottage now, and Ellen told them that Annie would be safer and more comfortable with her mother at this time. It was agreed that her husband would take her this same day.

"But I must return here to protect what is ours," Laren said. "I must keep the signal fire prepared should the English come raiding. 'Tis my duty."

"Good man!" the laird approved.

Ellen bade her patient farewell, and they rode back toward the keep. "He is a loyal man, Laren," she said as they traveled.

"But you did the right thing with the wife. I could tell she was frightened," the laird noted.

"Her fears of the English won't subside. They may grow worse once she births her child," Ellen said. "She is one of those lasses who is just naturally fearful. Would it be possible to put a man without a wife out on the moors? And perhaps give Laren a position in the village? Annie can't live with the loneliness out here."

"He could work with the cattle," the laird said thoughtfully. "I could put one of the older men, a widower perhaps, at the signal fire."

"Do it in the spring, after the lass has had her bairn. Her husband will have gone the winter without her, and she without him. He will be more amenable to making a change," Ellen said with a small smile.

"You're a very devious lass," Duncan replied, smiling back.

"My grandsire always said I had a practical streak," she replied.

He liked her, Duncan realized, and as the days passed he really began to understand what a great loss Lochearn was to and for her. She was meant to be the wife of a man of property. She had been trained from her birth for such a role. She knew how to nurture gently without coddling, and how to be strong as well. And she was certainly easy to get along with, he found. His sister, with whom he had had little association over the years but knew by reputation, liked her too. God only knew that Maggie was not an easy person, but Ellen MacArthur had quickly gained her respect and her friendship.

The Christmastide season came, and Maggie warned him to have some small gift for Ellen, but she would not say why. On Christmas Day, the first of the twelve days of the feast, he discovered why when Ellen shyly presented him with three fine new linen shirts she had made for him.

"Of course, the linen is yours, my lord," she told him. "Maggie found it for me in a storeroom, but the work is all mine. It is the only way I can thank you for sheltering me. I took one of your old shirts to make the pattern, but I can make any alterations needed once you have tried one of the shirts on," Ellen finished.

He carefully inspected her handiwork, and then praised it. "Your stitches are so small, Ellen, that I can barely see them," he said. "I have not had any new shirts in a long time. The last I recall came from my sister-in-law, Adair, several years ago. Thank you!" And then he smiled at her. "And as turnabout is fair play, lass, I thought you might want to make yourself a few new gowns." He handed her a key. "This will unlock the storeroom in the chamber my mother inhabited when she lived here. I did not know of it, but Maggie did. I realized most of your clothing was left behind at Lochearn but the little you brought to court."

Quick tears sprang into Ellen's soft gray-blue eyes. "Thank you, my lord," she said, her voice trembling just slightly. "I have, I fear, become a bit shabby."

Sister Margaret Mary gave a small smile as she watched her brother and Ellen. *Yes,* she thought to herself, *God will answer my prayers in this particular matter.*

The winter passed in relative quiet. The snows came down from the north and covered the earth around them. But the hall was warm, and the days began to grow longer. Ellen found herself managing the daily affairs of the keep when Sim, the laird's steward, began coming to her for this and for that. She did not wish to appear forward, but Maggie assured her that the place needed a woman's touch. And so the days seemed to fly by. In the evening they would sit, the three of them, close by the fire talking or sometimes playing chess. Maggie appeared to be particularly skilled at the game.

"You're too clever, sister," the laird said one evening. "And here I assumed you spent all of your time on your knees in prayer at your convent. It would seem otherwise."

"Chess," Maggie told her sibling, "is a game of strategy and skill, Duncan. Like most men you are too impatient. Check. And mate." She took his king and smiled.

Ellen burst out laughing at the look of surprise upon the laird's face.

Then Maggie laughed too, unable to help herself.

"So," the laird said, and a wicked look came into his eye, "you find my helplessness before this religious charlatan amusing, Mistress MacArthur, do you?" He stood up. "I think you need a lesson in respect for your host." He stalked her.

Still giggling, Ellen jumped up, putting a chair between them. "I am most respectful of those deserving my esteem, my lord," she told him. "Your sister certainly has my admiration for her dexterity in the game of chess."

"Ho! Now you have added insult to my wounded pride, mistress. You will have to pay the price for your impudence, I fear." And, swiftly yanking the chair between them away, he reached out and began to tickle her.

Ellen squirmed in his grasp, laughing until her eyes teared up. "Stop! Stop!" she cried. "Ohh, I can bear no more! Stop, Duncan!"

And suddenly he did. They stood staring at each other for a long moment. Ellen was flushed prettily. Her heart was beating too quickly, she thought. He wanted to kiss those cherry lips, the laird considered as he gazed down into her upturned little face. What would she think if he did? he wondered.

"Well," Maggie's voice came breaking into the magic of the moment, "I think we have all had enough excitement for the night."

"Aye," Ellen agreed, lowering her eyes from his. For the briefest moment she had been lost in his gaze. It had enveloped her like a warm coverlet, leaving her feeling weak.

"Aye," the laird said. He wanted to protect her. To care for her. To cherish her. But Ellen MacArthur was the king's responsibility. Duncan had no rights to her.

Chapter 4

The spring was coming. Work on the defensive walls surrounding Duffdour increased with urgent rapidity, for the milder weather and the melting snows would usher in a new season of border raids. The meadow nearest the keep was greening, and the laird's sheep and lambs were allowed from their pens. His small herd of cattle had been increased with the birth of several calves. And two of his mares had dropped foals, a filly and a colt. Large wooden gates banded and studded with iron were being built for the outer walls, which had been placed at the foot of the rise upon which the keep stood. Near the top of the rise the laird had decided to dig a moat.

"Will you enlarge the keep?" Maggie asked, curious,

Duncan shook his head. "Nay, but I shall erect a smaller inner wall about the house, which will allow us to withstand a siege should the outer walls be breached. The stream that cuts across the hill can be used to keep the moat filled. We will have a drawbridge with a portcullis, and smaller gates. We have a well already dug by the kitchens. My permission from the king says I may do all, whatever is necessary to secure Duffdour. The barn will sit in the larger outer courtyard, the stables within the smaller. If war comes—and it will certainly come again, given the current state of affairs between our King James and their King Henry—Duffdour will be safer than most. And the outer court is large enough for us to shelter my cattle, my sheep, and my cotters. I am tired of seeing them taken off by the English."

"You steal from them," Maggie noted.

"But I don't want to," the laird answered her. "I want to live in peace, with my wife and bairns about me."

"You have no wife," Maggie said pointedly.

"I will one day," he responded.

"Duncan," his older sister said patiently, "has it occurred to you that you are no longer a youth in your prime? You are well past thirty. *Well* past," she told him sharply. "You need to take a wife. *Now!* You need an heir. *Now!* Not one day."

"I won't marry until I find a woman to love," Duncan Armstrong said. "I well recall how my half brother Conal Bruce struggled to keep from surrendering to that tender emotion. We could all see he loved his Adair, but he could not bring himself to admit it to her. He thought to love was a weakness, but it is not. Love is an incredible strength, sister, and I would have that wondrous power for my own."

"You surprise me, Duncan," the nun said.

"Do I?" He smiled at her. "I am glad I can surprise you, Maggie. But tell me where I am to find a lass to fall in love with, and I will do my best to comply."

"What of Ellen MacArthur?" the nun asked.

"Ellen?" He smiled. "Her fate is in the king's hands and not mine, Maggie. I know I have said it is unlikely she will ever return to Lochearn. But there is always the chance the king will come to an accommodation with the MacDonald and his MacArthur piper for the death of Balgair MacArthur. He could choose one of his own strong supporters to wed with Ellen and hold Lochearn for him. I am the master of Duffdour. I cannot wed into the Highlands even for the king; nor would James Stewart ask it of me."

April came, and May. Then one day a royal messenger rode through Duffdour's newly hung gates and up to the keep. The parchment he handed to the laird, once unrolled, revealed a command to court. The laird of Duffdour was to come in the company of Ellen MacArthur of Lochearn, chaperoned by Sister Margaret Mary of St. Mary's convent, with all possible speed to Sterling, where the king was currently in residence.

Peigi packed up her mistress's few belongings, grumbling as she did that she was weary of being a nomad. That they had no more life than a tinker who traveled from place to place, with nothing to really call their own. Ellen restrained her amusement, reminding her servant that they had moved from castle to castle when they were with Princess Margaret's household. Peigi gave her a jaundiced look.

"Aye, tinkers," she said, sourly slamming the lid of the little wooden trunk shut. "Will we ever hae another place to really call our own, my bairn? I dinna see why we canna return to Lochearn. Ye were but defending yerself when ye killed the fellow. And ye tell me he did murder the old laird and poor young Donald MacNab." She would not dignify Balgair MacArthur by even speaking his name.

"All of that is truth," Ellen admitted, "but I suspect Balgair's father and the MacDonald might not see it that way. Lochearn is lost to me. The king said it himself."

They departed Duffdour several days later, arriving at the king's current residence several days after that. Ellen, Maggie, and Peigi were immediately brought to the king's aunt, where they would be sheltered. The laird sought out the king, who had just returned from hunting with his lords. James Stewart waved his companions aside and beckoned to Duncan Armstrong as a servant ran to take his kill, and another put a goblet of wine into his gloved hand.

"Duncan! Are your defenses built yet?" the king asked.

"The outer walls are just about finished and the gates hung," the laird said. "Perhaps in the autumn you will come and stay, my lord. The grouse hunting is particularly good about Duffdour. Mine isn't a large or great keep, but I think you will not find my hospitality lacking."

"I should like that," the king replied. Then he grew serious. "You have brought Mistress Ellen MacArthur with you, as I requested?"

"I have, my lord. She is chaperoned by her servant and my sister," the laird said.

"Give me an hour, and then bring them to my privy chamber," the king said.

"There is news from Lochearn?"

"There is news," came the reply. "One hour," the king repeated, quaffing the wine in his cup. "The matter shall be ended today, Duncan." Then he waved the laird from his presence.

Duncan Armstrong immediately sought out Ellen and his sister in the princess's apartments. He did not see them, but Margaret Stewart's chief serving woman said, "I will tell young Ellen, my lord, and she will be ready when you come again to escort her."

Upon hearing she was to see the king in an hour, Ellen called to Peigi to help her dress. "I cannot go into the king's presence dressed for the road," she said. "Unpack my spring green gown, and fetch warm water for washing." She sat down on a settle by the fire and began to unbraid her hair so she might brush the dust from it.

Peigi hurried off to do her mistress's bidding.

"One of the advantages of my position in life," Maggie said with a small grin. "Having no wardrobe but that which I wear I have only to wash my face and hands and shake the road from my skirts."

Ellen laughed. "Not fair!" she said. "But if truth be known I should far rather have my pretty green gown. It won't be as fashionable as what you will see here at court, but I am content, and no peacock. Your mother's storage chamber was wonderful!"

"You should have made more than two gowns," Maggie scolded gently.

Ellen shook her head. "Where would I wear them? Two is more than enough for a lass like me. And I was able to repair my other garments so they're no longer so shabby."

Peigi brought the warm water in a basin, and Ellen stepped behind a small wooden screen, washed herself, and put on her bright green gown. It was soft wool, and tight-fitting, with long sleeves that hugged her arms, a long waist, and a low vee neckline. Her girdle was leather, studded with rounds of green malachite. Her long red-gold hair was brushed and loose beneath a modest sheer veil of white lawn. She had no jewelry but a small silver clan badge that Grandsire had given her. She pinned it to her gown.

When they were ready to go she was surprised to find that the king's aunt was to accompany them. Ellen was not certain if she should be frightened by this or encouraged to have these three older women as her protectors. Did she need protection? She would soon find out. The princess led the way through the castle to her nephew's privy chamber, where James Stewart and Duncan Armstrong awaited.

Ellen curtsied low to the king and gave him a tremulous smile.

"We are pleased to see you looking so well, Ellen MacArthur," the king said, unable to keep his eyes from going to her breasts. Indeed, she was looking well, he thought to himself, and then, seeing his aunt's sharp look, he smiled at the girl. "Now, though I would not bring you pain, mistress, I would once again hear the story you told me last autumn when you begged my protection."

Startled by the request, Ellen repeated the story she had told the king several months back. Why, she wondered, did he want to hear it again?

"You say you killed Balgair MacArthur when he attempted to assault you?"

"Aye, my lord," Ellen replied.

"You are certain you killed him?"

"My lord, the groan he gave when I stabbed him was terrible to hear. After he fell to the floor he did not move again; nor did I hear a sound from him. It took me several very long minutes to compose myself, dress, and flee my bedchamber. It took time for me to get to the stable, to saddle my horse, to get through the postern gate and escape. At no time was the alarm raised, because I killed him and no one yet knew it. I have, under the guidance of Sister Margaret Mary, prayed each day for the repose of his soul, and for God to forgive my taking the life of another."

A look of tender compassion crossed the young king's handsome face. Then he said, "God has spared you a great sin, Mistress Ellen. Balgair MacArthur is not dead."

Ellen's small hand flew to her mouth. "God help me," she half whispered, and then she felt the nun's hand slip into hers and squeeze it hard.

"He is here, my bonny." The king tried to comfort the pale girl by using the nickname he had christened her with when she had lived with the court. "You must face him before you can be free of him." He turned to his personal page. "Bring him in, lad."

Duncan Armstrong's hand went automatically to his blade.

"Be brave, child," the king's aunt whispered.

Ellen began to tremble as the door opened.

Balgair MacArthur stepped into the king's privy chamber. None of them was certain which of them gasped at the sight of his face. A long, raised reddish scar traversed it from his left eyebrow, across his cheek, and

below his jawline. A small scar ran across his right cheek
to the edge of his mouth. He bowed to the king, and
then his eyes found Ellen. He attempted a smile, but the
scar on his right cheek made the smile crooked.

"Wife," he said to her. His cruel gaze mocked her.

"I am not your wife, Balgair," Ellen said quietly. But
her heart beat wildly.

"My lord, if I may speak," Balgair asked the king, and
James nodded his consent. "Despite her assault upon
me, an attack that almost cost me my life, I would hae
her back. I will wed her this day before God and before
ye, my liege. Send for yer priest, my lord!" His voice was
rough and whispery to their ears. "She was promised to
me by her grandfather, and I will hae her though she
be a treacherous bitch. Lochearn will nae be fully mine
wi'out her. I will nae go back wi'out her. She belongs
to me!" He turned and stepped toward Ellen, his hand
reaching for her. "Ye're mine, and I'll let nae another
hae ye, Ellen MacArthur!"

Ellen shrank back as fear filled her. Then she crum-
pled to the floor with a small cry of horror. Immediately
Peigi and Maggie were kneeling to tend to the fallen
girl.

Margaret Stewart looked sharply at her nephew, and
then she turned to Balgair MacArthur. "The wench will
be punished for her insolence, of course, my lord, will
she not? Your wounds are fearful, and was your voice
damaged by her knife? Your tones are low, rough, and
harsh."

"Aye, my voice was badly damaged, for when I regained consciousness I lay for many long hours crying
out for help that did nae come," Balgair replied, thinking he had an ally in the king's stern-looking aunt. "As
for my bride, I intend beating her every day until she
ripens wi' my seed, madam. But after she gies me my
son she will be beaten at least once a week to remind
her I am her master. She will learn to obey me wi'out

question, I promise ye. Her grandsire doted upon her to her detriment."

Margaret Stewart nodded. "You killed the old man, then, and his heir?" she said.

"Nay, he was kin. I would nae hae his blood on my hands. I hae one of my men kill him. But I did do the MacNab myself, and it gie me great pleasure, I can tell ye," Balgair said. Then, suddenly suspecting he might have gone too far, he explained, "Old Ewan hae nae right to gie away MacArthur lands to a MacNab. When my da heard of it he was rightly angered. We came to Lochearn and attempted to make the old man see the wisdom of our way, but he would nae listen to us. When we came again to steal the lass, she was gone. It was some time before we learned where. We hae nae choice but to take Lochearn, but while the clansmen hae accepted me, for I am their kin, it will be better if Ellen is my wife and gies me my bairns."

"Indeed," Margaret Stewart said, and turned again to look straight at the king. "Well, nephew, what say you in this matter?"

Ellen had just regained consciousness and lay in Peigi's arms, terrified and listening as the king began to speak. She was verging on hysterics, which she fought down.

The king was silent a long moment, as if deciding with himself what to do. Then he spoke. "Is it that you share the same name that gave you cause to believe you were entitled to Lochearn, Balgair MacArthur?"

"Nay, my lord. My family is kin to old Ewan. His grandfather was the eldest son in his generation. He hae a younger brother who married a lass from Skye. That is how the MacArthurs came to live there and to serve the lord of the isles. We are their pipers. My ancestress's family hae nae sons, and they were the lord's pipers. They taught my ancestor, and the lord accepted him, and ever since that day MacArthurs hae piped for the MacDonald. But we came originally from Lochearn. Why would the laird make a MacNab his heir when he had male kin?"

"That I would have to ask old Ewan MacArthur, but alas, you have killed him," the king noted dryly. "However, while I condemn all that has happened, I have no wish to offend the MacDonald. We have communicated about this matter and together come to this decision: You will have Lochearn, and you will be its laird, for you are kin to the former lord. But you will not have Ellen MacArthur. There is too much hate between you, and you burn for revenge on this maiden. I see it in your eyes. I sense it in your heart, which is hardened against the lass. She would not live a month in your care. I will not have the death of an innocent on my soul, Balgair MacArthur. Go home now."

"But I need her to impress my authority upon my clansmen," Balgair protested.

"Your strength and your leadership should impress your authority upon your clansmen," the king said. "And you have the MacNabs to worry about. They will want their revenge on you for killing their kinsman. Go home, my lord. You have all you will gain from me. Though the MacDonald is a great and proud lord, 'tis I, James Stewart, who is the king of Scotland. You would do well to remember that."

Balgair cast a dangerous look at Ellen, who now stood, the older women surrounding her protectively. "I'll hae my revenge on ye one day, Ellen MacArthur. Ye'll ne'er be safe from me wherever ye may go," he said bitterly. "Well, if I canna hae ye, then yer half sister, Anice, will hae to do."

"I have told you that Anice is no blood kin to the MacArthurs, Balgair." She turned away from him, unable to look at what she had obviously done to his formerly handsome visage. She hadn't realized when she was fighting him off that her dirk had touched his face. Ellen could remember only her weapon stabbing and stabbing and stabbing at him in her terrified efforts to escape him and the rape he was attempting.

"Escort the laird of Lochearn out," Margaret Stewart said to the king's page. And when Balgair was gone the king's aunt said, "Forgive me, nephew, but I have some questions as to this matter. I cajoled that fool into admitting his responsibility for two murders, and yet you let him walk free. What kind of justice is that, Jamie Stewart? Ellen MacArthur has lost her home, her inheritance, and I suspect she would know your reasons too. What is to become of this poor lass now that she has been impoverished?"

"Come and sit by my side, my bonny," the king invited Ellen, motioning to a small stool by his chair. When she had seated herself he said, "I had no choice but to allow Balgair MacArthur to go free. The MacDonald seeks an excuse to start an uprising in the Highlands, and would have used his piper's boorish son to fuel that uprising. Eventually I will break that proud lord's hold on the north, but now is not the time. You could not have returned in safety to Lochearn, my bonny. I am sorry, but I think you already knew that."

Ellen nodded. "Aye," she said, and she sighed. "I did, my lord. But what is to become of me now?" She turned to the king's aunt. "Peigi and I would serve you, my lady, for but a place to sleep and our daily bread. Peigi is not young, I know, but I am, and I am strong. I would work hard for you, my lady. *Anything.* Anything you asked of me I would gladly do."

"Of course I will take you in, my child," Margaret Stewart said, and she felt tears behind her eyelids. *The poor lass,* she thought.

"There is no need, Aunt. Ellen needs to wed, and wed she will," James Stewart said. His blue eyes were twinkling as his aunt looked questioningly at him.

"My lord, I would gladly marry, but I have no dower, and who would have a lass with no dower?" Ellen replied.

"But you do have a dower, my bonny," the king told her. And he held up a black velvet bag. "In this bag are twelve pieces of gold, ten silver pennies, ten silver half-pennies, two dozen coppers. You may be bereft of lands, my bonny, but you are a very well dowered woman this day. Now, will you accept my choice of a husband for you, Ellen MacArthur? I have chosen a good man, I promise you." He jingled the bag at her.

"But, my lord, where did you find a dower for me?" she asked.

"Surely, my bonny, you didn't expect me just to let Balgair MacArthur have Lochearn?" The king chuckled. "Nay, my bonny. The MacDonald, at my behest, purchased Lochearn from you, for you are Ewan MacArthur's rightful heir and closest kin, not the MacArthurs of Skye. On the old laird's death Lochearn became yours to do with as you would. Why do you think Balgair wanted you so desperately? The MacArthur clansmen would have given you their first loyalty. Your grandsire was forced before he was so cruelly slain to make Balgair his heir. This sale is his punishment for the theft and the murders. The MacArthurs of Skye owe their loyalty to the lord of the isles. They will not betray that loyalty. When Balgair returns north to *his* lands he will learn they are not his at all. He will discover he but holds them for the MacDonald. And should he at any time betray his overlord, the lord of the isles will not hesitate to kill him, as would I any man who betrayed me. The monies in this purse are what was paid for your lands, Ellen MacArthur. You have a dower. Now, answer my question. Will you accept my choice of a husband?"

"James, do not force the lass to make a decision this day," Margaret Stewart said.

"The man you have chosen," Ellen said slowly, "he is a good man?"

"The best, my bonny!"

"Your Majesty has always treated me with kindness," Ellen responded. "I must therefore trust your judgment, for I know you would not see me unhappy. I will accept the man you have chosen for me, and thank you for what you have done on my behalf."

"Are you not curious as to who your bridegroom is, my bonny?" The king's blue eyes were dancing merrily, and there was a smile on his face.

"I do not have to ask, for you will certainly tell me, my lord. I can see you are bursting to do so," she teased him back as sudden relief poured through her.

"I think you will be content, my bonny," the king answered. "And you, Aunt, will not be unhappy. I have chosen the gentleman who has kept you safe these past months. You are to marry Duncan Armstrong!" he crowed.

The nun gasped, surprised, and then she smiled broadly. Ellen did not think she had ever seen Maggie Armstrong really smile, but this was indeed a smile. And the princess nodded, smiling too. Ellen's gaze turned to the laird, and she caught the total surprise upon his handsome face, which he quickly masked with a neutral look. The king had obviously not consulted him beforehand. Remembering her months at court, Ellen recalled that the young king loved surprising those about him. Ellen remembered Maggie saying her brother had the fanciful notion of marrying for love, but few marriages were based upon that nebulous emotion so often sung about. Marriage was a practical matter for people of their station that usually involved land or gold or both.

"Are you not pleased, my bonny?" James Stewart chortled.

"Your Majesty has chosen well," Ellen said, slowly struggling for the right words. And she supposed that he had. If she had to be married—and a respectable woman really did have to wed, or join a religious order, for which Ellen admitted to herself that she had no leaning—then better she be wed to a man she knew and respected. A man, however, did not necessarily have to marry, although men of property usually did. She knew the laird liked her, but just how did he honestly feel about being leg-shackled to her for the rest of their lives?

"You'll be wed today," the king said enthusiastically.

"Today?" Both Ellen and the laird spoke in unison.

"There is no need to wait," James Stewart said. "Duncan must get back to Duffdour as soon as possible. The banns can be waived. I'll send to the archbishop at once. My own priest will perform the ceremony in my private chapel."

"Then," the king's aunt said, "we must go and make certain that Ellen and Peigi are ready to depart once the deed is done. Come, ladies!" And she shepherded Maggie, Peigi, and Ellen from the king's privy chamber.

When they had gone, James Stewart turned to Duncan Armstrong and said, "Say what you need to say, my lord, so we may be done with it."

"You might have warned me, my lord," the laird said.

"It's past time you were married, Duncan," the king told him.

"You are not wed," the laird pointed out sharply.

"I am much younger than you are, and besides, I would convince those whom I must that Meg Drummond should be my queen." His eyes grew soft when he said her name. "The Drummonds have already given Scotland two queens. Why not a third?"

"I will pray that Your Majesty gains his heart's desire," the laird told him, "but why did you choose me to wed with Ellen Armstrong?"

"You know her, and she you. It would appear there is no dislike between you. And she has a fine dower, Duncan. Besides, 'tis you who returned her to my protection."

"I could have hardly allowed her to fall back into Balgair MacArthur's clutches," the laird said indignantly. "You yourself saw the kind of man he is. He would have killed Ellen in short order, or she him. She is a gentle lass."

"And you are a good man who will treat her well," the king responded. "She will make you a fine wife, Duncan."

"I know that," the laird said. "Almost immediately my steward, Sim, deferred to her. My household ran more smoothly with Ellen managing it than it has since I inherited Duffdour. She has intelligence and a kind heart. But I am not certain I am ready to wed, my lord."

"Few men are ever ready to wed," the king said with a wisdom far beyond his years. "But wed we must for our families, for our estates. If my memory serves me readily—and it usually does—you are well into your thirties, Duncan Armstrong. When you were naught but a younger son with little to offer you were wise to eschew marriage, but that is no longer the case. You are the laird of Duffdour, and you have a duty to your people to gets bairns on a wife so your family may continue and prosper."

"But why choose me?" the laird persisted.

"Because I cannot marry her into the north. Any from that region would attempt to regain Lochearn and cause clan dissension. It is best she be as far from the western Highlands as possible, and so marrying her into a border family seems the proper course for me to take. And you need a wife, my old friend."

Duncan Armstrong laughed. "It is obvious I cannot convince you otherwise. I had always planned to wed for love, but Ellen is a good companion, so I will be satisfied."

"You diplomatically did not mention that you have no choice, as I have ordered you to do so," James Stewart murmured mischievously.

"Nay, my lord, I did not," Duncan replied.

The king handed the laird the velvet bag of coins. "Her dower," he said.

Duncan Armstrong took the bag and tucked it into his leather jerkin. "Thank you," he replied.

A young page was admitted to the king's privy chamber. "My lady the princess says the marriage must take place on the morrow after prime, for then the couple will have the whole day to travel. There is no time left today. And you must speak with the bishop, my lady says." The lad bowed to the two men.

"Tell your mistress it will be as she wishes," the king said, and the boy, bowing again, hurried out. "We should celebrate your impending nuptials tonight, then," James Stewart said with a grin. "My aunt means for you to be out and gone tomorrow."

"With your permission, my lord, I would go and speak with Ellen first," the laird said. "I would reassure her that all will be well."

"Go," the king said with a wave of his hand.

Duncan hurried through the castle halls to Princess Margaret's apartments, and, after asking permission of the king's aunt, he led Ellen into the castle gardens, where they might have a modicum of privacy while they spoke. "I did not know what the king proposed," he began. "Nor of the dower he obtained for you from the MacDonald."

"I know," she told him. "The look of surprise on your face when he announced you were to be my intended bridegroom was wondrous to behold, my lord." Ellen giggled mischievously. "And then you hid it so quickly."

"Are you content with this?" he inquired of her.

"My lord, you are aware that we are not being given a choice, aren't you? We are commanded to marry, and so we must. I am content with the king's decision. I like you. I like your sister. I like Duffdour. But if there is another who has a place in your heart, my lord, I will ask the king to reconsider. I would not part you from a true love, Duncan Armstrong, especially when you have been so good to me," Ellen told him.

"I love no other," he admitted, and as he did he realized that if he had said he did she would have insisted the king free him from this obligation. But for some reason he did not want to lie to her. If he did then what would happen to her? The thought of someone being unkind to Ellen MacArthur disturbed him deeply. "We will wed on the morrow," he said. "And then we will leave immediately for Duffdour. Do you mind if we go quickly, Ellen? We need to get home."

"I agree," she said with a small smile. "The defenses need to be completed. It won't be long before the English come raiding again. And Laren needs to be replaced out by the signal fire. Have you decided whom you will send?"

They spoke for a time of Duffdour as they walked through the spring garden. The sky above them was bright with the sunset when Duncan Armstrong finally escorted Ellen MacArthur back to the apartments of Princess Margaret. They lingered before the doors a few moments, and then Ellen went inside. Peigi had saved her a bit of meat, bread, and cheese from the supper she had missed. Ellen ate slowly as her servant chattered away.

"We'll be safe at Duffdour, my bairn. The laird is a good man. Ye couldna hae a better husband, I'm thinking. What will ye wear on yer wedding day?" Peigi asked.

"I have not a great deal of choice. Perhaps it is better I wear this gown I now have on, for the wrinkles are gone from it. It would be foolish to unpack my trunks now, when tomorrow they will go right back on the cart. 'Tis a pretty garment, and the color suits me well enough."

"Ye should be wed in the hall at Lochearn in yer finest gown," Peigi grumbled.

"Lochearn is gone, and I've not a doubt Anice is wearing my finest gown," Ellen remarked ruefully. "Still, to be wed in the king's private chapel is an honor, and my green gown is very nice. I'll have a good husband, and my dower portion is a very respectable one. I would not have thought Lochearn was worth so much."

"Well, I'll nae say the laird isn't a good man," Peigi allowed. "Ye did terrible damage to Balgair MacArthur's face, my bairn."

Ellen shuddered. "I barely remember," she said. "I just wanted to get away from him. I do not recall attacking his face, just going at him with my dirk."

"I should hae been wi' ye," Peigi said.

"I thank God you weren't. I could not have gotten away had you been, for I would never leave you behind, and you are not a woman for horses," Ellen reminded her servant with a mischievous smile. "I was fortunate to catch up with Duncan when I did."

"Do ye love him, lass?" Peigi wanted to know.

"Love him? I don't know," Ellen responded with a small shrug. "He seems a reasonable man. I have not seen him show temper or cruelty. But I do not know him well enough to have formed any kind of attachment to him. I will be a good wife, though, Peigi. He and the king have saved me from a terrible fate."

"Ye'll hae to bed him," Peigi said frankly. "Yer first duty will be to gie him a son. Hae ye even kissed him?"

"Why would I kiss him?" Ellen replied. "There would be no reason to kiss him."

Well, that was true enough, Peigi thought. "There are things ye should know before ye go to yer marriage bed."

Ellen laughed. "I know what I must know," she said to her surprised servant. "You cannot live to the ripe old age of nineteen without learning certain things. Anice was always speaking of men and their attributes. The lasses who were with me when I was a part of the princess's household. Even Margaret Stewart herself. She said all lasses should know about such matters if they were going to keep from getting themselves seduced, as she once did. I know of manroots, and that there will be pain when we are first joined. I know men like to fondle women's breasts. I am ready to do my duty."

"I am glad to hear it," Margaret Stewart said sharply as she joined them. "Now, tell me, Ellen. Are you truly content with this marriage you will contract tomorrow? If you are not you have but to say it, and I will convince my nephew otherwise. I do not want him to be responsible for your unhappiness. Jamie is wildly in love with his Meg, and he wants everyone else to be as happy as he is. But you and Duncan are not the king and Margaret Drummond."

"I must marry, madam," Ellen said quietly. "And I have found Duncan Armstrong to be a good and fair man. And I know him enough not to be afraid. I am content to be his wife. Duffdour is smaller than Lochearn, but a comfortable house. Its people have been friendly toward me. I believe I can be both content and happy there."

The princess nodded. "Then so be it. Now get to bed, Ellen. Prime is celebrated at six o'clock in the morning, as you know, and your wedding vows will be spoken immediately afterward. Peigi, tuck your mistress in and then come to me. I have instructions for you regarding your journey on the morrow."

It had been a very long day, preceded by several long days. And now on the morrow she would wed, then turn about and go right back from whence they had come. *I don't think I want to travel again for a very long time,* Ellen thought as she grew drowsy. *I will be content to remain at home. Home. I'm going to have a home again. And a husband. It's not at all what I thought it would be.* And then she slept.

When she was awakened it was already growing light. Two young maidservants were dragging a small round oak tub into the little chamber where she had been housed for the night. Several young serving men hurried in, each carrying two buckets, which they dumped into the tub. Peigi oversaw it all. When the other servants had gone Ellen arose and stripped off her chemise.

"A bath!" she said joyfully. "And the water is hot!" she exclaimed, seating herself.

Peigi handed her a washing cloth and a small sliver of soap. "Dinna forget yer neck and ears," she said. "I've yer gown all brushed and ready."

"I wish there were time to do my hair," Ellen murmured, but she knew that there wasn't. She washed herself quickly and then, rising from the water, stepped from the tub and dried herself with a warmed drying cloth.

"Here's a nice clean chemise for ye, my bairn," Peigi said, handing it to Ellen.

Ellen slipped it on and then, seating herself on the edge of the bed, undid the heavy, thick braid of her hair and began to brush it out. When she had finished she put on her green gown and slipped her feet into her sollerets. When they began their journey home later she would change again, but she would not go into the king's chapel in her boots and traveling clothes. Ellen would wear her red-gold tresses loose, denoting her virgin status. Peigi gave the long hair a final brush, and then she set a chaplet of fresh flowers atop her mistress's head that Margaret Stewart had sent for the bride.

Together the two women left the little chamber, which opened into the princess's large antechamber. The vast room was almost empty at this early hour but for several servants dusting and sweeping. Margaret Stewart joined the women, and they walked together to the king's own chapel, entering it to find the king, Maggie, and Duncan Armstrong waiting, along with the king's confessor. The priest said Prime, and then he called the laird and his lady before him. His assistant brought the marriage contract, which had been drawn up the previous evening, betrothing Ellen MacArthur of Lochearn to Duncan Armstrong of Duffdour. The dower was listed at ten gold pieces and ten silver pennies.

Ellen looked at the laird. "There was more," she said.

"It is yours," he replied. "A woman should have something of her own."

Ellen's eyes filled with tears. She was astounded that a man would be so thoughtful. Two pieces of gold, ten silver halfpennies, and two dozen coppers were hers! "Thank you, my lord," she whispered to him.

Duncan Armstrong silently brushed a tear from her cheek.

"Please sign the contracts or make your mark, my lord, my lady," the priest said.

First the laird and then Ellen took the inked quill from the assistant priest and signed their names. The king's confessor looked slightly surprised to see both signatures, especially the woman's. He was not certain he approved of women who could write. It generally meant that they could read too, and women who could read became dangerous. The signatures were sanded. Then the witnesses—the laird's sister, the king, and his aunt—signed. Their signatures were sanded. Sealing wax was carefully dropped onto the document. Both the priest and the king pressed their seals into it. The assistant took the documents away. One copy would be kept by the church; the other would be given to the laird before his party departed shortly for the borders.

"Kneel," the priest commanded the couple. A little too quickly, Ellen thought, the king's confessor muttered the words of the marriage sacrament. When asked, both Ellen and Duncan accepted each other although with the contracts already signed it was but a mere formality. He wrapped their hands together, saying, "Let those whom God has conjoined be not rent asunder by others." He blessed them, concluding, "It is done now. Go and be fruitful, my children."

They arose and for a moment stood awkwardly, not certain what to do next. Then the king's aunt spoke. "Come along now. I have had a small wedding breakfast laid in my own private dining room." And she led them out of the royal chapel.

They were five at the table, Peigi having gone to the little chamber to lay out the clothing Ellen would travel in shortly. It was a wonderful meal. There were individual half trenchers of bread filled with oat stirabout into which had been mixed bits of dried apple, pear, and cinnamon. There were eggs poached in a cream sauce that had been flavored with marsala wine and dusted with nutmeg. There was half a ham and a large rasher of bacon as well. There was fresh warm bread, sweet butter, plum jam, and a hard, sharp cheese. The wine was ruby red and rich. The quintet did full justice to the breakfast the king's aunt had ordered. As the meal was coming to an end the king stood and raised his goblet to Ellen.

"I have not failed you, my bonny Ellen. Be happy now, and put the dark memories from you. God bless you and your bridegroom!" Then the king drank, as did the other four at the table.

Now Duncan stood and raised his goblet. "To you, my liege. I thank you for the blessing of a fair wife. I am, as always, your most loyal servant." The laird bowed to the king. Then he turned to Ellen. "And to my bride, who has already brought goodness and happiness to Duffdour! May we have many years and many sons together." He raised her little hand up with his free hand and kissed it, his look piercing her. Ellen blushed prettily. Then the laird drank, as did the others.

With the two toasts the meal was concluded, and, kissing her on both cheeks, the king left his aunt's apartments. The nun excused herself as well.

"I will go and see to the horses," the laird told the women, and he hurried off.

"We will say our farewells, Ellen, when you are changed and ready to leave," Margaret Stewart said to her. "Come and see me then."

"Thank you, madam," Ellen replied. She found Peigi waiting to help her out of her green gown and into her traveling garments. She put on her linen breeks and her shirt, fastened a wide leather belt about her narrow waist, and donned her doeskin jerkin with its horn buttons. She pulled a pair of knitted foot coverings over her feet, and then yanked on her leather boots. Then Ellen sat down and braided her long hair up. She would not again wear it loose and flowing in public, for now she was a married woman.

"Are we ready?" she asked Peigi when she had finished her hair.

"We are, my lady," Peigi answered. "I'll have the men load this last wee trunk on the wagon. 'Tis fortunate we did not unload the rest of it two days ago when we came. I never thought to be going back to Duffdour, but I'll not be unhappy to see it again."

Ellen sighed. "I lost Lochearn," she said. "Perhaps if Balgair had let me become more familiar with him I should not have been so afraid when he attempted to have me. Perhaps I could have managed to live with him and be a good wife to him. If I had we should be at Lochearn now."

"That foreign MacArthur is a wicked man, my lady. There would hae been no living wi' him. Those northern island men are barely Christians, and many, I hae heard, keep more than one wife. You saw that already he was consorting wi' Anice. He wouldna put her aside for ye. Ye're well rid of him, though it cost ye Lochearn. Ye've a better man in the laird than ye would hae in Balgair MacArthur," Peigi told her mistress firmly. "Now let's be off for Duffdour, my lady!"

They left the little chamber together and found Margaret Stewart with her ladies. Ellen went to the king's aunt and knelt before her. "Madam, it is time for me to depart."

The princess smiled warmly, taking Ellen's two hands in her own. "In your time in my household you served me well, Ellen MacArthur. My nephew has chosen a good man to be your husband, but I think you already know it. Be glad, my child, and know that you will always have a friend in Margaret Stewart." The king's aunt leaned forward and kissed the kneeling girl on both of her cheeks. "Go now, and be happy."

Ellen lifted the two hands in her own and kissed them. "Thank you, madam, for all you have done for me.

I am but a simple Highland lass, but you treated me with kindness, and I will never forget you. I would not sound bold or above my station, my lady, but you will always have a friend in me as well. I bid you farewell." Then Ellen stood, curtsied, and backed from the princess's presence.

"Godspeed, child," Margaret Stewart called after her as Ellen and Peigi left her apartments. She was genuinely sorry to see Ellen go, but it was the way of the world that people came and went in one's life. She suddenly reflected on her daughter, but impatiently shook off the thoughts. Little Margaret was where she belonged.

In the stable yard of the castle they found the laird and his men awaiting them. The cart was standing at the ready. One of the clansmen hurried to help Peigi up onto the bench next to the driver. Maggie was then helped up next to Peigi. It wasn't meet that she sit next to a man. The laird helped Ellen to mount, and she smiled at him. He smiled back, suddenly very aware now that she was his wife. *A wife.* He had a wife. Conal and Murdoc, his brothers, would certainly be surprised. He grinned as their party moved forward and in short order left Sterling Castle behind.

When the noon hour came they stopped after several hours of riding to rest and water the horses. There was bread, cheese, and meat from the castle kitchens. They sat in the green grass and ate.

"I will miss this," Sister Margaret Mary said. "I had forgotten how delicious freedom is. I haven't had a picnic in the grass since I was a child."

"Will your superior allow you to come to Duffdour if we invite you?" Ellen wanted to know. "I will always plan picnics when you come, Maggie."

The nun laughed. "We are fairly cloistered, Ellen. I was allowed to come because the king requested it and my mother superior considered it an emergency. Perhaps she will let me come when you are having a bairn."

"*A bairn?* Oh, aye," Ellen said, and she found herself

blushing again. She would have to give the laird children, of course, but that would require some degree of intimacy, and they hadn't even kissed. Remembering Balgair's kiss, she wasn't certain she would even like being kissed again. And there was more to creating a child than just kissing.

"We'll reach St. Mary's at the end of our ride today," Maggie said. "You're staying in our guesthouse tonight," the nun informed Ellen.

"That will be nice," Ellen replied absently. Would he bed her in a nunnery? There was something almost wicked about such a thing, Ellen thought with a shiver.

Maggie's convent was small and neat. They were greeted by the mother superior, and said their good-byes to the laird's sister. Maggie's demeanor the moment she entered the cloistered convent became silent and subdued.

"Your sister will spend the next few months in solitude and prayer," the mother superior said in stern tones. "She must cleanse her spirit of the sin and filth of the outside world in which she has been forced to dwell these many months."

"She has spent most of her time at Duffdour," the laird said quietly, "and I am most grateful you permitted her to come and chaperone my wife."

"I was given to understand it was the king's ward who needed a chaperone," the mother superior said.

The laird explained briefly.

"Ah," the mother superior said, her lean face showing a bit of emotion. "I understand completely. How good of the king to give her a husband, considering that she has lost everything. Even the poorest girl entering my convent brings a dower."

"The king wheedled a dower for her from the MacDonald in exchange for her lands," the laird explained.

"Aha! Ha! Ha!" The nun barked sharp laughter, surprising him. "A clever laddie is our Jamie Stewart," she remarked. She turned to Ellen. "You are a fortunate woman, my lady," she said.

"Aye, I believe I am," Ellen agreed.

"Your wife and her servant may spend the night within our convent walls, my lord," the mother superior said. "You and your men, however, must shelter outside the walls. It is rare that we allow any man but priests within. A hot meal will be brought to you tonight, and in the morning after the Mass."

"We'll leave before Prime," the laird said. "The sun will be up, and with luck we will reach Duffdour before it sets."

The nun nodded. "The English seem quiet for now," she told him. Then she picked up a small bell upon the table and rang it. When a young nun hurried to answer it the mother superior said, "Escort the lady and her serving woman who waits outside to our guesthouse, Sister Mary Michael. The laird, I am certain, can find his own way back through our gates."

"I will see you on the morrow," Duncan said softly to Ellen as he walked with her from the mother superior's privy chamber. "This is hardly a place to spend a wedding night, now, is it?" His eyes twinkled at her, and he gave her a smile.

"I had honestly not thought about it," Ellen said softly.

He paused, and then he said, "We will have time to know each other better in the coming weeks, Ellen. You need not fear me." Then, taking her hand, he kissed it and left her, to find his way back to his own men outside the convent walls.

Ellen sighed. She had spent her entire life preparing for marriage with one man, only to find herself married to another. Despite the few months she had spent at Duffdour, her new husband was still a stranger to her. She knew everything a good chatelaine should know of housewifery, but she really knew little of men. Even her time at court had not really prepared her for the other side of marriage. Margaret Stewart had not encouraged the young women in her charge to flirt and play at love, although most of them certainly did. But Ellen had been betrothed and, faithful to Donald MacNab, she had avoided any situation that might have compromised her reputation or brought embarrassment upon her family or the MacNabs.

And now she was married to an Armstrong and not a MacNab. She would live in the borders and not the Highlands. She knew her first duty was to give her husband heirs. And she knew what was involved in gaining those bairns. The manroot injected its seed into the woman's womb. The seed took, and the child grew until it was time for it to be birthed. It seemed a cold process, Ellen thought, and yet she remembered the other girls in Margaret Stewart's household returning from trysts with their sweethearts flushed, starry-eyed, and dreamy. There had to be something more, but Ellen couldn't imagine what it was. She supposed that Duncan would tell her. He really was a very nice man.

Sister Mary Michael led them to a small stone house by the gates. "You will find the makings of a fire inside," she said quietly. "Your meal will be brought shortly." Then she hurried off.

"They dinna speak a great deal, these nuns," Peigi noted.

"The order is a strict one, Maggie said," Ellen told her servant as they entered the little house. It was but one room with a large hearth. Ellen added some wood to the tiny fire that had obviously just been recently begun. The flames sprang up, and gradually the damp, chilly room began to warm.

"Here are the pallets," Peigi said, opening a pair of doors set in the stone wall by the fireplace. She pulled the pallets out and shook them hard several times. "No bedbugs," she noted, pleased, and laid them on the floor before the hearth. "It won't be the most comfortable bed we've ever slept upon, my lady, but 'twill nae be the worst."

The room was very spare in its furnishings. There was no charm to it at all. There was a single table and two stools. A broom stood in the corner. A knock sounded upon the door. Another nun entered carrying a tray, which she set upon the table. She nodded to them, then silently glided out. Ellen and Peigi went to the table and looked at the meal that they had been sent. There were two trenchers filled with a steaming-hot vegetable pottage, a thin wedge of cheese, and to their surprise a small round cottage loaf. There was also a carafe of watered wine and a single wooden goblet.

"I suspect the bread and cheese are for the morning," Ellen said. "My lord told Mother Mary Andrew that we would depart at first light."

"We'll hae to keep it safe from the mice and rats, then," Peigi said in practical tones. She walked across the room and opened up the cabinet that had held the pallets. Reaching in, she felt around the enclosure for any opening that would allow a rodent through. She searched carefully, but she could find none. "In here," she said, beckoning to Ellen to bring the loaf and the cheese. "Wrap the cheese in the napkin, my lady. It will prevent it from getting hard overnight."

The bread and the cheese stored, the two women sat down to eat the vegetable stew that had been ladled into the stale bread trenchers. It was hot, well flavored, and surprisingly tasty. They scraped their trenchers dry, and then sat by the fire slowly eating them until not a crumb remained.

"They didn't stint us," Ellen remarked, sipping wine from the cup, and then handing it to Peigi to drink.

Their meal over, the two women used the chamber pot, then lay down in their clothes to sleep, pulling two thin blankets over themselves. Neither of them slept well, and consequently arose just as the first light began to tug at the edge of the darkness in the sky. They arose. There was no water for bathing, so they straightened their garments and their hair, ate their bread and cheese, and exited the guesthouse as the skies above them lightened to gray. Their horses had already been brought from the convent stables and were tied waiting by the gate. Ellen pressed a copper coin into the hand of the porteress, and thanked her as, with a smile, the nun opened the gates to allow the two women out. The laird and his men were waiting and, seeing the two women, they mounted up. The clansman driving the cart pulled Peigi up to her seat, and they were off for Duffdour.

Chapter 5

The day was long because it was almost summer, and the light lasted until late, time enough to reach Duffdour. The laird had sent a rider on ahead to alert the keep to their arrival. The baggage cart was at least an hour behind them, but riders were sent to escort it safely to Duffdour in the shimmering twilight.

Sim, the steward, came forward, a surprised look upon his weathered face when he saw Ellen MacArthur. "Welcome home, my lord. Welcome back, Mistress Ellen."

"Mistress Ellen is now your lady, Sim. We were married at Sterling Castle by the king's own chaplain two days ago," Duncan Armstrong said.

"My lord!" Sim smiled broadly. "I offer my felicitations to you and to your lady. Duffdour has not had a mistress since your mother's time, for your brother was never of a mind to wed. I know that everyone will be happy to learn this news."

"You are free to tell them, Sim," the laird said. "Is there a hot meal ready?"

"There is, my lord. It awaits you in the hall," the steward answered.

"Peigi and the cart are an hour behind us. Have the

watch be on the lookout for them. And see that the woman is fed. She's not young, and will be tired after our trip." He turned to Ellen and swept her up in his arms. "Welcome home, madam," he said as he carried her over the threshold of the keep and into the hall.

Startled at first, she then laughed. "Why, my lord, you are a man of tradition, I see," she said as he put her back on her feet. She looked about her. "It is good to be back, Duncan. I know I can be happy here. I hope I can make you happy."

He smiled down at her, and then, tipping her chin up, he brushed his lips across hers. "I know there is much we have to learn about each other, and I am a patient man, Ellen. You have said you can be happy here, and I want you to be. I was not expecting to return home with a wife, but I must tell you that while our marriage was unexpected, I am not unhappy to find you by my side, lassie."

She was briefly breathless with the gentle kiss, and he saw the surprise in her eyes when his mouth had taken hers.

"Have you never been kissed before, Ellen?" he asked her. Her sweet mouth had possessed an untried quality.

"Only once," Ellen admitted. "When Balgair attempted his rape he mashed his mouth on mine. I found it disgusting, for his breath was foul and I thought him rough. But your kiss was gentle, my lord. I liked it."

He smiled a slow smile at her, and she saw how his eyes crinkled at the edges when he did so. "I would like to spend more time kissing you," he told her.

"Will we share a bed?" she suddenly asked him candidly.

"Of course, you are my wife," he told her. "Did you think otherwise?"

"I know some ladies have a bedchamber, and their husbands have a bedchamber," Ellen explained. "That is what I was told by the princess, and the girls in her household have often discussed such things."

"Duffdour is a keep, not a castle," the laird said with a chuckle. "We must share a bedchamber, lassie."

"I see," she said in somber tones. "Tonight?"

"Aye, tonight, and all the nights of our life together," he responded.

"Oh." Her pretty face wore a look of consternation.

"We need not consummate our union until we have gotten to know each other better," Duncan said, "but you might as well get used to sharing a bed with me, for you will be doing it for a long time, I hope. Ahh, I see the food being brought in. Come on, lassie, and let us have our meal." He took her hand, led her to the high board, and seated her in the seat traditionally belonging to the lady of the house.

Ellen looked out over the hall. Oh, she had sat at this high board before, but then she considered herself a guest, and Maggie had sat where she was sitting now. This was *her* home now. This was *her* hall. *Her* fire that burned brightly. The loom sat by the hearth. *Her* loom with the half-finished tapestry she had left behind when they had gone to Sterling. She would spend the rainy days and the evenings finishing it. Absently she helped herself to the dishes presented to her.

There was rabbit stew with a rich brown gravy, carrots, and tiny onions. There was trout sautéed in butter and white wine and sliced on a bed of watercress. There was a small joint of venison, the last of the autumn hunt. It had been well braised, and sat on a platter surrounded by roasted onions. Fresh bread, sweet butter, and a quarter round of hard yellow cheese was set upon the board. Red wine filled their goblets.

"The cook is to be commended," Ellen said as she ate.

"She'll be pleased to know you approve," Duncan replied. "She's yours to command now, lassie. Frankly I prefer simple meals."

"I shall remember that," Ellen told him. "Tell me, how far away do your brothers live? Will I get to meet them soon?"

"Cleit is a good day's ride from Duffdour, but aye, you'll meet Conal and Murdoc soon enough. I'll send a messenger tomorrow to Cleit to tell them I have a wife. My sister-in-law will come with all haste to meet you." He chuckled. "Adair has been used to being the only lady in the family for some years now. She will want to know everything about you, and where you have come from, and that you will be a good wife to me. She's English born and bred, but I'll leave it to her to tell you her tale."

"Is she beautiful?" Ellen wanted to know.

He grinned at her. "Aye, she is, but very different from you. She is tall, with black hair and violet eyes. She suits my brother well. You, however, suit me well. I have a fondness for red hair and little lasses," he told her.

"You are much taller than I am," she agreed.

"But we will fit together nicely, lassie. Of that you may be certain," Duncan said softly, and, taking up her hand, he kissed it first on the back, and then on the palm.

A shiver ran down Ellen's spine. Her gray-blue eyes widened with surprise, and he smiled into those eyes, rendering her weak. She could not have risen from the board even if she had wanted to stand up.

"Amazing," he said, low. "A year and a half in the royal Stewart's household, and you are still as innocent as a young doe." His hand now caressed her face with delicate fingers that ran down her nose and over her lips and up her jawline.

Ellen finally found her voice. "Are you making love to me, my lord?" she asked.

"A little," he admitted. "I find, now that you are mine, lassie, that I am having a difficult time keeping my hands off of you. But I would not frighten you."

"You don't frighten me, Duncan," she responded. "You are a most gentle man."

Reaching out, he cupped her head in his hand and drew her to him. His lips brushed across hers, touching, tasting, before he took her mouth in a passionate kiss. Her lips were silken, firm, and sweet. She sighed, and her breath tasted like wine in his mouth. He felt a tightening in his groin, and was genuinely surprised by his reaction. He wasn't a lad with his first maid, but there was something so sensual and yet so innocent about Ellen that he could not help but be aroused by her.

"Oh, my," she whispered as he drew away. Her cheeks were pink.

"I will want to do more of that," he told her softly. "You are a most kissable lassie, Ellen MacArthur, lady of Duffdour."

"That was ever so much nicer than Balgair's kiss," she told him. "After he kissed me, I thought I would not like kissing, but now that you have kissed me I realize that it depends upon who is kissing you, doesn't it, Duncan? I will want to do more of that with you as well." Her gray-blue eyes twinkled at him.

He laughed aloud at this.

Sim came to the high board to tell them that the cart had arrived and Peigi was having her supper in the kitchens.

Ellen stood up. "I had best go and greet her," she said. "Sim, will you show me the way to the kitchens? Then have the men bring my belongings to the room I slept in before. I don't want to fill our bedchamber with my possessions until Peigi and I have sorted through it all," she explained to the laird.

He sat with his wine when she had left him and considered that just sleeping with her might prove to be more difficult than he had anticipated. She excited him, and her soft young body next to his was going to be very tempting. She had deliciously round little breasts, like the plumpest apples. His hands itched to fondle them. He contemplated the image of her with her long red-gold hair spread upon the pillows. She would be the most tender morsel, and he would eat her up. Suddenly Duncan Armstrong realized that his cock in his breeks was hard and aching. *God's wounds!* What was the matter with him? Was he actually lusting after his own wife? Aye! He was indeed.

He struggled to consider other, less inflammatory matters. It was time to drive the cattle to the high meadow. Perhaps he would overnight with his herders in the fields. Mayhap instead of sending a messenger to Cleit he would ride over himself. He hadn't seen his brothers in months now. Aye, it was the better way to inform them of his marriage. He wouldn't mind their teasing either, nor Adair's many questions. He could remain away at least three or four days. Possibly longer.

Ellen returned to the hall. "Peigi is very glad to be home," she said with a smile. "I want to settle her in her own little chamber myself. Do you mind?"

"Nay, I have some business in the stables, lassie. You know where the lord's chamber lies. Find your way there when you are tired, and surely you are after our ride." He hurried from the hall.

Now what was the matter? Ellen wondered. Was he being thoughtful and allowing her time for herself before he joined her? Or was he experiencing a certain amount of shyness himself? She hurried upstairs to find Peigi rooting through the trunks. "Tomorrow," Ellen said, "we will get your trunk into your chamber, my dearie."

"My chamber?" Peigi said, surprised.

"Aye, your chamber!" Ellen told her, smiling. "There is a wee room just for you at the end of the hall. Sim has readied it." She led her servant down the corridor and opened the door, stepping inside. " 'Tis not very big, but it has its own hearth, a bed, and room for your trunk. And a window. Its shutter is open now, but you can close it when it suits you, Peigi. I thought you were deserving of your own quarters."

Peigi looked about her, and her eyes grew misty. "Thank you, my lady," she said.

"I will leave you then to your bed," Ellen replied.

"What? And who is to get you prepared for your wedding night?" Peigi demanded to know.

"My lord and I have thought it best to learn each other's ways before we grow more intimate," Ellen explained. "We will share the bed. No more."

"He's a sensitive man, he is," Peigi said. "Very well, then, my lady, if you do not need me I will retire. I must admit that my bed looks tempting."

Ellen walked back down the hall to the lord's chamber and entered it. It was a comfortable room. Tapestries hung upon its stone walls. There was a fire burning in the hearth, which was flanked by carved stone manikins. A double window facing southeast was hung with linen draperies pulled back to reveal the open wooden shutters. Outside she could hear a night bird calling. There was an oak table before the window with a small tray, two little goblets, and a carafe of wine. On either side of the table, and flat against the wall on either side of the windows, two high-backed oak chairs had been placed. Each had a woven rush seat topped with a small linen-and-burgundy-velvet brocade cushion. The large bed had two great turned posts at its foot, with a carved wooden headboard and canopy. It was hung with the same linen and brocade that covered the cushions. On both sides of the bed was a candle stand with a taper-stick. There was a low, large rectangular chest at the foot of the bed, and Ellen saw that her own trunk had been placed along a wall opposite the window wall. On one side of the hearth was another small table holding a pottery basin. She saw the matching pitcher, which she knew held water, in the edge coals of the fireplace. There was a small drying cloth and washing rag.

Ellen went to her trunk and lifted out a clean chemise. Then, taking the pitcher from the coals, she poured water into the basin, then set the pitcher back in the fire. She needed a bath, but that would have to wait until the morrow. Stripping off her clothing, she washed herself as best she could. There was only a sliver of soap. She would have to ask Sim if there was a larger cake, and she should probably make a goodly supply for the year, Ellen thought. There was a small garderobe off the bedchamber. How civilized, she considered. There had been no such amenity at Lochearn, although the royal dwellings had had them both public and private. She used it, giving herself a final wash, then donned her clean chemise, brushed and plaited her hair, and climbed into bed. Which side did he prefer? Well, she would ask him when he came to bed.

But she was asleep when he came into the bedchamber, and Duncan Armstrong found that he was actually relieved. It would be easier to lie next to her if she were sleeping. He stripped off his garments and, naked, climbed into bed. She was wearing her chemise, he saw immediately, and his anxiousness was lightened a bit more. And her glorious hair was modestly braided. No temptation there. But he could not sleep. She was warm against his back, and smelled faintly of some fragrance that tickled at his nostrils. She breathed softly, and he felt her breath soft against his bare flesh. The laird gritted his teeth, closed his eyes, and tried to will himself into slumber. He finally succeeded when he managed to relax his own body and decided to enjoy her warmth and sweetness as she lay against him. How many nights of this could he endure? he wondered. Aye, he would go to Cleit tomorrow, and then he would help move his cattle to their summer pasturage. As her husband he had every right to Ellen's body, but he really did want her to be ready. Perhaps she might even come to love him, and love was the one thing he had always sought in a wife. But left to his own devices would he have found it? He wasn't certain of the answer to his own question.

Ellen awoke at first light to find her husband by her side. *And he was naked!* She could see his broad shoulders, his arm, and a bit of his back. He was unclothed.

It hadn't occurred to her that he slept nude. But then, what did she really know about how men slept? What should she do? Even the servants wouldn't be stirring quite this early.

"I didn't realize until I got into bed last night that you would sleep clothed." His deep voice startled her.

"I didn't realize until I awoke a few moments ago that you would sleep naked," she answered him.

He rolled onto his back, and she could see the dark hair upon his chest. "Do I tempt you, madam?" he teased her. His blue eyes danced wickedly.

Ellen raised herself up, clutching the coverlet to her breasts. "I suspect I may tempt you far more, my lord," she said pertly.

"Aye, you do," he admitted, and then, reaching up, he pulled her down to kiss her. "How clever of you to note it, but you have not answered my question. Do I tempt you?"

"I am not familiar with flirtation or lovemaking, and until I awoke I had not even a small knowledge of the male body unclothed," Ellen answered him. She sat up again, for his closeness, she found, was far too heady. The male scent of him awoke something in her that she did not understand, and her heart was fluttering oddly. "I do not think I am ready or even capable of being tempted, but I will admit to curiosity, my lord."

Duncan chuckled, running a finger down her straight little nose. "Do you always say what you are thinking, Ellen?" He wanted to kiss her until she was breathless.

"Usually, unless my words would be hurtful to someone," Ellen replied. When he touched her she felt nervous. Not afraid, but fidgety. It was very disconcerting.

"I am going to make a quick visit to Cleit to inform my brothers of our marriage," he said. "And then I will be moving the cattle to their summer meadow. Will you be all right if I leave you for a few days?" he asked her.

She nodded. "You do not want me to ride to Cleit with you?"

"Not this time, Ellen," he told her. Then he pulled her back down into his embrace and said against her lips, "I want you to have time to grow used to being the mistress of Duffdour, to sleeping in this bed, to accepting that the next time we share a bed you will become my wife in more than just name." Then his mouth closed over hers, and, rolling her over onto her back, he kissed her softly at first, but as he found she could respond to his lips on hers, his kiss became more passionate, more intimate, more demanding. And then he lifted his mouth from hers. "I will leave you now, Ellen," he said, rising from their bed. Then he turned to face her. "This is what a man full-grown looks like, *wife*." He gave her time to look at him in his nakedness, his blue-veined cock aroused, before, turning abruptly, he walked across the room to dress himself.

Ellen's heart was hammering with a mixture of fright and excitement. She had actually gasped softly when he had turned to face her. He had broad shoulders and a broad chest that was covered with a small mat of dark curls. It matched the thick curls at the junction of his groin that cushioned what she suspected was a very impressive manhood. His waist and hips were narrow— nay, sleek. He had very long legs and long, slender feet. His arms were muscled. When he had turned she had admired the graceful line of his back and his tight buttocks. His body was beautiful, if indeed a man could be called beautiful. She wondered if he would find her body beautiful.

"I will see you in a few days," he told her, dressing and leaving their bedchamber.

The sky outside the room was now light, but the sun had not quite risen. Ellen lay in the big bed. She would be alone for the next few nights, and then . . . She shivered. He had said it plainly: When he returned he would make her a woman—take her virginity and use her body. Ellen shivered again. She knew enough to know the details of the coupling. What she didn't know was whether she would like it. What if she didn't like it? How many times did they have to do it to create a bairn? Would he stop when she had given him the heirs he needed? There was so much she needed to know, and there was no one whom she could ask. *Peigi, bless her, can't tell me what I need to know,* Ellen thought. She would have to learn with experience, she decided. She would have to rely on Duncan, who surely had great experience where women, their bodies, and lovemaking were concerned. Ellen rolled over, drawing the coverlet up over her. He would be gone now, she thought as she fell back asleep.

And he was. He had gone directly to the stables, saddled his own horse, and left through his new gates, telling the watchman that he would be at Cleit. He realized an hour later that he hadn't bothered to stop in the kitchens and take a day's rations. He'd be very hungry by the time he reached his half brother's keep. At least the day was fair. When the sun was high and he had been riding for several hours, he stopped to water his horse, and considered that he should have taken several men at arms with him. It was early summer, and he hoped not to run into any raiding parties.

The day was long, and before dark he sighted Cleit Keep ahead on the crest of a hill. The laird of Cleit's cattle grazed in one field, his sheep in the other. Duncan Armstrong rode down the hill onto the narrow road leading to the stone structure. He knew that the watchman had spotted him as soon as he had come over the rise, for Conal Bruce was a careful man where the safety of his family was concerned. Reaching the keep, he dismounted in the small courtyard, turning his horse over to a stable lad, and entered the dwelling, going directly to the hall. His sister-in-law, Adair, saw him first.

"Duncan!" she exclaimed, and, rising, came to greet him.

"Adair," he said, bussing her on both cheeks. "You are

beautiful as always, madam," Duncan told her, spinning her about. "Where are my nephews and my niece?"

"In the nursery with their nursemaid. How early did you leave Duffdour? You look tired and hungry."

"I left just before dawn, and I forgot to take something to eat with me," he admitted to her. "I am starving, and could use some of Elsbeth's good bread and meat."

"Fetch some meat and bread for my lord," Adair instructed a serving girl. "And wine! Do not dally."

"Where is Conal?" the laird of Duffdour asked her.

"In the village on the other side of the hill. The English raided last night and took some livestock and three women. He's gone to get the details, and will go raiding tonight to see if he can regain what was stolen. It's unlikely the English will expect the Scots quite so soon, so we may have the advantage. I'm glad you're here. You can go with him. Is all well at Duffdour?"

"I have news, but I would prefer that you and Conal hear it at the same time," the laird said.

Adair pouted. "Why can't you just tell me now?" she demanded.

He chuckled. "Because if I did, sister, you would blurt it out to Conal as he came into the hall, and it's my news to tell."

"Ohh," Adair said. "It must be very good news."

"Or very bad," he teased her.

"Duncan!" The laird of Duffdour's younger half brother, Murdoc, came into the hall.

"Ho, laddie! I swear you have grown another foot since I last saw you," the laird said, hugging his youngest sibling warmly.

"Duncan has news, but he won't tell me until Conal comes home," Adair said.

"I'll bet I know," Murdoc replied with a mischievous grin.

"You *do*?" Adair and the laird said in unison.

"Tell me at once, you wicked lad!" Adair said to her younger brother-in-law.

Murdoc shook his dark head. "Nay, 'tis Duncan's news."

"How could you know?" the laird asked.

"I have just come from St. Mary's," Murdoc said. "I needed advice in a certain matter, and when Mother Mary Andrew heard what it was she allowed Maggie to speak with me. I have news too, and I will not wait for Conal to come into the hall. I have decided to become a priest. I am not comfortable as a fighting man, and I have naught to offer a lass, neither land nor coin. For younger sons such as myself there is only one other way, and that is the Church. Once I have been trained and ordained, I hope Conal will offer me a place here at Cleit."

"If he doesn't you can come to Duffdour, laddie," the laird said. "I would welcome a priest, and I even have a church for you. The priest there now is ancient."

"Thank you, Duncan," Murdoc Bruce said.

"What are you thanking him for?" Conal Bruce said as he came into his hall. "Duncan, what brings you to Cleit?" He took a goblet of wine from the servant, who had finally brought them, along with the laird's bread and meat.

"I've made up my mind, Conal. I'm going to St. Andrews to study for the priesthood," Murdoc said.

Conal Bruce nodded. "I thought it might come to that," he said. "I'll pay your way into the priesthood, Murdoc. After all, we share both father and mother."

"If you can manage to support a priest when I'm through I would like to return to Cleit, but if you cannot Duncan has offered me a place at Duffdour. 'Twas why I was thanking him," Murdoc Bruce explained.

"Why would you need a priest?" Conal Bruce asked his elder sibling.

"I have a church, and an old cleric who will eventually die or need to be sent to a comfortable cottage," the laird of Duffdour told the laird of Cleit. "My people are glad to have a priest among them, and I'll eventually need to replace him."

"Duncan has come with news!" Adair said excitedly, her violet eyes dancing.

"You're married," Conal Bruce said drolly.

His wife swatted at him. "Don't be silly, Conal. When Duncan marries we'll all come to the wedding, dance, and drink to his health and that of his bride."

"Then raise your goblets," Duncan Armstrong said, "for Conal is correct. I was married at Sterling in the king's own chapel, by the king's own confessor, almost a week ago. Her name is Ellen MacArthur."

Adair shrieked. "Why didn't you call for us to come, you wretch!" She hit him on the arm. "Now you must tell us all. Sit down, the three of you, at the high board, and we'll eat and speak on this. How did you meet this lass? Who are her people? How old is she? And why were you married in the king's chapel by his confessor? God's wounds! The girl is enceinte by the king, and he wanted to give her a husband. That's it, isn't it, Duncan? You'll be raising a king's brat such as I was!"

Duncan Armstrong burst out laughing. He was still laughing as he seated himself at his brother's high board. He laughed so hard he almost choked on the last bit of bread and meat he had crammed into his mouth. "Adair, Adair," he finally said. "That is quite a tale you have just woven, but 'tis not even near the truth. Ellen MacArthur was her grandfather's heiress. She was to wed with a cousin, Donald MacNab," he began.

"Northern names," Conal Bruce said. "Is she a Highlander, then?"

"Aye, she is," Duncan replied. "A distant kinsman, however, was offended that Ewan MacArthur would give his only heiress to a MacNab. He attempted to convince this laird to give the girl to his son, but the old man was adamant. Suspecting his kin would bridenap Ellen, he sent her to the king, asking that Jamie protect her. This the king did, putting her with his aunt's household. Over a year later a message came from Ewan Mac-

Arthur asking that Ellen be returned home to Lochearn to be wed to her cousin Donald MacNab.

"It was at that point I arrived at court asking the king's permission to fortify Duffdour. The king gave me permission in exchange for escorting Ellen home, which I did. When we reached Lochearn we found the old laird and the bridegroom slain by his MacArthur kin. They had forced Ewan MacArthur to sign papers making this same kin's son his heir, and betrothing Ellen to him."

"How terrible," Adair exclaimed. "The poor girl."

"I had six men with me, and there was no way I could get her out of there. I managed to extract a promise from the bastard that he would not wed her for a month, so she might mourn her grandfather and her bridegroom. Then I took my men and departed with all haste. That night, however, her betrothed husband attempted to rape her. She defended herself and cut him up quite badly with her dirk. Then she fled Lochearn and came after me. I returned her to the king, who put her in my care until the matter could be straightened out to everyone's satisfaction. Maggie came from St. Mary's to chaperone Ellen. She remained at Duffdour all last winter.

"Several weeks ago the king recalled her to Sterling. She had not, sadly, dispatched Balgair MacArthur—that is his name—to hell, where he certainly belongs, but she had done a lovely job of carving him to bits. He was a horror to behold, and his hatred for Ellen oozed from him," Duncan continued. "Once the snows had melted and he had healed so he could travel, he had come down from the Highlands to reclaim her. The poor lass was terrified. The king questioned her once again, but she did not waver in her story. Balgair, however, blustered, boasted, and demanded the return of his *bride*, but the king is no fool. Balgair's father is one of the MacDonald's pipers. For the sake of peace between the lord of the isles and King James, he could not detain Balgair and punish him for the murders he had committed. Balgair even admitted to the murders before us all, for he was proud of having Lochearn retained as MacArthur family property.

"Instead the king told him that while he would be laird of Lochearn, Ellen would not be turned over to him. Jamie said he saw the anger Balgair had for her, and it was obvious that she detested him. There was too much hatred between them ever to be mended, the king said, and he sent him home. Ellen thanked him for saving her once again, and asked the king's aunt, who had been with us, if she would take her into service, as she now had nothing for a dower.

"Jamie laughed, and told Ellen she had a very comfortable dower. It seems that after Ellen's escape from Lochearn the king had gotten in contact with the MacDonald regarding the murders of Ewan MacArthur and Donald MacNab. After some negotiation they had agreed that Ellen could not return to Lochearn, but that she should be compensated for the theft of her dower. The lord of the isles paid a more than fair compensation for Lochearn and for the old laird's murder. As for Donald MacNab, it is a certainty that his kinfolk will have their revenge on Balgair, not just for Donald's murder, but for the loss of Lochearn's lands. And I would enjoy being a shadow in the chamber when Balgair MacArthur learns that Lochearn does not belong to him." Duncan laughed heartily. "He dare not defy the MacDonald, who is his overlord, and even his own father will not defend him against his master. All his scheming has come to naught. He has neither the land nor the lass."

"But he was certainly encouraged by his family to take Lochearn by force," Conal noted, and the others nodded in agreement.

"Aye, he was, and I have no doubt the MacDonald knew of the MacArthurs' plans. But I doubt any anticipated the level of violence that would be done. Balgair was not content to force the old man to sign a document making him his heir, or to sign another giving Ellen to Balgair as his wife. He lured young MacNab to Lochearn and then murdered both of them in cold blood. It was unnecessary. Ellen would have returned home and been forced to the altar. Would the MacNabs have objected? Aye, they would have, but it would have been done. There might have been a bit of warring between the two clans, but then a penalty would have been paid for the MacNabs' disappointment. Ewan MacArthur was not a well man. He would have died in a year or less. There was no need for Ellen to come home to find her grandfather and her bridegroom with their throats slit, tied to chairs at the high board."

"I cannot even begin to imagine her horror at such a sight," Adair murmured.

"She's a braw lassie," Duncan Armstrong said. "She kept her head about her and was able to successfully escape." There was just the hint of pride in his voice when he spoke of her, and while his brothers did not particularly notice it, Adair did.

"How did she end up your wife?" she asked her brother-in-law.

Duncan smiled. "The king and his aunt agreed she must have a husband. Jamie asked her if she would accept his choice, and she said she would. Since she had lived at Duffdour all last winter and was familiar with me, and since I did not have a wife, the king decided that I should make her the perfect husband."

Adair giggled. "Was it a shock?" she asked him mischievously.

"Aye," he responded with a grin. "It was, but I could not say nay, could I?"

"You were wed that same day?" Conal Bruce wanted to know.

"The next day," Duncan said. "Jamie wanted us on the road immediately thereafter. The king's own confessor married us after Prime. We returned Maggie to her convent and departed the next day for Duffdour, reaching it late that second day, yesterday. I left my keep early this morning to ride to Cleit to share my news with you."

"You left your bride alone to herself?" Adair was shocked.

"I wanted her to have a little time to take in all that has happened to her in the last seven months, and be settled in her mind." He sighed. "Unlike you, Conal, I had hoped to find love—true love—in the woman I married."

"You do not think you can love her?" Adair said softly.

"I do not know, because I don't really know Ellen," Duncan replied. "She spent just about all of her time last winter with Maggie. Maggie seems to like her, though."

"What does she look like?" Murdoc asked his eldest sibling.

"Oh, she's fair, very fair. The king calls her bonny," Duncan said. "Ellen is petite and just slightly rounded. Her eyes are a soft, misty gray-blue, her skin luminescent like a pearl. But 'tis her hair I love. It is long, thick, and a glorious red-gold in color."

"It would appear you like her," Conal Bruce said dryly to his elder half brother.

"I do!" Duncan said. "She's pretty, intelligent, and amusing, not to mention brave. Of course I like her."

Adair smiled a little cat's smile. "Then there is hope, Duncan, that you will come to love her. Be certain to tell her when you do. Do not be like your brother."

"Will you never leave off naggling me about that?" the laird of Cleit said, irritated. "I finally said it. I'll say it now, Adair. I love you!"

Duncan and Murdoc laughed, remembering how difficult it had been for Conal Bruce to admit that he loved the woman who was now his wife.

"When do we get to meet your bride?" Adair asked.

"I'll stay with you a day or so. Perhaps, Conal, I can ride out with you when you go raiding tonight. Then I must oversee the moving of my cattle to a summer pasturage. Come in another week or ten days."

"We'll come in a month," Adair said. "You need

time alone with your Ellen, you great lout. The poor lass will begin to think you don't want a wife if you don't spend some time with her." She laughed. "I do believe that you are shy of her, Duncan, and I have never known you to be shy with the lasses. How Agnes Carr would laugh."

He reddened. "Damn, madam, you have too sharp a tongue."

"And a sharper eye," Adair told him. Then, reaching out, she took his hand in hers. "You're a good man, Duncan," she said, and she squeezed his hand. "Any lass would be fortunate to have you as a husband. The king and his aunt saw it. I suspect your little Ellen sees it too. But remember, if you are shy of her, she is even shyer. She's been raised by her beloved grandfather. She'll need your reassurance, gentleness, and good heart. And in time she will learn to love you, and you her. This is not a bad thing, this marriage. I doubt if you would have ever had the courage to ask a woman to wed with you. I don't know what it is about big, strong men that they cannot say certain words."

"I love you," Conal Bruce murmured in his wife's ear, and she turned, smiling, as she released her brother-in-law's big hand.

"I love you," she told him, and he grinned as if he had never before heard the words from her lips. Then she patted his rough cheek. "Be careful out there tonight," she said. "The moon is almost full, my lord."

"Do you know who has been raiding?" Duncan asked. "It's been very quiet at Duffdour, but I suspect my walls no longer make us so easy a target. And you've always been safe here on your hill."

"It's my village on the other side of the hill. They are vulnerable to raiders," Conal Bruce told his brother, "and my keep isn't big enough to shelter them all. The English have discovered that. The raiding parties all seem to be directed by the same man, Sir Roger Colby. He is, the gossip would have it, a friend of King Henry."

"I thought we had a peace with the English," Duncan said.

"We were supposed to," Adair said, "but even as the two kings signed the document, the Tudor king's ships were attacking Scots ships in our own waters. The three-year truce has lasted but eight months, I fear."

"Where did you learn all this?" Duncan was curious.

"Hercules Hepburn comes now and again to hunt with Conal," Adair said.

"And you know my wife is most interested in politics," the laird of Cleit observed. "It is her upbringing, I fear. I can't seem to wean her from it."

Duncan laughed. "You shouldn't. She learns all manner of fascinating facts."

Encouraged, Adair continued as they helped themselves to the dishes being brought now by the servants: mussels in mustard sauce, trout in white wine, a large, fat roasted capon with a cherry sauce, a small roast of venison, lark pie, rabbit stew, braised lettuces, fresh peas, bread, butter, and cheese. "King Henry is working very hard to make King James's government unstable. His agents are coming privily to the border lords in hopes of getting them to switch their allegiances from Scotland to England. Those who refuse, or who they think might refuse, are being raided. The price of peace here on the border right now is loyalty to the Tudor king."

"The Tudor king is *not* Scotland's king," Duncan said grimly. "And Sir Roger is King Harry's chief agent, I am assuming."

"Aye," Adair told him. "He is, I am told, a ruthless man, much like his master."

"Then this is why Jamie made mention of a lad who claims to be your half brother, Richard. He is being championed by the Duchess of Burgundy, Margaret Plantagenet," Duncan said.

"Both Edward and Richard are dead!" Adair said. Tears sprang to her eyes. "The young page who escaped Middlesham after King Richard was killed at Bosworth

Field came to me and told me so. He saw the boys strangled and their bodies carried away. The murderers would have been Lancastrians, of course, although in whose pay we will never know. Henry Tudor has killed or imprisoned any other Yorkist claimants to the throne who remained in England. Poor Warwick languishes in the Tower."

"I fear our King James seeks to pay back in kind the Tudor's behavior toward him, and toward Scotland. If he supports this lad's claim to England's throne, who knows to where it will lead, Adair?"

"The English are comfortable now with this king of theirs. They are tired of warring. They will not support any pretender, no matter who advocates for him. Especially a Scots king. If Scots borderers are bitter over the constant raiding, so too are the English borderers weary of it. But they will fight if need be for King Henry," Adair said. "If this Sir Roger Colby has been appointed by the Tudor to cause havoc and dissension, the English borderers will support him, I fear. It is our way of life here in the borders to steal one another's cattle, sheep, and women, but it is not usual for it to be done with such violence as has been seen of late."

"We'll only seek out where Sir Roger holes up," Conal Bruce said, "and return with our livestock and women. I have an idea where he is. But next time we will burn his house to the ground." He flashed a wolfish smile. "But you, Murdoc, shall not go. If you are to be a priest you want nothing more on your conscience than is now there, lad. I'm certain your exploits in Agnes Carr's bed are more than enough for our priest to tolerate." The laird of Cleit chuckled, enjoying the flush on his little brother's face.

"The priest visits Agnes now and again. He says it is to pray with her. She says he comes to fuck her first, and then he prays afterward with her for forgiveness," Murdoc told them with a broad grin. "She says for an old man he is quite lusty."

His brothers and sister-in-law burst out laughing.

"God bless Agnes," Duncan said.

"She'll be heartbroken to learn you have a wife," Murdoc said.

"Aye, I have a wife," Duncan said, smiling.

"May I go and meet her while you are off raiding and herding cattle?" Murdoc said. He was the youngest of his late mother's five children, and his siblings had a tendency to be protective of him. Cleit's cook, Elsbeth, adored him.

Duncan thought a moment, and then he nodded. "Aye, ride over to Duffdour tomorrow and meet Ellen. You need not wait a month or more. 'Tis foolish."

"I'll go with you," Adair said. "When you have finished your raiding, Conal, you may join us there. And we'll wait for Duncan to return from his cattle herding before we return home. I'm sure his lass will welcome a bit of company."

"Will you bring your bairns?" Duncan wanted to know.

"Gracious, no! We don't want to frighten the poor lass," Adair replied with a small smile. "My noisy lot might put her off bairns, and you need an heir."

When it was fully dark Conal Bruce, his brother Duncan Armstrong, and their men rode out and headed across the Scots border into the English border. The night was still, and an almost full moon lit the landscape. The laird of Cleit had been told by a passing peddler that Sir Roger Colby had a house in the region known as the Devil's Glen. As they neared it they slowed their horses to muffle the sound of their hooves.

" 'Tis well named," Duncan murmured softly as they entered the narrow passage into the little valley. Sheer rock walls and heavy stands of trees surrounded them.

"Aye, it's a good hidey-hole," Conal agreed.

At the end of the glen they saw a large stone house, barns, and pens filled with cattle. At the Bruce's upraised hand they stopped. The house was dark, indicating that its master was not in residence. Or perhaps on this fine summer's night he was out raiding once again. A dog barked twice, but they could not see any indication of men guarding the cattle pens. Obviously Sir Roger felt secure in the Devil's Glen.

"Where do you think the women are?" Conal said to his brother.

"Probably the cellars, and I am certain there is household help, but how many servants and how well armed is the question," Duncan said. "Look, at the top of the house—a light. I'll wager the servants sleep there. If we could get into the house and then into the cellars we might be able to find the three women without rousing anyone. We can take the cattle afterward."

"We'll have to move quickly," Conal Bruce said. "I don't want to get caught at the end of this glen, or in the narrow track leading back to the moors."

"I'll go into the house," Duncan said, and he signaled to two of his clansmen.

"No," his brother said. "I'll go into the house. The lasses are more apt to recognize me than you. You haven't lived at Cleit in several years. You start taking the cattle from their pens."

"How many do you want?" the laird of Duffdour asked.

Conal Bruce grinned wickedly. "My own, and as many others as we can steal," he replied. Then he gestured to several of his men and, dismounting, went toward the house. Soon the shadows of the raiders disappeared.

Duncan Armstrong spoke to the men surrounding him. "Take all of the cattle, lads," he said. The two pens were opened, and as the cattle began to stream out slowly the clansmen herded them away from Sir Roger's house and back toward the moors. The laird of Duffdour directed them with soft words and hand signals as they worked. Soon the cattle were gone from his sight, but he remained, waiting for Conal. And finally the laird of Cleit came from the house with his men and the three women who had been stolen. The clansmen mounted, pulling the women up behind them. Then, the two lairds leading the way, they made good their escape from the Devil's Glen.

Out on the moor the sky above was now black, the long summer's night coming to an end slowly before the dawn. The moon shone brightly as they rode, the noise of the cattle's and horses' hooves thundering rhythmically as they galloped along. They instinctively knew when the English border became the Scots border. And finally, as the night gave way to the false dawn, they reached Cleit. The clansmen riding with the three kidnapped women headed toward the village on the other side of the hill to return their companions back to their families.

"Why don't you take some of the cattle for yourself," Conal suggested. "You'll be heading for the high meadows at Duffdour. And you did do much of the work last night while I sought out the lasses. The English used one of them, and at first she didn't want to return, for she was so ashamed. She isn't certain her husband will want her back. I have said I would go and speak to her man. Poor lass. I know I couldn't put Adair away if something like that happened to her. What would you do, Duncan, if your wife were stolen away, and forced?"

"I don't know," Duncan answered. "I haven't yet bedded Ellen, although I mean to when I return home. I suppose if I loved her I would be outraged, but whether my anger would overcome my love is a moot point, because I barely know the lass."

"You think too much," Conal said with a grin. "Always did. I thought you might be the priest in the family. Never considered young Murdoc."

"He'll be a good priest," Duncan responded. "He is pious without being pompous. And his heart is both good and kind."

"And he understands human weaknesses, having several of them himself," Conal agreed. "But I wonder if can he refrain from fucking Agnes Carr. The rumor is that her two bairns are his." He shrugged. "But if the priesthood is his choice, then so be it."

"His conscience is between him and God. And although it's banned, there are plenty of priests even today here in Scotland with hearth mates, or who pay regular visits to the village whore on the pretext of saving her wicked soul."

They had reached the keep. The sun was coming up over the eastern hills.

"Drive them out into the pastures," Conal Bruce ordered his men. Then he and his brother entered the tower house.

Adair greeted them. "You're back safe, praise God and his Blessed Mother. Come and eat. Elsbeth has prepared an incredible breakfast for you."

"We rescued the women," Conal Bruce told his wife. "And we came back with a rather fine herd of cattle. Duncan will take some with him when he rides home."

"Murdoc and I are ready to leave for Duffdour now," Adair said. She bent and kissed her husband. "I'll see you in a few days, my lord. Try not to get into any trouble while I am away from you. Jamie's birthday is next week. I've left his gifts in the low chest in our bedchamber. Before you come to Duffdour be certain that their nursemaid knows. And he'll be six, Conal, since I know you don't remember." She laughed. And then she was gone from the hall, the elusive scent she always wore wafting behind her.

Duncan and Conal ate a hearty breakfast and then sought their beds. It had been a long night. When they awoke in early afternoon the captain of the men at arms informed them that all was quiet, and no strangers had been spotted from the heights during the day. He would post an extra watch this night, however. The bulk of the cattle had already been taken to the summer meadows. The two dozen that the laird of Duffdour wanted were now penned in the barns and out of sight.

The two brothers spent a companionable evening

talking and playing chess. The night remained calm, and in the morning Conal Bruce and Duncan Armstrong parted, one to drive his new cattle to Duffdour, and the other to strengthen the defenses of his home. They would meet again in a few days at Duffdour.

Chapter 6

$\mathcal{E}$llen was very surprised when Sim came into the hall to announce visitors.

"The lady of Cleit and my lord's youngest brother, Murdoc Bruce," he said.

Rising, Ellen went to greet her guests, her eyes quickly scanning the beautiful woman with the dark hair and the startling violet eyes who came in the company of a pleasant-faced young man with Duncan's blue eyes.

"I am your new sister, Adair," the woman said, "and this is our husbands' youngest brother, Murdoc. I hope you will not think us rude, but once Duncan told us he had married, we could not wait for a proper invitation to meet you."

"You are more than welcome to Duffdour," Ellen replied. "Sim, some wine. Our guests have had a long day's ride." She led her two visitors to places by the hearth where a small fire was burning, taking the chill off the hall.

They seated themselves, and the servants came with wine. As they waited silently, Ellen was suddenly aware she didn't know what to say, and it was apparent that Adair didn't either. She was indeed curious that her new sister-in-law had come unasked.

Finally it was Murdoc who spoke. "You're even prettier than Duncan told us," he said. "He should be back in a few days, and he'll be bringing Adair's husband with him to meet you. You're a Highlander." It wasn't a question, but a statement.

"Aye, I was, but no more," Ellen replied, and there was a touch of sadness in her voice. "But your borders are lovely, Murdoc."

"Aren't they!" Adair had found her voice. "I was raised on the English side."

"How did you come to marry the laird of Cleit?" Ellen asked.

"I was taken in a border raid. Conal bought me and my old Nursie at a Michaelmas fair. I was to housekeep for him, and Elsbeth would cook."

"Oh, my!" Ellen exclaimed, blushing. She knew what happened to women taken by raiding parties, and they didn't usually end up as wives.

"They saved us from burned porridge and weeviled bread." Murdoc chuckled.

"And you never saw your family again? That is so sad," Ellen said softly.

"My parents were long dead," Adair said. "I was six when they died."

"My grandsire raised me," Ellen responded. "My parents died in a winter epidemic. I had no brothers or sisters. It was just Grandsire and me. I was to marry my cousin Donald, but he and Grandsire were murdered by a distant MacArthur kinsman who coveted my family's lands. I will never see Lochearn again." She sighed sadly.

"And Stanton, which was my home, is destroyed. It is best to put such things in the past," Adair said. "I grieved far too long for Stanton."

"Oh, you misunderstand me," Ellen quickly said. "I am past grief. I will always remember with happiness both my childhood at Lochearn and my grandsire. But I am not a lass to look back. Memories are but empty dreams that can never be rekindled. I have been given an honorable man for a husband. And is not this keep a fine one? How can I bemoan a fate such as this, my lady?"

"Adair. My name is Adair," the lady of Cleit said. "What a sensible lass you are. Does Duncan understand that yet? Or has he been too busy adjusting to the fact that he has a pretty wife?" Adair chuckled. "You are well matched, you know. My brother-in-law is a very sensible and practical fellow."

"We hardly know each other," Ellen admitted. "Though I spent all last winter here, I kept company with Maggie. Duncan was at the board in the evening. Sometimes we played games or listened to music, but he and I had little to say to each other."

"He is an easy man to know," Adair assured Ellen.

"And he is kind and thoughtful too," Murdoc chimed in. "Why, he brought me to Agnes Carr himself my first time." Then he blushed beet red, realizing what he had said to his new sister-in-law.

"Murdoc!" Adair scolded the younger man. "Agnes Carr is not a subject to be discussed with an innocent bride." She turned to Ellen, briefly explaining. "Agnes is the village whore. She's actually a nice lass, but a lad's whore is not something to be spoken of in a lady's hall. You know better, Murdoc. You had best learn to guard your tongue if you truly mean to be a priest." But Adair was smiling slightly as she spoke. Murdoc, the youngest of the siblings, was still very ingenuous in his manner.

"I do beg your pardon, Ellen," the young man said, and his look was contrite.

"We had a whore at Lochearn, but I wasn't supposed to know about her. She taught me how to darn a sock and mend a hem," Ellen said with a twinkle.

Her companions laughed, and both the visitors from Cleit silently decided that the laird of Duffdour had not gotten a bad bargain in his new wife. Ellen was distressed to learn that Duncan had gone raiding with his brother, but Adair told her bluntly that it was simply a way of life in the borders.

"You will have to get used to your man riding off," the lady of Cleit said.

"Are you used to it?" Ellen asked.

Adair shook her head. "Nay, I have never gotten used to it, but what can I do?" she said. "At least the Bruces of Cleit do not raid or plunder until provoked to it. The English came and took some of our cattle and three village lasses the other night. You never know if a borderer is going to sell the woman or use her for his whore. Conal and Duncan retrieved both the cattle and the women. The English were out raiding, and no one was left behind to guard their hidey-hole, for they thought it well hidden. Of course, now they may come raiding again, or not. It is a vicious cycle here in the borders, and men are not apt to cease their warring until forced to it by a higher authority." She sighed. "It is so difficult to raise the bairns under such a constant threat." Then Adair smiled at Ellen. "Are you with child yet?" she asked pleasantly.

Ellen blushed to the roots of her red-gold hair. "Nay," she managed to say.

"You're certain?" Adair continued. "Do you know the signs?" she queried.

"We are but newly wed," Ellen protested faintly, and her cheeks were hot.

"Still and all, it can happen the first time, you know," Adair continued.

"It hasn't," Ellen squeaked, wishing she were anywhere else right now. How could she admit that she and Duncan hadn't yet coupled? Her husband would be publicly embarrassed if the fact that he hadn't consummated their marriage became known. A man was expected to do his duty on his wedding night, and devil take the hindmost.

"Well, it will," Adair said cheerfully. "Conal's gotten five bairns on me so far, though one died at her birth. And I've heard it said that our young priest-to-be has fathered at least two wee ones on Agnes Carr, though she will not say who the father of those bairns is," Adair continued with a chuckle. "But then, perhaps she doesn't know, although there was a time when Murdoc plowed that mare exclusively, wasn't there, little brother?"

"Adair enjoys being outspoken," Murdoc said quietly to Ellen. "I hope she has not shocked you. We excuse her because she was born English, don't we?" he teased his brother's wife wickedly.

Adair swatted him fondly. "If you mean to deny yourself the pleasures of a woman's body, Murdoc," she said, "it cannot harm you to at least know those pleasures before you take your vows. A cock is a cock, even beneath a holy cassock. Agnes's wee lads look just like you, and will always be taken care of and considered Bruces, as you well know. But the woman is too old for you. She never before allowed herself to conceive a child. I think she just wanted her own bairn and chose the best sire. She is honorable in her own way too, as she did not point a finger," Adair concluded.

While a trifle shocked by her sister-in-law's frank speech, Ellen was relieved to have had the subject changed from herself. "I'm so glad for your company," she told her visitors. "While we wait for the others to return you will tell me all about Duncan, for there is not a great deal that I know of him except that he is honorable and brave."

"Aye, he is!" Murdoc responded with a warm smile at Ellen. He had guessed her secret, although he would never say it. Still, it was like his oldest brother that he would give his bride a chance to become comfortable with her situation and her surroundings before bedding her. The startled look on her face when Adair began prying had given Ellen away, although Adair had been far too curious to notice.

"He has a grand sense of humor," Adair noted, "and

as I have previously said, he is the most sensible of the three brothers, isn't he, Murdoc?"

"He is," Murdoc agreed, not in the least offended.

"He is intelligent and extremely clever," Adair continued. "Of the three brothers he is the wisest. 'Twas he who figured out how to marry me to my Conal when I had said I would not until the man admitted his love for me," she recalled with a smile. "Duncan could serve the king well if he chose."

"He is too canny to involve himself with the king and his court," Murdoc noted. "He remembers the king's late father, and with whom he chose to surround himself."

"I don't understand," Ellen said.

"Old James, the third of his line, preferred useful and artistic companions to the great lords, who became jealous of those favored few and at one point rose up, slaying the former king's friends," Adair said.

"I had heard our king's father was deviant in his liking of other men," Ellen murmured, a blush suffusing her pale cheeks.

"Perhaps he was, and perhaps he wasn't," Murdoc replied. "He did his duty by Scotland and sired several children on his queen. And when she died he was devastated and mourned her deeply. Who knows what the real truth of it all was?"

"James the Third lost his father at a young age, and his mother was a great influence on him and on his life," Adair explained. "She was an elegant lady from a cultured court, a niece of the Duke of Burgundy. It was from his mother that James the Third gained his love of the arts. He was only nine years of age when he became king."

"What happened to his sire?" Ellen wanted to know.

"King James the Second had a love of gunnery. At the siege of Roxburgh he was supervising the firing of a canon when it exploded and killed him instantly. When she learned of it, the queen immediately hastened to Roxburgh with her oldest son. Once there she urged her late husband's commanders onto a victory, which they accomplished, and a week later King James the Third was crowned at nearby Kelso Abbey, his reign begun with a victory. Then a long-term peace was made with my father, King Edward the Fourth."

Ellen gasped, surprised. "You are a king's daughter?" she asked.

"A king's brat," Adair replied, "for all the good it did me. It's a long story for another day, Ellen."

"Then tell me more of this history of which you know," Ellen said, somewhat taken aback by the casual way in which Adair referred to her birth. "Though I lived at court for well over a year, actually almost two, little is spoken there of the past. The women gossip endlessly on men and fashion. Only my mistress, the king's aunt, spoke on more important matters, for she is very wise, but she rarely spoke of her brother, the late king. All her efforts went into aiding her nephew, our young king. She is devoted to him. Tell me more of our king's father."

"The queen was a great influence on her eldest son, and it is said that he looked more like her, with his dark eyes, olive skin, and black hair. Like her he was pious and loved the arts, a knowledge that she imparted to him. But she died when he was twelve, and two years later his mentor, the wise and beloved bishop of St. Andrews, also died. The king was seized by the Boyds of Kilmarnock, who forced him to approve their coup d'état. They sought to secure their power over the king by marrying Lord Boyd's son to his sister, Princess Mary. And when he was eighteen years old, they arranged for James the Third to marry King Christian of Denmark's daughter, Margaret. But once he had the love of a good wife, King James the Third came into his majority, as his father before him had done. He punished the Boyds for their presumption in seizing his person, and attempting to rule through him, as his father had chastened the Livingstone family who had controlled his minority. Lord Boyd and his son fled Scotland, dying in exile. Others in the family were executed, or penalized with fines and the loss of their lands," Adair said. "Kings love excuses for confiscating other people's lands. They use them to bribe others," she said with a grin, and then continued. "Queen Margaret was a good queen, a good wife, a pious lady. She gave her husband three sons. But the king was more interested in the arts and acquiring paintings and musicians than he was in ruling. His extravagances cost the people. And what could not be forgiven was the fact that he chose his close friends and advisers from among those who, like him, had a passion for beauty. They were not men from great families. The great lords were offended, and they more often than not bridled against him. This king of theirs could not ride well, could speak French and Italian but not the language of the Highlands, and disliked hunting and carousing." Adair chuckled mischievously. "Scots do love their wine and their hunting."

Ellen nodded in agreement. "What happened next?" she asked.

"As our King James grew older," Adair went on, "the lords rallied about him until several years ago a battle ensued between the father and the son, the result of which was that the old king was killed, and James the Fourth ascended to the throne of Scotland. I have often wondered just how involved in that business our king really was. He claims he did not wish to depose his father or see him dead, but any sensible person knows that a country can have only one king," Adair concluded.

"King James is an honest man," Ellen defended the monarch. "He would never have had any part in the murder of his father. But tell me, how is it that you know so much?" Ellen asked.

"I was raised at my father's court, and am well educated," Adair told her. "You cannot grow up in a royal court and not listen to what is being said or see what is going on about you. And if you are wise you say naught, but retain what you know to use when it can be of help to you." She smiled at Ellen, realizing the girl was intrigued by her words and her manner.

"Can you speak foreign tongues?" Ellen inquired.

"I can," Adair admitted.

"I can speak my Highland tongue, French, and church Latin," Ellen said. "I learned to speak as you southerners do when I lived at court. I wonder if I am the proper wife for a man like my husband. What if one day he decides to offer his services to the king?"

"Duncan will not leave his lands without very good cause," Murdoc told Ellen. "The king once hinted to him that he would be welcome at court, but my brother refused. His name is not a powerful one; nor does he have the resources to make a career at court."

"And you would appear to be just the kind of wife he should have," Adair said. "You are pretty. You know housewifery. Your servants, I can see, already respect you. You are, I suspect, loyal. Give Duncan heirs and you will be perfect," she teased the younger woman, laughing.

During the next few days that followed, Ellen learned enough about her new family to realize that she was going to get on well with them. Her sister-in-law, the beautiful Adair Bruce, was proud but kind, if outspoken. Her brother-in-law Murdoc Bruce was a gentle young man with a tender heart. And then the laird of Cleit arrived to join them, and Ellen was at first startled by the resemblance between her husband and his younger half brother. She remarked upon it.

"We favor our mother," Conal Bruce said. "Murdoc looks more like our father." The laird of Cleit looked his new sister-in-law over carefully. She was a very pretty lass, with her gray-blue eyes and her red-gold hair. He was amazed that Duncan had sheltered her for several long winter months and not even attempted to seduce her. That round little figure of hers was extremely tempting. But listening to Ellen speak of Donald MacNab, her grandsire, and Lochearn, Conal Bruce suddenly under-stood the depth of honor Duncan Armstrong had ex-hibited. But he was her husband now. How long did he intend to remain away from such a delicious treat?

And after a week had passed during which Ellen had fed them, and housed them, and ridden out to hunt with them, and they had spoken at length on a variety of sub-jects, the laird of Duffdour returned home to be greeted by his relations and his young wife, the latter of whom welcomed him sweetly with a kiss on his lips.

"I have a tub ready for you, my lord," she said, smiling.

"A tub?" He was surprised. Why would she have a tub? He was hungry and wanted a hot meal. He was tired and wanted his bed.

"You have been gone for some days, my lord," Ellen said. "I will bathe you myself, as I was taught by Lady Margaret at the court. But first come to the table and eat." She led him to his high board, where his servants hurried to bring him several dishes steaming hot from the kitchen. There was a bowl of freshwater mussels with a mustard sauce for dipping; a large rabbit pie, its flaky pastry oozing a rich brown gravy; a fat roasted duck, its skin crisp and black; warm, fresh bread; sweet butter and cheese.

Duncan Armstrong ate greedily, noticing as he finally slowed the pace of his chewing to drink half of his wine-filled goblet that his guests were happily consuming the contents of the bowls and platters too. There was more than enough food. He couldn't remember since he had come to Duffdour as its laird his table being so well laid, and he realized at once that the credit belonged to Ellen. He turned to her with a smile and, taking up her little hand, kissed it. "Thank you," was all he said, but she fully understood him, and smiled back.

"Your servants but needed direction, my lord," Ellen murmured. "Your sister, being a nun, was more abstemi-ous in her manner. Maggie had never run a household, as she was raised to sing and pray. She did her best by you last winter. I did not feel it was my place to interfere or guide her. Had she asked I certainly would have rendered my aid, for I was raised to manage my husband's house."

"The sauce for the mussels was excellent," he told her. "I was not aware my cook had such talents."

"The sauce was one I learned from the cook at Lochearn," Ellen explained. "I am glad to have pleased you, Duncan."

"There are other ways in which you would please me, lass," he said, low.

She blushed, but nodded. "I am ready," she told him softly.

"Because it is your duty?" he asked her, scanning her pretty face.

"Aye." Ellen nodded candidly, but then she added, "And because I like you, my lord." She blushed again at her bold words.

He chuckled. "I like you too," he said with a grin.

And Ellen laughed. Then she arose from the table. "I will go and prepare your bath for you, my lord," she said. She smiled at her guests, curtsying. "I bid you all a good night," Ellen said, and hurried from her hall.

"She's bonny," Conal Bruce said to his brother. "You're a lucky man."

"That's what the king has always called her. 'My bonny,'" Duncan replied.

"You don't think—" Conal began.

"Nay. He never touched her. Of that I am certain. He thinks of her as he would a younger sister, a fond companion. They play chess together. He told me she was the best opponent he had ever had, and she plays to win, having no regard for his rank whatsoever." Duncan chuckled. "And she teases him about it when he loses to her." The laird of Duffdour thought a long moment. "I truly believe that they are good friends."

Conal Bruce nodded. "I would not have thought Jamie could be friends with a woman he didn't bed."

His brothers laughed, as did Adair.

Then Duncan Armstrong arose. "I believe my wife is awaiting me," he said. "I will bid you all a good night." He bowed and hurried from the hall. When he reached the bedchamber he shared with Ellen he found a tall-ish oaken tub set up by the fireplace. "God's blood!" he swore softly. "Where did you find it? I haven't seen that old tub since I was a lad here. Our mother, in her chemise, used to get into it with Ian, Margaret, and me to wash us. Maggie was so small she would stand on a stool, while Ian and I stood with the water up to our necks," he recalled.

"I realize it may seem odd to you," Ellen said, "but I like bathing in warm water. I had Sim search the attic and the cellar, because he said he remembered a tub. We found it, and the cooper rebanded it with fresh iron straps and tarred the inside. It's quite watertight now." She was standing in her chemise as she spoke, her hair pinned up.

"Will you get into the tub like my mother did?" he asked her.

"Of course! I cannot wash you from outside the tub," Ellen told him. "Get out of your garments, or do you need help?" she asked.

"Nay, I can undress myself. I need no coterie of servants with tasks like 'stocking peeler,' " he responded as he began to pull his clothing off.

Ellen climbed up the steps to the tub and stepped down into the water as he did so. It wasn't as hot as she would have wished, and it was already beginning to cool. She moved to the far side of the tub, and her back was turned when he entered it. Only then did she turn about, a washing cloth in hand. "Let's start with your face," she said, and she wiped the soapy rag over his face, carefully cleansing the dirt of several days from his nose, around his eyes, and his forehead. She rinsed the soap off quickly and cleaned his ears, moving next to his neck.

"You will make a good mother one day," he said softly.

She caught his gaze with hers. "Before we get to that task you must be clean," she told him frankly.

"You have a delicate nose then," he remarked teasingly.

"I cannot believe a man's lust is so great that he would prefer a woman smelling of her own filth and sweat to one who smelled fresh and clean," Ellen replied. Her cloth swept across his chest, with its dark-furred mat. "Turn about." And when he complied she washed the back of his neck and his upper back to the waist. Still standing behind him, she washed his two arms. Then, before he realized what was happening, she dumped a pitcher of water over his head.

"You're drowning me, lass!" he protested.

"Stand still!" she ordered him sharply.

He felt her fingers begin massaging soap into his dark hair and realized that she was standing on the tub's stool. She rinsed, soaped again, rinsed again, and then began picking through his hair with swift fingers.

"No nits!" she pronounced, pleased.

"You haven't done the naughty bits," he teased her, turning about and wrapping his arms about her as she stood on the stool. "Shall I stand on the stool for you?" His blue eyes danced wickedly.

"Lady Margaret always said a man is capable of washing his own privates," Ellen replied primly, but her cheeks were flaming.

She had engaged his lust, and his cock was hardening as he stood in the water, his arms about her soft body. Had she had any experience he would have pressed her back against the tub's wall and had his way with her. But she was still a virgin, and he didn't think it would make for a good deflowering to do such a thing. Instead he pulled her wet chemise from her body and kissed her mouth—a long, slow kiss. His big hand couldn't resist closing about a small round breast and squeezing it gently. Then he teased at the nipple for a moment, his mouth still on hers.

"Oh." She had not meant to gasp, but it had all come as a sudden surprise to Ellen. One moment she was washing him; the next she was naked, and his hands and mouth were doing wonderful things to her.

"I like it when you bathe me," he said against her mouth, and his tongue encircled her ripe lips. "We must bathe together frequently, Ellen."

"I've already washed," she managed to say. "The water is cooling. You must get out before you catch an ague, my lord. There are towels on the drying rack by the fire." If he didn't stop caressing her breast she was going to melt into the tub.

"Aren't you going to dry me?" he asked mischievously.

"Then I would be in danger of an ague," Ellen told him.

"Stay in the water until I am dry," he told her as he climbed back out of their tub.

"Why?" she queried him. His buttocks were very firm and tight. She had never before considered a man's backside, but his was certainly pleasant to view.

"Because after I've dried myself I mean to dry you," he told her.

"Oh." The thought of those big hands roaming over her body sent a flush of heat through her. Briefly she wanted to flee him, but where would she go dripping wet? She stood quietly, listening to the beat of her heart in her ears. And then she heard his voice.

"Come now, my pretty wife, and step from the tub," he said.

"You will see me as God made me," she replied.

"Indeed, I mean to see you as God made you. And make love to you as God made you. Lovers should not hide behind anything, either pride or garments, Ellen."

As she arose she could not help but admire his nakedness. His limbs were long and well made. His chest was broad and his belly flat. He stood unabashed before her gaze, and for some reason it gave her courage she hadn't realized she had. She stepped up from their tub, down the narrow wooden steps, and into the warmed towel he held out for her. The brief chill of the chamber was erased as he wrapped the cloth about her.

Slowly he rubbed her skin dry, using the corners of the towel to reach portions of her flesh. He dried her shoulders, back, buttocks, and legs; and when he had he sat her on the edge of their bed, kneeling to dry her feet. The towel rubbed moisture from her arms and chest. And then, taking each breast individually, he dried it, kissing the nipple as he finished. He took up a hand, glossing over the palm and then drying the fingers. Then he took two of her fingers, putting them into his mouth to suck on them slowly, sensuously, his blue eyes staring into her gray-blue ones.

Ellen felt a wave of weakness sweep over her. She couldn't move or speak. The sensation of his tongue encircling her fingers in his mouth was something that in her wildest dreams she had never imagined. She knew nothing about lying with a lover, but if this was an example of what was to come, Ellen realized she was eager to learn. She drew her two fingers from his mouth and, imitating him, took one of his big fingers into her mouth to suck upon it, but only briefly.

She couldn't know, of course, Duncan Armstrong realized, what she was doing other than following his actions. He thought her adorable at that moment. Reaching out, he dried the thick fluff of red curls at the junction of her thighs and belly. Then, tossing the damp towel away, he stood up, pulling her with him. They stood, bodies touching, and the weakness swept over Ellen again. She would have fallen but that he was holding her tightly. Was she breathing? She wasn't certain as she tipped her face up to his.

"You are so fair," he said, and there was a catch in his voice when he spoke. His hand caressed her face, fingers brushing against her cheek, running over her lips.

"I can wait no longer to possess you, Ellen. I don't want you fearful or repelled, but I cannot wait, lass. Can you forgive me?"

"You are not Balgair MacArthur," Ellen said quietly. "I am your wife, Duncan, and it is my duty to pleasure you, to give you an heir. We cannot do that if we do not . . ." She ceased speaking, blushing rosy.

"Nay," he said, low, "we cannot, can we? Let me make love to you, my wee wife. Trust me not to harm you, for I know you to be a true virgin. Your innocence is your gift to me, and the greatest gift a woman may give to a man, for once taken it cannot be returned or given again." He brushed her lips tenderly with his own.

"Do you desire me, my lord?" she asked him. "Or do you do a duty?"

In answer he took her small hand and brought it to his groin, where his manhood was already hard and eager for her, and when her fingers wrapped themselves about his cock he groaned. "Here is the proof of my desire for you, Ellen," he told her.

She felt the thick rod of flesh pulsing with life within her gentle grasp. "Is it alive?" she asked him almost fearfully as she loosened her grip on him.

"It beats with life, my darling," he said. "It yearns to plunge deep into the hot, wet softness hidden between your legs. It needs desperately to feel the walls of your sweet sheath closing about it." His hands closed about her little waist, and he lifted her up, holding her so he might lick at her small, round breasts.

Her head was spinning. Her heart was hammering. His tongue played over the firm flesh of her breasts, and then his mouth closed over a nipple, sucking it.

"Oh, holy Mother!" Ellen cried, startled by the emotions that engulfed her.

He laid her upon their bed, looking down at her for a long moment. Then he joined her, gathering her into his embrace, his mouth finding hers, kissing her with long, slow kisses that sent wave after wave of heat through her body. She felt his hard length against her leg, and bridled nervously.

"Nah, nah, lassie," he said softly, pushing back the sudden fear that threatened to rise up and overwhelm her. His hand stroked her breasts and belly gently, his fingers tangling themselves amid the thick curls covering her plump mons veneris. He could feel the wet heat rising up from her. An exploratory finger brushed down her shadowed slit, slipping into the moisture between her nether lips. She murmured, but neither struggled nor forbade him. Without difficulty he found her little love bud. The ball of that single finger rubbed against it again and again until Ellen began to whimper.

With another man her lack of knowledge might have been terrifying, but Ellen had instinctively trusted Duncan Armstrong from the moment they had met. When he told her he would not harm her, she believed him. And certainly the delicious feelings he was arousing in her were more exciting than frightening. Her body seemed to grow tenser and tenser as that wicked finger of his teased at her, and then it was as if something inside her burst, and she shuddered as a wave a pleasure washed over her. And as it did the finger moved past the sensitive nub of flesh, and without warning began to push into her body.

"Nah, nah, lass," he crooned at her again as she stiffened. The single finger began to move back and forth within her, and then she realized there were two fingers. His mouth found hers again, his tongue mimicking the motion of his fingers, and Ellen's head spun. His lips brushed against her closed eyelids. "I want to be inside of you," he whispered in her ear, his breath hot. "I need to be inside of you, my wee wife."

Her hips had begun to move in time with his fingers, and it wasn't enough, Ellen realized. She wanted him inside of her. She needed him inside of her. How could this be? And how could she know it? And yet she did.

"Yes!" she managed to gasp. "Please, yes! Tell me what to do, my lord! Tell me!"

"Open your legs for me, my darling," Duncan gently instructed her. "Tonight I will do all the rest." He pushed her knees up, sliding between them. His hot cock was engorged with his desire, his need for her. Carefully he guided himself into position. He had already ascertained that her maidenhead was tightly ensconced. He pushed carefully, slowly into her tight sheath, sinking himself carefully.

"Are you too big?" she questioned him nervously.

"Nay," he assured her. "Your body will shortly yield to me, my darling; I promise you. Trust me, Ellen."

"I have heard it said that my deflowering will hurt," she whispered.

"Only once," he said honestly.

"And after?"

He could see the blue-veined pulse in her slender throat leaping against her creamy flesh. "Only pleasure," he promised her. "Now wrap your legs about me so I may sink deeper into your sweet body, my wee wife." And when she had complied with his request he kissed her a fierce, hard kiss, absorbing the cry of pain that escaped her when he thrust against her maidenhead. Once. Twice. A third time, and the membrane finally shattered, letting him drive deep into her. He licked the tears from her cheeks, his hot tongue tenderly caressing the salty moisture from her skin. Then he began to move rhythmically within her, slowly, slowly, until she was moaning low against his mouth, her body straining against him, seeking everything he wanted to give her.

It had hurt! Mother of God, it had hurt! But then as quickly as the pain had driven through her, it was gone. And in its place was a feeling of fullness. She was full of him, and he fit her like a well-made leather glove as he plumbed her depths, unleashing feelings such as she had never known existed. Ellen clung to him. Unable to help herself she sank her teeth into his shoulder, biting down hard, and she heard his rumble of laughter as he swore softly. He increased the tempo of his rhythm, and her nails clawed at his back as she wanted more and more.

"Little wildcat," Duncan growled deep in his throat. He caught her wrists, pressing them back on either side of her head. "Look at me, Ellen! *Look at me!*"

With great effort she opened her eyes, although her eyelids felt leaden. Her gaze met his, and she saw the passion between them reflected. She cried out, and he laughed low as she said, "I canna look more. It is too much! Too much!" Her head was spinning again as her eyes closed, but now behind her eyelids stars burst over and over again. She cried out again, but the sound was lost in the roar of his shout as his juices burst forth within her, and his big body shook with desire fulfilled.

Afterward he lay upon his back, breathing deeply, with Ellen half-conscious upon his chest, and he considered that he was the most fortunate man in all of Scotland. She was a passionate woman, and it had been his good fortune to have awakened her. He stroked the long, soft red-gold hair, now loose, flowing down her shapely back and over her creamy shoulders. She was his wife. His wife! And no one would ever know the fire within her but him. He felt sated and more relaxed than he had in months. Reaching down, he drew the coverlet over them and smiled at her faint murmur of contentment as he did so. He was going to love her. He was! How could he not?

When she awoke several hours later, for she had drifted into sleep within the comfort of his strong arms, Ellen considered her wedding night. She had slept better than she had in many months. She was safe. She was a woman now. How gentle he had been with her. Were all men thus? Balgair wasn't. But she didn't have to know anything else, because she was Duncan Armstrong's wife, and there were no other men in the world for her but him. The coupling between them had been . . . She sought for a word, but even *wonderful* didn't quite sum up her thoughts. At least they were compatible, she considered. Would they do it every night? Would it be as marvelous as it had been last night? And he had said there would never again be pain when he entered her.

"You're awake." His deep, masculine voice startled her.

"Aye," she replied softly.

"You are all right?" he questioned her.

"Perhaps a trifle sore, but that, I expect, is natural," Ellen admitted.

"Your maidenhead was lodged tightly," he told her. "I'm sorry it had to hurt you as much as it did." His hand stroked her head.

"At least you have no doubts now about my chastity," Ellen replied. "I know some considered that the king might have trifled with me because we were friends."

"I never doubted your innocence," Duncan told her quietly.

"But you could not be certain until last night," Ellen said, but she believed him, for he wasn't a man who lied easily. "I'm glad I was a virgin for you, my lord."

"A virgin no more," he murmured softly, his hand moving past the ends of her hair to fondle her bottom. "I find I am hungry for you once more wee wife." His cock was engorged again with the delicious lust he felt for her.

"But it is light outside our windows," she protested softly.

"Lovemaking may be accomplished at any time of the day or the night, and in any place. I think I must make it my duty to love you in all manner of loci." He chuckled, delighted by her little shocked gasp. Rising from the bed he pulled her up, leading her to the windows. He set her with her hands braced against the sill, bending her forward just enough, and then, taking her by the hips, he whispered to her to spread her legs for him. When she did he slipped his length deep inside her and began to pump himself against her. "You see," he whispered hotly in her ear. "Anytime. Anywhere. Let me begin a list of the places I shall fuck you, my wee wife: before the hearth here in our bedchamber, and the hearth in the hall, and in the darkness of a horse stall in the stables, and out on the hillside in the heather, and in our tub, and in my lap. I shall take you on your back and from behind; I shall take you on your knees and sitting astride me. You excite me, Ellen, and the thought of educating you arouses me greatly." He pressed a hot kiss on the back of her neck.

He was so big inside of her, and yet her body accepted him easily. The friction of his cock against her sensitive hidden flesh was the most exciting thing she had ever experienced. She could not have imagined being taken in such a manner, or the other ways and places to which he referred. He dominated her with his mastery of passion, but she would one day learn to dominate him, Ellen vowed. The landscape before her blurred, and she sighed as she let herself be carried away again into the heights. She sighed again deeply, and then she shuddered with her release even as he shuddered with his.

It had been every bit as wonderful this second time, Ellen thought as the countryside beyond the windows came into focus again. "I believe I shall look forward to the many times and different places you propose, my lord," she said softly, and she felt his lips on her neck again.

"You're a braw lass," he told her, laughing low. Then he picked her up and tucked her back into their bed again.

Ellen gazed at him through half-closed eyes as he climbed into the oak tub again, and quickly washed himself. The water would be cold now, but he didn't seem to mind. She watched as he briskly toweled himself dry and pulled on his garments. But then he did something that surprised her entirely: He took the earthenware pitcher from the hot coals of the hearth and poured the warm water into the matching ewer on the little table.

"You'll want to bathe a bit, I suspect," he said. "I'll await you in the hall, wife." Then he left her, unbarring the door, closing it behind him.

Ellen climbed quickly from their bed. She was shocked at first to note the bloody brown mark on the bedsheet that matched the stains on her thighs. Honest evidence of her innocence lost, she realized. She washed herself slowly, thoughtfully. How odd life was. All her life she had known she would marry Donald MacNab and live her life in the same house in which she had been born. She would be the lady of Lochearn. Yet her fate had been changed in an instant the moment the MacArthurs of Skye had descended upon her home. And now she was a border lord's bride, and far from Lochearn, and all those she had loved were dead at the hands of their treacherous kin. She wondered if Balgair MacArthur had learned yet that he was not the laird of Lochearn except with the permission of the lord of the isles. Or had the MacNabs exacted their revenge over Donald's death? It was unlikely she would ever know.

Ellen pulled on a clean chemise and then a fitted blue velvet gown with long, tight sleeves and a vee neckline. The blue was more the color of a sunlit sea than the sky. Sitting down upon the bed, she brushed out her hair and plaited it into a single thick braid, which she fastened with a dark blue ribbon. Standing again, she slipped her feet into her leather house clogs and hurried down to the hall. Her guests would surely be up, and she did not know if they would leave today or remain to visit with Duncan.

The Bruces of Cleit remained one more day to visit. Ellen noted that the brothers spent a great deal of time together laughing, and it was obvious the two Bruces were teasing their Armstrong half brother. She could but imagine what it was all about, and every time Conal Bruce looked her way she felt her cheeks getting hot.

Noticing it, Adair said, "Pay them no mind. Their bodies grow, but men are still boys at heart. Are you all right?"

"Shouldn't I be?" Ellen said.

"He was gentle?"

"Aye," was the answer.

"You are uncomfortable speaking with another woman about these matters," Adair told her sister-in-law, "but you must not be. Certainly your old nurse cannot tell you what you must know, still being a maiden herself. But then, servants exchange information." She smiled. "You should have someone younger to serve you."

"Peigi would be heartbroken," Ellen said.

"Not if your new servant is in Peigi's charge," Adair replied.

Ellen laughed. " 'Tis clever," she admitted, and then, seeing Sim, the steward, she called to him to come to her. "Whom among the women would you choose to serve me when Peigi grows too old?" she asked him. "I would like someone who might be trained to my likes and dislikes by Peigi."

"Young Gunna, my lady," Sim answered. "She is sweet-natured, and quick to learn. Her mother is our cook, but Gunna has no talent for it, I fear." He smiled. "I would tell you before someone else does, she is my niece."

"Send her to me," Ellen said. "The lady of Cleit will help me decide. And Sim—not a word to Peigi. She will not be pleased by my decision."

The steward bowed politely. "I understand, my lady, and if I might suggest it, I would send Peigi to you first, that you may explain to her what it is you wish to do. Then she might have a hand in helping you to decide if Gunna is suitable."

"Aye!" Ellen responded. "That is a fine idea, Sim. Thank you."

Sim bowed again, and then hurried off to find both Peigi and Gunna.

"You are fortunate to have such a man as Sim overseeing your house," Adair noted. "And clever to accept his good advice."

"It *was* good advice," Ellen replied. "Oh, there was news at court you might find interesting. I am astounded I forgot, for it would certainly be of interest to you. The Duchess of Burgundy is sending the Duke of York to Scotland. She seeks King James's aid in restoring him to his rightful throne."

Adair grew pale. "My half brother is dead!" She gasped. "He and Edward, his elder, were murdered at Middlesham after the battle of Market Bosworth. The Tudor faction tried to imply that King Richard had killed them, but he didn't. They were alive after the Tudor stole the throne."

"Nonetheless I did not misunderstand what was being gossiped about. Margaret of Burgundy champions this young man, and the king wishes to repay King Henry for his treachery along the border. He will irritate the English mightily by sheltering this prince."

"He is no prince!" Adair said heatedly. "He is an impostor, a pretender! And King James knows it, for we spoke on it several years ago. He knows my half brothers are dead, God assoil their innocent and sweet young souls. The page who slept hidden in their bedchamber saw the murders done, the bodies carried off, and he fled to me at Stanton to tell me of it."

"Where is he?" Ellen asked. "Perhaps he could help expose this alleged duke."

Adair sighed. "He was killed the day Willie Douglas raided my home and carried me off," she answered.

"Then your only witness to this deed is himself dead," Ellen pointed out. "But perhaps this man who calls himself Richard of York is indeed your half brother, and did not die after all," she suggested.

"I do not believe it. The Duchess of Burgundy has every reason to hate Henry Tudor. She is sister to my father, King Edward the Fourth, and my uncle, King Richard the Third. She would hold the Tudors responsible for the downfall of the House of York. She is a Plantagenet, and there are other male heirs of their line with far stronger claims on England's throne than Henry Tudor has. As much as I dislike King Henry I know this is simply a grab for power," Adair told her companion.

"I am amazed by you," Ellen said admiringly. "You are a simple bonnet laird's wife, and yet you know even more than most of the great lords at court."

Adair smiled. "I have not forgotten my early training, for all that England deserted me. I would rather be a Scot, Ellen, and a bonnet laird's mate than to go back to what I once was. There is no future in the past, but I am no fool. I know what it is King James is about. He had best be careful that this duplicity he aims at Henry Tudor doesn't turn about to harm him. The Tudors are ruthless, and I do not think our young King James is."

Chapter 7

The English had always been a thorn in Scotland's side, James thought as he sat by the fire in his privy chamber, a page dozing by his feet. Had there ever been peace between the two kingdoms? Real peace? He thought on the history of his country. Was there ever a time when Scotland and England had not been intertwined? He didn't believe so, but James believed the two lands had become more seriously involved when the Norman Duke William had conquered England over five hundred years prior.

The Anglo-Saxon heir to the English throne, Edgar, had fled north with his sisters to the court of King Malcolm of Scotland. Malcolm was known as Ceann Mor, which had several translations, James thought, smiling. Big head. Headman. Great chief. Edgar's eldest sister, Margaret, was very beautiful not just physically, but in character as well. Malcolm already had a wife, Ingeborg of Orkney, the widow of a Norse earl. She had given him three children. But Malcolm had married Ingeborg in a pagan ceremony. He married his Anglo-Saxon princess in the Christian rite, and was devoted to her for the rest of their lives. She gave him six sons.

But Malcolm miscalculated the time it would take William the Norman to consolidate his conquest of England. The Scots king attempted to expand his territories, believing that William would be so occupied in the south that he would not be able to defend the north of England. When William quickly marched north, Malcolm realized his own resources were not equal to that of the Norman. He welcomed the new English king at Abernethy, and took a public oath to be his man. Such action may have saved the day, but it boded badly for future relations between the two countries.

The peace did not last. When did peace between the two lands ever last? Five years later Malcolm once again attempted to expand his territories, and lost more than he gained. King William's eldest son, Robert, built a castle on the Tyne. His younger son, and eventual successor, William Rufus, built another at Carlisle. Fourteen years later King Malcolm died during his fifth invasion of England, this one, however, justified by the provocation of William Rufus. His eldest son, Edward, died with him. Queen Margaret, a devout woman, died shortly thereafter, resigning herself to the will of God.

James IV considered what happened next as Scotland had fallen into near anarchy. He sighed. Always the English throughout the centuries. Even in his father's reign they had attempted to destabilize the country with their constant plottings. It had been Edward IV and his brother, later King Richard III, who had encouraged King James III's younger brother in his attempt to overthrow Scotland's king. *And now,* James thought, *here I am offering to shelter and sponsor the young man who claims to be the younger son and nephew of those two kings.*

He recalled that his distant kinswoman, Adair Radcliffe, wife of Conal Bruce, the laird of Cleit, had said the two princes were murdered by Lancastrians after King Richard III was killed. But still he considered the delightful havoc he could cause the English king by championing this young man. He sought the quiet counsel of his aunt. "The Duchess of Burgundy says he is without a doubt her true nephew," James said when his aunt had finished reading the missive that had been sent to Scotland.

"Yet Adair Radcliffe says her half brothers were killed at Middlesham after Richard's death," Margaret Stewart said.

"But she wasn't there," the king argued. "A servant brought her word. How can we be certain he wasn't lying, hadn't been sent by King Henry to cover the princes' escape?"

"Margaret of Burgundy has always hated the Tudors," his aunt replied. "And King Henry is not yet entirely secure upon his throne. She seeks to help the Yorkists, Jamie. You say Adair wasn't at Middlesham when her brothers were killed. Neither was Margaret of Burgundy, my lad. Is it so important to you to irritate Henry Tudor?"

James smiled mischievously, but then he grew serious. "I'm tired of the constant raiding along the border, and the attempts to subvert my border lords," he said. "Perhaps the English and I could come to an accommodation if I had something with which to bargain. Henry will have many a sleepless night if I take this *son* of Edward's into my keeping, and champion his just cause. What if he is the genuine article, Aunt?"

"There is one way to find out," Margaret Stewart said quietly. "Adair will know for certain, for she was raised with young Richard of York."

"She last saw him when he was ten," the king reminded his aunt. "She might not recognize the man he has become."

"That is true," the lady agreed, "but he would certainly recognize her, for Adair was grown when she left court, and she visited at Middlesham after the two princes arrived there from London. You must arrange to have Adair see this Richard."

"Conal Bruce won't bring her to court, and there is no reason to invite them," the king noted. And then a light came into his eyes. "But I could go into the borders to hunt grouse in the autumn, and visit with the Bruces. In the meantime I will invite the Duchess of Burgundy to send her *nephew* to Scotland so we may become better acquainted. I shall then take my guest with me when it is time to go hunting." He chuckled.

"Will you stay at Cleit?" Margaret Stewart asked.

"Aye, and I shall spend a night or two at Armstrong's holding to inspect the fortifications he has erected. That shall give me another excuse. I shall say I would like his brothers and Adair to join us there as well," the king decided.

But it was late autumn before the young man calling himself Richard of York arrived in Scotland. The king decided to *invite* the lairds of Cleit and Duffdour, along with their wives, to celebrate Christmas at his favorite castle, at Linlithgow. There could be no refusing such an invitation, but at his aunt's suggestion James had invited Duncan Armstrong, because he knew Conal Bruce would be less apt to complain if his brother and Ellen were to come. He even saw that a small chamber was set aside to house the two women. Their husbands would have to find their own place to sleep, like most of the other guests. An invitation to join the king at Christmas was an honor no matter the difficulties of housing the guests.

"I won't go," Adair told her husband.

"You'll go," Conal Bruce said grimly. "He wants us both there for a reason, and we cannot refuse him. He's the king."

"I'm not leaving my holding in the winter weather to prance about the court with a lot of idlers and hangers-on," Duncan Armstrong told his wife.

"Oh, yes, you will," Ellen responded. "If the king calls, it is our duty to answer him." She gave him a quick kiss. "Besides, I have not played chess in months, and I know the king will want to play. If you won't learn, Duncan, my lord, then I must feed my passion for the game at court." She gave him another quick kiss.

"You're a bad lass," he grumbled.

"Aye, I am," she agreed, and slid into his arms. "Will you teach me better?" Her mouth was now practically brushing his.

"Nay, I like you bad," Duncan Armstrong said, his arms tightening about her. Her round, sweet breasts against his chest felt wonderful. He nibbled at her lower lip. "Remember I once told you that I meant to have you in many different places?"

Ellen reached down between them and caressed the length now hardening within his breeches. "Is now one of those times, my lord?" she murmured softly, her fingers closing about him, encouraging him in his intent. Her little tongue snaked out to lick at his lips.

"Aye," he drawled slowly. "Here. Now. In the hall." He backed her over to the high board, gently forcing her up on the dais and turning her about. "Bend, wench, and put your hands on the table," he ordered her.

"Duncan!" Ellen squealed nervously. "What if the servants see us?"

"There are no servants in the hall, and should one enter he will quickly leave," he told her. "They want an heir to Duffdour as much as we do." He pushed her skirts up and ran his hand down her graceful back and over her bared buttocks. "Such a delicious little bottom," he said softly as he loosened his clothing, freeing his cock.

"This is very wicked," Ellen protested. *And exciting.* "Ohhh!" His fingers had found their way between her nether lips and were now encouraging her juices to release themselves. She squirmed and pressed against his hand.

Finally satisfied that she was ready to be penetrated,

he took his cock in his hand and guided it to its destination. Then with a single smooth thrust he drove into her.

"Ahhhh," Ellen cried softly as he filled her full.

Reaching forward, he forced her back into an arch so he might fondle her breasts. His fingers squeezed gently as he stood quietly, his manhood filling her. She stirred beneath him and murmured a soft protest. The laird laughed low. "Do you want to be fucked, my precious?" he asked her.

She did not answer him.

"You must tell me," he teased her, "or I shall not know what to do."

Still she remained silent.

"Then I shall leave you to yourself," Duncan said, pretending to pull away from her. He grinned to himself, awaiting her protest.

"Fuck me, damn you!" his wife hissed at him.

Laughing, he began to move on her. Thrusting deeply. Withdrawing in a single smooth motion. Thrusting again, and again and again until she was whimpering, straining beneath him, her rounded buttocks moving in time with him. His hand now held her hips in a firm grasp as he drove into Ellen, now eliciting little cries of pleasure from her throat. And then she cried out, and he released himself into her.

"I can't breathe," Ellen finally said, struggling to get out from beneath him. "Get off me, you great lump!"

Duncan sighed deeply as he lifted himself from her. "You have an absolute talent for passion, my little wife," he told her with an answering sigh. Then he stood and pulled her skirts down for her before turning her onto her back half on the table, pinioning her beneath him and kissing her soundly. "Next time *on* the high board," he told her with a wicked grin.

Rosy, her lips swollen with his kisses, Ellen pushed him away and stood. "Only in the middle of the night," she told him. "I don't want to get caught in such behavior."

"But that's half the fun of it," he teased back as her blush deepened.

"Only if you promise me you'll go to Linlithgow for Christmas, and not complain," Ellen said.

"I'd rather spend our first Christmas as a newlywed couple here in our own home," the laird of Duffdour protested to his wife.

"So would I," Ellen agreed, "but he wants us there for a specific purpose, else he would not have asked an unimportant border lord and his equally unimportant wife to join him. I have a distinct feeling that he may have asked the laird of Cleit too."

Duncan took his wife's hand, and together they walked back to the hearth, seating themselves upon the settle. "Why do you think that?" he asked her.

"There were rumors at court before I left it last spring that the Duchess of Burgundy was claiming that the younger of her brother's sons had survived and was with her. She is looking for allies to help her revenge her family on the Tudors. What could be better than to claim she has the son—her nephew—of the last two kings before Henry Tudor? And King James is still young enough to enjoy an opportunity to strike a blow at England without having to raise an army to do it. What if he has invited the Duchess of Burgundy's protégé to Scotland, and would legitimize his status by having Adair recognize him and claim him as her half brother? She did tell me that she was raised at the court of her father, and knew the two princes well."

"If what you say is so, why invite us?" Duncan Armstrong wanted to know.

"Adair Bruce will not want to go to court at Christmas, Duncan. Like you, she will resist the invitation, but her husband will insist, being the king's loyal man. James is clever enough to know that if we must go too it will make it more palatable for her," Ellen explained. "He is not, cannot be certain this *prince* is the real one. He knows that Adair will be able to tell him. That is why he wants her at court."

"This business between kings is a damned waste of time," Duncan grumbled, "and 'tis always the simple people who get caught in the troubles that follow."

"I know," Ellen agreed, "but is it not the way of the world, my husband?"

He put an arm about her, and Ellen laid her head against his shoulder. "You are proving to be a good wife, lass," he told her. "I believe that in these past months I have come to love you, and I always thought it a good thing that a man love his wife."

She was astounded to hear such a declaration from him. He had come to love her? But did she love him? She hadn't considered it, Ellen thought, surprised at herself. He was a good companion. A fair and just man. He treated her with kindness, and she had to admit in finding pleasure in their bed sport. "I am not certain what love is, or is not," she told him, for such a pronouncement deserved an honest reply. "I do not think I loved my cousin Donald MacNab. He was simply the man I was to marry one day, and we liked each other. Our fate was set from childhood. It was what was expected of us," Ellen explained. "I never knew anyone who loved another."

"Does the king not love his mistress?" the laird wanted to know.

"James Stewart lusts after his women," Ellen said with a chuckle. "I do not believe his heart has ever been engaged by any, although he must like them, but perhaps Meg Drummond is different."

"Do you mind that I love you?" Duncan asked her.

"Mind? Why would I mind?" she replied. "I consider myself fortunate, my lord, that you love me. And I believe that once I come to understand love more fully I will come to love you as well. I hope you are willing to wait."

"Forever," he declared softly. "Until the heather ceases to bloom upon the hills of Scotland!"

"You are extravagant in your promise, Duncan Armstrong," Ellen said. "I quite like it. You make me feel cherished, and never before have I felt that way."

"Then I need not fear some court dandy will lure you from my side when we go to Linlithgow," he remarked with a small chuckle.

"Nay, I am quite satisfied to be your border bride, Duncan Armstrong," Ellen told him, and she snuggled closer against him.

They sent to Cleit and learned that the Bruces had indeed been commanded to come to court for Christmas. They arranged to meet on the road to Linlithgow and arrive together, *en famille*. The December weather grew cold, and there was snow on the road when the Armstrongs of Duffdour set out for Linlithgow. The trip had been planned in brief stages, for the mid-December days were short, and they did not want to be caught upon the road by the early darkness. It took them twice as long as it would have in the summer months. They had a rider going ahead of them to arrange for their evening shelter at the homes of several acquaintances, at two convents, and a monastery. They finally met up with the Bruces of Cleit at an inn on the road to Edinburgh. It wasn't a particularly reputable establishment, but the food was good, and the number of men-at-arms with their Bruce and Armstrong badges guaranteed the two lairds and their wives a night of safety along with a hot meal.

The innkeeper fell over himself at their arrival, bowing and smiling as he ushered them into the building. "Welcoom, my lords, my ladies! Ye'll be staying the night, of course, as 'tis almost dark. We're most crowded tonight with all the traffic to the king's court, but I can offer ye an apartment at the rear of the house on the main floor, my lords, my ladies." He bowed again.

"You'll offer us an apartment on the second floor," Duncan Armstrong said quietly. "I may be from the borders, but I know better than to stay on the main floor of a public house. I am the laird of Duffdour, and this is my half brother, the laird of Cleit. Both he and his lady are kin to the king, and personally invited to the Christmas revels. You will want to keep us safe, innkeeper."

"Indeed, my lord, indeed," the innkeeper agreed heartily. He grabbed at a passing serving man. "Find Lord Brodie in the taproom, and tell him we have had to move him to the main floor. If he asks why tell him I must house the king's kin tonight."

Duncan Armstrong smiled just slightly, his gaze meeting that of his half brother.

"Just a few minutes, my lords, my ladies," the innkeeper assured them. "May I offer ye a wee dram in my own privy room? Please follow me." He led them to a small chamber off the noisy, bustling taproom.

"You'll see to the horses and our men," Conal Bruce said, and the innkeeper assured him he would. "And send my captain to join us here," he continued, effectively dismissing the man.

"There is refreshment on the tray," the innkeeper said with a wave of his hand, and then he hurried off.

A good fire burned in the room's hearth, and both women went to stand by it, pulling off their gloves and holding out their hands to the warmth. Then two men poured small dram cups of smoky peat-flavored whiskey for themselves and the ladies.

Duncan Armstrong drank his down in a single gulp. "By God's own nightshirt, our host keeps good stock." He poured himself a second dram cup.

"At least for himself," Conal Bruce agreed, joining his sibling in another libation.

Both Ellen and Adair sipped more delicately, letting the liquor warm them slowly as they now sat by the fire.

"I'm not certain I can feel my toes," Ellen said. "Today was bitter riding."

Adair nodded. "Aye, and I'd rather be home at Cleit with my brood. My bottom has turned to leather these last few days." She didn't look happy at all.

"He needs you," Ellen replied softly. "You know he does."

" 'Tis a fool's errand," Adair said. "My half brothers are both dead."

"But maybe, just maybe—" Ellen began.

"Edward and Dickon are dead," Adair responded firmly. "Anthony Tolliver did not lie to me. If you had seen him when he came to my home at Stanton and begged sanctuary of me, Ellen. His eyes were positively haunted. He had had to hide in my brothers' bedchamber watching while they were murdered, in fear of his own life. He never got over it. He could barely sleep because he dreamed of that terrible night over and over again. And poor Anthony always felt guilty that he had been unable to do anything to help Neddie and Dickie. He was a lad himself. Had he stepped forward, or even cried out, they would have killed him too. So Anthony fled to me in the confusion of Uncle Richard's defeat so someone would know the truth. He was killed, poor laddie, when Willie Douglas raided Stanton and carried me off. I think now that it was a mercy," Adair said softly. "I do not know who this man claiming to be my half brother is, but I know he is an impostor."

"The king needs to be certain," Ellen answered her. "You know that is why he has asked you to his Christmas court."

Adair shook her head. "Bless you, my little Highland sister-in-law, you are still an innocent despite your year at court. The king is a ruthless man like all the Stewarts. Whatever he does, he does with a purpose in mind. But then, he is, I expect, no different from any other king in any other land. I think you must be unflinching in your direction in order to rule successfully." She sighed.

The innkeeper returned and personally escorted them to their rooms above. They were surprised to find a pleasant dayroom along with a large bedchamber with two large beds. "Lord Brodie was anticipating entertaining this evening," the innkeeper said dryly.

"A large entertainment, no doubt," Duncan Armstrong responded with an amused quirk of his dark bushy eyebrow, and the laird of Cleit laughed aloud.

"He was more than pleased to give up the apartment to ye," the innkeeper answered. He did not tell his guests that a strong sleeping draft had been put into Lord Brodie's cup when he protested the move, and that when he collapsed he had been carried off to while away the night in a deep and dreamless slumber. By the time the man awoke the following day, the two border lords and their wives would be reaching Linlithgow, the innkeeper would declare that none of it had ever happened, and Lord Brodie would leave for court himself, bemused and confused. "I have arranged to have a good hot supper brought up," their host said, smiling and bowing again. "I hope it will be to your liking, my lords and my ladies." He then bowed himself out even as the serving women were coming up the stairs with their plates, platters, and bowls.

A male servant preceded them, and he quickly laid the table for four. Then he directed the women to set the serving dishes down, poured the goblets full with wine, and departed. It was a surprisingly good meal. There was a large pie with a flaky crust that oozed gravy and was filled with a mixture of game birds. There was a platter of roasted rabbit, already cut into pieces. There was a platter of sliced salmon laid upon a bed of watercress that caused both lairds to raise an eyebrow, for salmon did not show up in public houses as a rule. It had obviously been poached, but the innkeeper was not fearful of being caught, which meant he had obtained it from an important servant of some lordling, maybe even the king. A round plate held a small ham. The bread was hot and very fresh. The cheese was of the best quality, and there was a tub of sweet, newly churned butter. And finally a dish holding several warm roasted apples with cinnamon and honey, along with a little pitcher of thick golden cream.

"No wonder the place is so crowded," Duncan Armstrong observed as he quaffed some wine. "The man keeps a good table, and has a good cellar."

"And probably preys on the unsuspecting," his brother replied.

There was a knock at the door, and both men let a hand go to their sword. But the door opened to reveal the Bruce captain, who stepped quickly into the room. "The lads, both ours and Duffdour's, have all been fed, my lords," he reported. "I shall set four men at arms at the door in two-hour shifts for the night. Is there anything else?"

"We'll depart at first light," Conal Bruce said. "Make certain the men are fed, and see that the innkeeper is paid."

"Aye, my lord," the captain responded, and then, bowing again, departed the room.

The two couples each took a bed and slept. Used to awakening early, they arose while it was still dark and dressed quickly. But Ellen and Adair each took more care this early morning, for they would arrive at court just after midday. Their gowns were velvet and all of one piece, although the fashion in England and France was now to have bodice and skirt separate. The garments were tight fitting, with long sleeves and deeply veed necklines that exposed their breasts. Adair was garbed in a rich burgundy color, and Ellen in a vibrant green. The long hooded cloaks, lined in warm fur, that they would wear on their ride matched their gowns. They departed the inn at first light, having eaten oat porridge and fresh bread with butter and cheese.

Linlithgow Palace was located between Edinburgh and Sterling. It sat on a headland that projected out into the southern end of Linlithgow Loch. It was called the fairest royal house in Scotland, and the Stewart kings loved it. It was in a perfect defensive position, surrounded on three sides by water. They were not the only ones going to court that day, and the kirk gate leading to St. Michael's Church was crowded with horses and traveling carts.

"I thought never to see this castle again," Ellen said softly.

"You did not expect to return to court?" Adair asked.

"Nay, like you, I am happiest in my home. And I am not of any importance."

"He asked you so I would come," Adair replied softly.

"Aye, that is exactly why he asked us," Ellen answered, chuckling. "So, here we are, and I suppose we might as well enjoy ourselves, for how likely is it that either of us will ever come again to the king's court? James Stewart is fortunate I was not with child and refused to travel."

Adair grinned. "Damn!" she said. "I should have pleaded my belly!"

Linlithgow Palace was of a simple design. There was a gateway that led to the outer close. Beyond and to the left was the peel, or palisade, that had been built by the English king, Edward I, to defend the fortress. The inner close had square towers at each of its corners. Spiral staircases known as turnpikes gave access to each tower. At the southwest was the king's tower. The great hall and the chapel were housed in the southeast tower, the kitchens in the northeast. The northwest tower was the queen's, although James IV had no queen currently, and his aunt resided there.

The ground floor of the palace housed the guardrooms. Below them were the wine cellar, the kitchens, and a large prison chamber where prisoners were thrust from the guardrooms above. The main living quarters were on the first floor. The great hall had been built between two towers, and was called the Lyon Chamber for the great tapestry that had been woven in Bruges and hung there. Its design was of the lion rampant of Scotland's royal house. The hall had a hammer-beamed roof but for its southern end above the fireplace, which was vaulted into the stone walls. It was there that the dais supporting the high board was set. At the north end of the Lyon Chamber was an oak screen supporting the minstrels' gallery above.

As they passed through the palace's gateway and into the outer close, Ellen found the memories flooding back. The memory of departing Linlithgow in the dark heading north for Lochearn. The memory of returning, numb with shock after the murders of her grandfather and Donald MacNab, terrified of being forced back and into marriage with Balgair MacArthur. Leaving and returning, and then leaving again as Duncan Armstrong's wife. She had always liked Linlithgow, but it had always seemed that something affecting her life happened whenever she left it.

The king was in the great hall surrounded by his friends and those who would be his friends. There were several ambassadors, and many ladies, including the king's aunt and hostess, Princess Margaret Stewart. The two lairds and their wives joined the throng of guests greeting acquaintances and friends as they made their way to the king to pay him their respects. He was speaking with his good friend Patrick Hepburn, the Earl of Bothwell, but he saw them, his eyes lighting up with pleasure.

Duncan Armstrong and Conal Bruce bowed. Adair and Ellen curtsied.

"We are pleased you accepted our invitation," James Stewart said.

"How could we refuse *you*, cousin?" Adair said sweetly.

Both the king and the earl chuckled.

"You are a headstrong woman, my lady of Cleit," Patrick Hepburn said.

"And here is my bonny Ellen," the king noted. "You look happy, poppet."

"I am happy," Ellen told him, smiling, "but I should far rather have spent my first Christmas as the lady of

Duffdour in my own home, my lord. You do not need me for the nefarious purposes you have in mind," she said boldly.

"But I did," the king admitted. "My good cousin would not have come without you, would you, Adair?"

"Nay, I would not," Adair responded candidly.

"We will speak privily on it later," James Stewart said. "Now go and enjoy yourselves, but first pay your respects to my aunt."

"Go and find yourselves some wine," Ellen suggested to her husband and brother-in-law. "We will visit with the Lady Margaret." She turned to Adair. "Have you ever met the princess? She is a woman of much intellect."

"I have not met her before," Adair replied as Ellen directed their steps across the Lyon Chamber to where Margaret Stewart sat holding her own small court.

The princess's eyes lit up as she saw Ellen. The younger woman knelt prettily and, taking the lady's hands up, kissed them. Margaret Stewart smiled warmly. "Ah, here you are, Ellen MacArthur. Jamie said you would be coming. And who is this beauty with you? The lady of Cleit, if I am not mistaken."

Ellen stood up, drawing Adair forward. "Aye, my lady. May I introduce to you my sister-in-law, Adair Bruce."

Adair curtsied to the king's aunt. "I am honored, my lady," she said.

"Come and sit by my side, lasses," the princess invited, offering them seats on two low stools. "Tell me of your journey."

"Slow and cold," Ellen said succinctly, with a mischievous grin.

The princess laughed. "My nephew will have his own way," she noted.

"What is this gossip we hear in the borders of an English prince?" Ellen asked innocently. "They say he is King Edward the Fourth's son. Is it so, my lady?"

"Whether it is so or not," Margaret Stewart replied, "I have no idea."

"Is he here? At Linlithgow?" Ellen queried. She looked about the hall. "Is he in this hall now? I have never seen a prince of England."

Margaret Stewart chuckled knowingly. "Ellen, for shame! Do not play the gullible fool with me, for I know you far better. You know you were asked to court in order that the lady of Cleit be pressed into obeying my nephew's summons. Your husbands, bless them, are good, loyal border lords, and would bring you to any place that the king demanded of you." She turned to Adair. "King Richard, for my nephew insists he be addressed thusly, is not in the hall tonight. He is dining with the Gordons of Huntley and their daughter, Katherine. Would you know your half brother as a grown man, my lady of Cleit? Would you know young Richard of York after all these years?"

"Aye," Adair said quietly. "I would know Dickie, but my brother is dead, madam. He was murdered at Middlesham, as I told King James several years ago."

Margaret Stewart nodded. "This will be something for you and my nephew to determine," she said. "I know you do not believe it, but there is always the faint possibility that your brother survived the attack that took his elder sibling's life."

Adair's lips compressed themselves in a thin line. "As I was not there at the time of my brothers' murders, I will concede that anything is possible, but the page who brought me word of the foul deed was an honest lad."

Margaret Stewart nodded. "I will admit," she said, lowering her voice so that only the two young women could hear her, "that I am not convinced of this man's authenticity." She sighed.

"I know well the games kings play," Adair replied, her tone almost bitter. But then she smiled. "But despite it all I found happiness."

"Be grateful then," Margaret Stewart told the younger woman. "Happiness is an elusive thing. Sometimes it is like trying to hold a ray of sunlight in your hand."

"But you are happy, my lady," Ellen remarked. "I always thought you happy."

"Aye," the princess said, "I am. I am not beholden to any man, not even my dear nephew, the king. I have my own home, although I rarely get to it these days, my books, and enough friends to keep me amused. I am an independent woman, which is, in our world, as rare a thing as a golden goose." She chuckled.

Ellen and Adair remained by Margaret Stewart's side until the meal was announced. She left them to join the king at the high board. The two young women sought for their husbands, then found places at the trestles below toward the end of the great hall. Servants bustled about with platters and bowls and pitchers of ale and wine. After the meal the tables were once again pushed to the side of the hall and they were treated to entertainments. The king's piper played. There were three jugglers, who performed both separately and in concert with one another. And then came a troupe of Gypsy dancers who stamped with bare feet and whirled about, tossing their colorful skirts up to show supple legs beneath as they clapped rhythmically in time to the wild music.

It was during this part of the entertainment that a very young page came to their table announcing, "My lord the king would speak with the lady of Cleit and her sister, the lady of Duffdour. If you will attend me, please." The lad turned and moved away even as Ellen and Adair arose to follow him.

Between the great hall and the chapel was a room called the Chamber of Dease, which was a withdrawing room where the king usually went first after departing the high board. Ellen had assumed that the page was leading them there, but he did not. Through the chapel they followed the boy, and into a hall that Ellen knew led to the king's own rooms. She was at first surprised, but then she realized James would want complete privacy for what was about to come.

"Do you know where we are?" Adair asked her as they hurried along.

"We are going to the king's own apartments. He has a little privy room for himself. We have often played chess together there. It allows him to escape the formality of the court," Ellen answered. "Ah, here we are."

The privy chamber was empty, however, when the page left them there.

"Does he bring his mistresses here, I wonder?" Adair said.

"Aye, he used to bring Marion Boyd, old Bell the Cat's niece. She's a nice woman and gave him two children, his firstborn, Alexander, and a wee girlie, Catherine. He's married her off now, and he has fallen in love with Lord Drummond's sweet daughter, Margaret. He is a man for romance, our king," Ellen said with a fond smile.

"Did you ever . . . ?" Adair couldn't resist asking.

"Me? Nay." Ellen laughed. "I am not at all the king's fancy. We were naught but friends."

"And still are, I hope," James Stewart said, entering the little chamber where the two women were awaiting him. "Sit, my ladies, and let us speak on a matter of great importance to Scotland." He motioned them to a small settle by the hearth and took the chair opposite them. "You have heard the rumors in the borders, my aunt tells me."

"Of a man who claims to be young Richard of York? Aye, my lord, we have," Ellen said. "It is a most troubling rumor."

"Have you nothing to say, my lady of Cleit?" the king asked Adair.

"Do you think I do not know what you are about, my lord?" Adair burst out. "This is a burr to place beneath Henry of England's saddle, isn't it? Repayment for all the troubles he has caused you and continues to cause you."

"Aye, it is exactly that," James Stewart admitted. "But could your brother Richard have escaped death? Could he have been smuggled to Flanders and then to the court of the Duchess of Burgundy? Could this young man indeed be Edward's son?"

"Nay, it is impossible!" Adair cried. "Anthony Tolliver would not have lied when he fled to me from Middlesham after my uncle Richard was slain."

"Improbable, but not necessarily impossible," James Stewart said.

"Do not fret yourselves," Ellen broke in. "The solution to this conundrum is really a very simple one, my dear lord."

"Ah, my sweet bonny," the king said, turning a smile on Ellen. "And what would you propose be done to settle this matter once and for all?"

"Introduce Adair to this man, my lord, but do not tell him of her connection with Edward IV. See if he recognizes his sister. He should, you know. Adair was grown when they last saw each other. If he is really King Edward's son, then he will know her for certain. If he is not, then he will not, and you will know he is a fraud."

James Stewart grinned. "A deceptively simple plot, my bonny, and quite worthy of you. It is discreet—provided, of course, that the lady of Cleit will cooperate. Will you, cousin?" The king smiled winningly at Adair.

"How can I be certain you will not speak with this man who calls himself my brother and warn him of me?" Adair demanded. "I know what you are about, cousin. You want an advantage, or at least a perceived advantage, over Henry Tudor."

"You are no friend of that king," James Stewart said.

"Nay, I am not," Adair agreed, "but I will not sully the memory of my father's sons with some cruel hoax so you may get back at your English rival."

"You are a difficult woman," the king said, "but I must know the truth of this matter, and you, Adair, are the only one who can tell me that truth."

"Does it matter to you if he is true or false?" Adair wanted to know.

James Stewart smiled a slow smile, and then he said, "Nay. I will use him against Henry Tudor nonetheless. I merely seek to satisfy my own curiosity."

Ellen sat transfixed, listening to them. She was shocked. This was a James Stewart she did not know—an unrelenting and merciless king, not the young man she beat at chess and then teased about it. Nay, this man was powerful and determined. If she had not known that what he did he believed was best for Scotland—and Ellen did know, for she had seen his love for his kingdom during her time spent at court—all of her illusions would have been entirely shattered. But Ellen did know that James Stewart had a kind heart and was a good man.

She suddenly realized that it was not easy being a king. There were power, wealth, and pomp to be sure, but there was also the responsibility for an entire kingdom. In the north, the king had to struggle against the power of the MacDonald lord of the isles. In the south, he had to be concerned for the English raiders who attacked not only his border lords, but the small villages and farms under their authority. And this man was not like his late father, the third James, who cared only for his own pleasures, who had not seen the misery of his subjects. Nay, this fourth James was a caring man.

"To assure you of my honesty, since I suspect you doubt it," the king said to Adair, "I will tell you that he of whom we speak will be back in the palace later this evening. When he comes I will point him out to you first, and then introduce you."

"Very well," Adair replied, and then her manner softened. "Forgive me, cousin, for my suspicion of this man. I would be as glad as you to do Henry Tudor a bad turn. If this fellow were indeed Dickie I would fall on his neck and praise God for such a great mercy. I would ride the length of England declaring Richard of York king over that usurper now astride England's throne. But many things concern me." She paused, and then said, "If Margaret of Burgundy truly believed that her nephew had survived murder, and knew where he was, then why did she not at least tell Dickie's mother before Elizabeth Woodville died almost three years ago? The duchess is a mother herself. Certainly she would have considered her sister-in-law's feelings, even if she did not particularly like her. None of my father's family really liked his queen."

"Perhaps Elizabeth Woodville's desire to see her grown daughter queen of England outweighed her love for her youngest son, who would have been a child king. As I recall, she and her Woodville relations attempted to seize control of her eldest son when his father died. She would have been allowed no power or part in her younger son's rule. And her own power base had been destroyed by King Richard."

Adair nodded. "What you say is true, I will agree. But had it been my child who had survived an assassination, I should have gone to be with him in exile." Then she shrugged. "But then, Elizabeth Woodville was never particularly maternal. She spawned her offspring, and after that had little interest in them except for what they could give her. I suppose if Dickie did survive his murder my father's wife carefully weighed and balanced the situation, finally deciding that my sister Elizabeth's chances were better and offered more than a little boy's."

There was a faint scratching at the door of the king's privy chamber, and it opened to reveal the page. "My lord, a servant has come to say that King Richard has returned, and is now in the great hall."

"Thank you, lad," James Stewart said, standing. Then he turned to his companions. "May I escort you back to the great hall, my ladies?"

Ellen and Adair arose together, and, following the king, they returned with him to the Lyon Chamber.

Chapter 8

$\mathcal{I}$n the great hall, a group of courtiers and ladies were gathered around a young man. He was tall and extremely handsome, with dark, wavy hair and fine blue eyes. He smiled easily, and his charm was evident even from a distance.

"There is the young king," James Stewart said, pointing. "What think you, cousin?"

"Dickie did not have dark hair. He was, like all of my father's children but for me, light-haired. But then, his queen was fair, and my mother had jet-black hair. All of Elizabeth Woodville's offspring were blondes, or redblondes. None was dark among them, my lord."

"Let me introduce you," the king suggested, "so you may be certain."

"He does have the look of a Plantagenet about him," Adair admitted slowly.

The gaggle of courtiers and simpering ladies parted as the king reached the young man with his two companions. "My lord Richard," he said, "may I present the lady of Cleit, who, like you, is English-born, and her sister-in-law, the lady of Duffdour."

The handsome young man bowed and kissed first

Adair's hand, and then Ellen's. "Are there no ugly women in Scotland, my lord James?" he asked, captivating the other ladies about them, who tittered appreciatively. Then he fixed his gaze on Adair, but his eyes held no recognition. "You are English-born, madam?"

"Aye, my lord, I am. My family name was Radcliffe, and our seat was at Stanton, which is on the English side of the borders," Adair explained.

"My uncle of York kept a tight rein on the north," the young man replied. "Did you or your parents ever meet him? He was not a kind man."

Adair kept her temper in check, for she needed to know more of this fellow. "Aye, I did meet him on several occasions, but not at Stanton. My parents were killed, and I was sent to court into the king's protection." *If you were really Dickie*, she thought, *you would not repeat that Tudor gossip about Uncle Dickon, who was the kindest of men.*

The young man's brow furrowed, and then he said, "We did not meet, did we? But, of course, I was in the royal nurseries under the care of that bitch Margaret Beaufort, the mother of he who usurped my throne. I have always suspected she was involved in the plot to murder my brother Edward and me. My aunt of Burgundy believes it too."

"Oh?" Adair could think of nothing to say to such an accusation, for as ambitious as Margaret Beaufort had been for her son, she was not a woman to stoop to murder.

"It was in the Tower, you know," the young man said confidentially. "They came and took Edward away one night. I never saw him again. But then those still loyal to the House of York came, secretly gaining entrance to my apartments. I was smuggled to the coast, and from there to Flanders, where I was put with a family called Warbeck, who told me that while I was now England's true king I would be killed like my brother if anyone knew. I was to answer to the name of Perkin Warbeck until I might one day be restored to my rightful place as England's king. And two years ago my aunt of Burgundy came for me and brought me to her court in preparation for my return to England."

"Oh, Your Highness was so brave!" one of the ladies said.

"Aye, 'tis quite a tale you tell," Adair said with a small smile. Then she curtsied. "If you will excuse me, sir, I must seek out my husband, for our day has been long." She looked at James Stewart. "With your permission, my liege?"

"I will help you find your laird, madam," the king said. "I must have words with him regarding a matter of the border." His hand grasped her elbow, and they moved away, Ellen with them. When they were out of hearing of the others, James Stewart asked, "Well, is he your half brother, or is he a false prince?"

"He did not show any sign of recognition for me," Adair began. "I gave him my family name, and that of Stanton. I said I was brought to court as a child. I did not, however, tell him I was raised in the royal nursery, for he should have known me if he were the true prince, my lord. But he did not know me. The real Prince Richard would have, for everyone at court knew my history, and that I was the king's brat. And saying that his uncle Richard was not a kind man was a patent lie, for Uncle Dickon was the most loving of men to all the children who crossed his path. And that Banbury tale about the Tower! As soon as my uncle Richard became king he moved the boys to Middlesham for their safety, knowing the Woodvilles would attempt to gain custody of the boys and cause difficulties. How Margaret of Burgundy could delude herself is beyond me. But perhaps she does not fool herself. Mayhap it is to irritate Henry Tudor that she sponsors this hoax. You are her cat's-paw, cousin, as the Irish before you who supported this man. I would expect it of the Irish, but not of Scotland's king, who should be wiser."

"You are too bold by far to speak to me like that," the king said, stung.

"I told you he was a fraud before I ever laid eyes upon him!" Adair snapped.

"Seek your husband, madam," James Stewart said, stomping off.

Adair curtsied, but when Ellen did the same the king reached out and took her by the arm. She looked up at him, surprised. "She should not have spoken to you that way."

"I am too ill tempered to rejoin the court," he admitted to her. "We will go back to my privy chamber and play a game of chess. I need better mastery of myself before I face anyone else." He practically dragged her along.

Ellen stood stock-still, forcing the king to stop. "Your humor will be the worse if you lose to me, my good lord," she gently teased him. "And Duncan will be wondering by now where I have gotten to, and he will worry."

"I'll send someone to him to tell him where you are," was his reply.

"Oh, he will be very reassured to learn that I am with you in your privy chamber. I don't even know where we are to sleep," Ellen protested. "I am a country woman, and not used to these hours you keep here at court."

The king snorted, disbelieving, at her complaint. "Everything has been arranged for my guests, and considering that I invited the Bruces and the Armstrongs to court, I am hardly likely to leave you without a bed," he said. He hailed a passing manservant. "Go back into the Lyon Chamber and seek out the laird of Duffdour, Duncan Armstrong. Tell him that I am playing chess with his wife."

"Yes, my lord," the servant said, eyeing Ellen curiously. She did not seem at all like the king's type, but then he shrugged and hurried off.

"I can but imagine what the man makes of your words," she said irritably. "By morning it will be all over court that you and I were alone. A page would have been more discreet, my lord. Would you sully my reputation?"

"If I meant to *sully* your good name, my bonny, I should have done it long since," James Stewart said dryly with a grin. He was beginning to feel a little bit better. Ellen had always had a knack for restoring his good humor in spite of himself. "And I order you not to beat me tonight. I need a victory, no matter how small. I knew it! I knew that Margaret of Burgundy was a duplicitous bitch. When could the English ever truly be trusted?" He flung open the door to his privy chamber and drew her in. "Set up the chessboard, my bonny, and I will fetch us some wine to take the chill off the evening."

Ellen did as she had been bidden, finding the chess set where it had always been, bringing the checkered board to the small game table that was set between the chair and the settle before the hearth. She then fetched the rectangular chased-silver box that held the pieces, which were fashioned from ivory and dark green agate. Placing the pieces in their proper order on either side of the board, she sat down to wait for her partner. Shortly the king joined her, handing her a goblet of sweet wine and seating himself opposite her.

"If you knew the Duchess of Burgundy could not be trusted, why did you take this Perkin Warbeck into your care?" Ellen asked.

"Because there was always the chance he was the genuine prince, but I suspect he is the by-blow of one of her Anjou Plantagenet relations," the king responded.

"Will you expose him for the fraud he is?" Ellen asked, moving a piece thoughtfully.

"Nay. I mean to use him, as the old duchess knew I would, even if I did find her protégé out. And I shall go on as if I believe he is young Richard of York," the king said. "He can be more useful to me actually than he will be to Burgundy."

"How?" Ellen asked.

"First I'll use him to put a stop to the Earl of Huntley's disobedience. The Gordons have caused me difficulties for several years now, but the earl came to court this Christmas. The beautiful Katherine Gordon, who has been in my aunt's household, has fallen in love with my faux prince." The king chuckled. "I mean to marry him to her."

"You think Huntley such a fool?" Ellen said softly.

"I think Huntley an ambitious man. The thought that his daughter might one day be queen of England will be much too much for him to resist." James Stewart laughed again. "And with that marriage, and the faint hope of his daughter's queenship, the Gordons are mine once again. How can he betray the man who gave his child a throne?"

"There will be no throne, my lord, and you well know it. Whatever happens, poor Katherine Gordon will be caught up in it. The Gordons will hardly thank you for that," Ellen told him seriously.

"I will plead that I was as duped as they were," the king said.

"You have become ruthless, my lord," Ellen responded softly. "I have never before known you to be such."

"You have never before seen that side of me," James Stewart said. "I am a royal Stewart, my bonny, and we are ruthless. It is our nature to be so. It is said that a king may be loved or he may be feared. I intend to be both loved and feared."

Ellen shook her head as she moved her knight. "Katherine Gordon is a proud girl, and I cannot say that I like her particularly well, but I must now pity her for what you are doing in this game you play."

"Do not pity her, my bonny," the king said. "The wench fancies herself in love with our faux prince, and is as ambitious as her sire. She already pictures a crown upon her head." He chuckled. "I have told you that my family is merciless in its desire to rule well. Now let me tell you a tale of my great-grandfather, the first James. Check and mate, my bonny," James Stewart said, ending their game.

"Either you have grown more skilled at this, or I have not been paying proper attention," Ellen complained, but she was smiling, for she had restored his good humor.

He laughed. "Will you stay and hear the story of James the First?"

Ellen nodded. "Aye, I will."

"That James had been sent from Scotland at a young age. He was to go to France, for he was his father's only surviving son. That king feared for his life, as he was aged, and was no longer certain he could protect his little son. But the lad's ship was captured by English pirates, and the young prince taken to the English court, where he was well treated and grew up. When he returned to Scotland with his English wife, Joan, he was welcomed, and became beloved.

"But in the north the MacDonald lord of the isles, like all his kind before and after, warred against the king's authority. James the First had slowly and carefully built a network of spies in the north, but the one thing he lacked was someone close to the MacDonald. And then that lord sent his bastard brother, the MacDonald of Nairn, to court to spy upon my great-grandfather. At the same time Black Angus Gordon, the laird of Loch Brae, arrived with his mistress, Fiona Hay. The laird was deeply in love with his mistress, and intended to wed her when they returned home.

"My great-grandfather, however, saw that the MacDonald of Nairn was very taken with Fiona Hay. He coerced Nairn's cousin, a young woman wed to a border lord, to entice him into kidnapping Fiona Hay as she traveled back to Brae. Then he sent Black Angus south to fetch his English queen's cousin and bring her back to court. Fiona Hay prepared to depart the court of James the First, but before she went my great-grandfather told her that he and his queen wanted Angus Gordon to wed with the queen's English cousin, so she must step aside for the royal wishes.

"She was, my ancestor's diaries reveal, devastated. Next the king said that word of a plot by the MacDonald of Nairn to kidnap Fiona Hay had come to his ears. She would allow it, and go north with Nairn to spy for her king. She finally agreed, but not before extracting a promise from my great-grandsire to repair her home and deposit a sum of monies for her with an Edinburgh goldsmith. The bargain was struck, and Fiona Hay reluctantly went north to do as she had been bidden.

"Of course, Angus Gordon was not meant to wed with the queen's cousin at all, and he was devastated to learn of his mistress's disappearance, but according to his king no trace of the lass could be found, although a great search had been made. He returned to his home at Loch Brae heartbroken," James Stewart told Ellen.

"Did this MacDonald of Nairn kidnap Fiona Hay?" she asked.

"He did, and he married her. Some few years later my ancestor marched into the Highlands. He shamed the chieftains he had called to Inverness. A short while later they burned the town in retaliation. King James the First marched into the Highlands to punish the chieftains. The MacDonald of Nairn was killed in the ensuing battle, and his castle burned and destroyed. Fiona Hay took her children, for by then she had three, and returned to her tower home near Brae. It was there, shortly thereafter, that the laird of Loch Brae found her, and they were reunited and wed."

"So there was a happy ending after all, despite King James the First's perfidy," Ellen noted. "But you are as ruthless as your great-grandfather was, my lord. And you are not ashamed of it, for you relate this story with pride." She worried her lower lip with her teeth. "I do not know this man you have revealed to me tonight. The James Stewart whom I know is a kind and caring man. He would not use an innocent girl's dream of becoming a queen, for most girls dream like that, to further his own purposes. I am suddenly afraid of you, my good lord. What will you do to gain your own will, and where will it stop?" Her gray-blue eyes were wet with unshed tears, and she was shocked to have seen this other side of a king she had always admired and trusted. Now she didn't know what to think.

"I have never betrayed you, my bonny," James Stewart said quietly. "Indeed, when I gave you to Duffdour it was because I could see you liked him, and that he was already a little bit in love with you. It pleased me to see you both happy."

Ellen flushed with the half rebuke, but then she said, "If you saw that he cared for me, and that I did not find him repulsive, my lord, then you put us together to bind him ever closer to you. Had I been an heiress of importance you would not have given me to Duncan Armstrong, and we both know it. It cost you naught to see us wed, and you gain from it, do you not?"

The king chuckled. "Is Duffdour aware of how clever you are, my bonny? You think like your husband, with a sharp clarity, and you have an honest tongue. There are so few who will speak plainly to a king. I value you for that, and always have."

Ellen stood up and shook her green velvet skirts. "Please, my lord," she said. "I am fair worn-out by our trip to Linlithgow. I would find my husband and seek our bed."

He nodded, smiling at her. "Aye, your day has been long, Ellen. Will we still be friends despite the fact that I have disappointed you?"

"Oh, my lord, I am not disappointed. I am surprised you have revealed this side of yourself to me. I must think on it, but you will always have my friendship and my loyalty. The mistake was mine. I have ever thought of you as a man, and you are not just a man. You are a man who is king of Scotland." She curtsied to him, then backed from the privy chamber. Outside the door she found the young page waiting. He escorted her back to the great hall, where she quickly found her husband.

Duncan Armstrong slipped an arm about his wife. "Are you all right?" he asked her anxiously, for Ellen seemed pale to him. "Adair returned to the hall in a high fury."

"Did she tell you?" Ellen wanted to know.

"Tell me what?" he countered.

"Then she has not." Ellen sighed. She glanced about. "Where is Adair?"

"She and Conal went off to find a private spot," the laird told her.

"We must find a quiet spot as well, so I may tell you all that has transpired," Ellen said, low. "Come, I know a place." And she led him through the Lyon Chamber and into the chapel. It was empty. Taking his hand, she led him to the front of the chapel and, pulling Duncan aside into a corner, Ellen began to speak. She told her husband that Adair had told the king that the prince was indeed false, but that the king insisted he would not expose him, and indeed would marry him to Katherine Gordon. "Adair is furious, and would expose the Duchess of Burgundy's pawn if she could, but she must consider what the king would do if she did, for he has his own plans."

"She must think of Cleit first," Duncan said sternly. "This matter between kings has little to do with us. Adair must remember Conal and their children. Let our King Jamie tweak the nose of the Tudor king if it pleases him. It should not matter to us."

"Adair is angry that someone would impersonate her dead half brother. This young man showed absolutely no recognition of her. It is obvious that whoever trained this fellow did not know all the intimate details of King Edward's household. All he knows would have been public knowledge. I suspect he might not even be English," Ellen told Duncan. "But Adair loved her siblings. This masquerade hurts her."

"But it has naught to do with her," Duncan Armstrong said in practical tones. "She knows her brothers were murdered at Middlesham, although the only witness to the deed is now himself dead. This pretender—the reasons behind his appearance—is nothing to Adair. Certainly she understands the reasoning behind it all. She must turn her head away from it. In a few days we will return home to the borders. We were invited for but one reason, and, that reason satisfied, it is unlikely we will come again to court."

"I wish we might go home right now," Ellen said, putting her head on his shoulder.

"So do I," Duncan Armstrong agreed, "but for now I think it incumbent upon us that we seek where we are to lay our heads this night, and for the next few nights."

Returning to the great hall, they found Conal and Adair looking nonplussed.

"You and I have been given a bed in a tiny chamber," Adair told her sister-in-law. "Our husbands must find their own place to sleep."

Ellen couldn't help but giggle, and the giggle grew into a burst of unrestrained laugher. "Oh, how typical of the court. Because we were specially invited they have provided a bed for you and me, Adair, but our men must fend for themselves, for they only escorted us. Well, Linlithgow is not a huge palace, and from what I saw in the Lyon Chamber tonight, everyone of even the smallest importance is here for the Christmas revels. I suppose we are fortunate someone thought to give us a bed at all."

"How can you laugh?" Adair demanded. "We have traveled for several days in this damned winter weather to get here, and if the truth be known we wouldn't have come at all had it not been a royal command, and then there is no bed for us?"

"Let us see this chamber you have been offered," Duncan Armstrong said in practical tones. "If it is large enough we may all share it, eh?"

Adair huffed angrily.

"Do you know where it is?" Ellen asked quietly.

"The servant said it was in the northwest wing of the palace," Conal answered. "Do you know the way, Ellen?"

Ellen nodded and led them from the hall. When they reached the wing in question they found an upper servant waiting at its entry. "The lord and lady of Cleit, and the lord and lady of Duffdour, please," she said.

The servant glanced at the list he had been given. "A chamber has been set aside for the ladies," he said, repeating what they already knew. "Third door on the right down this corridor, my lady."

"Do you think it's large enough for us all?" Ellen questioned gently. She knew very well from her year at court that the servant would have already heard numerous complaints about the housing. She smiled at the man.

"You can look," he said, grateful for her soft tones, "but there is only one bed."

"Do you know if it has a trundle?" Ellen pressed further.

The servant shook his head. "Nay, lady."

Accepting the taperstick he offered them, they followed the corridor to the chamber in question. It was a very little space, and the bed took up the entire room. Even if there had been a trundle beneath the bed, and there was not, there would not have been any room to pull it out. The saddlebags in which they had packed their clothing lay flung carelessly upon the bed.

Adair stamped her foot. "This is intolerable!" she declared.

"Perhaps," her husband said with an effort at humor, "if you had identified the faux prince as the true one, our accommodations might have been changed for the better."

Both Ellen and Duncan snickered, and Adair shot them a venomous look.

"You and Conal take the bed," Ellen said. "I know the palace, and I can find a place for Duncan and me to lay our heads. There will be some nook empty."

"Nay," the laird of Cleit answered her. "You and Adair will share the bed, as was planned. My brother and I will find an empty space somewhere. But we will change our garments here, for I'm of no mind to show my bony legs in public." And before either of the women might argue, the two men withdrew, leaving them alone.

"I'll leave on the morrow," Adair said. "If my cousin can offer his own kin no better place to lay her head then he may celebrate the holiday without me."

"How are you related to King James?" Ellen wanted to know.

"We both descend from King Edward the Third of England, albeit through different lines," Adair explained. "My descent is through that king's third and fifth sons. King James's line comes down from the fourth son. It is a nebulous connection, to be sure, but it amuses King James to claim it with me, and if truth be known it enhances my small reputation to have him address me as *cousin*."

"When I lived in Lady Margaret's household and the king would call upon me to play chess with him we would often speak. Actually I listened, for the king had far more to say than I ever did." Ellen smiled. "He spoke of you now and again. Of your beauty, but more often of your intellect. He says 'twas you who suggested he send out ambassadors to France, England, and the other lands across the water."

"When you are brought up in a sophisticated court, as I was," Adair said, "you can learn a great deal if you keep your lips sealed but to ask questions, and if you listen carefully without making judgments. My father was self-indulgent and amoral, but he was a good king, Ellen. No one was more clever at manipulating people than Edward Plantagenet of York. He might have been great had he been more interested in being a king and less of a sybarite. But he did have charm."

"Your life has been so different from mine," Ellen said. "I was just a Highland lass raised mostly by my grandsire, a simple laird. Yet we have become friends."

Adair smiled. Her humor was already restored being in Ellen's company. Duncan's wife was a sweet lass by nature, but not as dewy-eyed as she appeared. It was a pose she took on to put people at their ease. Adair thought her actually quite clever, else her brother-in-law would not have been as happy as he appeared these days. Duncan Armstrong, of the three brothers, was the most intelligent, and quite clever to boot. He was really quite wasted at Duffdour. He would have made a fine adviser or diplomat for King James. "Your time in Lady Margaret's household was not wasted," Adair remarked. "It gives us something in common besides our husbands."

The two women continued chatting amiably as they prepared for bed. They did so quickly, for the tiny chamber was icy, and it had no hearth. Though the single little window's wooden shutter was tightly closed, there was still a bit of a draft, and Ellen would have sworn that there was hoarfrost upon the chamber's stone walls. The bed the two women shared was comfortable, however, with a good featherbed beneath them, and a thick coverlet of down and a heavy fur rug to snuggle under.

In the morning it was agreed that they would remain for a day or two more to enjoy the company of the court. They hunted in the hills about Linlithgow one day, but the following day dawned cold and rainy, and while there was jousting in the courtyard, the day was generally unpleasant. The king, having gotten what he wanted from Adair, no longer cared whether they were there. On the third night of their stay he announced to the inhabitants of the great hall that Lady Katherine Gordon would wed with King Richard of York after the New Year.

"Let us leave on the morrow," Ellen suggested to her companions. "Unless, of course, any of you have a desire to see the wedding between the Gordon and England's *trew* king," she teased them, grinning.

"A pallet in a monastery guesthouse will be more comfortable than where Conal and I have been sleeping," Duncan Armstrong said.

"And just where have you been sleeping?" Ellen wanted to know.

"In an unused garderobe at the top of the east wing," her husband told her.

"Ohh, poor Duncan!" Ellen sympathized, but her eyes were dancing.

"It's just big enough for one," he said. "We take turns, with one of us inside the garderobe and the other on the stone floor outside of it. It's cold, and it's uncomfortable besides," the laird of Duffdour complained.

"Then we had best take our leave of the king now," Ellen said, and the two couples walked across the Lyon Chamber to where the king was now seated; they waited for him to recognize them. When he did Duncan Armstrong stepped forward and bowed.

"My liege, the court is crowded, and while we are honored to have been asked to join your Christmas revels, we should with your permission take our leave of you on the morrow. Our journey home will be hard in the best of circumstances, and neither my brother of Cleit nor I should want to find ourselves caught in a blizzard."

James Stewart looked at the two couples standing before him. "Do you not wish to remain and be witness to the wedding of our cousin Katherine Gordon and England's *true* king?" he asked them innocently, noting as he spoke the fury that leaped into Adair's eyes, and the sad, almost chiding look in Ellen's.

"You are more than gracious, my liege," the laird of Duffdour said, a wry twist to his lips. "I am certain that the happiness of the young couple will be guaranteed without us, else we would certainly remain to assure it."

James Stewart laughed aloud. "You are wasted in the borders, Duncan," he told the handsome laird. "You would make me a fine diplomat if I could but convince you to leave your beloved Duffdour. Aye, you have our permission, my lords, to return to your homes." He turned to Ellen. "Are you still disappointed in me, my bonny?" he asked, low, his blue eyes searching her face.

"Nay, my lord," she told him. "I am coming to terms now with what it really means to be a king. I never before understood. But I owe you much, and I will always be your most loyal liege woman, my lord." She curtsied to him.

James Stewart leaned forward and kissed Ellen's rosy cheek. "Godspeed, my bonny," he said softly. Then he looked to Adair. "Thank you, cousin. Though you disapprove of my actions, thank you for your discretion."

Adair curtsied to him. "I may be the wife of a simple bonnet laird, my lord, but I was raised a king's daughter. Beware, however, of the English lion. His claws are sharp, and his memory for a fault is a long one. I should not like to see you harmed."

The king grinned. "I am younger and more agile than Henry Tudor," he declared. "Godspeed to you also, my lady of Cleit."

Adair curtsied again, and then, taking her husband's arm, she backed from the royal presence. Then the two women sought out Margaret Stewart and bade her farewell.

"You are not remaining for the wedding?" the king's aunt asked. "Pity."

"Did he tell you?" Adair asked her.

The older woman nodded. "I do not know if my nephew is being exceeding clever, or exceeding foolish," she said. "Go home, my lasses, and escape the mayhem of the court's political maneuverings. I think the border may prove a safer place."

"Perhaps if it snows," Ellen said, "but then, thanks to the king, Duffdour is now well fortified. Come the spring, however, the raiding back and forth will begin again." She kissed the hand held out to her. "Farewell, my lady. God keep you safe."

* * *

In the morning the two brothers, their wives in tow, departed Linlithgow in the company of their men at arms. They traveled together for several days, parting finally as the road south of Edinburgh divided. The weather was cold, and it was gray most of the days as they rode, but the rain and the snows held off. Only as the laird of Duffdour and Ellen found themselves and their men a few hours from home did the snow begin to fall. It was midday, and Duncan Armstrong was glad he had forced the pace. By the time the walls of his house came into view the snow was falling thickly. They rode through the gates and up before the house, dismounting. One of their men at arms took their horses and started for the stables. Hand in hand the laird and his wife entered their house.

No sooner had they stepped through the door than they were surrounded by armed men who hustled them into their great hall, where a handsome gentleman lounged at their high board, the laird's frightened servants hurrying to serve him. "You've done a fine job of fortifying your house, Armstrong," the man said.

"Who the hell are you?" Duncan demanded.

"Lord Roger Colby, at your service, sir," the gentleman said, standing and coming down to greet his host. "I'm sorry you were not here when I arrived."

"I built walls to keep the English out," the laird replied dryly.

"Aye, and fine walls they are. Unfortunately you did not teach your people how to keep your gates locked. By slowing our pace and not appearing threatening we were able to ride right in this morning." He grinned. "There's going to be hell to pay here when I'm gone, isn't there, Armstrong? Still, I thought it only fair that, as you had visited my home some months back, I should visit yours."

Duncan Armstrong laughed, for he saw the humor in the situation, as dangerous as it was. "You'll be remaining the night, my lord," he told his guest. "We come heralding the blizzard behind us, I fear." He drew Ellen forward. "This is my wife, the lady Ellen, my lord. Sweeting, go to the kitchens and see that they know our guests are remaining at least the night. And tell cook I am quite hungry after our ride."

"Aye, my lord, and I will see that a bed space here in the hall is prepared for Lord Colby." She curtsied to her husband, then, turning, hurried off.

"A most fetching armful," Lord Colby drawled. "She's not border-born."

"Nay, she's a Highlander. She was the king's ward, and a favorite of his aunt. They saw us wed, as I needed a wife and Ellen needed a husband," the laird replied.

"You are so important that the king himself picked you a wife?" Lord Colby was intrigued by this scrap of information.

"I am of no import at all," the laird answered him. "I had simply done the king a small favor. He wished to repay me in kind. And Ellen's betrothed husband had been killed. The king's aunt, in whose household Ellen lived, wished to see her wed. I was in the right place at the right time. 'Tis no more than that."

The laird's servants, more at ease now that their master was home, came with cups of wine for the two men lounging by the fire. The hall had once again taken on an air of normalcy. The servants moved quietly back and forth, setting the high board up for the meal that was to be served. In the kitchens Ellen reassured the cook and her helpers that Lord Colby would not harm them. He was merely visiting.

"Since when do the English *visit* the Scots in such a manner?" the cook, who was named Lizzie, wanted to know. She was a tall, bony woman with perpetually rosy cheeks.

"Since the fools standing guard at the gates let them ride through," Ellen said. "There aren't that many of them. Only the lord and six men at arms."

"We can kill them then!" the cook said enthusiastically, grabbing a particularly large and dangerous-looking knife up from the table.

Ellen held her hand up in a cautionary gesture. "I do not believe there is any necessity for that," she quietly told the kitchen staff. "If Lord Colby had meant us any harm it would have long ago been accomplished, and he would have brought more than six men with him. The laird ordered the gates barred behind us when we returned. Our walls are strong and secure. There is a blizzard raging outside. I do not believe any of us are in any danger, cook. Now," she said briskly, "you have seven more mouths to feed, at least until this storm has blown itself down into England. And be warned that my lord is hungry, and ready for a good meal." Ellen then turned and hurried from the kitchens. On the stairs she met Sim and drew him aside. "How did this happen?" she asked him. "Did my lord not give instructions when we departed that the gates were to be kept closed and locked at all times? There is a very dangerous man in our hall right now."

"My lady, Artair, the captain of the guard, has been ill. He put his eldest son in charge of the gate, and Father Iver had gone out to visit an elderly cottager. The lad thought it was safe to leave the gates open until he returned."

"The lad has been brought up here at Duffdour," Ellen said sharply. "His father is a soldier. What kind of fool was he to think he might leave the gates open? And when he saw seven riders coming, why did he not close them? At least until he learned their business? Lord Colby knows that now that he has gained entry to our house we will not abuse the laws of hospitality, but he is the enemy nonetheless."

"Lady, I have not yet learned the truth of this matter, but I will. Artair, I am told, arose from his sickbed, and beat his son bloody for what has happened," Sim said.

"No one was hurt then by this incursion?" Ellen asked her majordomo.

"Nay, lady. Other than the fact that we have seven English in the house, all is well," Sim replied. "They must have come for a specific purpose, else they would have brought far more men to Duffdour," he noted.

"My lord will learn their purpose soon enough," Ellen responded. Then, picking up her skirts, she said, "I must get back to the hall. See that a hot meal is served promptly." She moved off up the stairs now, and back into her hall. Joining Duncan and their guests, she smiled. "Your unexpected arrival has frightened my servants, my lord," she chided Lord Colby, "but we will soon have food upon the table. You have wine? Ah, good, you do." Ellen looked about, and instantly a servant was at her side with a goblet. She took it from him and drank deeply. All she had wanted was to gain her home, have a good supper, and then climb into her bed with Duncan. Instead she must entertain this unwelcome visitor who eyed her with a much too bold look.

"I apologize, lady," Roger, Lord Colby, said with a charming grin. "My men and I were but out for a ride when we came upon Duffdour, and it looked so inviting we could not resist coming to call."

Ellen was forced to laugh, but Duncan did not look pleased at all.

"Open gates are always inviting," he murmured darkly.

"Sim tells me that Artair is quite sick," Ellen told her husband.

Duncan nodded. "I will speak with him later," he said grimly.

Lord Colby listened to this cryptic exchange, amused. He and his men had ridden through the open gates to discover a group of young men at arms surrounding two very pretty girls, laughing and chatting away with them. They had looked totally surprised when they realized that seven armed men had just passed through their gates, and one of the youths had demanded with great self-importance to know their business. It hadn't been difficult to overcome the inexperienced men at arms and enter the house. He could only imagine Duncan Armstrong's chagrin, and expected that there would be hell to pay when the laird of Duffdour got to the bottom of the matter. In the meantime he knew that he and his men were protected by the laws of hospitality, which not even the most wicked borderer would contravene. He smiled pleasantly at his host, and sipped his wine.

"Has Lord Colby yet spoken of the reason for his visit?" Ellen gently pressed her husband. Duncan was angry, but he was being forced to restrain his anger for the moment, and that was but feeding his anger further.

"I will discuss it with your good lord after the meal," Lord Colby said before the laird might speak up. "It is not a matter that you need trouble your pretty head about."

"I share all with my wife," Duncan said in hard tones. "Anything affecting me or Duffdour affects my wife. Therefore she is always kept informed of what I am thinking, and what is happening."

"How very modern of you," Lord Colby murmured. "You must value your wife quite highly, my lord. And you, madam, do you feel treasured by this man? For you should. It is rare that a man will admit to accepting his wife's counsel."

Duncan could feel his temper rising further, but Ellen's gentle hand on his cooled his ire as she spoke to the Englishman.

"I do indeed feel treasured, my lord. How clever of you to understand. I shall look forward to learning the nature and reason for your visit after we have dined."

"The meal is ready, my lady." Sim had quietly joined them.

Ellen arose. "Come, my lords," she invited them, "and let us settle ourselves at the table. I'm sure the cook has set forth a fine meal." She was pleased to see that her servants had placed the fine silver plates upon the table. They had been a wedding gift from Margaret Stewart, along with matching silver spoons. Their best goblets were also silver, studded with green agate. They were very old.

"Wine or ale, my lords?" Ellen asked them, and the appropriate beverage was poured into the goblets. Both men took ale, but Ellen preferred watered wine. She wondered about her appearance, for she had not had time to change, nor had she even seen Peigi or Gunna. They would undoubtedly be awaiting her upstairs. She had entered her hall wearing breeches, for she far preferred riding astride to riding sidesaddle, as most women did. Yet Lord Colby hadn't been in the least shocked.

The cook had conjured up a fine meal. Ellen watched as the servers brought platters of sliced trout, a fat roasted capon, a haunch of venison to be carved, and a ham. There were bowls with creamed cod, and lamb stew, a meat pie, a dish of braised lettuces, fresh bread, a crock of sweet butter, and half a wheel of a hard yellow cheese.

"You keep a good table," Lord Colby praised, and he ate like a man starving.

She and Duncan, Ellen saw, were a bit more abstemious, for she knew that they were more concerned with why the Englishman had violated their home. What did he want? Why had he come to Duffdour? When the meal had been cleared away the trio once again went to sit before the fire, where they might learn the nature of their guest's visit. They had to admit they were very curious.

The laird of Duffdour spoke first. "You have, sir, entered my house uninvited and unannounced. I have honored the laws of hospitality. Now, what is the purpose of your visit, my lord?"

"I come with an offer from King Henry," Lord Colby began.

"I do not know the fellow," Duncan Armstrong said rudely.

Lord Colby smiled briefly. "This young king of yours

will not last long upon his stolen throne, Armstrong. He is not well liked, and eventually will be pulled down. My master, King Henry, would offer you, and several others here along our shared border, the chance to give your allegiance to England. Do so, and you will be safe when this James Stewart is replaced."

"The eldest surviving son of a reigning king can hardly be called a usurper," Duncan said slowly. "The throne belongs to James Stewart, the fourth of that name, heir to James the third of that name, now deceased. And those who swear to your master that James is not well liked are badly misinformed; or perhaps they just have their own agenda and wish to hoodwink your king to gain their own purposes. King James is already adored by the people. He is not his father, who did not listen to his own lords, and who wasted the treasury on trifles while ignoring the cries of his own people. This James Stewart listens, is frugal, and is already beloved of his people. He is as comfortable conversing with a foreign ambassador in his own language as he is in a Highland hall speaking in the northern tongue of our people. I am his man, and I will never betray him."

"Your king is a foolish young man," Lord Colby said. "This adventure he has embarked upon with Margaret of Burgundy's pawn proves that."

"Ahh." Duncan Armstrong began to chuckle. "So our Jamie has indeed managed to put a burr beneath your king's saddle with the lad they call the *true* king of England."

"Henry Tudor is England's true king," Lord Colby said, irritated by the laird's sharp and accurate barb. "But, aye, he fears another useless civil war should anyone flock to the banner of this Plantagenet bastard Burgundy attempts to foist off on the world as King Edward's surviving son. Those two unfortunate princes disappeared, and no one truly knows what happened to them, although it is believed King Richard had them slain to protect himself after his brother died. And the queen is most distraught by this pretender. It but brings back sad memories she would sooner forget."

"So your king seeks to cause trouble for Scotland as Scotland is causing it for England. Well, my wife and I have just returned from court. We have seen this lad who calls himself your *true* king. Whether he is or nay I could not tell you, for I would not know one English prince from another, my lord. I'm a simple man, a bonnet laird. I am not a man for political maneuvering or plotting. When this storm is over you and your men may leave in peace, and we will not follow you. I seek no enemies if I can avoid it. But I will never betray James Stewart."

"I came to you first, Armstrong. He who offers King Henry his loyalty first will be rewarded handsomely," Lord Colby said.

"You came to me first because, while I am a simple man, I am well respected among my fellow lairds here in the border. You came to me because my Bruce half brother is kin to James Stewart. What a coup that would be for you! You hoped by subverting me you could gain the trust of the others. Do you take me for that great a fool, my lord, that I would not divine your purpose? Because my family name is not of great import, because I eschew the halls of power and prefer to live my life quietly here in the border does not mean I am stupid, my lord."

Roger, Lord Colby, flushed with the strong rebuke. "Nay, I do not think you a fool, Armstrong, but I believe you ill place your loyalty to this king of yours. God's wounds, man! He slew his own father to gain his throne."

"The death of King James the Third was not the king's fault," the laird said. "We have never been able to learn who killed that unfortunate, but that it was a man who claimed to be a priest to the two women who sought one for the wounded man they did not know was their king. If someone sent this assassin, if the assassin was someone who saw what he thought was an opportunity to gain favor with an important lord, that man has never stepped forth. He would not have dared to admit to the deed once the depth of the king's grief became apparent. King James wears an iron link beneath his garments in penance, and to always remind himself of what happened. As for your king, there is blood enough on his hands, my lord. Shall we speak on the death of King Richard, and many of England's good sons?"

"Even if you do not join us," Lord Colby said, "there will be those who will. In the end we can keep the borderlands roiled up with strife. You think the raiding in the past has been hard? It will be worse soon enough. You would be well protected if you joined us. The Scots do not have to know of your change of loyalties. But you could be safe from any attacks from the English borderers."

"You seek my small influence, yet you would keep my part in your nefarious scheme secret?" The laird shook his head. "You are either mad or desperate. Perhaps you are both. My answer is nay. It will always be nay. There is nothing you can do that would change my mind. I am my king's loyal man. When the storm has blown itself out, my men and I will personally escort you back over the border, my lord." Duncan Armstrong stood up. "Sim!" he called to his majordomo, and when Sim came the laird said to him, "Show Lord Colby where he is to sleep tonight." Reaching out, he pulled Ellen up to stand by his side. "I bid you a good night, my lord," he told the Englishman. Then, hand in hand, without another backward glance at the man, he walked upstairs with his wife. He was still angry at all that had transpired.

Ellen sensed it. When they entered their bedchamber she turned to face him, and his arms closed about her. "He has been insulting since the first moment he entered Duffdour uninvited," she said. "His request is insulting. If he were an honorable man he could not be induced to solicit treachery from others for his king. It says nothing good about this Henry Tudor." Reaching up, she stroked his strong face. "Do not be angry, my lord. Or if you would, then release your anger in passion for me." Ellen brushed his lips with hers, pressing herself against her long, lean husband.

The laird could feel his fury begin to slink away, and he kissed her back hard. "What magic is this that you weave about me, you Highland witch?" He felt his body eager to respond to the silent invitation she was offering him. It had been days since they had been able to share an intimacy with each other. Duncan pressed kisses over his wife's heart-shaped little face. His finger began to unlace her shirt.

"Ummmm," Ellen murmured, reaching down with a hand to encourage the burgeoning she felt between his legs. "Ohh, such an eager and randy laddie," she teased.

His hand slipped into her now open shirt, past her chemise, and cupped a soft round little breast. He had adored those breasts since he first laid eyes upon them. They were plump and round, like autumn apples. His thumb rubbed across her nipple.

Ellen squirmed in his arms, for she had discovered from the first time they had made love how very sensitive her breasts were. He was rousing a fire within her, and she could feel the moisture already bubbling up between her nether lips.

With a groan of impatience the laird suddenly ripped his wife's shirt and chemise open in order to have full access to those tempting breasts. His big hands fitted themselves about her narrow waist, and he lifted her up so he might run his tongue between the valley separating her breasts. Her flesh was sweet to his taste. He turned his head and captured an already puckered nipple in his mouth, and began to suck upon it in a leisurely fashion.

Ellen murmured with her pleasure as his teeth grazed her gently. He walked across their bedchamber, still suckling her, to lay her down upon her back on their bed. His hands now free, Duncan undid the belt at her breeches, pulling the garment down to her boot tops. His mouth never left her breast as he did. The sensuous tugging on her flesh, first on one side, and then the other, was setting her aflame with lust. And then his tongue was licking across her half-naked torso in long, hot strokes, and she moaned.

It wasn't loving, but he wanted her, and he wanted her now. The boots still on her feet, the breeches tangled atop them, made it difficult to spread her for his lustful purposes. Duncan pulled back momentarily, and then he quickly turned her over, delighted that she understood his intent, and pulled herself up onto her knees. He pushed his own breeches down, and, grasping Ellen's hips, he drove into her, almost weeping as he felt the hot walls of her sheath embracing and closing about his eager cock. He groaned, and she echoed the sound as he began to piston her.

Was it right to be so eager for your husband? Ellen wondered muzzily as his length filled her. Then he began to move upon her, first with slow, deep, leisurely strokes, then with hard, quick thrusts that set her head spinning and her own lust skyrocketing. "Oh, God!" she cried softly. "Yes! *Yes!*" She was trembling with her need for him. From the first their bed sport had been good. He had taught her how to please him, and together they had discovered what pleased her. Tonight, however, their lust was high, and they found the heights together in a hot rush of mutual desire that had Duncan crying out as his cock burst forth with its juices, and Ellen almost screaming as pleasure overcame her, sending her into a half swoon.

When they came to themselves once again Duncan was still atop Ellen. He marshaled his strength as best he could and rolled onto his back. They were both breathing heavily, and his long legs hung over their bed. Finally the laird sat up and pulled up his breeks. Ellen was still sprawled upon her face. He ran a big hand over her bottom, and she pleaded, "Oh, don't!"

"Why not?" he teased her. "You have a most fetching bottom, madam."

"I'm overwhelmed with lust, my lord, and when you touch me I want more," she said bluntly. She was so weak she could barely speak, let alone move. Their coming together had been incredible tonight. She sighed.

He chuckled. "How fortunate that I am also possessed with an *overwhelming* lust, my adorable wife. Shortly I will want more of you," he told her, and his hand patted the little bottom turned up to him. "But first I think we need to take off our boots and our garments, and crawl into the bed beneath the coverlet." He bent and pulled his boots off. Then, standing, he drew off Ellen's. When he had relieved her of the footwear, she turned over, and looked up at him with half-closed eyes, watching as he took off the rest of his garments before her admiring gaze.

"Are men supposed to be beautiful?" she asked him as she sat up and kicked off her breeches, then pulled off her torn shirt and chemise.

"Women's bodies are more pleasing, I am inclined to think," he told her as he sat beside her and began to undo her thick braid. When it was undone he opened his fingers and combed her hair out so that it spread itself like a mantle about her white shoulders. "I love you, Ellen," he told her softly, his hand brushing a stray lock from her forehead.

"So you have said of late," she replied, smiling into his warm blue eyes.

"Nay, lass, what I said was that I thought I was coming to care for you, but now I realize that I do. I love you. You are not just beautiful; you are intelligent and you are brave. I watched you tonight in the hall with Lord Colby. You might have said much, but you did not. You were clever and discreet."

"You are the lord of Duffdour," Ellen answered him. "It was your place, your duty, to speak for us all, Duncan."

"Other women—my sister-in-law, Adair—would have put forth their own thoughts, but you did not," he replied.

"Perhaps I had no thoughts of my own," Ellen suggested.

Duncan laughed. "Nay, wife, there is much you might have said, but you did not. And now the Englishman will go away knowing that at Duffdour we are united in our loyalty to King James Stewart, the fourth of that name."

"My lord," Ellen said impatiently, "do you really wish to converse with me on our evening in the hall, or do you wish to continue our bout of lust in our bed?" Reaching down, she tweaked his manhood mischievously, giggling when it stirred strongly.

"You're a wise woman, Ellen, my wife," the laird of Duffdour said, and he yanked her into his arms, kissing her strongly.

"Aye, Duncan, my husband, I am that indeed," Ellen answered, kissing him back.

And outside of their bedchamber window the storm blew and raged the night away as they made passionate love with each other, finally falling into a restful sleep as the faint gray light of dawn began to slip through the drawn curtains of the room.

Chapter 9

When Ellen went down into the hall the next morning she was surprised to find their unexpected guest and his men at arms gone.

"They left at first light, my lady," Sim told her. "There was still a bit of light snow, but most of the storm had gone. We did see that they were fed."

Ellen nodded. " 'Twas well done, then."

"Mistress," Sim began, "we could not prevent them from gaining the hall once they passed through the gates. I hope the laird understands."

"I think you will find the laird in a better mood this morning, and especially as he does not have to ride out in this cold," Ellen told her majordomo with a small smile.

Sim bowed, relieved. He was not responsible for the incursion at the gates. That was a terrible error that could cost Artair his position as captain of Duffdour's men at arms. But perhaps the laird would be merciful, for there had been no real harm done.

When Duncan Armstrong came into the hall a few minutes later he learned his uninvited guests had gone. "Good riddance!" he muttered. Then he called for Sim, telling him, "Send someone for Artair and his son. What is the lad's name?"

"Mathe, my lord," Sim replied. "Artair may not be well enough to come into the hall, for he has been ill, which is why Mathe had the gate," the majordomo reminded his master. "I will go myself to see before I send for his son."

The laird nodded. "Aye, he's always been a good man. Go." He took his place at the high board and began to eat the food that had been laid out for him.

"I think," Ellen said, "that Artair may have put his son in charge because he has hopes of the lad taking his place one day. I have been speaking with some of the maidservants. They all like Mathe, but say his interest in the lasses is great. And he fancies himself perhaps a bit too much. He's good-hearted and good-natured, they tell me, but not the cleverest lad at Duffdour."

Duncan nodded. "I believe I know him. He has not the qualities to follow his father one day, but Artair's younger son, Evan, does."

"It won't be easy for Artair to pass over his eldest," Ellen said.

Duncan scraped the last of his porridge from the bread trencher. "Nay, it won't," he agreed, "but I am laird here at Duffdour, not Artair."

"Yes, my lord," Ellen said mischievously.

He grinned at her. "You're a saucy bit, wife," he told her.

Ellen smiled at him, and then she surprised him by asking, "Have you really come to love me, Duncan Armstrong? Or did you speak in the throes of passion?"

"I love you," he told her without hesitation. "I always said I would not be like Conal, who avoided love until Adair made him realize that without love he would not have her. My father loved my mother. My stepfather loved her too. I saw that love was a good thing. I swore I would not wed unless I loved the woman who was to be my bride. But then the king made a match of us, more for his convenience than for ours, of course. I was your husband, and while we knew each other after a fashion, we were more strangers." Reaching out he took her hand in his and, turning it, kissed first her palm and then her wrist. "But as I have come to know you, Ellen, I have realized that fate did us a good turn. I could not have found a better wife myself, and I have come to love you for your sweetness, your intelligence, and the passion you give me."

She felt tears pricking at her eyelids. "Thank you," she said softly.

"Do you think that one day you can love me?" he asked her gently.

"Aye, I do," Ellen told him. She did care for him already, but she wondered if what she felt was the kind of love that he felt for her. Would she ever feel that way? She smiled into his face. "You are the best husband any lass could have, Duncan Armstrong," she said, and, pulling his head to her, Ellen kissed him a soft, sweet kiss.

The sound of someone entering the hall brought an end to the embrace. They turned to find Sim and Artair approaching. Duncan Armstrong waved the two men forward, but raised a questioning eyebrow. Sim nodded and, turning away, left Duffdour's captain of the guard to his master. Artair bowed, and then waited for the rebuke he knew was about to come.

"I know he's your eldest," the laird began, "but Mathe is not the man you are. Why the hell did you give him charge over the gate?"

"My lord, I was ill with a flux—" Artair began.

"I know you were ill," the laird said. "And I know if you lay abed that you were truly ill, for you are not a man to slack his duties. But you know Mathe is a buffoon, and not at all suited to being a man at arms. He left the gates wide-open, and then he spent his time preening and prancing before the lasses. And while he did, the most dangerous man on the English side of the borders rode into Duffdour with six armed men. You're damned

lucky he didn't ride in with a full troop and slay you all."
Duncan Armstrong's voice was rising with his growing
anger.

"My lord, I beg you to forgive my son. Mathe is young,
and filled with the juices of life. He did not mean to allow
Lord Colby and his men entry," Artair pleaded.

"Now that we have walls about the house, and a moat,
the standing order is that the gates be closed at all times.
Your son was more interested in the lasses than he was
in obeying my orders. His disobedience could have cost
innocent lives. He is not fit to stand watch. Does he have
another talent we might put to good use?"

"He will do better, my lord. I swear it!" Artair
pleaded.

"Nay, this is no small infraction, Artair, and you know
it," the laird said. "And it is not the first time Mathe has
failed in his duties. The lad is as big as a bear, but his wits
are small. I will not have him among the men at arms
any longer. Now, your younger son, Evan—he has all the
makings of a good soldier. Train him, and perhaps he
will eventually take your place one day."

"I've risen from my sickbed to beat Mathe," Artair
said. "He has been punished."

"The lad is no bairn," Duncan Armstrong said.

Mathe now slunk into the hall, escorted by Sim. He
was a big lad with a too-handsome face that did not
belong with the rest of him. Both of his eyes had been
blackened, and there was a large purple bruise visible
on his chin. He stood, head bowed, before the laird.

"Well," Duncan said, "the lasses won't be finding you
as pretty for a while, Mathe, will they?"

"Nay, m'lord," Mathe muttered.

"You're no soldier," his master continued.

"I try," Mathe replied, but he did not sound very
convincing.

Ellen leaned over and whispered something to her
husband.

He nodded, and then said, "If you were not a soldier,

Mathe, what would you like to do? Besides chase the lasses, I mean."

The big man did not hesitate in his reply. "Horses, m'lord! I like working with the horses, and I'm good with them. It's almost as if I understand what they are thinking."

" 'Tis true, my lord," Sim said. "Mathe is excellent with the animals."

"Then why the hell isn't he working in the stables, instead of being allowed to let the enemy pass through my gates unchallenged?" Duncan demanded. "Artair, your oldest son is good with the beasts. From now on he will work in the stables. You'll learn from old Tam, lad, and if he approves you can have his position one day, as he has no son to follow him. And as for you, Artair, go back to your bed. I'll manage the men until you are well again. And train Evan, for he is the soldier."

"Thank you, m'lord, thank you!" father and son said in unison, and then they left the hall in Sim's company.

The laird turned to his wife. " 'Twas a good suggestion," he said.

"Well, the lad had to be useful in some manner," Ellen replied.

"We'll see what Tam says after a month or two," Duncan replied. Then he said, "I'll want to send word to Conal about Lord Colby. I'll have him alert the Hepburn. Let the great lords decide what to do. My task is to keep faith with the king, and to keep my own Duffdour folk safe."

"We'll keep Duffdour safe together," Ellen said, slipping her small hand into his big hand. "For now we have a winter to get through, and the raiding will be kept to a minimum with the weather being what it is. But come the spring, my husband, we will truly have to be on the alert. Colby may attempt to make an example of you to intimidate some of the other lairds into aligning themselves with the English, but why they would seek to solicit the smaller families I do not know."

"With allies on this side of the border," Duncan explained, "they would have a place in Scotland from which to attack the rest of us. And they could raid deeper into the land if they didn't have to hurry back over the border into England. And who would at first suspect that the king's own subjects were betraying him? And when it was public knowledge it would harm the king's authority and prestige not only in Scotland, but abroad as well. That cannot be allowed to happen."

"How wickedly clever," Ellen said slowly. "But if other families are cajoled by Lord Colby, how can we stop it?"

"I will send to Conal, and he will send to the Hepburn. As I have said, let the mighty handle it. But I will keep an ear to the ground," Duncan told his wife.

January passed. The weather was cold and gray with occasional storms of snow. By the end of the month, and into February as the ewes lambed, they noted that the days were growing longer again. By March the snows began to slowly melt away; the sun felt warmer on faces and shoulders. The winds had a faint warmth to them on certain afternoons, and the precipitation turned from snow to icy rain to rain.

Duncan grew more concerned as the winter eased toward spring. He prepared for the coming full moon, knowing that if the weather were clear then the raiders would be out. He had sent a message to Cleit advising his brother to inform the Hepburn, now the Earl of Bothwell, of Lord Colby's visit. He had heard nothing since. Whatever the king and his advisers wanted to do, they would do. The laird of Duffdour's concerns had to be for his own clanspeople. He had trained his men at arms hard over the winter, bringing in a dozen or so more men. The gates were kept closed and barred at all times. The new walls were patrolled the day and night long. The Duffdour folk knew they could seek shelter with their laird when the raiders came.

During the winter months, Duncan Armstrong had instructed each cotter to dig a small shelter beneath the stone floor of his cottage. If the raiders came at night, and there was no time for the inhabitants of each cottage to make an escape, they were instructed to flee to the shelter. The entrance to each of these underground hidey-holes was concealed by one of the floor's large stones. Even if the cottage above was burned, the stone floor would remain unscathed, and those hidden beneath it safe. Each shelter had a small barrel that was kept filled with water, a bucket, and some coverlets.

The March full moon came on a cloudless night. On the walls of Duffdour the men at arms spotted a fire on the far hills just after midnight. The bell in Father Iver's church pealed out a warning, while the laird himself rode into the village to speak with the clanfolk. "It looks like Johnston's Keep, between us and the Bruces," he told them. "They can come either way—to Cleit or to Duffdour. Gather your families up. Shelter behind the walls of Duffdour House. We'll know better on the morrow what is happening. I want no lives lost if we can manage it."

In response the cotters gathered up their families and followed the laird back behind the walls. Ellen took the women and children, along with some oldsters, into the hall, where they could be settled down. Then she joined her husband on the heights of the walls to watch. The night deepened and finally waned into morning, but no one had come. Still the laird was cautious, for he had noted, as had Altair, the faint, irregular shadows on the hillsides.

"What are they?" Ellen asked when he pointed them out to her.

"Raiders," Duncan Armstrong said. "Their garments are the colors of the hillsides, and when they lie upon their bellies they are almost invisible to the eye."

"How many are there?" Ellen wanted to know.

"Probably only a few, come to see if our gates are open," the laird said wryly.

Ellen gestured with her head to remind him Artair was also somewhere along the parapet too.

He grinned at her, giving her a quick kiss. "I think it's time to send our visitors home," he said. Then the laird called for his longbow, took it up, nocked an arrow into it, and sent the missal flying into the pale gray of the early morning hillside. He smiled, satisfied, as a howl of pain broke the silence, and signaled to several of his men at arms to prepare to shoot their longbows. "That is your only warning, lads," he called out. "By the time I count to ten you had best be on your way across yon border, or my men will begin shooting. And please tell Lord Colby that the laird of Duffdour sends his compliments." Then he began to count.

Suddenly the hillside sprang to life, and five men arose, two of them dragging a sixth man between them as they stumbled to escape the arrows shortly to come.

"Ten!" the laird called out. Then Duncan Armstrong turned to his men. "Don't hit them, lads. Just help them along on their way," he instructed.

The men on the walls let fly their arrows, carefully placing them near enough to the fleeing English borderers to hurry them along. And the other men at arms laughed loudly as their enemies made their escape.

"You might have done better to kill them," Ellen noted. "We would have at Lochearn, my lord. Why leave your foes alive to fight another day?"

"I made the point I wished to make, wife," he explained. "Better to have six mouths babbling about Duffdour's readiness against raiders. The next time they come I will show no mercy."

But while other villages and keeps along the border felt the fury of the English that spring, Duffdour did not. Conal Bruce rode over to visit his older brother one day in late May to tell Duncan Armstrong that there was talk being circulated among the border families that the laird of Duffdour had made some accommodation with the English that was keeping his house and villages, his cattle, horses, and sheep safe. The question was, had he paid the English to keep away, or was he involved in some form of betrayal to Scotland and to the king?

"But I am the one who warned the king last winter of Lord Colby," the laird said.

"Aye, 'tis truth," Conal said, "and I sent to several of the families myself on the advice of Patrick Hepburn. But you still remain unscathed while the rest of us have suffered losses, Duncan."

"This is Lord Colby's revenge on you, husband," Ellen spoke up. "You refused to help him when he attempted to gain your aid last winter. He has now made you seem guilty by leaving us alone here at Duffdour. 'Tis cleverly done. I suspect the loudest voices against you may be those whom the English have subverted."

"We must call a meeting of the border lords," Duncan said. "We cannot be entrapped into fighting with one another, for that but serves the purpose of the English."

"I'll send the word out, and hold the meeting at Cleit," Conal Bruce said.

"Arrogant bastard Colby," Duncan said. "If he meant to turn me because I had nowhere else to go he is sadly mistaken. I will never betray the king!"

"I'll have Patrick Hepburn at the meeting to attest to your warning last winter," the laird of Cleit told his brother. "We'll straighten this out."

"Aye, we will," Duncan said. "And before someone tumbles my walls down and burns my house to the ground. I will give our neighbors no excuses to steal my stock."

Conal Bruce returned to Cleit and sent out invitations to most of the border lords to come to his hall on the tenth day of June to discuss the gossip about his brother. The laird of Duffdour would be there himself, and could prove that he was no traitor. Patrick Hepburn agreed to come as well to testify to Duncan Armstrong's innocence.

This would be a meeting of clansmen, and Ellen would not travel with her husband to Cleit. She was content to remain at home, for old Peigi had not been well. The winter had been a difficult one for Ellen's longtime servant. And the proof that she did not feel well was the fact that she was allowing young Gunna to do more and more of her work. Ellen didn't want to leave Peigi at this particular time, for she worried that her last link to Lochearn could soon be no more if Peigi did not improve with the warmer days.

Duncan Armstrong arrived at Cleit to find that his brother had invited lairds belonging to the families along the immediate border such as themselves. There were Elliots, Kerrs, Johnstons, Douglases, Fergusons, and even some Hays. Several of them glared at the laird of Duffdour with open distrust, but Duncan Armstrong refused to be cowed. He looked each man in the eye, and shook his hand. Adair was nowhere to be seen; nor were any maidservants. Only men filled the hall.

The laird of Cleit saw that his guests were served some of his fine smoky whiskey, and then he called the meeting to order from his place at his high board. "There have been rumors," he began, "that my brother is in league with the English. It is not so, and I have invited you all here today that he may tell you this himself."

"He can say whatever he chooses to say," Ian Johnston said, "but I for one find it odd that while all of us along the border have suffered losses over the spring months, Duffdour has remained unscathed."

"The Armstrongs of Duffdour are known to be the most honorable of men," Andrew Hay spoke up. "Before you go accusing them, Johnston, at least allow the man to speak in his own defense. Yours isn't the only holding that's lost stock and folk."

"I lost my house!" Ian Johnston said, his voice decidedly louder now. "And my wife lost the bairn she was carrying from the terror she endured. 'Twas a lad too!"

"Blame Lord Colby then," Duncan said in a quiet but commanding voice. "He is the man who directs the raiders."

"And how the hell do you know that?" Ian Johnston demanded.

"Because last December when my Ellen and I returned from court, where we had gone at the king's request, I found Roger Colby in my hall waiting for me."

"How did he get past your fine new walls?" Robert Elliot asked.

"My captain was ill, and the youngsters on guard left the gates open. The Englishman came with six men, and ambled through my gates while those on guard flirted with some lasses," the laird of Duffdour said irritably.

Several of the other men snickered. They were jealous of the walls that Armstrong had been given royal permission to erect about his house and barns. Without the king's permission most of the border keeps were vulnerable.

"You find it amusing?" Duncan said. "I did not. The Englishman wanted me to give my allegiance to his king, and in exchange Duffdour would be free from attack. Had there not been a blizzard outside my house, and had not the laws of hospitality bound me, I should have thrown the arrogant bastard out in the same moment the words left his lips. But there was a blizzard, and I was bound by common decency. I refused his offer and told him I would notify Cleit, and Cleit would notify others as to his attempts to subvert the border lords. I told the Englishman that I was loyal to King James, and should never betray him. He put forth some veiled threats against me, against Duffdour, but in the morning when my wife went down to the hall he and his men were gone."

"So you admit he offered to keep Duffdour safe from raiders?" Ian Johnston said. His tone and his stance were bellicose.

"Aye, I do," the laird of Duffdour said. "And I also told

you I turned his offer away. And on that next morning I sent to my brother here at Cleit, telling him what had transpired, and asking him to inform Lord Bothwell."

"And Conal Bruce did indeed inform me," the Earl of Bothwell said from his place by the fire, where he had been listening to the exchange among the lairds. "And I informed the king of the English duplicity."

"Then why the hell has Duffdour been kept safe?" James Elliot wanted to know.

"Is that not obvious to you and the others, Elliot? I will admit this Colby fellow is clever. He sought Duffdour's aid in order to dragoon others of you into his plot, for the Armstrongs are respected in the borders, but Duffdour turned him down. So rather than attack Duffdour, he leaves it be so that the rest of you grow suspicious of the Armstrongs. Without this meeting you would soon all be quarreling with one another, some championing Duncan Armstrong, others not. By fighting with one another you would weaken yourselves, leave yourselves more open to attack by the English. You should all find yourselves warring on two fronts. Against the English. Against each other. Is that what you really want? Other than the fact that Duffdour has been left unscathed, what proof do any of you have that the Armstrongs have betrayed the king or their neighbors? You have no proof. Will you start a contretemps over an empty suspicion?" the earl asked them. "Know that if any of you should attack Duffdour acting on these baseless doubts, you will find yourself facing me as well."

"And me," Conal Bruce said.

"And me," Andrew Hay chimed in.

"And I should wonder," Patrick Hepburn continued, "that the man so determined and eager to place blame on Duncan Armstrong might perhaps be guilty himself of betrayal and treachery." He looked around the hall at the other men there. "Did Lord Colby pay any of you a visit too, my lords?"

There was a dead silence, and several of the men

looked away, shuffling their feet. There was no doubt that Lord Colby had visited them as well.

"What, my lords, no denials?" the earl demanded scathingly.

"We sent him away," Ian Johnston said.

"And so did I," Duncan repeated.

"But they burned my house the very same night!" Johnston shouted. "Your home stands untouched, your wife safe."

"Because I have walls about Duffdour," Duncan replied. "And gates that are kept barred at all times now. I have men patrolling those walls and hidden in the hills around my home to give me early warning of an enemy's approach. What have any of you done to secure your premises? Even my cotters are protected from danger should they not be able to gain the safety of my walls in time. Walls can be breached, my lords."

"And why have you all sat these past weeks like a gaggle of geese waiting to be plucked?" the earl asked them. "Why haven't you ridden out and attacked the English in kind? When do you intend to defend yourselves, my lords?"

"We are few," James Elliot said. "We're bonnet lairds with small holdings and barely enough men to protect ourselves. If we leave, who will look after our women and the bairns? And who will protect the stock and the fields? 'Tis all well and good for you to lecture us, Hepburn. You've men and arms enough, thanks to your good fortune as the king's favorite. We're only simple men."

"Band together into a single large force," the earl told them. "That's what the English have done. They're no better off than you are but that Colby allied them."

"And you think our clansmen should join forces?" James Elliot asked.

"Why not?" the earl responded. "A dozen clansmen can do little, but fifty or sixty men can put a terrible fear into the hearts of the English. Raise enough havoc on their side of the border, and Colby will find his forces dwindling away, for they won't want to leave their own holdings vulnerable to us."

"Won't we be vulnerable to them?" Andrew Hay wanted to know.

"Aye, but not at first. Three or four hard strikes will come as a complete surprise to the English. Colby will then have to change his tactics," the earl told them.

"You can fortify your homes more than they are now," Duncan Armstrong spoke up. "I'm sure Patrick Hepburn will speak on your behalf with the king, will you not, my lord? Whatever can be done to deter the enemy should be done. Certainly the king will not object to low walls of stones or wood or brush—brush that can be fired to deter the enemy even more. Make the doors and windows of your house less accessible. If you don't have a well in your kitchens, then dig one. A man can live without food, but water is absolutely necessary."

"I agree with the Hepburn," Conal Bruce spoke up. "We need to band together to stop this Englishman before he causes any more difficulty."

"Aye," the others muttered—all but Ian Johnston, who continued to glare hard at the laird of Duffdour. "And who is to lead us?" he demanded to know.

"I think Duncan Armstrong should," the Earl of Bothwell said.

"Aye!"

"Aye!"

"Aye!" the others agreed, even James Elliot, but Ian Johnston was silent.

"There must be someone else," Duncan protested. "What about my brother of Cleit, who already has a quiver full of bairns? The Bruces have always been leaders of men, my lords. Choose Conal to lead you."

"Nay," Conal said quietly. "*Fuimus* is our motto. 'We have been.' The Bruces are Scotland's past. The Armstrong motto is *Invictus maneo*. 'I remain unvanquished.' You are the man to lead us at this time, and you have the king's friendship."

"But not his coin," Duncan quickly replied, and the other men in the hall laughed uproariously at the remark.

"Duffdour also has that walled keep, a good place for a gathering of clansmen to meet," the earl said. "Let us decide the matter now. All in favor of making Duncan Armstrong the chieftain of our combined forces say aye!"

The hall erupted with a chorus of approval but for the silent Ian Johnston.

"Then 'tis done," said the Hepburn Earl of Bothwell.

Adair, the lady of Cleit, had prepared a fine supper for her guests. There was roast boar, roast venison, broiled salmon, and trout. There were several large pies filled with duck and rabbit, the pastry atop golden and flaky, their vents pouring forth a fragrant steam scented with wine that flavored the gravy. There were fresh summer peas, warm loaves of bread, sweet butter, and several kinds of cheese. The men ate heartily, and their goblets were kept filled with good ale. And when they had finished the clansmen played outside on the hill, wrestling with one another, shooting arrows at targets, tossing spears at a butt that had been set up. Then one by one the men drifted back into the hall at Cleit and were shown to bed spaces, where they collapsed gratefully.

Conal Bruce, the Earl of Bothwell, and the laird of Duffdour sat huddled by the large hearth in the hall, speaking in low tones.

"Don't trust Johnston," Patrick Hepburn said. "There is something not quite right there. He suffered far more damage than did any of the others, and I don't believe it was because he turned Colby down and Colby made an example of him. You turned Colby down, and you are far more important to the English than is Ian Johnston."

"Aye," Conal Bruce said. "The English come and go quickly. They would have had to be at Johnston's for quite a while to have inflicted the damage they did. And I know for a fact that Mary Johnston suffered her bairn's loss *before* the English raided, and not *after*. Agnes Carr entertains Johnston now and again. She's friends with some of our women. He came to her one night complaining that his wife cannot seem to bear him a healthy son. I'm surprised he hasn't used the English raids to do away with her."

Duncan Armstrong's eyes narrowed. "Money. It will be money that drives him. My fear is that he will send to Colby and tell him what we are doing. But I don't want him to know we are onto him either. We'll have to put a watch on him, and stop every messenger leaving Johnston's Keep. And we'll have to watch who comes to call," he said thoughtfully. " 'Tis sad. The Johnstons have always been an honorable clan."

"Ian is a member of the poorer and lesser branch of the family," the earl said. "His sire died when he was five. His mother, a proper bitch, would allow no one near him, for she feared someone might harm him. Consequently he had no guidance. But that notwithstanding, if we catch him in treason, we will kill him."

The two brothers nodded in agreement.

"I'll send one of my men to follow Johnston when he departs on the morrow," Conal Bruce said.

"What if he goes to Colby himself?" the earl asked.

"He'll have to be killed before he reaches him," Duncan Armstrong said. "But I doubt he would attempt to go himself. At least not now. He will want to keep suspicion on me if he can. Johnston's Keep is on my way back to Duffdour. I'll ride with him and see him safely home. You can have one of your men follow us, Conal, and then remain to keep a watch on Ian. On reflection, better send two men. If Johnston tries to sneak off, or if he sends one of his people, then your second man can bring us word while the other follows the messenger. But have the one who brings you word wait a short while to make certain Johnston hasn't sent a decoy messenger off."

"And that, brother, is why you are the leader of us all," Conal Bruce said. "You anticipate everything."

"No one can anticipate everything, Conal," Duncan replied. "Men make mistakes, and some of those mistakes are dangerous, while others are just foolish."

"And that," the Earl of Bothwell said, "is why I chose you to lead the others. You know how to look at the overall picture, and have not a small intellect. The king could use a man like you, my lord, but as you turned down Jamie himself, I doubt I could persuade you to take a greater role in Scotland's destiny."

"Like you, Patrick?" the laird of Duffdour teased. "Scotland's lord high admiral? You're the worst sailor in Scotland." He laughed.

The Earl of Bothwell grinned sheepishly. "Jamie meant to give the admiralty to Angus, but then they had that falling-out. Thank God for Sir Andrew Wood, who is the real mariner among us. I don't like the sea at all. I prefer the rolling hills of the borders to the rolling waves on the ocean."

His companions chuckled. They spoke quietly for a brief while longer, and then the laird of Cleit joined his wife in their bed while his guests found bed spaces, crawled in, and slept what remained of the night, for in summer the dawn came early. But as the birds were twittering with the soft light of early morning, the servants were coming into the hall with trenchers of bread filled with oat porridge, newly baked cottage loaves, butter, and cheese. A platter with a ham was placed on the high board, along with pitchers of watered wine and ale.

Adair Bruce was already in the hall overseeing her servants, directing her guests outdoors where they could relieve themselves, ushering them to table to eat. Many of the border lords had not been to Cleit before, and were well impressed with the hospitality shown them. Duncan announced that there would be a meeting at Duffdour in a week's time, for time was obviously important in this matter. Each of the border lords was to come with as many men as he could, for they would go a-raiding when they had all gathered, the English would not be expecting them this first time.

"We will make the initial raid a terrible one," Duncan told them. "Afterward we will decide how many men can be spared from each of you for the raids to come, which must each take a serious toll in its own way."

And then as Ian Johnston finished eating, got up, and prepared to leave, the laird of Duffdour called to him, "Ian, we ride the same way. My men and I will go along with you and yours. You came with but four, and I with eight. A dozen men at arms is a far better deterrent than just four, eh?" Coming over to Johnston, he clapped him on the shoulder in friendly fashion.

"There should be no danger to me ... uh, us, at this time," Johnston said sourly.

"Certainly you don't object to our joining forces, since we are going the same way?" Duncan persisted cheerfully. "I have to tell you I'll ride easier with twelve good men at my back, won't you, Ian?" He grinned.

"Sorry you're not going my way," Andrew Hay remarked. "I've but six with me."

"I'll want to leave now," Ian Johnston said. "Mary is always nervous when I'm away at night and don't return earlier in the day. She's a frail woman, you know."

"I'm ready, and so are my lads," the laird of Duffdour said. He walked across the hall to where his sister-in-law, Adair, was seated at her loom. "Farewell, lassie," he said, giving her a quick kiss on the cheek.

"My love to Ellen," Adair replied. "Tell her I'll see her at the summer games."

"I will," Duncan said, and then, giving a friendly wave to the others in the hall, he followed after Ian Johnston, who was already in the courtyard. His reluctant companion was not a friendly traveler. He hardly spoke a word during the next few hours as they rode along, and when they reached Johnston's Keep he did not invite the laird of Duffdour in for a bit of refreshment. Duncan looked carefully about him as they briefly stopped. Ian Johnston's tower house appeared to be in good condition, and his few fields were green with ripening grain. His outbuildings were burned to the ground, but his cattle did not seem diminished, and his flock of sheep seemed rather larger than smaller. Duncan Armstrong began to consider just how great the man's losses were.

"For all his talk he doesn't seem to have suffered greatly," Artair, his captain, murmured. "I made it a point to talk with his men. They're all afraid of him. They say he beats his wife when he drinks, and he drinks a good deal of late. That's how she lost her bairn. And only the old women will serve the lady Mary, for Johnston is like a randy billy goat, and will fuck any young lass he can get his hands on, they say. He's sired two bastard daughters already, and another cotter's daughter has a big belly by him now."

"He may be consorting with the English," the laird told his captain. "Two of Cleit's men followed us, and will keep a watch on Johnston's Keep. If he attempts to contact Lord Colby the messenger will be stopped."

"It's a good plan, my lord. While I'm grateful Duffdour has been safe so far, I realize we won't remain unscathed forever. Best to catch the rat in his nest, eh?"

The laird chuckled. "I could not have said it better myself, Artair," he told his captain with a grin. He had long since forgiven the man for his elder son's misstep.

By midafternoon they reached Duffdour. It sat quietly upon its hill in the summer sun, the waters of its narrow moat sparkling. The party of horsemen brought a man at arms to the closed gate. The small square peephole was pulled back.

"Who goes there?" a young voice demanded, although the owner of the voice could see quite well who the keep's visitors were.

"Duncan Armstrong, laird of Duffdour," came the answer.

The peephole was closed with a little bang. The iron portcullis was slowly winched up, creaking and groaning.

When it was tucked high above the gates they opened slowly, and just enough to allow the laird and his men to ride through one by one. The laird slid off his horse, tossing the reins to a stableman. Then he turned and addressed the young man at arms.

"That was well-done, lad. Evan, isn't it?"

"Aye, my lord!" The boy's eyes sparkled with pleasure at the praise.

"Now, this one is a soldier, Artair," the laird said to his captain.

"Thank you, my lord," Artair responded, pleased his younger son had made an impression upon their master.

The laird clapped father and son upon their backs, signing his approval, and then, turning, hurried across the wide courtyard, across the little bridge spanning the moat, and into his house. As he entered the hall Ellen ran to meet him, throwing herself into his arms with a glad cry. He lifted her up, kissing her hard and swinging her about so that her green skirts billowed out.

"You're home!" She kissed him back. "I missed you, and your laddie."

"My laddie and I missed you too." He chuckled, setting her down on her feet. "But I wasn't gone that long, lassie. I can but wonder at the kind of welcome you'll give me when you've been without me for several days."

"Where are you going?" Ellen demanded to know. "You can't go! You've just gotten home again. I won't let you go!"

"I'm not going anywhere, but in a week's time we'll have a houseful, wife." Taking her hand he led her to the hearth and sat with her upon the settle. A servant hurried up with a goblet of wine for him. "We're going to strike back at the English for all these raids this spring. Patrick Hepburn suggested we ally ourselves to make one large force. I've been elected head of this wee army." He drank a long draft from his cup.

"What of the gossip that you could be in league with the English?" Ellen wanted to know. "Who stood up for your honor besides the Bruces?"

"The Hays and the Hepburns. James Elliot was willing to hear me out, and Ian Johnston wanted to condemn me. From all that transpired the earl thinks that Johnston may be the one among the border lords who was willing to betray us all. We've set a watch on him so he cannot warn Lord Colby. In a week's time we'll all meet at Duffdour and go a-raiding, wife."

"I dislike all this warring back and forth over the border," Ellen said slowly. "Why must you lead the others? Colby has let us be so far."

"Only to cast suspicion upon me, and set us to quarreling among ourselves, wife," he explained. "The Scots haven't gone raiding this year because we are trying to keep peace, but now when he least expects it we will hit him a hard blow. Not once or twice, but several times, and in quick succession. It is to be hoped that Lord Colby's men will desert him for fear of losing everything they possess. If they cease raiding, then so will we. And we all want to be able to feed our stock and ourselves this winter. If we strike now we can end this, at least for the time being," Duncan concluded.

"It seems a logical plan," Ellen agreed, "but how can you be certain the English will stop raiding and agree to a peace in the borders? The peace made earlier that was to last three years between our kingdoms lasted but eight months. We are natural enemies, and it seems to be our nature to fight with one another."

"This spring's raids have not just been the snatching of a few cattle or sheep or the stealing of women; it has been brutal, with a lot of killing, looting, and burning. This is more like war than just the usual game we play," Duncan responded. "We have to reply in kind, and make the English hurt as much as we have been hurting. Lord Colby can fire them up for king and country, but once they find their farmsteads and keeps being burned, their stock being driven off, and their people slain, it will be a different matter. There are no winners in our border warring, lass. Raised in your Highlands, you would not know that or understand it."

"I doubt your border raiding is any different from the clan rivalries in the north, husband," Ellen told him. "If a MacArthur thought a MacCrae's greeting insulting, a small war would start over it. North or south, we Scots are really much alike, I fear." She arose from the settle. "You'll be wanting your food, husband. I should see to it."

Reaching out, the laird pulled her into his lap, one big hand caressing Ellen's small heart-shaped face. "I was well nourished at Cleit. Adair does not stint her guests," he said. "You, my lass, are what I hunger for, and what I need." He brushed his mouth across hers, and the hand caressing her face moved to the laces of her shirt, untying them with quick, supple fingers, sliding beneath the opening in her chemise to cup a breast. His thumb rubbed slowly over the nipple, encouraging it to tighten.

Ellen sighed with pleasure. From the first moment he had made love to her she had enjoyed all of his attentions. Now, used to the hands and lips that offered her such pleasure, she welcomed his touch. "Ummm, there are servants in the hall, my lord," she murmured softly, but she shifted herself to allow him greater access to her body.

"It is to be hoped that you have trained them well enough to look the other way," he whispered back. "God's blood, wife, I have missed you. I was away but two days, and yet it seemed like forever. I slept in Cleit's hall surrounded by a group of men, all snoring and groaning in their sleep, while I could think of nothing but you, Ellen, lass." He kissed the side of her neck, nipping gently at it.

"Do you not think that those men were missing their wives too?" she asked him.

"Their wives do not drive me mad with lust like mine does," Duncan told her, and he gave her nipple a little pinch. *"I want to fuck you,"* he breathed in her ear.

Ellen gave a little squeak of surprise. "Not here!" And she yanked his hand from her blouse and, jumping from his lap, straightened her garments.

"Then you had best hie yourself upstairs right now, madam," he said.

She turned and ran, picking up her skirts to climb the stairs quickly. As she hurried down the hall to their bedchamber she heard him coming behind her. The thunderous sound of his boots on the stairs was both exciting and frightening. She burst through the door of their chamber and spun about to face him. His look was deliciously dark and wicked. Slamming the door to the room shut, he twisted the key in the lock and turned to face her. Then, before she could think what she should do next, Duncan reached out and pulled her hard against him.

Her breasts were crushed against his hard chest. Her breath was coming in short bursts. She almost swooned as, reaching up with one hand, he tenderly cupped her face, bending his head to meet her mouth with his own. Ellen sighed as her lips softened to accept his delicious kisses. His tongue licked at her lips, and she parted them to allow him entry, meeting his tongue with hers. The two digits entwined about each other in a sensuous exercise of passion. A hand kneaded urgently at her small, round breast. Reaching down, she stroked the hard ridge burgeoning beneath his breeches.

"Ohh, my," she purred in his ear. "You are a randy lad, husband." Her fingers undid the breeches, and, slipping her hand inside the garment, she grasped his cock with her hand as he had taught her. "Such a bad thing it is," she whispered against his mouth.

Turning her about, Duncan backed her up against the door, where his long, lean body held her a willing prisoner. He pushed his breeches down and they fell to his ankles, where he stepped from them, kicking the apparel aside. Then, with a quick movement, he yanked her skirts up, lifting Ellen as he did so. His hungry gaze met hers as lowered her onto his raging manhood, and she, with a sigh, wrapped her legs about him.

She was almost faint with the sensation of him buried deep inside her. He was hard and hot. His turgid cock throbbed with its lustful need for her. He shuddered with his desire restrained, and then Ellen whispered once more against his lips, "Fuck me!"

With a growl, his hands cupping her round bottom, he began to piston her. She threw back her head with a glad cry, and his lips pressed kisses on the exposed flesh. Again and again he drove himself within her until she sobbed with her release, but he was not yet finished. His raging cock buried within her, he turned about and walked slowly across the bedchamber until he reached their bed. Lowering her down onto her back, he unhooked her legs from about his torso, pressed them back over her shoulders, and began to ream her fiercely, his manhood driving into her again and again and again. He ripped her blouse open and buried his face between her round breasts with a groan, suddenly enveloped in the fragrant scent of white heather that she favored.

Ellen cried out with the incredible pleasure he was giving her. She tore at his shirt, sliding her hands up his long back, raking her nails down the flesh as she felt herself losing control. "Duncan! Duncan!" She cried his name, overcome by the passion she always felt with him, and the sudden realization of the love that had begun to bloom within her heart for this man who was her husband. "Oh, holy Mother!" she sobbed as he pounded against her, and her passion peaked a second time.

"I love you, wife!" he cried out to her as his crisis overcame him.

And then the only sounds in their bedchamber were the crackling of the fire and the whimpering gasps of release from them both. Finally Duncan managed to stand up. He pulled Ellen from the bed, wrapping his strong arms about her, kissing her face, and murmuring to her how much he loved her. She nestled against him, wondering if she was truly coming to love him, or if it had merely been her desire for him. How did one know? But it felt wonderful, and it was comforting to know that this big man loved her. *I think perhaps that I do love him*, Ellen considered. *I'll tell him soon. Aye, I will! But not quite yet. I need to be certain.* And yet, did it really matter? She was his wife no matter, and he did love her.

Chapter 10

They came to Duffdour under the cover of darkness. Hays and Elliots. Kerrs, Stewarts, Hepburns, and Bruces. There were a few Scotts, and several Fergusons from just west of Dumfries who had heard there was to be a fight with the English and, having time between the haying and the harvest, had come along to help. They showed neither clan badges nor plaids, and Ian Johnston was very visible by his absence.

The laird of Johnston's Keep had sent word that his wife was sick, and he could not leave her side. He had sent two messengers out to warn Lord Colby of the border lords' plans, but each of these men had been taken and killed by Bruce clansmen. When the first of his men had not returned, the traitor considered that Lord Colby might have had him remain at his keep, but, concerned, he had sent a second man. When he had not come back, Ian Johnston began to consider that his treasonous behavior might be known, and he was afraid.

Knowing what her man had been doing, Mary Johnston realized that sooner than later border justice would be meted out to her husband. She had tried to flee to her brother's house, but had been caught. Angry at what he considered his wife's lack of loyalty, and now in terrible fear of his own life, Ian Johnston had beaten his wife so severely that she was near death.

At Duffdour, Ellen had been preparing for a week for her guests. Duncan and his men had spent a great deal of time hunting in order to bring in enough game to feed their many guests. The cook and her helpers had baked enough meat pies in the past two days to feed a small army, and the pies were stored away in a cool, dry place safe from vermin. The first of the clansmen arriving in the dusk of the late twilight were greeted by the fragrance of roasting meat, and their pretty hostess. They had not met Ellen MacArthur Armstrong before, and were charmed by the laird of Duffdour's pretty wife. And seeing how he doted upon her, even the most flirtatious among the border lords minded his manners. They were here to fight the English, and not one another.

Soon the hall was filled to overflowing, the men at the trestles below the high board enjoying a hearty meal of roasted venison, cold meat pies, a pottage of vegetables, bread, and cheese. Ellen's well-trained servants saw that the cups were never empty of ale. And at the high board the laird and his fellow lordlings sat talking. It was agreed that they would ride at moonrise, crossing the border and doing as much damage as they could that night before returning to Duffdour.

"What about Sir Roger's fine house?" Andrew Hay asked.

"Devil's Glen can be reached only by riding through a narrow passage," Conal Bruce said. "It's too dangerous for such a large group. Duncan and I raided it with a small force once to get back my cattle and some village lasses. Colby was off on our side of the border, and his house seemed sparsely staffed, but that may have changed by now. Besides, Colby poses no danger without his own large force. It's our job to cause enough dissention among the English that they will not follow him any longer for fear of losing what little they have."

Several of the lairds had brought pipers with them, and now those pipers played for the assembled men. The music began with lyrical tunes, but slowly the songs played became more martial in sound and spirit. And then Artair's younger son, Evan, came into the hall. Going up to the high board, he murmured something in Duncan Armstrong's ear. The laird nodded, and then he stood up.

"Men, I am told the moon is just peeping over the hills. It is time to ride!"

A cheer went up, and the hall emptied quickly, but Duncan did not get away before Ellen found him. As the sound of laughter, braggadocio, and boots echoed around them, the lady of Duffdour stood before her husband.

"Be careful, my lord," she told him.

"Why?" he teased her. "Do you want me back then, madam?"

"We have a son to make," Ellen replied seriously.

"Is that all?" he asked, looking into her fair face.

"Why would you ask such a thing of me, Duncan?" Ellen wondered.

"Because of late I have had the feeling that there is something you are keeping from me, wife. I am an intuitive man, lass." His eyes searched hers for an answer.

"Come back then because I love you," Ellen said quietly. "I but sought for the right time to tell you, and this, it would seem, is it." She reached up and touched his face with her hand. "I cannot lose you now, my lord."

His great heart soared at her simple declaration. He took the hand touching his face and kissed the palm. "You love me," he repeated softly. "You love me!" he almost shouted, and the servants in the hall stared a moment at their master in surprise.

Ellen laughed aloud. "Aye, I love you, you great, tall man. Now go and take your men over the border to wreak a bit of havoc among the English. But you are not to take chances; nor do I want you to get wounded, Duncan. Come home in one piece, if you please, my lord." Standing upon her tiptoes she gave him a hard kiss, then pushed him out of the hall, walking outside with him to where a stable lad was holding his stallion.

He mounted his horse, but then, reaching down, he pulled her up and kissed her a long, hard kiss that left Ellen breathless. Around them the men cheered. "I'll be back," he said softly. "Be waiting for me, madam." He set her down again, and, turning his horse about, he raised his hand, signaling the great troop to proceed.

Ellen stood watching as they rode through the gates of Duffdour, and the gates closed behind them. She climbed to the top of the house and watched until the shadowy forms in the pale moonlight disappeared over the hill. Then, returning to her hall, she directed her servants as they restored it properly, seeing that the bed spaces were prepared for the other lairds when they returned. Their clansmen would sleep in the barns and stables. Then, having seen to all the preparations necessary, Ellen retired to her own bed.

When morning came she arose and, having dressed, visited her old nurse, Peigi, who was sitting up in a chair by the window in her chamber. Young Gunna had brought Peigi a bread trencher of hot oats, and was coaxing her into eating it.

"Cook put honey and cream on it," Gunna said cheerfully.

"What are these bits?" Peigi demanded querulously. "They look like wee beetles." Her spoon poked at several tiny dark objects amid the porridge.

"Cook had some raisins," Gunna said. "She thought you might like them."

"Raisins, is it? Cook is getting fancy," Peigi observed.

Ellen came and sat by the old woman. "How are you feeling today?" she asked.

"I'll nae die today, lass," Peigi answered her, "but one

day soon. And I ne'er thought to die so far from my Highlands."

Ellen patted Peigi's hand. "If I thought there was a corner for you back at Lochearn, and you wanted to go, I would send you myself," she said.

"Go back to Lochearn? Never, lassie! I could nae bear to see that bold whore Anice lording it over all in the hall," old Peigi declared.

"He may not have wed her," Ellen remarked. "He's the son of the MacArthurs of the isles, and he who is the favored piper of the great MacDonald lord himself. I somehow do not believe Balgair would wed the by-blow of a Gypsy woman and some unknown man. He has too much pride for that, Peigi. He will have kept Anice as his mistress, for her lust is well suited to his, but he will have taken a younger daughter of some Highland chieftain to wife. I pity her, poor thing, but if she does her duty by Balgair and gives him a son or two she will be safe from him."

"And what of you, my chick?" Peigi asked. "When are you going to give your husband a child? I had hoped to live to see it, but I fear I will not."

"The child will come, and you will be here to see it," Ellen said, patting her hand again. "How can it not come when we love each other so deeply?"

"Ahh," the old lady said, "so you've come to love him. He loves you, you know. He has since almost the first moment he laid his eyes upon you. You've told the man, I hope? You haven't sent him off not knowing?"

"I've told him," Ellen said with a small smile. "And he'll come home to me; never fear. We have a son to make." She stood up. "I must make certain there is food enough for the men when they return, for they will be hungry after the long night." She bent and kissed Peigi's cheek. "I will come and see you later. Gunna, see that she eats."

"Yes, my lady," Gunna said. "We talk, and she gets it all down eventually."

Ellen patted Gunna's shoulder with a smile and then hurried off. In the hall all was in readiness for the return of the clansmen, and shortly before the noon hour the watch at the gates called out that a great party of men was even now approaching Duffdour. Ellen ran from the house and, climbing up the ladder to the catwalk along the walls, watched the approach of the riders. She immediately recognized her husband in the lead, but would not allow the gates to be opened until she was certain all was well. Then, climbing down from the walls, she greeted the laird as he rode through the now open gates. "Come into the hall, lads," she called to them. "There is food for all, and then you will want to rest. From the look of you it has been a hard night."

Duncan Armstrong slid off his stallion and put an arm about his wife. Together they walked into the hall, and she led him to his place. Then Ellen hurried to fill his plate with hot food and his cup with cool wine. She then sat herself next to him and waited quietly to learn how the night had gone. The men looked tired. Some appeared to have wounds, but nothing looked serious. She would take care of them after they had eaten. Their faces and hands were covered in dirt and soot.

"Did you lose any?" she asked softly when he had cleared his plate and was reaching for more bread and cheese.

"Nay, not this time," he answered her. "We'll go again tonight. They'll not be expecting us two nights in a row."

"I'll tend to the wounded when everyone has eaten," Ellen said quietly.

He nodded. "We'll sleep the rest of the day and into the night."

"And there will be food before you ride out again," she assured him.

"Come to bed with me," he said, low.

"When the wounded are cared for, my lord," she

promised him, and turned to Conal Bruce. "Did you surprise them?"

The laird of Cleit laughed. "Aye, we did. We burned two villages to the ground, and drove off some fine cattle and sheep that we hid in a secluded meadow near here. They won't be easily found. It was a perfect night for it. We learned Colby and his men were meeting at Devil's Glen."

"How did you learn that?" Ellen wanted to know.

"The villages had only women, children, and the elderly," he replied.

"And they just told you?" Ellen probed further.

"Some of the men sported themselves with some of the women," he said candidly.

Ellen sighed. She knew what he meant. There had been rape, but then the English thought nothing of amusing themselves with Scotswomen when they came raiding. It was the way of it, and while she didn't like it, she knew it happened. It always happened when men warred. The borders were no different from the Highlands in that respect. Men fought. Women suffered.

"No one in the villages was killed," Conal Bruce said, as if to reassure her.

"But their homes are gone now," Ellen answered.

"Aye, and they'll rebuild. They do the same to us," the laird of Cleit replied.

"I know," Ellen said, "but it's sad." Then she stood up. "Men, if you have wounds I will gladly tend to them before you sleep. Sim will show you to my apothecary when you are ready." Then, excusing herself from the high board, she went off to get ready for her patients. The wounds she saw were mostly cuts and bruises. One man had broken his arm, and could not ride out again. He swore bitterly until Sim said sharply, "Mind your mouth before my lady, man!" And the clansman asked her pardon, then grew silent as Ellen, swallowing back her laughter, finished tending to his arm. Her grandfather had often used language far worse. When those who needed her care had been serviced, Ellen went upstairs to join her husband. As she passed through her hall she heard the snores of the lairds already abed, and the servants moved quietly about so as not to disturb them.

Entering their bedchamber, she saw that Duncan had stripped off his clothing and was carefully tending to a bruise on his shoulder. "You're wounded!" Ellen exclaimed, hurrying over to him. He smelled of sweat, leather, and horse.

" 'Tis naught, wife. A goodwife struck at me with a shovel," he said. "She wasn't happy that we were firing her house, and several of our men had taken her daughter off for a bit of fun. The girl was overripe, and hardly seemed distressed."

Ellen made a face at him, her fingers carefully examining the wound. She was relieved to see the skin wasn't broken. "You'll live," she told him.

He pulled her into his arms. "I waited to have my bit of fun," he teased her.

"Did you, my lord?" She pulled away from him and began unlacing her gown. "Well, I suppose the mighty conqueror is entitled to his pleasures." She shrugged the gown off and, reaching up, began unplaiting her long red-gold hair.

Stepping in front of her, he undid the ribbons holding her chemise closed. Then he pulled it off of her as Ellen kicked her house slippers from her feet. "God's wounds, wife, you are so perfect in every way," he said, and, spinning her about, reached around to cup her two round breasts. "These are like little apples," he told her. He squeezed them gently. "I long to see our son suckling upon them, but until he comes to do so I shall have the only pleasure of them." Turning her back, he lifted her up, and his mouth closed about a nipple. He sucked on it, murmuring contentedly as he did so.

Ellen felt the tug of lust between her legs that she always felt when his mouth suckled upon her. Her fingers kneaded his muscled shoulders, and he winced as she touched the bruise. "I'm sorry," she whispered. "Take me to bed, my lord, and have your way with me, for you must sleep before you ride again tonight."

His mouth released its hold upon her nipple, and, sweeping her up, he carried her to their bed and laid her down. She opened her arms to him, and he slipped between her milky white thighs. His cock was hard and eager. He sheathed himself quickly and easily as Ellen wrapped her legs about him. Her teeth nibbled upon his ear, and she licked at it as he began to ride her. Her nails raked down his long back as he moved faster and faster upon her. She cried out as her crisis overcame her, but he was not yet satisfied.

Withdrawing from her, he rolled her onto her belly, whispering instructions to her. Ellen tucked her legs beneath her, raising her bottom up to him and resting upon her arms. She felt his manhood sliding into her female channel, delving deeply. He began to piston her, and when he had found his rhythm he released his hold upon her hips and, reaching about, took her two breasts in his hands, crushing them, pinching the tight little nipples as he strove to find release. And when he did she came with him, crying as his love juices flooded her, and he groaned with pleasure, collapsing atop her. But even in his delight the laird remembered his petite wife, and rolled off of her. When Ellen managed to regain herself as her satisfied lust drained away, she discovered that her husband had fallen into a deep sleep. She smiled, amused. Their fierce and hurried coupling had released all the tension of the night past for him, and she was glad of it.

For five nights in a row the clansmen, led by the laird of Duffdour, raided over the border into England, causing much damage. After the third night the English knew that they were coming, but each night they rode from a different direction, completely flummoxing the English, who weren't at all certain where this great raiding party was coming from or where they would strike next. Stock was taken. Fields were fired, along with houses, and many young women found themselves on their backs entertaining their unwelcome guests. And then the Scots went to ground. Hidden at Duffdour, they waited to see what would happen. But all was suddenly quiet. It appeared as if their fellow borderers had understood the message they had sent them.

"Either that, or they are planning to retaliate in kind," Hercules Hepburn, who had brought a contingent of his clansmen, said.

"We'll have to send out men to spy upon the English," Duncan Armstrong replied. "We need to know if Colby's forces are being increased, or if his forces have scattered. The English fields need to be replanted now, if they and what stock we haven't taken aren't to starve this winter. We'll draw lots to decide whose men go."

"What are we going to do about Johnston?" Andrew Hay wanted to know.

"Let him twist in the wind," Conal Bruce said.

"Aye." The laird of Duffdour chuckled. "It is likely he has lost his credibility with Sir Roger for not warning him of our plans. And he'll know, if he doesn't already, that we are onto him. The traitor would piss his breeks if any of us came calling. We'll leave him be for now."

There was a murmur of assent, and then several clansmen were chosen by lot to leave that night to spy upon the English. One returned two days later to tell them that he had followed a raiding party back over the border. Ian Johnston's few fields had been burned, his stock driven off, his small village and his tower set afire. Johnston himself had been taken off with those of his clansmen remaining with him not killed, and any of the cotters who could be found. His wife had not been seen, but when the English had gone the Scots clansman had discovered a new grave near the tower.

"Before I left to return to Duffdour," the clansman said, "I found a small group of women who had managed to hide themselves in the heather and not be caught in the chaos. One old hag told me that Johnston had beaten his wife so severely that she had died a few days before. The English led him away, a rope about his scrawny neck."

"Good riddance!" Hercules Hepburn said. "I hope they hanged him."

"Colby will want to know what he believes Johnston knows first," Duncan said. "And Johnston may have talked his way out of it, given the chance."

After several more days, all of the men sent out returned with the same tale to tell. Sir Roger's band of raiders was mostly dispersed now but for his own personal men at arms. The others had returned to attempt to restore their homes and replant their fields before another winter set in. The Scots had succeeded in bringing a peace of sorts to the borders for the interim, and so the border lords and their clansmen returned to their own homes satisfied they had bested the English for the time being.

The remainder of the summer was more peaceful by far than they had seen in several years. In the autumn the king came to hunt grouse, bringing with him the false Richard of York and his wife, Katherine Gordon. The king, used to visiting in the borders, had not brought his mistress, Margaret Drummond, and was content to sleep simply. But Katherine Gordon, a fine horsewoman and hunter, had insisted on accompanying her husband. Ellen gave the *royal* couple the bedchamber she shared with her husband, but Katherine Gordon was not pleased at all. If her husband was to be England's king one day, then she was England's queen.

"Have you no better chamber than this?" she demanded of her hostess.

"I have given you the finest in the house, my lady," Ellen said.

"Your Highness," came the reply. "You must address me as Your Highness. And please keep your head covered while I am in residence. I cannot allow you to show your hair, for it is much the color of mine, although mine is finer in texture and purer in color."

"Of course, *Your Highness*," Ellen said pleasantly. "I should not want you mistaken for me based on the color of your tresses."

"How can you speak so sweetly to that little bitch?" Adair, who had come from Cleit with her husband, wanted to know. "She is far above herself, especially given that she is married to an impostor. My blood is more royal than hers."

"I knew her at court," Ellen answered. "It is her nature to be overproud. Let her enjoy herself while she can. We both know she will never be queen of England, and I think in her heart she knows it too."

"You look pale," Adair said.

"I am pale by nature," Ellen replied with a smile.

"Nay, you are paler than normal," Adair insisted.

"I believe I may be with child," Ellen said softly. "Do not squeal, Adair! Until I am certain I do not want to tell Duncan."

"How many cycles have you missed?" Adair wanted to know.

"Two, and soon a third," Ellen responded.

"Are your breasts tender?"

"Aye!"

"And your gowns are beginning to feel perhaps a wee bit tight?" Adair probed further.

"Aye," Ellen answered her sister-in-law.

"Are you nauseous?"

"All the time, though I hide it, for a puking woman lacks charm," Ellen said with a mischievous grin. "And I have a terrible hunger for cheese all the time, and all I desire to do is sleep. Such a thing is not natural for me."

Adair laughed. "There can be no doubt. You are with child. I have gone through what you are experiencing enough times to know the signs of a breeding woman. You must tell Duncan. It will make him so happy."

"Oh, dear," Ellen said. "We have been ... Can we still ... Will it harm the bairn?" she asked the older woman.

Adair giggled. "Just be careful, but if you are it should not harm the bairn. I am always very lustful just before I deliver my children." She chuckled. "Conal loves it, and doesn't seem to mind my big belly."

The royal hunting party departed after a few days, and the Bruces of Cleit left as well. Back in their own bed-chamber, and cuddled up with her husband that first night, Ellen told her husband that she would give him a child in the spring. Adair had calculated, Ellen said, probably at the end of April, the beginning of May. As her sister-in-law had predicted, Duncan Armstrong was ecstatic.

"A son," he said. "You are giving me a son!"

"It might be a daughter," she reminded him. "It is in God's hands, husband."

"Nay," he insisted, "it will be a lad. Armstrongs throw lads."

"What of your sister?" she asked.

"One lass but two lads, our mother bore our da," he said. "Nay, you'll give me a boy," he said in a determined tone.

"I shall name her Mary," Ellen teased her husband.

"I shall name him William Kenzie, after my father and my Bruce stepfather," the laird told his wife, and he hugged her tightly to him. "You are the most pre-cious thing in the world to me, Ellen MacArthur," he told her.

Ellen nestled happily against him. Would her life at Lochearn with Donald MacNab have been as con-tented? she found herself wondering. Nay, it could not have been. Lochearn was as far away in her heart and mind now as the moon in the sky was.

The autumn finally came to an end. Duncan and his men had done well in the hunting, and their cold larder was well stocked. The first snowfall came at the beginning of December. Old Peigi, who had been fading away, was suddenly revived by the news that her own nursling was with child. She would live, despite the winter months, to see the bairn, she told her mistress with a toothless grin.

"It is amazing," Ellen told her husband. "She can hardly walk, but her mind is as sharp as ever. And I am relieved to say that she is teaching me much I need to know about caring for our bairn. Growing up with no siblings about me, I know little of bairns, but Peigi surely does."

The winter months passed, quickly it seemed that year, and then it was April. Ellen was enormous with her child, and, being petite, she now resembled a rather large, round ball. She waddled when she walked, and the child within her was very active. Her usual sunny attitude had long since vanished, and only old Peigi could speak to her without being castigated. Both the laird and his servants were cautious in their manner about her. But finally, on the last day of April, the lady of Duffdour bore her firstborn child. It was a lad, as his father had predicted, and he came so quickly that Ellen barely had the opportunity to acknowledge that she was in labor.

Howling, purple-faced, a tuft of bright red hair upon his head, William Kenzie Armstrong entered the world, his small arms and legs flailing with his outrage. He was a large child like his father, but his mother, to her amazement, scarcely felt his coming. The midwife had come hurriedly from the laird's village in response to Gunna's arrival. Picking up her skirts, she had run through the gates, across the large courtyard, over the little drawbridge, and into the house to find the child half-born, the maidservants fluttering, distressed and not certain at all what to do about their mistress, who was swearing in her northern tongue. But the midwife could imagine just what was being said, for she had heard it all many times before. Taking charge of the situation, she quickly delivered the child, and then tended to its mother while the baby was cleansed and wrapped tightly in swaddling clothes before being placed in his mother's arms.

"God's foot!" the laird said as he gazed upon his son. "How did such a wee lass give me such a sturdy bairn, wife?"

"You'll give me a lass next time, Duncan," Ellen said firmly. "Or a smaller lad."

The midwife chuckled as she gathered up her basket. "God bless him, my lady," she said. "And God bless yourself and the master. Ye're a wee thing, but you're made for birthing bairns. She is, my lord!" Then with a curtsy the midwife departed.

Old Peigi was helped into their bedchamber, and once she was seated the baby was put into her arms. Tears ran down her withered cheeks. "Ye've done well, my lass. Verra well," she said, lapsing into her Highland tongue. " 'Tis a fine heir ye've given yer man, and yer grandsire would be proud of ye." She looked down at William and began to croon to him. The baby, fretful since his quick birth, quieted, his eyes closed, and he fell asleep in the old woman's arms.

"That settles it," Ellen said. "You cannot die, Peigi. You have another nursling to care for, and I know you will do your duty. You'll have help, but you must look after Willie for us. And the brothers and sisters who will follow."

"I will stay as long as the blessed Lord will let me, my lass, but you must nae count upon me. I've taught Laria well. She's a sensible woman. I'll remain long enough to see that she does her duty as she should," Peigi said.

Ellen felt tears pricking at the back of her eyelids. She knew the effort that her old nurse had made to stay alive to see this child. When Peigi died Ellen's last link with her past would be gone. But Peigi meant more to her than that. This woman had mothered her all of her life; had taken her courage in hand and come down from the Highlands to serve her when Anice had proved so unreliable. Peigi was her best friend.

The spring now burst into full bloom. And once more the raiding began from over the border. But this year it was not a great party of English borderers burning and raising havoc; it was small groups of men grabbing what they could: cattle, sheep, and a stray lass here and there, and then scuttling back to their own keeps and villages. And the Scots were following their lead.

Summer arrived, and a flux of watery bowels struck the laird's village. Ellen learned from Sim how many families were involved, and then made up a nostrum that would cure it. Putting her elixir into little stone bottles, she delivered them to the cottagers needing them. And within a few days the affected families were well again. But the flux had moved beyond the village, afflicting several cottages beyond the village. Dutifully Ellen made up another batch of her potion and, riding out, delivered it to the clansmen and -women in need. She returned several days later to check on her patients.

In the last cottage, one located several miles from Duffdour Keep, she found a woman with several children ranging in age from an infant to several unruly lads, and a nubile young girl who looked to be about fourteen. All the children were ill but the girl, and Ellen feared most for the infant, who looked to be the age of her own Willie. The two men at arms with her waited outside while their lady hurried in with her basket of medicines. Examining the boys, she turned with an encouraging smile to the woman. "I'll give you some herbs and an elixir for them," Ellen told her. "You must see that the bairn keeps nursing. They should all be fine in a few days. This flux has just about run its course through the village. Where is your man?" she wondered curiously.

"Died," the woman said shortly. "In the last raid the laird made on the English."

Ellen nodded, wondering if the woman's husband was the baby's father.

"My lady . . ." The cottage wife hesitated, and then said, "I'm sorry!"

"Sorry?" Ellen replied. "For what are you sorry, woman?"

The girl by her side snickered, looking sly, and the woman burst into tears.

"I had no choice, my lady," she burbled. "They said they would kill my bairns! I had no choice! 'Twas the lass who brought them on us, my lady! The baggage has made a whore of herself for a few ha'pennies to buy ribbons from the peddler who travels this way during the year. Forgive me, my lady!" And the woman fell sobbing to her knees at Ellen's feet, clasping her bairn with one hand, the other grasping at Ellen's skirts.

A cold chill ran down Ellen's spine as she heard a vaguely familiar voice. "I have been waiting for you, madam." Turning, she faced Sir Roger Colby, who stepped from the farthest shadows of the cottage. "Cry out, madam, and your men will be dead." Then he said to the girl, "Go outside and do what you do best, wench, but see those two well occupied. Tell them your mistress has more to do here than she anticipated and will be a while longer. Keep them happily entertained, and I'll have a bright silver penny for you the next time we meet. I have been good to you, haven't I?"

"Aye, my lord," the girl replied, and quickly slipped through the front door of the cottage, not opening it wide enough for Ellen to see her men, and closing it quickly.

"Now, madam, so we understand each other. I have a rather large score to settle with your husband, and so you will come with me now," Sir Roger said.

"Why would I do that?" Ellen said coolly. "You are

alone, and I have two armed men outside the cottage door."

"Think, madam," Sir Roger said. He was an elegant man of medium height and of an undetermined age. "I have managed to seduce the rather foolish lass belonging to this cottage into betraying her family, and into betraying you. If you do not come with me willingly I will personally slay every inhabitant here, and then force you to come with me. Shall I start with this puling bairn?" he asked her, swiftly snatching the infant from its frightened mother. The baby howled loudly.

"My lord, give the infant back to its mam, and let us discuss this in a reasonable fashion," Ellen said. But she was truly afraid. "What do you want of me?"

"Your husband has caused me to lose favor with my king, and so I must repay him in kind by taking something he treasures. You are the laird of Duffdour's weakness, madam," Sir Roger told her with a small, cold smile. "All know it."

"I have a child," Ellen said. "My son will die without my milk."

"Even better," Sir Roger answered her.

"Duncan will come after me," Ellen said.

"He will not find you until I wish it, and then when he comes I shall kill him. I made a grave error with your husband, madam. I underestimated him. I was not aware that he had both intelligence and a natural ability to lead men. And that mistake has cost me King Henry's favor, for I was charged with keeping this section of the border in an uproar. Because of your husband, I failed. But he will pay the price for thwarting me, madam. Now take up your cloak and follow me. Just over the hill behind this cottage my men are waiting for us." His knife pricked at the baby's small arm, drawing a drop of blood forth. The child howled louder, and its mother whimpered, anguished, her eyes pleading with Ellen to do something.

"Very well, I will come with you," she said to him.

And once outside she would run shrieking for her men to come to her aid.

Sir Roger handed the infant back to his mother and, walking over to where the woman's three older sons lay abed, reached out and yanked the smallest up from the bed.

"This lad comes with us," he said. "When we have reached the safety of my men I will let him go." He looked at Ellen. "If you should attempt to scream or run, madam, I will slit the boy's throat without hesitation, and I will come back to see all here are slain. Do you understand me?"

The cottage wife moaned, low, tears pouring down her face as she clutched her baby to her breast. Her desperate eyes pleaded with Ellen. "I'm sorry! I'm sorry!" she whispered.

" 'Tis not your fault," Ellen said quietly. "Do what this villain says, and do not fear. I won't let him harm your lad. And the laird will find me and kill this English bastard who very much needs killing."

Sir Roger barked a sharp laugh. "I have always enjoyed women with spirit," he said. Then he rounded on the frightened cottager again. "You and your bairns will remain here in your home until your slut of a daughter returns from entertaining the lady's two men." He moved cautiously to the small window by the door and peeped out. A smile creased his face, and then he said, "There is nothing like the enthusiasm of youth, madam, is there? She is sucking his cock for all it is worth right now. Your man will give her a good ride, for the little bitch has a talent for keeping a manhood going for longer than he thinks he can. All my men have said it, and I have experienced it myself." He moved away from the window. "Remember what I told you, woman," he warned her. Then, his hand firmly grasping the neck of the lad's shirt, he directed Ellen to the rear entry of the cottage and out the door. "Hurry!" he hissed at her. "Up that small hill, madam. Do not dally. I will kill this little

Scots vermin if you make any attempt at escape, or try to delay us. We must be gone from this place quickly. We are near enough to the border to be over it before that little trollop finishes with your men."

The day was a gray one, and the skies were darkening with the approach of a rainstorm. There was just enough of a wind blowing to take the edge off of the silence. Ellen did not dare slow her pace, for she truly feared for the life of the boy with them. She didn't doubt for a moment that Sir Roger would murder the lad in cold blood, given the excuse to do so. They reached the crest of the hill, and at the bottom on the other side several men waited with horses.

Reaching them, Sir Roger flung the boy at his men, instructing them to hold on to him for the moment. Then he forced Ellen to mount one of the animals. Turning around to look at the boy in his men's custody, he bent and spoke face-to-face with the lad. "Go home and tell your mam that Sir Roger Colby keeps his word. Enter into the cot through the same door we exited. And remind your mam she is to give no alarm until your sister returns from the chore I set her to, boy. Do you understand me?" His fingers dug into the boy's small arm as he glared at him menacingly.

The little boy, who was no more than five, nodded, frightened. A small sob escaped him.

"You remain here until we are gone from your sight," Sir Roger finished.

The boy nodded again.

"Stop frightening the lad," Ellen said, irritated. "Don't be afraid, laddie. It's all right. No one will harm you. Wait just a bit, and then do as Sir Roger has instructed you to do. Tell the laird the lady said to give you a ha'penny for being so brave." She smiled down at him, and the child looked less fearful now.

Sir Roger mounted his own stallion and, taking the lead rein to Ellen's horse, signaled his men forward. The lad barely had time to scramble out of the way of the animals' hooves. Ellen turned to be certain he was all right, but he had not been harmed.

"You have a soft heart for the bairns," Sir Roger said.

"And you are a bully intimidating helpless women and children, turning an innocent lass into a whore," Ellen said.

"The cottage wench?" Sir Roger laughed. "The lass was more than willing to spread herself for a bit of coin. I had her first, and she was a virgin. She yelled most satisfactorily when I took her maidenhead, as I recall. My men enjoy her greatly. She's an adventurous little trollop, and more than happy to do whatever you want of her. In time she will give Agnes Carr over at Cleit a run for her money."

"Agnes, I am told, has a kind heart," Ellen responded. "That lass has no heart, that she could betray her family and her laird. When you get your ransom from my husband I will see the girl is taught better than you have taught her."

"I don't want a ransom from Duffdour," Sir Roger said as they rode along. "I want your husband to suffer with the loss of you, as I am suffering from the loss of my king's favor and approval. I do not need gold or silver, madam."

"Duncan knows where Devil's Glen is located. I believe he paid you a visit several years ago, but alas, you were not home, so he took what he came for and returned to Duffdour," Ellen said sweetly. "I believe he will do the same thing again, but if he finds you in residence, my lord, he will probably kill you."

Sir Roger laughed. "God's nightshirt, madam, you are a spirited little creature, but this is just the beginning of our acquaintance. It will be interesting to see whether I can break your spirit, or if you are capable of keeping it as we get to know each other better. We are not going to Devil's Glen. Wily foxes always have more than one den in which to hide, and I have several. I do not believe any of the others are known to the Scots, but time will tell us that, of course."

They rode through the long summer's twilight, and the three-quarter moon was so bright that with only two periods of brief rest they rode through the entire night. They were well into England now, and Ellen knew it. As the sun came up, Ellen realized that they were riding west across northern Cumbria. And then as the afternoon came, and she was beginning to fall asleep in her saddle, he spoke to her.

"Look ahead, madam. There is my ancestral home on the cliffs overlooking the sea. Have you ever before seen the sea?"

"I was raised in the Highlands," Ellen answered him. "No, I have never before seen the sea, my lord, but Duncan will find me no matter where you hide me."

He laughed. "Aye, he probably will, but not until I wish him to find you."

Ellen looked straight ahead. The building he claimed as his home was a small castle. It had four square towers, and was built about a courtyard, she discovered as, clattering over a drawbridge that spanned a wide moat, they entered into it. Serving men wearing badges with a fox's head on their black livery came quickly forth to take the horses, holding them steady for the dismount.

Sliding off his stallion, Sir Roger lifted Ellen from her horse. As her feet touched the ground her legs buckled beneath her, to her embarrassment. He quickly caught her up saying, "You have not ridden for so long a period before."

"Put me down!" Ellen said angrily.

"Your limbs are yet weak," he said as he started toward a door.

"Put me down!" she told him through gritted teeth. She drew several deep breaths so that as her feet touched the ground this time she was able to keep her balance, although at first she wobbled a small bit. But then she was fine, and followed him into the building. When they had gained his hall Sir Roger called his sergeant to him.

"Take the lady of Duffdour to the dungeon chamber that has been prepared for her," he said. "See that she is given something to eat and drink."

"You would put me into a dungeon?" Ellen was outraged.

"For now you are my prisoner, madam," Sir Roger said to her. "Perhaps later you may become my guest, and I will house you more suitably. Now go with my sergeant."

Furious, Ellen followed the soldier from the great hall of Colby Castle. He led her down a corridor and then, opening a door, ushered her down several flights of steps. At the bottom of the stairs they were met by another man at arms carrying a large ring of keys. He took them through what seemed to Ellen a maze of stone hallways that were lit with pitch torches. Finally he stopped before a small wooden door with an iron grate in it. Taking a key from his ring, he turned it in the lock. The door opened on silent, well-oiled hinges. How long had Sir Roger been planning this? Ellen wondered.

"In there, my lady," the sergeant said. "Put a torch in for her," he commanded the man at arms.

"I was told a clean pallet and blanket, a table, a stool, a bucket, and a candle," the jailer said in surly tones. "Nothing was said about a torch."

"You'll not leave a wee girl like this in the dark," the sergeant said. "I don't think the master would like it. And bring her some water and something to eat. I'll wait till you do, just to make sure that you do."

"If she's to be coddled and cozened then she should have a place in the tower, not here in my dungeons," the man at arms complained, but he went off to do as the sergeant had commanded, for he knew the man had more authority than he did.

"Thank you," Ellen said quietly, and she stepped into the cell, sitting down upon the three-legged wooden stool, for her legs were beginning to feel shaky again.

The sergeant nodded and, coming in after her, set his

torch into an iron holder upon the wall. "It will last for some time, for there is little draft here," he said.

They waited, and finally the jailer returned with a metal pitcher he slammed upon the table, and a tin plate with a hunk of bread.

"That's all?" the sergeant demanded to know. "The woman has been riding for over twenty-four hours, man. She needs hot food. You weren't told to starve her, were you? Get your skinny arse up to his lordship's kitchens and bring her down something hot in a trencher. I'm going to be checking on her daily, you mangy weasel. His lordship wants her housed here temporarily, not abused and starved. She's worth a great deal to Sir Roger. Do you want me telling him how you have greeted his honored prisoner?"

"Honored prisoner, is it?" the jailer said. "Again I ask you: Why is she here, instead of in the guest quarters above?"

"I don't know," the sergeant said irritably. "I'm not privy to his lordship's thoughts. What I do know is that this lady is the wife of a lord with whom our master has had a difference. He would bring the fellow to reason by holding his wife captive. But eventually he'll be sending her home, and she has to be as healthy then as she is at this very minute, so feed the woman, you wretched cur!"

"No need to excite yourself, Sergeant. I'll send my helper to the kitchens for a trencher of food for the lady." He hurried off.

"Thank you once more," Ellen said.

The sergeant nodded, but then he said, "Do not mistake me, my lady. I am Sir Roger's most loyal man, but I know he did not mean for you to be mistreated, despite his choice of quarters." Then he gave her a small bow. "I will leave you now." Closing the door behind him, he was gone.

The door, of course, was not locked, but Ellen did not bother to attempt an escape. She was exhausted with the very long ride, and she really had absolutely no idea where she was other than somewhere in northern England by the sea. She pulled her cloak about her. The cell was damp and chill. It was not a big space, and its stone walls were moist, the stone floor cold. There was no cup for her to drink from, and so Ellen raised the pitcher up and drank from it. The water was warmish and slightly fetid. The bread the jailer had brought her was as hard as a rock. She hoped the trencher would be better.

Her foot touched the pallet on the floor. It crunched with the sound of the straw filling it. Her body ached from the long, long ride, and the front of her gown was wet with the milk that was oozing from her breasts. Who was feeding her son? Ellen suddenly wondered. What would happen to her Willie if she was not there? For a brief moment panic rose up to claim her, but, catching herself, she took several deep breaths to calm down. When she hadn't returned, and they realized what had happened—that she had been kidnapped—old Peigi would rally. She would find a healthy wet nurse for Willie right away. Her baby wouldn't starve. But she would need something to stop her milk so that it didn't continue to flow. When the jailer returned with her food she asked him.

"Have you a midwife nearby, or someone in the castle who keeps the apothecary?"

"Aye," he said. "Have you been hurt?" The sergeant's warning had gotten through to him, and he didn't want this prisoner harmed.

"I was taken from my nursing infant. I need to stop my milk, as Sir Roger has told me I am to be held for some time. My gown is ruined already."

"I could help you out," the jailer said, leering at her. "Open yer gown and I'll suck you dry, my lady. From what I can see you have a fine pair of teats on you."

Ellen drew herself up and glared the jailer down. "Fetch me help, or I will make certain that Sir Roger knows of your lewd behavior," she said coldly. "I expect sooner or later he will come to see me."

The jailer shrugged. "I'll do what I can when I has the time," he told her. Then he left her, and this time she heard the key turning in the lock.

Ellen sat down at the table. The smell from the trencher was not unappetizing, and it had a spoon in it. She began to eat—vegetable pottage with scraps of bacon, but it was hot and filling. They had given her oatcakes, and Sir Roger had allowed her sips of wine from his flask, but they had stopped very little as they fled Duffdour. Her spoon scraped every bit of food from the trencher. Then, unfastening her gown, she got out of it, and, opening her chemise, she squeezed the milk from her swollen breasts into the trencher, giving her some relief. As an afterthought she took the chunk of bread the jailer had brought her earlier and put it in the trencher to soak. Who knew when the man would remember to feed her again?

Spreading her gown upon an end of the table, she attempted to sponge some of the milk stains from it with a little bit of water from the pitcher, using the hem of the gown to scrub at it. If she did not it was going to stink. She wiped the stains from her chemise in a similar manner, but dared not remove it. Then, wrapping herself in her cloak, Ellen lay down upon the pallet, hoping it was indeed fresh and free of fleas. She was quickly asleep, and she slept soundly for almost an entire day.

She did not hear Sir Roger by her cell's door. He looked through the grate at the sleeping woman, and thought she had been very brave so far. He would see in the coming weeks just how brave she could be, and he would enjoy pitting himself against the pretty Scots girl. She was most outspoken, and no coward, he had already discovered. He had called her spirited, and she was just that. It had been a long time since any woman had engaged either his interest or his lust.

If he must be forced to remain in this exile, punished for having been outwitted by a mere border lord—and the king had made it very clear he neither wanted to see nor hear from Sir Roger Colby for the interim—then at least he would have his amusement. The laird of Duffdour might eventually discover where his enemy had gone, but it would be some time before he learned of Colby Castle, which was located in a remote section of Cumbria on the sea. In the meantime he would play with the laird's wife like a cat with an adorable wee mousie. He would see if he could break her to his will. He had not had the luxury of such a game in some time. He briefly considered what the laird of Duffdour was thinking right now, and when he did Sir Roger Colby smiled wickedly and chuckled. It was the sound of a man well pleased.

Chapter 11

The laird of Duffdour stood in the middle of the cottage and tried to keep his temper, but it was a losing battle. He was angry at himself. He was angry at his men. And God help him, he was angry at this poor woman and her children. And now the littlest boy with the dirty face was looking up at him hopefully.

"The lady said the laird would give me a ha'penny for being so brave," the child said. "Are you our laird?"

"Tad!" his mother replied. Her tone was desperate.

"Well, she did, mam," the lad persisted.

Duncan Armstrong burst out laughing, unable to help it. Then, regaining a mastery of himself, he said, "I will give you the ha'penny my wife promised you, Tad, but first I need to know all of the story so I may find my lady wife." He looked at the woman. "Your name, for I am sorry, I do not know it."

"Machara, my lord. I was wife to Gair, the fletcher, who died in the last battle with the English," the woman said.

"I remember Gair," the laird told her. "He made the best arrows I have ever had. We have been without a fletcher since his death. You have one son almost grown. Was he not apprenticed to his da?"

"He was, my lord, but I did not know how to approach you to offer his services. And as you see, we have fallen upon hard times without a man to support us."

"Tell me what happened, Machara," the laird said.

"Evina, my husband's daughter, has taken to lying in the heather, and lay with some English lads."

"It was the lord that had me maidenhead first," Evina said proudly. "He's got a fine long and thick cock. I screamed when he took me, but then I liked it. I still like it," she said, smiling seductively at the laird.

"I raised her," Machara said, "but she's my husband's brat from another wife, who died. She would never listen, even when her father beat her. And now look what misery you have brought upon us, you dirty slut!" Machara slapped the girl angrily.

The laird thought he would have liked to smack both women, but instead he said quietly, "Tell me exactly what happened. Evina became involved with the English, am I correct? Who is the lord who is your lover, lassie?"

The girl giggled. "I don't know his name," she simpered. "His name means nothing. I care only for the size of a man's cock." She eyed him boldly. "You look as if you are as well hung as the bull in the meadow, my lord."

"Do not bother to flirt with me, lassie. There is no pleasure for me in traveling a road well trodden," the laird drawled.

"I heard the lady call him Sir Roger," Machara said helpfully. "He entered my cottage and threatened to kill us all if I gave him away. And then your good lady came to heal us. She is kind beyond measure, my lord, and I am so sorry this happened. This villain stayed hidden until the lady had almost finished, and then he revealed himself. He took the bairn at my breast and threatened to cut its wee throat if I cried out. Then he sent Evina outside to tell your men the lady would be longer than expected because the illness was greater."

Duncan Armstrong turned to the girl. "And you lifted your skirts for them, eh?"

"Well," Evina said, "I knew there would be plenty of time, and they thought they would have time for a quick fuck. I took my time with them, and they never noticed. First I sucked their cocks, and then we fucked and fucked and fucked. Our Scots lads are far more lusty than the English lads, my lord. And I had a copper off each of them for my troubles."

The laird gritted his teeth as she prattled on at him. "And while your daughter was *entertaining* my men, Sir Roger took my wife off?" he asked Machara, trying to control his rage.

She nodded. "He took Tad with them, and said if the lady made any attempt to escape, he would kill my son. We both believed him."

"Do you know where he had his horses?"

"I do!" Tad said. "We went up the hill behind the cottage, and down the other side six men and eight horses awaited. The lord was mean, but the lady was kind to me. She said you would give me a ha'penny for being brave," he repeated.

"Why did you not return quickly to the house, and give the alarm, lad?" the laird wondered. But he could see how young the child was.

"The mean lord told me I must stay where I was until he and his riders were out of sight. I am a good lad, my lord, and I have been taught to obey my betters."

Duncan nodded, and then looked to the boy's mother. "Why did you not give the alarm then?" he asked her.

"He threatened to return to kill me and my bairns if I called out before Evina was finished with your men and returned to the cottage. I believed him, for he has always been a man of his word, my lord," Machara told the laird.

"Indeed, and how would you know that?" the laird asked her.

Machara flushed. "Evina brought him to the cottage over a year ago. He came with several men. I did not know Evina had already lost her virginity to him, and when they sought to have at her I tried to protect my husband's child, and offered myself in exchange. There were nine of them, and each of them put themselves inside of me. All night long they used me over and over again. The bairn at my breast now, I do not know who his sire is. And then in the morning, when I came to my senses again, I found this wretched little slut riding them all, and filled with merry laughter. But the Englishman said he would pay me coin if a child was born of that night, and he did. He gave me a whole silver penny and three coppers, my lord, after the birth. He may be a villain, but he has some small honor. And he swore he would never harm Evina, and he has not."

"But he threatened to kill you and your sons if you betrayed him," the laird said. "Do you believe he would have? Truly? And how did he know my wife was here?"

"Aye, my lord, I do. He would have slain us. As for how he knew the lady was coming, the lady herself sent word she was coming to bring us her medicines. And Evina brought him word of it, for he had often railed to her about how you had outwitted him, but how he would have his revenge upon you eventually. So when he learned she was coming to the outlying cottages he came, and he waited two days before the lady arrived."

The laird nodded. "Do you know where he has taken my wife?" he asked her.

Machara shook her head. "I do not know, my lord. I swear it! I would tell you if I did, for you are my lord, and our allegiance is yours."

Duncan Armstrong looked to Evina. "And you, wench, do you know where Sir Roger would have taken my wife?"

"I do not know where he lays his head, my lord," the girl said, and oddly the laird believed her. She was a proper slut of a lass interested only in fucking, and in what she could get for her easy acquiescence.

"If I learn that you are dealing with the English again, wench," he told her, "I will drive you from Duffdour. I would do it now but that I honor the memory of your father, who was a loyal servant to me. You have betrayed me and your lady, Evina, daughter of Gair. My son is motherless now thanks to you. When I find my wife you will come to her on your hands and knees and beg her pardon," Duncan Armstrong said.

"I don't know why my Englishman wanted *her* when he could have *me*," Evina said sulkily. "Your wife is old, past twenty, while I am young and juicy, and barely past fifteen." She preened before them, swinging her long brown hair.

The laird looked to Machara's eldest son. He was but thirteen, but he already stood six feet tall. "When I am gone, beat the wench, and do not be gentle," he told the boy. "You are now the man of the family, and she needs to learn respect. And come to me with your arrows. If they are good you shall be my new fletcher despite your youth. What are you called?"

"Farlan, my lord," the boy said.

"Well, Farlan, son of Gair, you have a bright future, I suspect. Now, tend to your sister, and teach her respect and loyalty." The laird then turned and left the cottage. As he rode off he heard Evina shrieking with outrage, and the smack of a leather belt on bare flesh. He could have beaten the girl himself, he was so angry, but he suspected he might have killed her. He was not by nature a man for abusing women, but God only knew the little baggage would try the patience of a saint, as she had tried his. Reaching his house, he had Sim send for Artair, and when his captain stood before him he told him to have the men who had been so negligent in their duty driven from his lands.

"They may go with the clothes on their back and a single weapon. Nothing more. Their negligence has cost me my wife, and I have no idea where to even begin to look for her," the laird said.

Stony faced, Artair nodded and went off to do his lord's bidding.

The laird now sought out old Peigi in the nursery, and asked her what they were to do for his son, who would starve without his mother's milk.

"Bad news travels swiftly, my lord. I have already sent Laria to the village to find a nursing mother and bring her back with her own bairn so she may feed William as well as her own child. We will not let your son die. Now, go and find my sweet bairn, Duncan Armstrong. She is a braw lass, and will know you are coming after her."

"I'll find her, and I'll bring her back," the laird promised the old woman.

But even though he sent to Cleit to his brother, and Conal Bruce sent to the Hepburn Earl of Bothwell for his aid, and Patrick Hepburn spoke with the king, no trace of Ellen could be found. They scoured the countryside both near and far. The rode over the border into England, and straight into the Devil's Glen. But Sir Roger's house was darkened and obviously deserted. The king spoke with the Spanish ambassador, who spoke with his counterpart in King Henry's court, but all he could report back was that the English king had exiled Sir Roger from his court until further notice, being displeased with him.

"He has to be somewhere!" Duncan Armstrong said desperately. "He cannot have disappeared off the face of the earth with my wife."

It appeared, however, that that was precisely what Sir Roger had done. No one could recall seeing him in many weeks. The laird of Duffdour was beginning to despair. He just didn't know what to do now, but on his brother's advice he posted a large reward for information leading to Ellen's safe return. And then he reluctantly looked to his lands and to his son, for they needed his care and attention too.

The summer was passing quickly, but in her cell at the bottom of Colby Castle Ellen knew neither day from night, nor one day from the next. After what she thought to be seven days Sir Roger came to see her. He behaved as if she were in one of his best guest chambers, entering her prison and chatting away in a friendly and normal fashion. At first Ellen was stunned, then appalled, and finally angry. But she swallowed her anger long enough to ask for a healer.

"You are ill?" He sounded genuinely distressed, and peered at her closely.

"I need to stop the flow of my milk," Ellen told him. "You took me from my nursing infant, my lord. A healer can give me some herbs to stop the milk, as it is obvious I shall not be going home anytime soon. My breasts are painful, and it is unhealthy for me to be left in this state. That you wish to torture my husband I understand, but I do not believe that you truly mean for me to die while in your custody."

"God, no!" Sir Roger burst out. "I shall attend to it immediately, madam."

"Thank you," she said simply.

He arose, asking as he did, "Is there anything else you need, madam?"

"A comb would be of service," Ellen said. "I have tried using my fingers to keep my hair neat, but a comb would be better."

"Of course," he agreed, and then with a bow he left her.

She was visited several hours later by an old crone, who handed her a comb and then asked about her milk. How long had she been nursing? Was the child a male or a female? Had the infant nursed strongly? Given the answers to her questions the crone pulled a small bowl and pestle from her skirts, along with a handful of herbs. She ground the leaves into a fine powder, poured it into a small square of cloth, folded it, and tied it with a bit of twine, then handed it to Ellen.

"Take a goodly pinch on your tongue with water three times daily," the crone said. "Your milk flow should stop in a few days. If it does not, have the lord send for me again." Then she scurried from the room, reminding Ellen of the thin gray rat who visited her daily, and with whom she shared a bit of her bread.

The prisoner followed the crone's instructions, and before another few days had gone by her milk had dried up. Ellen wept, and wondered if she would ever see her son again. Would she see his father again? *Duncan! Duncan!* she called to him silently, but there was no response. How long had she been in this tiny stone cell? Each day she spent hours combing her long hair and sleeping, for there was nothing else to do. She spoke to the rat, who would sit watching her with intelligent eyes, but the only sound of a human voice she heard came when her food was brought to her twice a day. The silence was becoming deafening, and Ellen began to sleep more and more. Several times her jailer had had difficulty awakening her when he brought the food. And on those occasions she had fallen back into sleep without touching her food while the rat, realizing there was no danger, clambered up onto the small wooden table and feasted. She was sleeping more and more, eating less and less. Finally the jailer, realizing his prisoner could very easily die unless something was done, went to Sir Roger.

"I've seen prisoners get like this before, my lord," the jailer told his master. "She'll die if it goes on like this." He waited for his better to say something.

"What do you suggest?" Sir Roger asked after a long few moments of silence.

"Couldn't you keep the lady imprisoned somewhere other than my dungeons, my lord? I know it ain't my place to ask, but what has she done that is so terrible that you must put her in there? She's been there over a month now, sir." The jailer shifted nervously on his feet.

"I suppose," Sir Roger said, ignoring the man's question, "that we might put her up in the west tower now. Yes, I'll have something prepared. Bring her up to the great hall in an hour's time, jailer."

"Yes, my lord!" The jailer was relieved. He was frankly curious as to who the lady was—and she was indeed a lady. Even a lowly fellow like him knew the difference between a lady and a slut. And why had his master brought her to the castle and imprisoned her? For since she had been here Sir Roger hadn't seemed particularly interested in her. But it was not his place to ask aloud such questions.

Ellen was feeding her rat when the jailer entered her cell. He was relieved to see she was awake. The rat scuttled away. "You're to come with me now, my lady," he said to her. "The master wants to see you in the hall. I think you will soon have a change of quarters for the better," he confided to her with a wink.

Ellen said nothing, but she did give the man a weak smile and followed him slowly through the damp corridors and up the several flights of stairs and finally into the great hall of Colby Castle, where Sir Roger was awaiting her.

He was appalled when he saw her. She was paler than normal, and her hair was filthy. Her gown was badly soiled, and yes, yes, there was definitely a distinct unpleasant odor about her. "What has happened to you?" he asked her.

Ellen looked at him as if he had lost his mind. Or perhaps it was she who had lost hers. Finally she said in a weak voice, "How long have you had me imprisoned in your dungeons, my lord? You stole me away in the middle of July. How long have I languished in the dark and dirt of your cellars?"

"I did not realize so much time had passed since you came to the castle," he told her.

"What day is this?" she asked him.

"The nineteenth of August," he admitted.

"Then there is your answer, my lord," Ellen said with a small show of spirit. "For over a month I have lain in that fetid cell with no change of clothing or way to bathe. I am flea-bitten, and there are certain to be nits in my hair. I am not used to living in filth."

"I am moving you to a small apartment in my west tower," Sir Roger said. "I kept you hidden only so I could be certain you would not be seen, and your location reported back to your husband. I am not yet ready to deal with him, madam."

"My comb!" Ellen cried, and she looked to her jailer. "I have left my comb behind. Will you be kind enough to fetch it for me, good sir?"

"There are women's things in your new residence," Sir Roger informed her. "Rafe!" he called to the same sergeant who had several weeks back escorted Ellen to the dungeons. "Take the lady to her new quarters now."

"I will need clean clothing," Ellen said. "And I want a bath, and water to wash my hair, my lord."

"Rafe will see you have whatever you need, madam," Sir Roger replied.

"When will you let me free?" Ellen wanted to know.

"In time, madam," he said. "In time."

Her new quarters were indeed a great improvement over her old. At the very top of the west tower were two small rooms, each with its own hearth, a stack of wood by each. The sergeant escorted her into the apartment, and as he left her he said, "I will fetch a tub and see that there is water for it, my lady. Is there anything else I might do for you?"

"Who lived here once?" Ellen inquired as she saw the brush and comb upon a table, and opened a small trunk to reveal female garments.

"Sir Roger once had a mistress," the sergeant said tersely.

"What happened to her?" Ellen wanted to know.

"He found she was betraying him, and he killed her," the man answered.

"Was she?" Ellen looked directly at him.

"Yes," the sergeant replied. "His mother saw to it,

for he was needed to do the king's work, but he would not leave his mistress. Then his mother saw that her son learned of the betrayal. He killed them both. It was several years ago, my lady. There has been no one in these rooms since." He bowed. "I will go fetch the tub now."

"He kidnapped me," Ellen said. "He has a quarrel with my husband."

"It is not my place to know these things, my lady," the sergeant said, and he hurried off to find the oak tub, and to get her enough water to fill it.

When she was alone once more she wandered through the two rooms, examining everything. The tiny day room had a rectangular oak table that had been set beneath one of the two windows. On either side of the table, against the stone wall of the tower, was an oak chair with a woven seat and a tapestry cushion. Before the hearth was a small oak settle with a cushion made to fit over the wooden seat. The wood floor of the room was black with its age. The two windows had shutters that were now open, and there was glass in the casements. Ellen opened one of the windows and breathed in the first fresh air she had had in weeks. It was late afternoon, and the sun was bright.

She left the window open and walked slowly into the other little room. It contained an oak bedstead with natural-colored linen bed curtains embroidered with deep blue threads hanging from tarnished brass rings. There was a small round candle stand to one side of the bed, and a stool before the hearth. On the wall without the single window in the chamber was the trunk she had briefly opened earlier. It was still open, and looking inside she could see it was filled with colorful garments. She had but gazed into it before. Now she began pulling things out, and to her surprise she found the clothing was very much her size. Dropping the garments she went back out into the day room, as she heard the sergeant stamping back into the chamber.

He was carrying a round wooden tub, and he looked

to her. "Where do you want it, my lady? Sir Roger's majordomo found it, and said it belongs with your rooms. He does not know why it was still not in them. It is supposed to hang on an iron hook outside your door." He was red-faced from his climb, and puffing with his exertion.

"I think I should like to bathe before a fire if you would be so kind as to start one for me, Sergeant," Ellen told him.

"In your bedchamber," he suggested. "You would have more privacy there, my lady. Sir Roger has given orders that the door to these rooms be locked from the outside. You do not want someone catching you unawares as you bathe." He was most serious and deferential when he spoke to her.

"Aye," she agreed, and he carried the tub past her, setting it down before the bedchamber's little hearth.

"I'll start the fire for you," he told her, kneeling to arrange the kindling and then the wood, taking the lit candle she offered him, and lighting the fire. He stood up, giving her back the candle. "I hear the menservants coming with the buckets," the sergeant said. "Perhaps you would like to sit in your dayroom while the tub is filled."

Ellen went, doing as he suggested, waiting patiently for some minutes as four serving men came in and out of the room with buckets of steaming water. It took over half an hour for the little tub to be filled, for the servants had to make their way back to the kitchens to get the hot water. Finally the tub was filled, and two buckets were left for her to wash her hair. Ellen thanked the servants politely.

"I will leave you to yourself now, my lady," Rafe said. "Remember that the door is locked from the outside. It will be opened only by Sir Roger or by me."

"Thank you," Ellen answered him, and watched as he left her tower rooms, hearing the key as it turned and slammed the door's lock firmly into its place. She stood for several long moments after he left, growing used to this new silence that surrounded her. In her cell the quiet had been very complete, but here in her tower she could hear the birds outside, and the faint sounds of cattle and sheep in nearby meadows. There seemed to be no wind this late afternoon, but the air was sweet and it was fresh. She opened the twin casements in the dayroom to air out the mustiness, for it was obvious that these rooms had been closed up for several years. Still she had noted that the bed was freshly made.

Ellen went and made a fire in the dayroom hearth. She noticed almost at once that the wood beginning to burn was apple wood, for it had a lovely fragrance. She had almost forgotten such things during her monthlong incarceration. With a sigh Ellen went into the bedchamber and stripped off her dirty garments. Naked, she stood debating with herself for a moment, and then she put them on the fire to burn. There was no salvaging them. Then she climbed into the little tub, delighted to find that a small sliver of soap had been set on its edge, and a washing rag floated in the yet-hot water.

She scrubbed and scrubbed at herself until her skin was pink and tingling. Then she washed her long red-gold hair, relieved to find that despite her fears of nits she had managed to escape them. *A few more days in that dungeon,* she considered, *and I should not have been so fortunate.* She used one of the remaining buckets to rinse her hair free of soap and grime; then she exited the tub and dried herself and her hair thoroughly with the drying cloth that had been laid upon her bed. It felt wonderful to be clean again.

Wrapping herself in a pale blue silk house robe she found in the trunk, she sat down upon the little stool by the fire and began to brush her long hair until it was soft and dry. As she did she considered that she had never before thought of a bath and clean hair as luxuries, but after her month in the castle dungeon she certainly did. Carefully she plaited her hair into a single thick braid.

Then she went to the window of her bedchamber, leaning upon the stone sill to look out at the day again.

The castle stood upon a cliff overlooking the sea. Ellen had never seen the sea until the day she had come to this place. There seemed to be no end to the vastness of the water. It appeared to stretch forever. Today in the late-afternoon sunlight the water sparkled bright blue, and above it great white gulls soared on the almost invisible wind. And the air—it had a clean tang to it. She could see no boats in the sea or upon the bit of stony beach she could but glimpse. In the distance she saw a river emptying into this sea. But there were no other people. Colby Castle was obviously very isolated.

How on earth was Duncan going to find her there? Was he even searching for her after all these weeks, or had he given her up for dead? He had not been unhappy as a bachelor gentleman. Perhaps, having an heir, he was content without a wife. But he loved her! He had said he loved her, and he had said it before she had said it. Suddenly Ellen found herself crying silently. Aye, she was better off as the day ended than she had been when it began, but she was so alone. She had not even a rat to talk to now, not that she had really talked to the creature, but he—or perhaps she—had been company.

Flinging herself down upon the bed, she wept herself into a slumber. When she awoke the late-summer sun was sinking down into the far reaches of the sea. Getting up, she went to the window once again and reveled in the magnificent colors on the horizon. When had she last seen such beauty? She didn't understand why, but watching it strengthened her. All the sorrow and weakness she had experienced earlier vanished. If Duncan Armstrong couldn't find his wife, then she would find him. Of course, there was the small matter of escaping from Colby Castle to be considered. Ellen chuckled to herself. But she would escape no matter what it took to do so.

A knock sounded upon the door that led from her

dayroom into the hallway outside. Ellen went to the door, tightening her house robe as she did. "Yes? Who is it?"

"It is I, my lady, Rafe, the sergeant," came the reply. "I have brought a serving woman with your meal. May she enter?"

"Of course," Ellen answered him, and as she stepped back she heard the key turning in the lock.

The door opened, and the sergeant stepped into the room, holding the door to allow the servant carrying the tray inside. The woman scuttled quickly in, her eyes averted from Ellen, and set a tray upon the table. Then she hurried out, and Ellen heard her footsteps as she went down the stairs.

"Is there anything else I may do for you, my lady?" Rafe asked her.

"Could the tub in my bedchamber be emptied?" Ellen asked him.

He nodded and, going directly into the room, picked the tub up—to Ellen's amazement, for surely it must be heavy—and carefully dumped it out of her chamber window. Then he brought the tub out through the dayroom and, stepping out the door into the hall, hung it on the iron hook that stuck out from the stone wall. "Will that be all, my lady?" he asked politely. "I believe you have plenty of wood for your fires, and while the night will be damp, for we are by the sea, it is not cold."

"I shall be fine, Sergeant," she answered.

"Sir Roger wishes to know if you have everything you need," Rafe said.

"Tell him I would like my freedom," Ellen replied, and the sergeant grinned.

"I shall convey that message to him, my lady," he responded politely with a small bow. "Good night, my lady." Then, backing through the door into the hall, he drew the door shut and locked it.

She heard his footsteps as they echoed down the staircase, and sighed. Having someone to talk with even briefly and on mundane matters was very nice. She would look forward to his visits. Walking over to the table, she looked to see what nourishment had been given her tonight, and was pleasantly surprised. Her fare in the dungeon had consisted of either vegetable pottage or oat porridge in a small, stale trencher of bread. Neither had had a great deal of flavor. But there in a large fresh bread trencher had been laid a slice of ham, a little haunch of rabbit, and a piece of cold meat pie. There was a small bowl with some new peas with two leaves of braised lettuce, a wedge of cheese, and a peach. There was also a small silver goblet of sweet wine.

"What a great improvement," Ellen said aloud, and, pulling one of the chairs to the table, she ate it slowly, but she ate it all. She savored the peach in particular, devouring it as she once again leaned upon the stone sill of one of the casements and watched the bright twinkling stars popping out in the blue-black sky. The juice from the fruit ran down her hands, and she licked them clean before taking the napkin she had been given, dipping it in the remaining bucket of water, and wiping the stickiness from her skin.

When she had finished eating she sought about the apartment for a pitcher, and, finding it with its matching brass basin, she poured water into the vessel and set it into the hot ashes of her bedchamber fire so it would be warm for her morning ablutions. Then, being sleepy once again, Ellen left the dayroom and climbed into her bed. The bedding smelled of lavender, and was far more comfortable than her cell pallet had been. She was quickly asleep after burrowing into the featherbed and drawing the coverlet over her.

Her life settled once again into long, dull hours made only slightly better by the fact that she could look out the windows of her new prison to watch the sea and the birds. After a few days Ellen said to the sergeant, "Tell your master that I am bored with no one to speak with and nothing to do."

He nodded. "I shall tell him, my lady."

To Ellen's surprise Rafe returned shortly after he had left her. He carried a small basket and several garments. "What is this?" she asked him.

"My master says if you are bored then perhaps you would not mind mending some of his garments. He has no woman to do it for him. I have brought his late mother's sewing basket." He set the items down.

Ellen was at first outraged, and then she laughed. "Thank your master for providing me with something for my hands to do, but tell him I am still without lively conversation. Perhaps he could send me a serving girl for a companion."

"I will convey your request," the sergeant said with a little bow, and then he was gone again, locking the door behind him.

"One day you will forget to lock that door," Ellen muttered to herself. And then she looked through the garments she had been brought. There were three shirts, all the worse for wear, a velvet jerkin, its trim worn, and a brocade surcoat with a torn pocket. Ellen laid the clothing on the dayroom table and opened the small basket. Inside she found thread and needles, along with scraps of fabric and bits of ribbon. Sir Roger, Ellen decided, might own a castle, but he had no wealth, as his garments indicated. She set to work repairing the items in question, mending the tear in the surcoat pocket first, then replacing the trim on the velvet jerkin with some contrasting ribbon she had found in the basket. Then she mended the cuffs and collars on the shirts.

When her late meal was brought that day, Ellen returned the clothing to the sergeant. "Tell your master that if he will supply me with the fabric and return one of the shirts to me for a pattern, I will make him some new shirts. These have seen better days, and can be mended or repaired no more."

Following her custom, Ellen ate her lonely meal and then retired to the window to watch the sea. The horizon was dark today, and she thought as the darkness seemed to be coming toward her that there might be a storm soon. Her ears caught the sound of faint thunder, and the gulls were screeching noisily above her. Since she had been brought up from the darkness of the dungeon she had been able to keep track of the days. August had gone, and it was now early September.

She had tried not to think of why her husband had not yet found her. Admittedly Sir Roger's ancestral home was not well-known, and it was certainly isolated; but surely someone knew where the Englishman would hole up with his captive, and had been able to help Duncan seek her out. Yet no one had come. And what of her baby? She knew Peigi would have known enough to find a wet nurse for Willie immediately, but had her son thrived on another woman's milk? Or had he died? If Duncan's heir were dead she would kill Sir Roger herself, even if she went to hell and burned for eternity for the crime. As the dark thoughts began to take hold of her, she heard to her surprise the key in the door being turned. The door swung wide, and Sir Roger stepped into the chamber.

"Good evening, madam," he said pleasantly.

Ellen tensed. "What do you want?" she demanded of him.

"I am told by my sergeant that you have complained of a lack of company," Sir Roger told her. "Do you play chess? I have brought a chessboard and pieces," he said. He held the board out and showed her a box that he carried.

"I do play chess, my lord," Ellen said slowly.

"Excellent! Then we shall have a game or two," he replied. He immediately set the board and box upon the table, drawing the two chairs on either side of the table to the ends of it, and moving a footed candelabra near for light.

Ellen sat down and opened the box. She spilled the pieces out, admiring them as she did so. They were beautifully carved figures of ash wood and ebony. They were hand-painted, green being the predominant color for one set, the king and queen of which had gold crowns; and red with silver belonging to the other grouping. She set the figures up carefully, and when she had finished he turned the board about.

"I prefer the red figures," he said, moving a pawn.

Ellen nodded. Then she moved a pawn.

They played for a long time, and Ellen found herself rather pleased that he was a worthy opponent. "You play well," she finally told him.

"As do you, madam," he answered her. "Who taught you?"

"My grandsire," Ellen answered.

"You played only with him?" Sir Roger wondered.

"Nay, I often played with King James when I was in his aunt's household," Ellen explained to her companion.

"Did you beat him?" Sir Roger asked, curious.

"More often than not," Ellen said without embarrassment.

He laughed, genuinely amused. "Modesty is not your strong suit, madam," he told her. "This is a side of you I did not expect."

"Why did you kidnap me?" she asked him quietly.

"Your husband embarrassed me, and cost me my king's favor. I have told you before that I simply wished to take something of value from him, as he had taken something of value from me. He will find us eventually, for he is a determined man. You should know he has scoured the borders all summer for any trace of you, madam."

"When he finds me he will kill you," Ellen said.

"Or I will kill him. Check, madam, and mate," Sir Roger replied. "Another game?" He gave her a small smile. "Either way, I win this game we play."

"If you are dead I cannot see how you could possibly win," Ellen said irritably.

"Your husband won the first game by conducting those ferocious border raids late last spring and into early summer. I had gathered together a goodly group of English borderers myself, and had been successfully attacking on the Scots side of the border. But then the laird of Duffdour gathered a great grouping of borderers from several clans and came after us. Immediately my people began to flee back to their own homes and villages to protect themselves, to protect their women and their stock. Your husband destroyed my little army and won the second game. His actions caused King Henry to exile me from his favor for my failures here in the borders. That I had hitherto been successful made no difference. Your king's ridiculous support of the pretender has unnerved and irritated Henry Tudor greatly. England has had enough of civil wars."

"Then England should keep to its side of the border," Ellen retorted pertly.

"Alas, madam, neither the English nor the Scots are capable of doing that. It is a centuries-old dispute. You are from the Highlands, and it is difficult to explain to one who was not born to it. We shall never stop playing the game, and game three between the laird of Duffdour and Sir Roger Colby is now on. If I kill your husband I win, especially if I should keep you for my own. My prestige will once again be restored, and I shall be able to bring men to my side. We will raid into Scotland, and my king will be pleased with my actions. I shall again be in his favor."

"And if Duncan kills you, which he most certainly will?" Ellen asked him.

"I still win," Sir Roger said, "for I shall have died attempting to restore my honor, and England's, which will regain me, if posthumously, my king's respect."

"You are mad," Ellen told him. His reasoning frightened her.

"Perhaps," he said. "Pay attention, madam! If you move that knight the game will surely end, and when it does I will leave you."

Ellen stood up. "I can play no more," she said.

He looked across the table at her. "Sit down, madam," he ordered her in a cold voice. "You are behaving like a child." His hand swept the figures on the board away. "We will begin again," Sir Roger told her, setting all the figures back up, "and you will make the very first move."

His demeanor, his tone, angered Ellen, and she played him with a fierce concentration, determined to win.

"We will set a wager," he suddenly said. "If you win you get to slap me, which you very much wish to do right now. But if I win I get to take a kiss from your lips."

"I am a married woman, not your mistress!" she snapped at him.

"All women, madam, are whores and sluts at heart. I am a man of great experience, and *that* I know for truth. When you lose I will take my kiss, and I will wager you will enjoy it in your secret heart, even if you try to tell yourself that you feel guilt." Then he laughed again, and devoted his energies back to winning the game.

Furious, Ellen played skillfully against him. Her hand longed to smack his smug face. He was a horrible, horrible man! She must concentrate her energies into planning her escape from Colby Castle.

"Checkmate, madam," he said suddenly.

Ellen looked down at the board and realized her anger had cost her the game. She jumped up from her chair, not knowing what she should do or where she should go.

Reaching out, Roger Colby caught her hand and drew her around and away from the table. "You have lost, madam," he said softly. "You are now honor bound to pay your debt to me." He drew her closer, laughing softly as he saw the stubborn set of her face. "Do you truly think a small kiss so great a sin, madam?" One arm imprisoned her against him. His other hand tipped her face up toward his. "You are young, and very pretty, madam. I will wager your husband took much pleasure of you, and you of him. You have been gone from each other for almost two months now. Does your laird keep a mistress among his clanswomen, I wonder?" he asked her softly. "A lusty man cannot be too long without a woman. He sickens if his lust is not sated."

His voice was low and almost musical. It seemed to hold her in its spell. She struggled feebly against him. "Let me go," Ellen said, fighting to control the tremor that had taken over her voice.

In response he drew one of her small hands up to his lips and kissed it slowly, lingeringly, first her fingers, and then, turning it over, he pressed a second hot kiss on the palm. "Forgive me, madam, but I could not resist," he told her. Then he released her. "I have enjoyed our game," Sir Roger said. "Good night, madam." And he was gone through the door. The key turned in the lock, and Ellen heard his footsteps retreating down the stairs.

Shaken, she sat heavily down in a chair, and a shudder raced through her. All these weeks she had been separated from her husband she had thought only of her love for him, and her fears for their infant bairn. She had not considered that Duncan might be feeling lust. She had not felt lust. She had been far too concerned with surviving to feel lust. But then, men were different, as the king's aunt was forever telling her ladies.

Balgair MacArthur had repelled her. The thought of coupling with him had been repulsive. He had been dirty and rough, and his heart was black. She knew with certainty that he would never have brought her to passion. She knew better than to flirt with the king, but she had wondered once or twice whether, if she had, he would have flirted back. Made love to her? And then Duncan Armstrong had come into her life. She had found him attractive from the start, but had never dared to dream he would become her husband. But he had. He was the only man who had ever really kissed her, touched her, coupled with her. And she loved him.

Was Duncan being faithful to her? Truly faithful? Or was Sir Roger, who was a man himself, and certainly knew other men well, correct? Was Duncan sating his lusts with a mistress? God only knew that little slut Evina would have been happy to serve her lord in such a capacity. So here she was, Ellen thought morbidly, a captive heaven only knew how far from Duffdour, while her husband was amusing himself with some easy, nubile slut. It wasn't fair! He should be even now riding for Colby Castle to retrieve her and kill Sir Roger. Ellen burst into tears. It just wasn't fair!

But Duncan Armstrong wasn't riding for Colby Castle because he had yet to learn of its existence. "Where the hell can she be?" he demanded to his brother Conal. "It's as if the earth opened up and swallowed her. Jesu! You don't think the bastard killed her, do you?" The color drained from his handsome face.

"Nay, he'll not have killed her," Conal said, and the other men in the hall nodded, agreeing. "If he killed her there would be nothing more between you but revenge, and Roger Colby wants more from you than that. What we have to learn is where he has gone to ground, the wily fox. Since he's not in Devil's Glen, and it has remained deserted, according to our spies, then he must have another place to which he could run."

"It cannot be too far over the border," Hercules Hepburn said, "for after he made off with her she was not seen again by any."

"Any on this side of the border," Duncan Armstrong remarked. "How far could he have gotten if he rode the night through?"

"A good distance, but now we must wonder in which direction he rode," Conal Bruce noted.

"I want her home, and 'tis already early autumn. How will I find her if the snows come early? I need her! Willie needs her," the laird of Duffdour said brokenly. He had lost weight in the past few weeks. His face was gaunt from lack of sleep, his eyes haunted with the thought he somehow could have prevented this.

"Has anyone seen Johnston?" Hercules Hepburn asked. "He might know."

"No one has seen him since he was taken. I doubt that he would know anything of value," Duncan said. "If I ever get my hands on the man I'll kill him, the dirty traitor!"

"He's already been condemned by the king, and if is caught will be hanged," Hercules said. "Bothwell is not pleased."

"We'll have to send out parties of clansmen again to search for Ellen," Conal Bruce suggested.

"Nay, she's not in Scotland," Duncan said. "Of that I am certain. She's somewhere in England, and armed clansmen will hardly be welcome on the other side of the border, given our enthusiastic activity of the past few years. We will have to go into England in ones and twos, not wearing our plaids or our badges. We must travel discreetly, not drawing attention to ourselves. We can send out two dozen or more men in as many directions to track down the den into which our English fox has retreated with his captive. We will find Ellen, and we will bring her home," the laird of Duffdour declared. "And then I will kill Sir Roger Colby. No one else may do the deed. He is mine, and mine alone!"

And the men in the hall cheered both his declaration and his determination. You did not steal a man's wife and live to tell the tale.

Chapter 12

$\mathcal{H}$enry, king of England, the seventh of that name, was irritated beyond all measure. The king of Scotland had taken into his kingdom an impostor he was advancing as the younger son of King Edward IV. He had even married this fellow to the Earl of Huntley's beautiful daughter, Katherine Gordon, in his efforts to further the actions of that dead king's sister, the Duchess of Burgundy, in her vengeful cause against Henry Tudor. King Henry wondered how George Gordon felt about having his daughter put into such a tenuous arrangement, but then, it was said the foolish girl was wildly in love with the young man who claimed to be England's true king. Lady Gordon, however, it was said, had pleaded with James Stewart not to arrange the marriage.

Seated in his privy chamber with his mother, Lady Margaret Beaufort, and his own wife, Elizabeth, daughter of the late King Edward IV, Henry Tudor said, "He must know the man he champions is a fraud. He has to know!"

"Aye, he is aware of it," the king's mother said.

"How can you be certain of such a thing?" Elizabeth the queen asked.

"Your half sister will have told him," Margaret Beaufort said. "Remember that I spoke with her that last unfortunate time she came to court. She told me that the page who slept in your brothers' bedchamber had witnessed their murders and their bodies being removed *after* Henry defeated King Richard at Market Bosworth. The assassins never saw the other boy, and when they had departed Middlesham he fled north to Adair at Stanton. Adair has made a place for herself in Scotland. King James knows her relationship to King Edward, to you, my dear Elizabeth. You may be certain he has called upon Adair and shown her this impostor."

"But what if, in an effort to revenge herself on me, she has told James Stewart that this fellow is indeed Richard of York?" King Henry wanted to know. "I was not kind to her that last time she came to court. And if she inherited one thing from her father, King Edward, it was pride. And she was furious at the blackening of King Richard's name."

"She was always Uncle Dickon's favorite, although in fairness I should say that he tried not to play favorites," Elizabeth said a bit petulantly. "Still, it was obvious."

"You were not kind to her either," Margaret Beaufort said softly. "Any other woman would want revenge on the Tudors, and perhaps given the opportunity Adair would take it. But not in this manner. Adair had too much pride in her royal blood to lie over something as serious as this. Nay. She will have told King James this man is not her half brother. And I will wager he did not know who she was, and, of course, the real Richard would have known Adair Radcliffe."

"James Stewart is like a thorn in my thumb," Henry Tudor said. "A thorn that needs to be removed as quickly as possible."

"And who would you have as king of Scotland?" his mother asked astutely.

"I don't care who is king of Scotland as long as I can manage him," King Henry said. "He has a brother or two, doesn't he? Younger sons of kings are always eager to be kings themselves, and usually not too scrupulous as to how to gain their goals."

"Do nothing precipitously," Margaret Beaufort warned. "You are usually a cautious and thoughtful man, my son, but James Stewart would appear to be your bête noire. I suspect this championing of the impostor is done in an effort to keep you from the incessant border warfare that goes on. You have encouraged it, you know."

"Only to keep James Stewart out of mischief while I solidified my own position," the king said. "But of course that fool Colby caused so much havoc that the Scots struck back in force, and caused a great deal of damage on our side of the border. At least a dozen villages were burned and pillaged, fields burned, stock driven off. Women taken."

"It's always been that way in the borders, I am told," Margaret Beaufort said.

"Aye, but Colby attempted to gain my favor by trying to blackmail the Scots border lords into spying against their own king. Even I know that James Stewart is both popular and beloved among both his people and his lords. The Spanish ambassador wrote to me from Sterling that Colby managed to subvert one poor fool while attempting to make another of the Scots lords who refused his overtures look as if he were in collusion with England. Sadly the man he chose to be his scapegoat is both well liked and honest to a fault. It was he, with the Hepburn Earl of Bothwell's help, who raised a great force from among the border families and rode out against us. Colby has been exiled from my presence. The man is a fool at any rate, and of no real use to me."

But even as he said it Henry Tudor was thinking that perhaps Roger Colby could indeed be of use to him one more time. *What if I offered Sir Roger the opportunity of regaining my royal favor? What if I hinted that James Stewart's death would be pleasing to me? And if the bumbling fool actually succeeded in murder, not that I expect*

*he will, but if he did, believing he would regain my appre-
ciation, then I could expose him as the assassin. I would
deny all culpability, and Scotland would be thrown into
turmoil while a struggle for power emerged. It would certainly give me peace on my northern border.*

"Why are you smiling?" his young queen asked.
Henry Tudor did not smile often.

"No reason, Bessie," the king answered her.

Margaret Beaufort's eyes narrowed. He was lying,
but then sometimes it was better not to press her son.
He obviously had had an idea, and didn't wish to share
it.

And when he was alone again Henry Tudor considered whom he might use to gain Sir Roger Colby's ear.
He needed someone discreet and totally loyal to Henry
Tudor. There were many seeking his favor, and most had
their own interests at heart first. Henry Tudor needed a
man who would put the king's interests first. And then
he remembered Sir Lionel de Frayne. His family was old
and respected, but poor. Sir Lionel's family had no influence, nor coin to pay someone with influence to help
them. What would be of use to such a man other than
a bag of coins? A secure place in the royal household,
with its guarantee of housing, food, clothing, and a small
remuneration each Michaelmas? Aye! That was the lure
he would use.

The king called his favorite page to his side. "Find
Sir Lionel de Frayne and bring him to me here in my
privy chamber," Henry Tudor said. "And be discreet, lad.
Speak to no one of my request—neither my mother, nor
the queen, nor any man."

The boy bowed with the elegance of a practiced
courtier. "At once, my lord!" he said, and then he hurried off.

The king considered the plan forming in his mind.
He would be candid with Sir Lionel. Friendly, but not
too familiar. He would promise the man his position for
life. But how much to confide in the man? How trust-

worthy was he? What he desired of Sir Roger Colby wasn't something he would trust to parchment. Colby was the sort who would not burn a message from the king, but keep it as insurance. Especially a message asking him to assassinate James Stewart. Now, there was a word he did not want to use. *Assassinate.* It sounded hostile, unfriendly. But if he put it more obliquely, would Sir Roger understand? Of course, the only thing that would matter to Colby was the chance to regain Henry Tudor's favor. The man was one of those poor creatures who could not live without the excitement of the court, and the knowledge that he was a part of it. Henry Tudor scorned men like Roger Colby. He had no real use or purpose in life other than to see and be seen. Yet he had done well stirring up difficulties along the border. At least, until the Scots had struck back. Who knew the Scots could show such cleverness? But they certainly had, and had done far more damage in their several raids within that brief period than Sir Roger had done all spring and summer. He would have preferred having on his side, rather than Colby, that Scots lord who led those raids.

There was a scratching on the door to his privy chamber. "Enter!" the king said.

"Sir Lionel de Frayne, my lord," the page in the doorway said, and then stepped aside to allow the king's visitor through, closing the door behind him.

"My liege!" Sir Lionel bowed. He was an unimposing man of medium height, with brown eyes and brown hair. There was nothing distinguished about him at all. He was a man who would disappear into a crowd and not be recognized. And he stood patiently waiting for the king to speak.

"Sit down, Sir Lionel," the king invited his guest, waving him to a small stool across from his own armed chair. One should always keep a petitioner seated beneath you. It gave them a feeling of helplessness while making he who would grant their petition seem more omnipotent.

His clever mother had taught him that trick. "It would appear there will be an opening in the royal household," he began. "I am going to have need of a man of great discretion to carry out private commissions. If you accept, you will have a chamber of your own wherever I am, for you must always be near me. You will eat from my kitchens. You will be given an allowance for your clothing, and be paid each Michaelmas the sum of six gold coins. Would such a position interest you, Sir Lionel?" The king's gaze caught that of his companion, and held it.

"I would kill for six gold coins a year, and all that you offer, my liege," Sir Lionel said, eager excitement filling his voice.

Henry Tudor smiled a brief, wintery smile. "You shall not have to." He chuckled. "It is just that sometimes there are things I need done, but do not wish to share them with my councilors or anyone else. You shall be called the king's personal and private secretary, for want of a better word, Sir Lionel."

"I but live to serve you, my liege. I have neither wife nor child to keep me from devoting myself entirely to your service," Sir Lionel said.

"Excellent!" the king purred. "Now I shall need you to ride north to Colby Castle immediately, and speak with Sir Roger for me. You need only deliver your message, and then you are to return to me. You will tell Sir Roger that there is a thorn in the paw of the lion. I wish him to remove the thorn, and when he has he may to return to court."

"I do not understand, my liege," Sir Lionel said.

"Understanding will not always be part of your duties, my lord. Only obedience," King Henry told the man. "Can your conscience abide such a thing?"

Sir Lionel was silent for a long few moments, and then he said, "Aye, my liege, it can. You are my king. And kings can do no wrong."

Henry Tudor barked a sharp laugh. "Kings often do

more wrong than ordinary men," he said. "But then, kings are above ordinary men."

"There is a thorn in the paw of the lion," Sir Lionel said. "You wish Sir Roger to remove the thorn, and then return to court. Is that correct, my liege?"

"It is perfect," Henry Tudor replied. "You may go now. Let me know when you have returned, and what Sir Roger says to you. Before you leave the palace, however, find my household steward and tell him I would have you wear a garment with my own badge upon it. While your commissions will be secret, your position should not be."

Sir Lionel stood up and bowed once more to the king. "Thank you, my liege," he said to the king, and then he backed slowly from the privy chamber.

The king sat back in his chair, and considered what he had just done. Would Colby be clever enough to understand what was meant by the cryptic message? Aye, he would, for while he had no real intellect, he was as canny and sly as a fox. If he thought he could regain his royal master's favor again he would figure it all out and then do what needed to be done. And if he bumbled and failed, Henry Tudor of England would not be blamed. Indeed, England's king would leave the Scots to kill Sir Roger, which they probably would eventually do. *I don't like the fellow,* the king thought, and he stood up, walking over to a small table to pour himself a goblet of fine wine. He drained it quickly. Yes, peace in the borders was very much to his advantage, and Colby was no loss.

Sir Lionel de Frayne found the king's household steward, and was given a tunic with the royal badge. He took it, and then, packing it away carefully in a saddlebag, he found his horse and started north. He was careful not to exhaust his beast, for the animal was all he had. Of course, when he returned to court either just before or just after Michaelmas he would be paid his yearly stipend and could purchase a second animal. As he was to live wherever the king lived, his horses would be stabled in the household stables, which would cost him naught for stabling and feed but an occasional penny to the stable lad for goodwill. Sir Lionel de Frayne could not believe his good luck, but that continued good fortune would be predicated upon his utmost discretion. His total loyalty to Henry Tudor must be unswerving. Kings were God's own chosen.

The ride to the north and west was uneventful. After several days he came in sight of Colby Castle, a small stone structure overlooking the sea in the wilds of Cumbria. Its drawbridge was raised defensively, and so he waited on the far side of the moat to be recognized. He had put on his tunic with its royal badge of service that morning. Finally one of the few men at arms patrolling the heights saw him, and called down to him.

"Identify yourself!"

"I am Sir Lionel de Frayne, in His Majesty King Henry's service. I wish to speak with Sir Roger Colby," the horseman said.

"A moment, my lord," the man at arms replied.

Sir Lionel waited. It had been a gray and cloudy day, and even though he could see a slash of red from the setting sun on the horizon, the storm clouds behind him were piling up, and he could sense the coming rain. And then the drawbridge began to be winched down, squeaking and creaking as it was lowered. When it at last met the earth on his side he moved his horse slowly across even as the iron portcullis was being lifted. Riding into the courtyard he dismounted, and an ancient stableman came to take his animal. A man with a soldier's bearing came up to him.

"I am the castle sergeant," he introduced himself. "I will escort you to my master if you will be so kind as to follow me."

Sir Lionel followed the man into a great hall, where a man sat at the high board eating. Next to him sat a woman with wonderful red-gold hair. Sir Lionel bowed.

"Sir Roger Colby?" he asked formally, knowing this was the castle's owner.

"Aye! What do you want other than food and a night's shelter?" Sir Roger demanded roughly—and a bit rudely, his guest thought silently.

"I am King Henry's personal and private secretary—" Sir Lionel began.

"Join us then, and eat," Sir Roger said. "Sit here next to me." He gestured to his left, for the woman sat on his right. "Bring my guest some hot food and some wine," Sir Roger said to no one in particular, but his servants scurried to do his bidding.

Sir Lionel stepped onto the high board, nodding politely to the woman as he passed her. "My lady."

The woman nodded back.

"She's my guest," Sir Roger said briefly.

"I am his prisoner," the woman replied.

Roger Colby laughed smugly. "She's the wife of the laird of Duffdour, who led the Scots against us. I kidnapped her to teach the Scots bastard a lesson. She is very good company, are you not, my lady?" He felt safe now letting Ellen be seen. Sir Lionel would tell the king that Roger Colby was still strong. And Sir Lionel could not tell the laird of Duffdour where his wife was.

"He kept me in his dungeons for a month," Ellen said calmly.

"She lives now in my west tower," Sir Roger countered.

"He will not release me," Ellen responded, "nor will he ask for ransom. He took me from my nursling, an infant lad of three months then. I can only hope my son lives."

"If I was responsible for the death of one more Scot, then so be it," Roger Colby said coldly. "Your bairn will not grow up to kill honest Englishmen."

"You are a pig!" Ellen said angrily. She stood and, looking at Sir Lionel, bade him good night. Then she walked quickly from the hall.

"A hot-tempered vixen I will soon bring to heel," Sir Roger said. "Eat, my lord, eat! Then you will tell me what brings the king's man to my castle."

Lionel de Frayne found Roger Colby unpleasant. What business could the king possibly have with such a man? Despite his breeding there was obviously no honor in the fellow. To steal another man's wife for revenge and not ask for ransom was inglorious and disgraceful. He applied himself to the plate that was set before him. While the food was plain, it was hot and well prepared. Reaching for his goblet he found it filled with ale, and drank thirstily. When he had finished his meal he thanked his host.

"Why are you here?" Sir Roger demanded again.

"I have a message for you from the king," Sir Lionel said. "I do not understand it myself, but King Henry, my master, said that you would."

"Give me the message!" Roger Colby said eagerly. He was being forgiven! He had hoped that sooner or later the king would forgive him, and now it was happening.

"There is a thorn in the paw of the lion," Sir Lionel said. "The king wishes you to remove it. That is all. There is no more."

Roger Colby looked totally befuddled. "I do not understand," he said slowly.

"That is the message I was told to deliver. However, the king did tell me to say that when the thorn was removed from the lion's paw you would be welcomed back to court." He stood up. "I thank you for the meal, my lord, and for the night's lodging." Stepping down from the high board he went to the large hearth and held out his hands to the fire, letting the warmth penetrate them.

Sir Roger followed him from the high board. "There is a thorn in the paw of the lion, and he wishes me to remove it?" he repeated. "It makes no sense at all. The king sent no written instructions? You carry no parchment from him?"

"The purpose of my service is to deliver discreet commissions that only the king—and myself to some small extent—are privy to, my lord. I have no knowledge at all other than that which I have imparted to you," Sir Lionel said.

"Then I am totally mystified," Sir Roger admitted.

"Perhaps a good night's sleep, and it will come to you," Sir Lionel said. "I shall depart at first light on the morrow, my lord. I appreciate your hospitality." The king's man bowed politely.

"Rafe!" the lord of the castle shouted, and the sergeant came to his side. "Sir Lionel is leaving us in the morning. See that his horse is waiting at first light. And show him where he can sleep tonight." Sir Roger turned to Sir Lionel. "I thank you for your service," he said. Then he turned and departed the hall.

Lionel de Frayne watched him go. *An odd man,* he thought. *Perhaps even a touch mad.* He followed the sergeant, who showed him a bed space and bade him good night before leaving the hall. He wondered briefly about the captive woman, but realized that it was really not his business at all, despite the strangeness of the situation.

Roger Colby mounted the stairs to the west tower. He turned the key in the lock of the door at the top of the steps and walked into the small dayroom. "Where are you?" he shouted, and when no one answered him he repeated his question. "Where are you, madam? This is hardly the place to hide from me."

"I am not hiding, my lord. I was merely putting a house robe about myself, as I was preparing for bed," Ellen said, coming forth from the bedchamber. "What is it that you want?" She looked at him as if he were something distasteful.

"How dare you say what you said to the king's man!" Roger Colby said angrily.

"Do you think I wanted the man thinking I was something other than what I am?" Ellen responded. "I have little use for the English, but I would not have this man thinking I was some light-skirted creature of ill repute. You have kept me imprisoned for almost three months now. Have you not had your revenge on Duncan Armstrong? It is obvious he has no idea of where I am, for who knew that you had this den of yours to run to when you needed to hide. Devil's Glen is where you made your home in the borders. Give me a horse and let me go! I will find my own way home. Your king obviously wants you back, and now that you have that privilege your quarrel with my husband should be over and done with, my lord."

"King Henry has sent me a message. He has a problem he wishes me to solve, and then I may return to court. But his message is a riddle, and I do not understand it," Sir Roger admitted.

"What is the riddle?" Ellen asked him, curious. Perhaps if she could help him solve the riddle he would let her go.

"He has asked me to remove the thorn from the paw of the lion," Sir Roger said.

Ellen thought for several moments, and then she said, "The lion would be England, or your king. A thorn in its paw would be some sort of irritant." She thought again, and then as the reality of the message dawned on her Ellen clapped her hand over her mouth in shock. No! It couldn't be!

"What?" Sir Roger asked her. "What?"

"'Tis too wicked! 'Tis monstrous!" Ellen cried.

"What is?" he demanded of her again

"It goes against God's law," Ellen said.

And then a dawning understanding came into Sir Roger's eyes. A smile lit his features. "I am to kill James Stewart," he said softly. "Aye, that is it, for your king is a plague on mine! What an honor I have been given! The king has not lost his faith in my abilities to be of service to him! But I can do it! Aye, I can! I will need help, but I know just where to find such aid." Reaching out suddenly, he yanked Ellen to him.

Horrified, she attempted to push him away. Was he evil? Aye! He was evil. Was he mad? The light in his eye bespoke madness, but she was not certain. "Let me go," Ellen said quietly.

Instead his arms tightened about her. "Do you know why I brought you here, madam?" he asked her. "Aye, you know what I have told you. But you do not know all of it. Hiding you away from the laird of Duffdour has, I know, hurt his heart, but it is his pride I wish to scar forever. I thought by incarcerating you in my dungeons for some weeks I would break your spirit, but I have not. So I imprisoned you in this tower, hoping that you would be grateful to me for my benevolence. But you are not. I have kept you from all company but my own in my attempt to turn you toward me, but you can think of nothing but your husband and child. You are a strong woman, madam, but if I am to have my revenge upon Duncan Armstrong, I *must* break you so that I may break him. When I return you to him, my stamp must be upon you. Your lips must be swollen with my kisses. Your body must smell of my lust. I will know you better than he has ever known you. He will never be able to look at you without remembering that I have had you, that another man has plundered what is—or was once—his alone. Do you understand me, madam? Do you understand what I am saying to you?"

"You would dishonor me," Ellen replied quietly, and her heart was hammering with her fright. She would not permit him to see her fear, but she was indeed close to breaking after her months in Colby's custody. Now, her body pressed hard against his, she had to swallow down that fear, because should he see it, or suspect she was afraid, she would have no defense against this man.

"I will have you in every way a man can have a woman," he told her softly against her mouth. One arm wrapped about her; his other hand slowly caressed her buttocks beneath the house robe. "Have you ever had a man's cock in your ass, madam? I will wager you have not, but you will take mine there one day soon." He squeezed the flesh beneath his fingers. "And you will suck my cock sweetly, and I will fuck you until you beg me for mercy, but I will show you none. And then one day you will beg me to fuck you, because you will have come to enjoy my attentions, and need them."

"Never!" Ellen said through gritted teeth. "Not even if you lock me back in your dungeons for a thousand years."

He laughed. "I have told you, madam, that all women are whores and sluts. You will prove yourself such sooner than later, despite your overweening pride." Then his mouth found hers in a cruel and brutal kiss as he ripped open the house robe she wore, and then her chemise beneath to find one of her breasts. He squeezed the small, round globe, his fingers bruising the soft white flesh, pinching the nipple hard, her cry of pain lost in his mouth.

Ellen struggled against him, her memories of Balgair MacArthur overwhelming her. His tongue ravaged her tongue. She bit his lips, and he swore softly, pinching her nipple again so fiercely that tears came to her eyes. She managed to bring one of her hands up and clawed at his face. His hand wrapped about her thick braid, yanking her away from him as he slapped her. Stunned, but angry, Ellen slapped him back.

"You but whet my appetite, madam, but I have more important matters to attend to now than fucking you, although I am sorely tempted. Still, now you will understand that I mean to master you, and the sooner you accept this fact the better it will be."

Ellen gathered up her spittle and spit it all in his face as hard as she could.

Roger Colby swore viciously and slapped her again several times. "You will pay for that, madam," he snarled. Then, pushing her from him, he strode from the chamber, remembering to lock the door behind him as he went.

*   *   *

Ellen stood transfixed for what seemed a long time. Her cheeks burned from his slaps. Her heart hammered with a mixture of fear, outrage, and anger. She had to escape Colby Castle, but how? The door to her rooms was kept locked at all times, and the only other way out was by means of the windows. She went now to one of them, clutching her torn garments to her as she did. But the dark had already set in, and while she knew she was high up, Ellen could not be certain how high her rooms were. To jump would certainly kill her, and while death did certainly seem a better alternative to Roger Colby's plans for her, Ellen knew she just wasn't brave enough to die. Besides, if her tormentor meant to make an attempt on King James's life, she needed to escape so an alarm might be raised, and the king saved.

Closing the window, she repaired to her bedchamber, pouring water into her ewer, scrubbing herself free of Sir Roger's scent. She stripped the ripped clothing off, putting on a fresh chemise. Then she examined the torn robe to see if it might be repaired. The chemise was only damaged slightly in his efforts to paw her. Ellen sighed. It was repairable, and she would take care of it tomorrow. Climbing into her bed, she found she could not sleep. She thought, as she had every night since she had been kidnapped, of her husband and their child. Had Willie managed to survive? The thought of having lost her child caused her tears to flow. What if her bairn had died? What if Duncan would not forgive her because she had been soiled by another man? For the first time since she had been stolen away Ellen felt despair.

Of course, she did eventually sleep, although every creak and groan of the old castle startled her. Was it Sir Roger? Was he coming to violate her? She awoke feeling headachy and sore. After getting up and dressing, she gathered up her sewing basket. Then, sitting herself in her dayroom, she began to mend the garments that had been damaged yesterday. Outside the day was gray.

She felt sorry for Sir Lionel de Frayne, who would be leaving on what promised to eventually be a rainy day. He might stay ahead of the weather for part of the day, but it would ultimately catch up to him. She put another log on her hearth fire to encourage a bit more warmth from it. Come winter this tower would be cold, but of course, Ellen told herself, she would not be here when winter came.

She repaired the chemise, which had been only minimally torn. Then she started to work on the house robe, which required finer stitches, for the damage to it was greater. When she heard the rain beating against the window it dawned upon her that no one had brought her anything to eat that morning, and it was already into the afternoon. Sir Roger probably thought he could starve her into submission.

For three days she saw or heard no one, but late on the fourth day she heard the key turning in the lock of the door, which opened to reveal an elderly serving woman carrying a tray. She said not a word, but set her burden on the table and then shuffled out, locking the door behind her.

Ellen walked over to the tray to find a chunk of bread, a sliver of cheese, and a goblet of wine. Shrugging at the paucity of the meal, she nonetheless ate it, drinking down the wine, for she was thirsty, and her water supply was low, so she had been conserving it. The wine was sweet and tasted of ripe grapes. Picking up her sewing, she began to work again, but the light was fading, and she was genuinely tired tonight. Going into her bedchamber, she disrobed but for her chemise and climbed into bed. She quickly fell into a deep slumber.

As the almost-full moon streamed through the tower windows Sir Roger Colby opened the door to Ellen's chambers and stepped inside. He wore only a shirt, and carried with him a small woven willow basket. Walking quickly across the floor, he entered the bedchamber and looked upon his prey. She was sleeping soundly, as he knew she would be. He smiled a cold, pitiless smile, his face a feral mask as he drew the bedclothes down to reveal the young woman beneath, her chemise riding halfway up her body to reveal a goodly part of her slender legs.

Setting the basket upon the floor by the bed, Sir Roger removed a silken cord from it. He slid the length slowly through his hand, as if contemplating what he would do, but Ellen's sleeping deeply upon her back, one arm above her head, made his decision an easy one. Leaning over Ellen, he gently drew her other arm up and, bringing the two limbs next to each other, he tied them together carefully. Reaching back into the basket, he withdrew two more lengths of silken cord and tied each of her legs to the turned posts of the bed. Straddling the unconscious bound woman, Roger Colby took a small knife from the basket. Slowly he cut Ellen's chemise open, pulling back the halves of the garment so he might view her nakedness as he licked his lips in anticipation of what was to come.

Stripping off his own garment, he lay on his side next to her. She was lovely, he thought, and for the briefest moment he felt the tiniest twinge of guilt, but it quickly passed. If he had had more time he would have taken it to seduce her into his bed, but there was no more time. The royal messenger had left with Roger Colby's assurances that he fully understood King Henry's message, and would complete his commission before returning to the court. Sir Lionel de Frayne had ridden off in a light rain, and the master of Colby Castle had considered how he might best go about assassinating James Stewart, Scotland's king.

But first Roger Colby meant to despoil the lady Ellen, wife of the laird of Duffdour, before returning her to her husband. In doing so he would take Duncan Armstrong's honor, as the Scot had taken his. Rolling onto his other side, Sir Roger reached into the basket and drew out a glass vial filled with liquid. Turning back to the sleeping woman, he put an arm about her, raising her up. Uncorking the vial, he put it to her lips. "Drink, madam," he murmured softly in her ear. "Drink and enjoy."

She couldn't quite awaken at first, even with the voice droning in her ear, but she felt the glass at her lips and, opening them, drank thirstily, for her mouth was so dry. The cool, sweet liquid tasting slightly of some berry she couldn't identify slid easily down her throat. She finally managed to open her eyes, only to find Roger Colby smiling down on her like a large tabby cat contemplating a treat.

Ellen gasped and attempted to sit up, but she couldn't.

"Do not bother struggling, madam, for I have bound you hand and foot," Sir Roger said. "You have exquisite little breasts, you know." His rough hand fondled her.

"What are you doing?" Ellen cried. Oh, God, she was so confused and dizzy. What was the matter with her? "Do not touch me, you monster!"

He laughed softly. "The wine was drugged, you know. I only gave you that bit of food so you would not collapse where you ate. I wanted you in bed waiting for me." He tweaked the nipple on her breast, which had puckered tightly with his play.

"Do not do this, I beg you," Ellen half sobbed. She struggled to stay calm, but she could think of no way to extricate herself from the situation in which she found herself. If he had his way with her Duncan would no longer love her. How could he, when another man had used her body? "Kill me," she begged him. "Take my body home to Duffdour and throw it before the gates and make your revenge against my husband complete. Do not, I beg you, my lord, spoliate me. *Do not!*" Tears, unbidden, began to slip down her lovely face. Furious with herself, Ellen bit her lip.

"There, there, madam, is not one cock the same as another? Oh, perhaps one is thicker or longer, but is not a manly cock a cock?"

"I have known none but Duncan Armstrong," Ellen half sobbed. *Oh, Duncan, why has this happened to us?* she thought desperately.

"Indeed, madam, you were a virgin when you wed your husband? I had heard that all Scots girls were unchaste. You are all certainly free with your kisses, and many an eager lass I have swived on your side of the border." He bent to kiss her breast while a hand trailed down her torso in leisurely fashion.

"I was a virgin!" Ellen cried.

"Nay, you were a slut and a whore like all women, madam. And now you shall whore for me, won't you? Oh, perhaps at first you will play reluctant, but in the end you will beg for my cock, and I will fill your cunt with fire. You should already be beginning to simmer with your lust." He put the vial to her surprised lips again, shoving it swiftly into her mouth, tipping the remaining contents down her throat before pulling it out and dropping it back into the basket by the bed.

"What have you given me?" she cried, trying to regurgitate the liquid, but it had slid swiftly down her gullet, into her belly, and even now seemed to be pooling with a ferocious heat into her nether regions. Her body was suddenly awash with unsatisfied lust. Ellen's eyes grew wide and fearful. "What have you done?" she repeated.

"Just given you a little something to release your reluctance, madam. This mask of chastity and discipline you have worn these few months grows wearisome." His fingers slid into the bright curls at the junction of her thighs.

"Don't!" Ellen's voice was shaking. Only Duncan had ever touched her there.

He smiled down into her frightened face as a single finger insinuated itself between her plump nether lips seeking, seeking.

She whimpered.

And reaching the tiny bud of her sex, he let the ball of his finger stroke that little nub of flesh, finding its minuscule pearl as Ellen bit her lip till it bled to keep from crying out. "There, my pretty slut, does it not feel sweet? You mustn't be ashamed to tell me." He bent his head and brushed his tongue across her lips. "Shall I show you what else my tongue can do, madam?" He trailed the wet organ over her breasts, licking slowly at the nipples.

Ellen strained against her bonds, but they held her fast. She was so immobilized that she could not even bring her bound arms back over her head to hit him. Her body was burning with desire now—a desire not experienced by her emotions.

She was aching with her own lust because of the aphrodisiac he had forced upon her, but she would do whatever she could to prevent his violating her totally. She closed her eyes, still dizzy, as she sought to shut him out. She wanted to taunt him, but she knew that could prove dangerous.

Roger Colby was unsatisfied, but, to his annoyance, his cock lay limp. Where was the victory unless he could fuck her? Still, he had promised himself that he would not have her the first night. He would torture her tonight, leave her for the next two days to wonder when her final violation would take place, realizing with each passing hour that there was no escape for her, knowing that in the end her lust-wracked body would yield to him because she had no other choice. He stifled a groan of irritation, but she was disciplined, and he had deliberately avoided taking the aphrodisiacs he needed now to perform as a man. Had needed ever since his mistress had betrayed him. Angry with the memory he leaned over and drew an item from the basket. It was a large phallus made of polished ash wood. He would make her cry out as he had cried out before this night was over.

Bending over her, he said, "Open your eyes, slut," and when she did, he asked, "Do you know what this is, madam? It is called a dildo, and it has been modeled after my own cock. There is a small discreet shop in London where such things may be done. I was fed a stimulant, and when my cock was fully aroused it was well oiled, then covered in wax which was allowed to harden. The wax was then slowly, carefully slipped from my manhood and fitted upon a cold metal form. Then the shop's owner, a master carver by trade, carved this for me using the wax model as his guide. When he was done the next day I returned, and the now-cold wax form was slipped over it to show me it was indeed me. It fit perfectly, for the carver is a true artisan. I was then given the wax model to destroy, which I did."

Ellen's eyes were wide as she looked at the dildo. It was fascinating in a repellent sort of way. She shivered as he ran it along her lips, and then she watched with horror as he oiled the phallus slowly, carefully, holding it by a long carved silver handle.

Reaching into his basket, he pulled out a small, hard bolster pillow and jammed it beneath her hips. Now her sex was fully visible and available to him. He rubbed the tip of the dildo over the wet, swollen lips. Then he spread those nether lips and touched her love bud with the phallus.

Ellen shivered hard, biting on her lips again. Her body was afire with a terrible need. It was similar to what she felt with her husband, yet there was also fear mixed with her desire. It both confused and frightened her. There was no love here. No passion. Then why did she want to be fucked? And Ellen knew that she did. Was she indeed a slut and a whore, as he was so fond of saying? She felt the head of the phallus at the opening to her sheath, and shuddered with her need.

"Yes, my pretty slut," he purred in her ear hotly. "But you shall not have it tonight. You are really not quite ready for such passion. Tomorrow, my pretty slut, or perhaps the day after that, or in another week, and there will be no need for this delightful replica of my most excellent attribute. I shall mount you myself without delay. You will not escape me," Roger Colby told her as he freed her from her bonds. Then he arose from the bed, gathered up his basket and garment, and left her.

When she had stopped trembling, when her legs would hold her upright, Ellen got up from the bed and, after filling the ewer with water from the pitcher in the ashes of the hearth, scrubbed her body until it was red and raw. She took the chemise he had cut off of her and threw it into the fire, where it immediately burned. She tore the bedding from the bed and flung it out the window onto the rocks below. Then, dressing herself, she went into the dayroom and lay down before its hearth, sobbing wildly. Her body began to shake, and for some time she could not stop the tremors that rocked her, almost tearing her asunder. She had to escape Colby Castle. She had to!

Ellen knew she could not go through another night such as she had just experienced. She just couldn't! Having him touch her with his soft hands and put his mouth on her and that awful phallus he had displayed had been horrid. The next time, there would be no escape for her. In the end, Ellen realized—and the tears flowed as she thought it—she was going to have to throw herself from the windows of her tower prison. Would God forgive her? Finally she cried herself into sleep, exhausted, weary, and despairing.

In the morning, however, it was the sergeant who came to fetch her down to the hall. While she knew he was loyal to Sir Roger, she had found him a decent man.

"Did you fall, lady?" he asked her, sounding concerned and pointing at her face. "There is a bruise upon your cheek."

"Aye," she lied. "I did. Is my hair neat? My gown?" she asked him.

"Aye." He nodded. "All is well but for the bruise."

In the hall Sir Roger beckoned her to the high board, and the meal was served: oat porridge in bread trenchers, a cottage loaf, hard-boiled eggs, and bacon. Ellen nodded to the master of the house and sat down to eat.

"You will need your nourishment now," he said to her with a smirk.

Ellen said nothing, afraid if she did he would send her from the table hungry. She needed a clear head because she needed to think. There had to be a way to escape Sir Roger and Colby Castle. There must be!

"I have been considering the best way to rid my king of the thorn he has been complaining about. I will, of course, need a bit of help. While you were in your dungeon, madam, there was another prisoner there as well. Did you ever have the pleasure of meeting Ian Johnston?"

"The laird who betrayed our Scotland?" Ellen replied in a pleasant tone. "Nay, my lord, I have not met him. The other border lords were aware of his duplicity, and therefore did not invite him to their gatherings. He has been below?"

"Aye, but Rafe has gone to bring him up. If he helps me I will tell him he may have his freedom," Sir Roger said.

"If I were in your position, my lord," Ellen told him, "I would use him, and then kill him so he could no longer cause me difficulty."

Roger Colby laughed. "You're a clever lass," he said, nodding. "Perhaps you are right, and I should drown him in Solway Firth."

"Is that the water I see from my windows? I thought it was the sea," Ellen said.

"Solway Firth opens into the Irish Sea," he told her. "This castle sits on a small hook of land overlooking them both."

"Oh," Ellen said, feigning disinterest. *Now,* she thought, *I have a better idea of where I am. But what good will it do me?*

"Ahh," Sir Roger said, "here is our other guest, madam. Come in, Johnston! Come in! You are not looking well at all, I fear."

Chapter 13

$\mathcal{I}$an Johnston stumbled across the hall to stand before the high board. He was filthy, and stank so badly that even from her seat Ellen could smell his stench. His hair was to his shoulders, and his growth of beard hung lankly down his chest. It was obvious that he was having difficulty seeing in the daylight of the hall, and Ellen understood that from her time in Sir Roger's dungeons.

"You do not look well," Roger Colby repeated in solicitous tones. "I did give orders to keep you alive, you know. Surely you have not been poorly treated."

"How long have I lived in your cellars?" Ian Johnston's voice rasped roughly.

Roger Colby appeared to consider the query, and then he said, "At least five months, sir. It took us a good month to run you to earth after you betrayed me."

"I told you before that I did not betray you! I sent two men to warn you before the others attacked," the prisoner insisted. "I didn't know when, but I knew they would."

"Yet neither of these alleged messengers reached me," Sir Roger replied.

"Of course they didn't," Ellen said. "I told you, my lord, that the others were aware of this laird's treason, and did not include him in their plans. A watch was set on his tower, and his messengers were killed. Their deaths were quick and merciful, unlike that of his wife, whom this villain beat to death."

"Who is this bitch, Colby?" Ian Johnston demanded to know. "Your latest whore? Do not dare to point a finger at me, you slut! My wife was useless, and deserved every beating that I gave her. If she were stronger, she might have lived, but because she was weak she died, as the bairns I put in her belly died. Four of them in as many years, and she could not bring one healthy and whole into this world. A useless bitch."

"You see, madam," Sir Roger murmured in her ear. "Even he recognizes you as a whore and a slut." Reaching out, he pulled her over and then down into his lap, fondling her breasts as he did. "So, Johnston, she has cleared your good name for you. Thank her prettily, or I shall send you below again, and not give you the opportunity to return to my good graces."

"Who am I thanking?" Ian Johnston wanted to know.

"Why, this is the laird of Duffdour's wife, sir. I stole her away from him, and she will be well used by the time I send her back to him," Sir Roger said.

Ian Johnston grinned, showing blackened teeth. "God's hoary head, Colby, you truly are a devil. Armstrong's bride, is it? I hope you fuck her well before you let her go. 'Tis a bold fellow you are! I don't suppose you would consider sharing the loot?"

Roger Colby smiled. "I shall indeed consider it, sir. Now, I am going to need your help. May I assume you are not averse to killing James Stewart?"

Johnston's mouth fell open, but then, recovering, he said, "Nay. It makes no difference to me who sits on the throne, for I know it will never be me."

"Excellent," Sir Roger said. "Rafe, take our *guest* to clean up, and give him new garments. And, Johnston, you will bathe yourself with both water and soap. The stink of you is not a pretty fragrance, eh, madam?" He tipped Ellen's face to his and kissed her lips. "She takes to discipline well, as you can see," he told Johnston, turning Ellen's face to show him the bruise upon her cheek.

"I'm glad to see you aren't afraid to administer a bit of a beating to a recalcitrant woman," Ian Johnston remarked. "I can see she hasn't been eager for your attentions." And he laughed. "Have you fucked her yet?"

Roger Colby chuckled. "The wench is comely, sir. I have held her here as my prisoner for the past three months. What do you think? Go and get cleaned up now. We have much talking to do, and much planning." He turned back to Ellen, who sat uncomfortably in his lap. "Tonight, madam, you will yield all to me." His hand slid beneath her skirts, slipping up her leg to push past her nether lips.

His fingers played with her while Ellen made every effort to remain still and unfeeling. But when he pushed two fingers into her sheath and began to move them, slowly, slowly, then faster and faster, she could not contain herself. A sob escaped her, and then a small cry as she shattered with his obscene attentions. Shamed, she hid her face in her hands and wept softly.

He took his hand from her body. "Look at me," he commanded her, and she obeyed, her eyes widening with shock as he took the two fingers that had been buried within her and slowly sucked them noisily. "You are delicious, madam," he said.

And then suddenly Ellen was filled with an anger such as she had never felt before. She would not continue to be his victim. She would not! Still on his lap, his arm about her waist, she said, "So tonight you will complete your rape of me, my lord." Her tone, so filled with disdain, gave him a moment's pause.

"What do you suggest then, madam? You are hardly my willing victim now, are you?" His color was high, for she had indeed pricked at his vanity.

"Loose me outside your castle. Give me an hour's start. And then hunt me down as you would a helpless doe." She laughed. "But you would not do such a thing, because there is always the possibility that I might escape, isn't there? And you could not bear to lose your revenge against my husband," Ellen sneered. "So you will take the coward's way, and force me to your will, and then declare a victory. But I tell you, my lord Colby, that even though you have already ruined me in my husband's eyes he will still have your life for it, and I would too, given the opportunity!" Then, pulling away from him, she jumped off his lap, settling her skirts about her with an angry shake.

His face had darkened with every word she had spoken. She was baiting him. He knew it. Yet the sting of her scorn burned him nonetheless. He would prove her wrong. "You'll run barefoot, and in your chemise," he said. "And when I catch you I'll have you then and there with no niceties, and you'll remain my willing whore until I tire of you. Those are my terms, madam. Have you the courage to accept them?"

"When?" she asked, her heart beating with a mixture of both fear and excitement.

"Now," he said.

"You will give me the full hour?" she asked him. How far could she get in so short a time? Ellen wondered. Far enough to gain more time to elude him? She had to take the chance, because it was the only one she would have.

"I do have some honor left, and as there is no doubt as to the outcome of this wager I can afford to be generous," he told her.

"The time will start when I step through your gates," Ellen said boldly.

"Agreed," he replied with a chuckle. "You shall have every moment you are entitled to, madam, before my dogs and I run you to ground, and I fuck you." Standing, he led her down from the high board. "I shall escort you to the gates myself," he said, and he took her by the arm as they walked from the hall and out into the courtyard. "Open the gates," Sir Roger called to the men at arms standing by the closed entry.

They obeyed immediately. The portcullis was winched up, and the drawbridge was slowly lowered.

"Take off your shoes," he said, and then he helped her to do so. "Now your gown, madam." And when she had he took her across the drawbridge himself. When they reached the other side Roger Colby yanked Ellen into his arms, and kissed her hard. "In an hour listen for the sounds of my horse's hooves, madam, and the baying of my hounds as we come after you," he said. Then, turning, he walked back across the drawbridge.

She ran for the shelter of nearby copse, out of the castle's view, and then stopped briefly to consider in which direction she would go. He would assume she knew that his prey would go cross-country, and so he would ride in that direction. But Ellen had often hunted in her childhood Highland home with her grandfather and his clansmen. She remembered a time when they had tracked a magnificent twelve-point buck for hours, only to have the dogs lose the scent after they had crossed a stream.

"Damn!" her grandfather had sworn. "The beast has taken to the water."

She had asked him what he meant, and he explained that instead of fording the stream, the animal had instead stayed in it, working his way either downstream or upstream before stepping onto land again, where his scent could be tracked. There was no telling where the buck was at that point, and so they had gone home again. The memory sharp in her mind, Ellen looked about her, considered the position of the sun above, for the day was fair, and then she headed west toward the beach.

In short order she found a narrow path and picked her way down the side of the cliff. Along the way she plucked a thick handful of long grass, and when she reached the bottom she backed slowly toward the water, brushing the marks of her footsteps away as she walked.

She would wager Sir Roger would not have considered that she had that kind of knowledge. Ellen chuckled as she stepped into the water. She gasped, for it was icy.

She ran as quickly as she could in the water. Her feet were soon numb with the cold sea, but she did not stop. It was the middle of October, and while the weak sun offered her some small warmth, the breeze was chilly. Her chemise offered her little warmth, but it was better than nothing. Finally Ellen stepped from the water and onto the beach. If Sir Roger had gone off cross-country, as she thought he would, it would be at least another hour or two before he considered—if indeed he did consider—that she would have taken to the beach as a means of escape. Hopefully he would not find the imprint of her feet anywhere, and would be puzzled. Perhaps he would return to the castle defeated, yet more than likely he would ride along the sand until he found evidence of her again. Still, she could no longer bear the frigid waters of the sea.

When her feet stopped burning and tingling with her pace, and began to feel like her feet once again, Ellen began to run faster. She had not heard either the sound of pursuing dogs or a stallion's hooves, but she did not count herself safe by any means. And then ahead of her the distance between the land on either side of Solway Firth grew narrower and narrower. And the waters of the firth seemed to have receded in that space. Ellen could not believe her good fortune. Was it possible that she could cross the mudflats back into Scotland? Please God and his blessed Mother that she might. Finally, at what she judged to be the narrowest point between the land, Ellen stepped from the sandy beach onto the mudflats of Solway Firth. She walked carefully, for mud, she knew, could be treacherous, but she walked as swiftly as she could. It made no matter that the only sounds she could hear were the gulls soaring and swooping above her.

And then, when she had almost reached the other

side, she heard an odd roaring sound, and turning her head she saw a great wall of water coming swiftly up the firth and directly toward her. She stopped, terrified, unable for a moment to move. She heard shouting, and saw ahead of her several men upon the beach gesturing at her. One of them broke from the group, hiked up the robes he was wearing, and ran out into the firth toward her. The water was beginning to rise around her ankles.

"Hurry, lass, hurry!" the man coming toward her cried, and, reaching her, he put an arm about her and forced her to run.

The water now washed about her knees. It was like trying to run through honey, Ellen thought, but she kept on moving, the man's arm about her. The water reached her waist, and in a rush her shoulders. Gasping, she swallowed some of the salty sea. The man was swimming. He held tightly on to Ellen, bringing her along with him. But she could swim too. She kicked her legs and struggled to keep her head above water, even if the currents beneath and around them were strong. Finally she felt the bottom of the firth beneath her feet again, and with her rescuer she stumbled up onto the beach before collapsing onto the sand.

"What in the name of holy Saint Andrew made you cross Solway Firth with a full-bore tide upon you, woman?" her rescuer demanded to know.

"I did not know, and it was that or die on the other side," Ellen finally managed to gasp. She sat up, looking about her and at the men surrounding her. All were dressed in long brown robes. "You are holy men?" she asked them.

Her rescuer smiled. "Brother Griogair, lady," he said, pulling his robe back down. "We are from the monastery of St. Andrews just atop the hill." He pointed.

"I am Ellen MacArthur, wife to Duncan Armstrong, the laird of Duffdour. I was kidnapped by the English several months ago, and held captive until today, when I managed to outwit my captor and escape. When I saw the distance between England and Scotland so small I crossed. I was not aware of such a tide as almost overcame us, for the sea is not a thing familiar to me. I thank you, good brother, for helping me to shore. Now I must beg a boon of you. Can you shelter me, and send to my husband at Duffdour to come for me? I live in terror that my captor will find me, for he is not averse to raiding into Scotland."

"Let us return to our house," Brother Griogair said. "The prior must make that decision, but he is a kind man, and will have some good solution for your problem."

He stood and helped Ellen up, avoiding looking at her, for her thin wet chemise clung closely to her body, revealing all her secrets. Then with his three companions they walked up the hill to the monastery of St. Andrews. They housed her in their tiny guest quarters, and shortly thereafter Brother Griogair returned with clean, dry garments for her, a dry chemise and a brown woolen robe. "You could hardly see the prior, dressed as you are, lady," he said with a small smile. "I will return with him in half of the hour. Will that be time enough for you to make yourself presentable?"

Ellen swallowed a giggle. "Aye, and thank you," she said. When he had left she stripped the sopping chemise from her. The salt water had left her body sticky, but using a rough cloth and a pitcher of water provided, she managed to cleanse and dry herself. She donned the fresh chemise and the rough brown robe. It was long on her, and so, hiking it up, she tied it with the knotted rope that had come with it. There was nothing she could do with her hair without a comb, and so, squeezing the water from her soaking braid, she left it as it was. A knock sounded upon her door. "Come in," Ellen called.

The door opened to reveal Brother Griogair and a white-haired older man. "This is Prior Kenneth," the brother said. "I have already told him your tale, lady."

Prior Kenneth came into the guest chamber. "You will understand, my lady, that we are a community of men. A woman may not enter our premises, and so I must come to you." He sat down upon one of the two chairs near the hearth, and beckoned her to take the other. "Now, tell me, who was the villain who stole you away from your husband?"

"His name is Sir Roger Colby," Ellen said. "He has caused much trouble along the border in the last two years at the behest of his master, King Henry. Finally my husband, with the Earl of Bothwell's aid and the king's approval, gathered together a vast troop of clansmen from several border families. They completed a series of fierce raids into the English border, breaking up Sir Roger's own band of raiders, burning a number of villages, and looting. These actions caused Sir Roger to be discredited in the eyes of King Henry, and he swore revenge against my husband."

The prior nodded. What she was telling him wasn't anything he hadn't heard before, for he had in one form or another. This constant raiding back and forth between the Scots and the English was nothing new, but tragic nonetheless. "Go on, my child," he said to her. "How was it you were taken?"

"In midsummer a sickness swept through our village and out among the cotters. One day as I tended to a family at the farthest reaches of our cottages Sir Roger came and kidnapped me. He threatened the cottage goodwife, a widow, and her children. Her eldest daughter had been whoring for the English for coppers, and had betrayed me."

Prior Kenneth *tsked* and shook his head wearily. Was there no end to human perfidy? "You were taken into England?"

"To Colby Castle, where I have been imprisoned ever since," Ellen said.

"Tell me how you tricked your captor into allowing you to escape," the prior asked her. If she had been imprisoned for several months, why had she not previously attempted to escape? he wondered.

Seeing the doubt and concern in his eyes, Ellen considered how best to explain. "For many weeks after my capture I was imprisoned in the dungeons of Colby Castle," she began. "There was no opportunity for escape. And then when I sickened I was brought from the dungeons to be kept in a tower of the castle. The door to my rooms was locked from the outside. I saw no one but whoever brought my meals, either an old servant or the castle sergeant. And then Sir Roger began to visit me in an attempt to seduce me. I rebuffed his attempts, reminding him I was a chaste wife and mother."

Both the prior and Brother Griogair looked uncomfortable with her recitation, but Ellen continued on. "Finally this morning I was brought to the hall, where Sir Roger told me I would come to his bed tonight. He seemed to believe that by dishonoring me he could have his revenge on Duncan, my husband. I taunted him, calling him a coward, and saying he had not the courage to loose me, give me an hour's start, and then hunt me down, if indeed he could. He is a proud man, so he agreed, insisting that I be barefoot and wear naught by my chemise." Ellen laughed softly. "I am Highland born, and until I was sent to court rarely wore shoes. And I remembered my grandfather telling me that an animal could escape pursuit by taking to water. I suspected Sir Roger would believe I should run from him cross-country, but I took to the water instead."

The prior nodded, smiling. "It was cleverly done, my lady. But surely once your captor went down to the beach he would have seen your footprints in the sand."

"I gathered grass as I climbed down the cliff side, and brushed my footprints away as I went," Ellen said. "By now, of course, Sir Roger may have figured out what I did, but he will have to ride the beach in both directions, and when he finds no trace of me in either, I do not know what he will do."

"He is obviously a very wicked man," the prior observed.

"Aye, he is," Ellen agreed. Then she said, "Good Prior, I have no wish to endanger you, or St. Andrews. All I ask of you is that you send to my husband, so he may come for me and bring me home to Duffdour."

"I think I may have a better plan, my daughter," the old prior said. "Tomorrow Brother Griogair will take you to his cousin, Robert Ferguson, the laird of Aldclune. He is in a better position to help you reach your husband than we are. As you will be traveling in your brown robe with its hood up, you will appear to be nothing more than two poor monks to anyone you pass."

Ellen turned to the younger man. "Your cousin is to be trusted?" she asked him.

"Robert is an honorable man, lady. My hand to God on it," the monk answered.

"How long will it take us to reach Aldclune?" she questioned.

"If we leave at first light we will be there before noon," Brother Griogair said.

"I will be ready," Ellen responded.

"You will have to ride astride if we are to make the charade real," he said.

"I am used to riding that way," she told him.

"I will pray for you, my daughter," Prior Kenneth said.

"My husband will reward you for your kindness," Ellen replied. "Thank you."

The two monks withdrew, and shortly afterward a young monk came with a trencher of fish stew, a wedge of cheese, and a goblet of apple cider for her. Ellen thanked him. She did not sleep well, every sound causing her to waken, listening, fearful. She was only now realizing what a dangerous thing she had done when she crossed the mud of Solway Firth without realizing the tide was coming back. She would remember till the day she died the peculiar roar of the water as it spilled up the firth. If the monks had not seen her she would have surely drowned.

But better death than another night with Sir Roger. And what was she going to tell Duncan? Should she tell him that Sir Roger had touched her, fondled her, attempted to rape her?

Finally the early light began to show through the shutters of her shelter. She arose, eager to get started. She could hear the monks' voices raised in prayerful song as they celebrated the second Mass of the day, prime. The first Mass, matins and lauds, had been celebrated after midnight. Ellen washed the sleep from her face, undid her braid, which was now dry, and combed out her hair. She made a face at how sticky her hair was from the seawater, but she would have to live with it for a time, she knew. Replaiting her hair, she then put on the itchy brown robe and sat down to wait for Brother Griogair.

When he arrived shortly after, he carried with him a fresh chunk of buttered bread, telling her, "I thought it would be better to eat astride rather than waste the time here. I know how anxious you are to put as many miles between you and England as possible."

"Aye," Ellen agreed. "I will not feel safe until I am with my kin again."

The monk led her to the monastery stables, which contained three horses. None looked either young or fast. They saddled two beasts, led them outside, and, mounting, rode to the gates of St. Andrews to be let out by the porter.

"No one on the road or coming from the sea," the porter told them cheerfully.

They rode in silence, eating their bread as they went. What was there to say? Ellen wondered. The silence around them meant that everything out of the ordinary echoed and caused her to start. Ellen had to admit to herself that she was still very frightened that Sir Roger Colby would appear out of the void and carry her off again to his castle. How long had he sought her, and how must he have felt, realizing that somehow, some way, she had escaped him? She knew he had been aware that her taunts were meant to prick at his pride, but she had also believed that her challenge would appeal to that pride. And it had! But she had been very fortunate at finding the mile-wide cross of Solway Firth, and escaping drowning when the full-bore tide had roared back up that channel of the Irish Sea. And lucky that the monks had seen her, rescued her, sheltered her, and were now taking her to a place of safety.

They rode for several hours, and then on a rise a short ways ahead of them in a green meadow was a large stone house, much like Duffdour, but lacking in walls.

"There is Aldclune ahead of us," Brother Griogair said, breaking their long silence.

Reaching the house, they dismounted, and servants took their horses, greeting the monk warmly. He led her inside to a gracious hall where a man and woman were seated at a high board, being served the main meal of the day.

"Griogair!" the man said, standing. "What have you brought us?"

"Robert," the monk greeted his cousin. "My lady Anne."

Robert Ferguson suddenly stared hard at Ellen. "God's boots! You are the laird of Duffdour's wife, are you not?"

"How is it you recognize me?" Ellen asked him.

"I was one of the men at Duffdour late last spring when plans were made to stop the English raiders. I had heard you had been taken by that villain Colby. Your husband has ridden both sides of the border for months seeking you."

Ellen began to cry, and at once Anne Ferguson came down from the high board, putting her arms about the young woman, comforting her.

"The lady escaped yesterday from Colby, but she will tell you the tale herself, cousin," Brother Griogair said. "She damned near drowned crossing the Solway just before the tide came back in. Fortunately several of us walking the beach saw her."

"He ... he ... rescued me," Ellen sobbed.

"Oh, you poor thing," the lady Anne said.

"Can you send to Duffdour, cousin?" the monk asked Robert Ferguson.

"I'll send to Cleit first, for Cleit is nearer, and he is Duffdour's half brother," the laird of Aldclune said. "He can send to Duffdour, and my clansmen and I will escort the lady to Cleit. If we leave within the hour we can shelter at our cousin David's home tonight, and reach Cleit by late tomorrow. Does Colby know where she is?"

"Come and sit down at the high board," Anne Ferguson said. "You must eat before you continue on your journey. You can tell us, if you want, what happened." She escorted Ellen to a seat and, signaling a servant, saw a trencher of hot rabbit stew brought to her, along with a small goblet of ale. "Eat, my dear; you look fair worn."

Ellen gratefully ate the food placed in front of her. When she had finished she quickly explained what had happened, telling the Fergusons the same tale she had told Brother Griogair and Prior Kenneth. The laird of Aldclune swore softly, and his good wife *tsked*, shaking her head sympathetically.

"You're a braw lass," Robert Ferguson said when she finished. "I'll gladly ride with your husband when he avenges you, lady. But now we must hurry if we are to reach my cousin's home by sunset. Thank you, Griogair, for bringing the lady of Duffdour to us."

And then she was on the road again, but this time she had been given a decent horse, although she still wore her monk's robes. Brother Griogair rode away from Aldclune as Robert Ferguson, his clansmen, and Ellen started in the opposite direction. And they rode at a good gallop for three more hours, reaching their destination just as the late-October sun was setting. David Ferguson's wife, Sine, offered Ellen a change of garments, but Ellen declined, feeling safer in her monk's robes. She told her story again after the light evening meal was served, and was again met with much sympathy.

At dawn they set out again. David Ferguson and a dozen of his men had joined them. They stopped when the sun was at its zenith to rest the horses and attend to their own needs. They had oatcakes and cheese for nourishment, which they ate as they rode. And then as the day waned and the sun was sinking to the west behind them, Cleit Keep was before them. Ellen had never before in her life been as glad to see any place as she was to see her brother-in-law's home. The Fergusons were warmly welcomed into Conal Bruce's hall, and all the more so because of whom they brought with them.

Ellen fell into Adair's arms, suddenly weeping wildly again. And Conal Bruce himself felt tears pricking at the backs of his eyelids. He knew how much his older brother loved this woman, and how painful the last few months had been for him. When he heard Ellen's tale, however, he knew that those months had been far worse for her than they had been for Duncan Armstrong.

Adair, however, sensed that Ellen was not telling them everything. Seeing her sister-in-law's head drooping, she whispered to her husband that she would take her off and tuck her into bed. Leading Ellen to a small guest chamber, she took the brown robe, laughing. "Tomorrow I shall give you a respectable gown to wear."

"No," Ellen said. "I am safer in the monk's robe."

"What happened?" Adair said quietly.

"I have told you what happened," Ellen replied.

"You have told us the tale you wish us to hear, sister. Now I want you to tell me the truth. Whatever you say 'twill be between us. Did he rape you?"

Ellen began to weep. "Aye, and nay," she finally sobbed.

"He fondled you?"

"Aye. And he put his tongue on me where he should not."

"He touched you where only your husband should touch you? Tell me, sweeting," Adair cajoled. "I can tell this pains you. Tell me, and be rid of the pain."

"Sir Roger says women are all whores and sluts," Ellen wailed. Then she wept harder.

Adair had a sudden thought. "Did he give you anything to eat or drink before he began his seduction?" she inquired, curious. "As he grew older, my father often had difficulties making his body perform as he would have it do. He took potions that helped keep his lust well fueled. They call such thing aphrodisiacs, and many of them come from the East."

"I was left without food or water for three days, and then I was given bread, a bit of cheese, a cup of wine," Ellen said. "When he came to my chamber that night and woke me he admitted to having drugged the wine so I would sleep. Then he forced a vial of some liquid down my throat. Afterward I felt filled with such lust as I have never known. It was terrible. Everything tingled and throbbed and yearned to be sated. I tried to fight it, Adair. I swear to you that I did, but I could not!"

"I thought as much," Adair said in a satisfied tone. "Whatever it was that Colby gave you, Ellen, that is what forced your body to react to his wicked, lustful torture. But even so, you still attempted to resist. I think you are very brave."

"Then why do I feel so shamed?" Ellen said softly. "How will I be able to face Duncan, knowing that another man made me feel passion? And how can he share a bed with me, knowing I am less than chaste now?" And she began to sob again.

"Do not be such a little fool, Ellen," Adair said sharply. "You will tell your husband the exact same tale you have told us. That you were imprisoned in a dungeon for many weeks. That you were then kept in a tower alone and without company for more weeks. That of late Sir Roger had taken to fondling you and kissing you in his hall. That when you realized he meant to force you to his will, you taunted him in such a manner that you were able to escape Colby Castle," Adair said.

"Why did I not attempt to escape before that?" Ellen wailed.

"Because you were waiting, praying to our Blessed Mother for your husband to come and rescue you. And when you could wait no more, when you realized that possibly Duncan did not know where you were, you did what you did. The shock of your incarceration finally wore off as you realized the danger you were in, and that you had no one, no one but yourself, to rely upon," Adair responded. "God's nightshirt, Ellen! Surely someone must have known that Colby had a home somewhere else other than Devil's Glen. He's English, for God's sake! He reports to his king."

"Oh, merciful Mother of God!" Ellen cried. "I forgot the most important thing of all, Adair. Ian Johnston is alive, and Colby means to make an attempt on the king's life with Johnston's aid. Our king!"

"What?" Adair jumped up from the bed where she had been seated. "I must get Conal. Do not dare to sleep until we get back!"

Ellen nodded, watching as her sister-in-law ran from the little chamber, returning several minutes later with Conal Bruce.

"What is this about an assassination?" he wanted to know.

"Colby received a messenger from King Henry a few days ago. As his king had forbidden him the court, he was quite pleased. The message was in the form of a riddle, and Colby could not at first understand it. King Henry had sent to say that there was a thorn in the lion's paw. If Colby would remove the thorn then he would be welcomed back to King Henry's court. He told me the riddle, and I said the lion was obviously King Henry himself. As soon as I said it Colby realized that the thorn was our own King James! That King Henry was asking him to kill Scotland's king! Then he brought Ian Johnston up from his dungeons, where he had languished for months, and together they began planning. I know nothing more, because that same morning I tricked Sir Roger into letting me loose, and I fled."

"You must send to Bothwell," Adair said.

The laird of Cleit nodded. "I will dispatch two messengers in the morning. One to Duffdour, so Duncan may come and collect his wife, and the other to Hailes to Hercules Hepburn, so he may notify Patrick. I have no idea where he would be. Perhaps the earl is at Hailes. Perhaps he is with the king, but Jamie must know immediately what is afoot." He patted Ellen's shoulder. "You're a braw lass, Ellen MacArthur. My brother is fortunate to have you as his wife," he told her, and Ellen began to cry again.

Conal Bruce looked aghast. "What have I said?" he asked his wife.

Adair shook her head. "The shock of it all is just beginning to touch her," she told him. "I'm afraid she's going to be like this for a while. Go back to the hall, my lord." And when he had gone Adair said to Ellen, "I'm going to leave you to get some sleep. Hopefully it will settle your nerves. You were not to blame for what happened these past weeks. There is only one person to blame. That is Sir Roger Colby. I hope he is prepared to run, but he cannot run far enough, Ellen. Duncan, his brothers, and their friends are going to find him, and when they do they will kill him. If they do not he may kill our king, and we cannot have England telling Scotland what to do again." Bending, she drew the coverlet over Ellen's shoulders. "Go to sleep now, lass, and dream of the man you love, for I doubt he'll wait for his clansmen once he learns you are here safe at Cleit. Good night."

Ellen lay awake in the comfortable bed for some minutes after her hostess had left her. She was safe! And she was almost home. She thought of what Adair had said to her, and she knew Adair was correct when she said Ellen was not to blame for what had happened to her. Somehow she would save Duncan from torturing himself for not rescuing her from that evil man. *I will bear this burden even if it kills me!*

She slept, and in the morning when she awakened she felt much, much better. A serving woman came to ask if there was anything she wanted, and Ellen told her, "Tell your mistress I want a bath, and I have changed my mind. I want clean clothing!"

Adair came to fetch her and brought her down to the kitchens of the keep, where the oak bathtub was set up and already filled with hot water. Ellen climbed in, washing herself first, and then washing her sticky hair free of the salt and sand of Solway Firth. The toweling was hot from the fire, and Ellen wrapped both herself and her hair in it. Elsbeth, Adair's old servant, and her sister, Margery, helped Ellen into a clean, soft chemise and a green velvet gown.

"Green was never my lady's color," Elsbeth remarked, "but on you, my lady Ellen, with your fiery hair, it is a fine gown."

"Sit down, child," Margery said, "here by the fire, and we will get your hair dry."

The two women fussed about Ellen, who was almost brought to tears again by the comfortable female company she had lacked for so long. They rubbed her hair free of its excess moisture, and then took turns brushing it until it was shining and dry again. When they were finished Ellen thanked them both, and went up into the hall to break her fast.

She found Adair there with her children, James, Andrew, John, and Janet. Adair was instructing them in their letters. "We have no priest again," she said, "and they have to learn how to read and write in this world."

"Isn't Jan a bit young?" Ellen asked, looking at her niece, who was barely three.

"It is never too young for learning," Adair answered her. "Bring Lady Ellen some breakfast," she called to a serving woman.

It was raining outside, Ellen learned after she had eaten. But despite the weather Conal Bruce had dispatched two riders just before the dawn: one to Hailes with a message that Duffdour's wife had been found, and that she spoke of a plot to kill the king; and the other to Duffdour to tell Duncan Armstrong to come and fetch his wife. The Fergusons had departed early too, and Ellen was distressed because she had not had the opportunity to thank them properly for bringing her to safety.

"Do not fret yourself," Adair told her when Ellen had expressed her concern. "Conal thanked them profusely, as was right and proper, for he is Cleit's laird and your husband's brother. They were not in the least slighted. Conal invited them to come along when they hunt down Colby. They were quite delighted by the invitation."

"I would go with them when they hunt the Englishman down," Ellen said, much to Adair's surprise.

"Would you? You would go back into England after *all* you have endured at the hands of that man?" Adair asked.

"It is because of all I have endured," Ellen said softly. "I want to see him dead with my own eyes. I will never really feel safe until he is, and I know it without doubt. That he could come onto Armstrong's lands and snatch me so easily was terrifying. Until I see him dead I will never feel safe anywhere."

Adair nodded. "I understand," she said softly, "yet does not the same thing happen in the Highlands?"

"I suppose it did," Ellen replied. "But usually it was for a quick ransom, or just a bit of bride stealing among the clans. But they were Scots. This man was English. He came over our border, debauched one of our lasses, turned her to betrayal and treason, and then kidnapped me into England. And why? Because my husband had beaten him. Because he lost his own king's favor over it. Colby told me he wanted Duncan to feel the same loss as he had upon losing something dear to his heart. That he could equate the loss of royal favor with the taking of a man's wife still astounds me. Roger Colby is an evil man.

"I have thought of all you said to me last night. You are right, Adair. There is no fault in me. Perhaps if I had been braver I would have thrown myself from my tower window, but I was not brave. And somewhere deep within me I always had the hope that my husband would find me and bring me home safely to Duffdour. I gambled on it, and played for time.

"Only when I realized that I had no more time, and when Colby was so sure he was near to breaking my spirit that morning in his hall, did I dare to taunt him into allowing me outside. Within the castle I had no chance at all to escape the inevitable rape he was planning. But once outside I knew my chances were better. There was no certainty that I could escape him. The odds in my favor were slim, but I had to try."

"What if he had caught up with you?" Adair asked quietly.

"I would have drowned myself in the sea before I ever let him touch me again," Ellen said grimly. "I actually think that was part of the reason that I took to the water. Like that buck escaping my grandsire and his huntsmen, the water was my only chance of ever getting back to Duncan and our son. Tell me, Adair—I was so tired and confused last night that I never asked. Does my bairn live?"

Adair nodded. "I have not been told to the contrary," she answered Ellen. "But I must be honest with you. I never asked, nor did Duncan say, for his main concern was in finding you. But your old Peigi is like my Elsbeth. She would have seen to the bairn's safety, I am certain."

"Aye," Ellen agreed, and she smiled a small smile. "She would have, bless her."

The two women spent the remainder of the rainy day in conversation as they sat by the blazing hearth in the hall of Cleit. Ellen felt great relief in being once more in what she considered a normal setting. She enjoyed her nieces and nephews very much, especially little Janet Margaret, who was called Jan by her three older brothers. It was, Ellen thought, a perfect family, and the obvious love between Conal Bruce and his wife, Adair, was heartwarming to see.

The next day it rained as well. Ellen spent some time with Adair in her apothecary, helping to make a salve that was used to help cure winter chest ailments. It was made of goose fat that was rendered into its purest form, and menthol, which was an oil extracted from the peppermint that Adair grew in her herb garden. They also packaged dried peppermint leaves for tea, an excellent remedy for disorders of the stomach. Ellen wondered if Duncan would arrive by nightfall, but Adair told her it would not be until the morrow sometime.

The follow morning dawned fair, and Ellen spent much of the morning with Adair again, teaching the children, mending Jan's tiny garments. By afternoon she was restless, and Conal suggested she go to the top of the keep and watch for Duncan. Taking a cape, Ellen climbed up to the roof of the keep and stood staring in the direction from which he would come from Duffdour.

He saw her there as his brother's home came into sight. Her red-gold hair blew like a banner in the west wind. His heart began to beat faster *Ellen! Wife!* He called to her with his heart, and as if she heard him Ellen began to wave wildly. And then she was gone from the top of the keep. He imagined her running down the winding stairs, dashing through the hall as she called out to Adair, to Conal, to whoever was in the hall, that the laird of Duffdour was coming. He grinned at the pictures he was making in his mind, and put his heels to his stallion's sides to encourage him to move faster. And then he saw the doors to Cleit being opened, and she burst through them as if she were being propelled. Picking up her green skirts she ran toward him, and Duncan Armstrong pulled his horse to a sharp stop, leaped from his saddle, and ran to meet her.

He caught her up in his arms, swinging her about, laughing with the pure happiness that was radiating through him. "Wife!" he said, looking down into the little heart-shaped face that had haunted his dreams these past months.

"Husband!" Ellen responded, and the tears in her eyes now slid unbidden down her cheeks, although she was smiling radiantly at him.

And then he kissed her a hungry kiss, his arms wrapping themselves tightly about her as if he would never again let her go. And, kissing him back with equal fervor, safe within his embrace, Ellen knew that she would have the strength to protect Duncan Armstrong from Roger Colby, because the love she shared with her husband was everything good. And Roger Colby was everything wicked.

Chapter 14

Roger Colby had watched, amused, as Ellen had sprinted away from the castle. Turning, he walked back across the drawbridge and told Rafe to have his stallion and the dogs ready in an hour. "I am going hunting," he said, chuckling.

"The lady?" his sergeant asked, curious. "Is that why you let her go, my lord?"

Ordinarily Sir Roger would not have tolerated such a question, even from so faithful a retainer, but he was feeling mellow with thoughts of putting his captive on her back where he caught her and fucking her until she begged for mercy. "The lady said I could not catch her if I released her, and so I have released her. I will have her under me soon enough, Rafe. Is Johnston cleaned up?"

"Aye, my lord, he is, and awaiting your orders," came the reply.

"Let him wait," Roger Colby said with a grin. "Give him a cot in your barracks room, some food, and tell him I will speak with him tomorrow. I don't want to see him again until I send for him. Do you understand?"

"Aye, my lord," the sergeant said. "I'll go now and

give the orders for your horse and the pack." He hurried off.

Sir Roger sought his private chambers. He did not wish to see or speak with the Scot now. His mind was on Ellen, and what he would do to her when he caught her. And the nights that followed. He had actually grown to like her. She had spirit and was intelligent for a woman. A whore and a slut like they all were, to be sure, but he had no doubt she would prove amusing entertainment. Redheads were always extremely fair, their flesh delicate.

How she had writhed beneath his tongue as it had plundered the sweetness and sensitivity of her little jewel. His hand went to his cock, which had grown hard with his thoughts. He rubbed it soothingly, attempting to calm it, but his lascivious memories now considered what he would do when he caught her. He could but imagine her fear, the acceleration of her heart as she heard the hoofbeats of his stallion and the baying of his dogs, first faintly, but then, as they grew closer, louder and louder. The dogs would reach her first, surrounding her, yapping and leaping. She would be terrified. He smiled.

And then he would reach her, taking her up over his saddle, driving the dogs off. He would ride a small way while she struggled against him. Finally he would bring his animal to a halt. Dismounting, he would rip that thin little chemise from her, and, slapping her hard several times to remind her he was the master, he would fling her to the ground. Then, straddling her, he would strip off his jerkin and shirt, loose his cock from his breeches, and join with her. He would kiss her until her mouth was swollen. He would suck and bite upon her lush little breasts until he drew blood. And all the while she would fight him, he knew.

But finally he would mount her. He would push himself slowly, slowly into her tight, wet sheath. She would encase his flesh in her flesh, helpless to deny him. He would have pinioned her arms above her head with one hand. And when he was deep, he would reach out with his other hand and play with her little jewel until she was mindless. Then he would fuck her hard and deep while he impelled the cries of pleasure from her. But he would not release his juices. When she was weakened he would turn her onto her belly, driving himself into her asshole because she had admitted no man had ever had her there. But he would have that virginity of her, and she would sob as his juices released themselves there.

He remembered his mistress, a beautiful, ethereal golden-haired creature, whom he had introduced to this particular perversion. She had been the daughter of one of his farmers. He had seen her haying in the fields one summer's day, and he had taken her up on his horse and brought her back to the castle. Her name had been Eve, and there was no denying that she tempted him. She was a virgin when he took her for himself, and for two years her body had pleased him, for her intellect was lacking, and she was often like a child. As long as he cosseted her and brought her bright trinkets and colorful ribbons, she was content. His mother had been alive then.

His mother. She had been a bitch out of hell, and he had left her much to her own devices, for they had never gotten on. She had taken the captain of his men at arms for her lover, but he didn't care. The castle priest had taught Roger Colby that women were whores and sluts whose only use was to bear children. And his mother proved the priest right, for she was always seeking out lusty men for her bed. As she was a handsome woman, she had little difficulty. On one particular day she had annoyed him, and he had called her a whore, for indeed she was, despite her highborn status.

His mother had laughed at him. "You call me a whore? What about the little slut you sleep with?"

"Eve is my mistress. She is mine alone," he had replied.

"Is she?" His mother laughed again. "Come to my

chambers at moonrise, and see what you will see," she taunted him.

And so he had gone to her chambers when the full moon had risen that night, to find its silvery light spilling across the body of his mistress while both his mother and her lover took their pleasure of her. And Eve had giggled and sucked his captain's cock while his mother licked at the girl's little jewel until she was whimpering. Then as Sir Roger had watched, stony faced, his captain had fucked his mistress until she was screaming her delight, and, having pleasured Eve, the captain then set about to pleasure his mother, who was soon writhing and moaning beneath the big man.

Roger Colby had slit his captain's throat as the man rode his mother. Then, pulling the body away from the dazed woman, he drove his dagger directly into her heart. She had not even the time to cry out. He then turned his attentions to his beautiful mistress, Eve, who cowered in a corner of the bed, her blue eyes wide with fear. He coaxed her from her defensive position with gentle words, kissing and caressing her. Then, putting her on her back, he fucked her, and as he did he strangled her. The priest who had taught him had been right. Women, *all* women, were whores and sluts. And his Scots captive had been no different, despite her protests of chastity. When he caught her later this afternoon she would cry out with pleasure. He licked his lips again with the anticipation, his hand rubbing at his cock to calm it. He wanted all of his strength for his conquest.

The sand in the hourglass he had turned upon entering the room filtered away until the bottom half was full. Roger Colby turned it again. He would give her a little extra time, because the result of this hunt would end in the capture of Duffdour's wife. "I can afford to be generous," Sir Roger said softly, and he thought of her long and silky red-gold hair, of how he would have her brush his body with it. He sighed with his eager anticipation, and when the hourglass was half-filled both top and bottom he arose and, pulling on his gloves, gathered up Ellen's gown, directing his steps to the courtyard of his castle, where his sergeant awaited him with two horses and the pack of his hounds.

"I ride alone," he told Rafe.

"You will need someone to call the dogs in when the prey is sighted, my lord," Rafe said doggedly.

It made sense. "Come along, then, but as soon as I see her, take the dogs and return here to the castle."

"Yes, my lord," the sergeant replied. "Shall I give the gown to the dogs to sniff?"

Sir Roger tossed it to him, then mounted the stallion.

Having gotten the scent, the dogs began to bay, and headed across the courtyard, through the gates, across the drawbridge into the meadow. They stopped, sniffing noisily in and around the copse where Ellen had sheltered briefly to get her bearings. Then they headed for the cliffs overlooking the sea. Down the path they galloped, baying and yowling, but at the edge of the water they stopped, confused, milling about.

"Damned dogs!" Sir Roger snapped. "She didn't come this way. There are no footprints in the sand or on the path. Take the useless beasts back to their kennel. They've been idle too long. She's gone cross-country, for where else could she go?" He directed his horse back up the cliff path and galloped across the meadow.

Rafe watched him until he was out of sight. The sergeant smiled. The dogs were not wrong. She had gone to water like a clever doe would have. But he'd not correct his master. Rafe was loyal to Sir Roger, but he had never particularly liked his kidnapping of the laird of Duffdour's wife. She was not the reason his master had lost favor with King Henry. He had lost it because he had grown arrogant in his leadership, and the Scots had taken advantage of that fact, for while they were savage folk they were not stupid. But, of course, such a thought was not to be voiced aloud. He drove the pack of hounds back to their kennel.

Roger Colby rode cross-country in the direction of the border, for that, he knew, was certainly the direction in which she had headed. The countryside was not heavily wooded, although there were stands of trees here and there. Yet there was no sign of her. Had she come upon some traveler and begged aid? Heaven forefend, but if she had and he caught up with her he would claim she was his runaway wife. A man would always be believed over a woman. But though he rode for several long miles there was no evidence of Ellen, or of any other traveler.

A thought began to tug at him. Had the dogs been right? Had she gone down to the shore? But there had been no footprints. Perhaps the winds that afternoon had erased all evidence of her bare feet, and the beach would have been easier for her than the meadowland. If she had gone for the water then she was far more clever than he had given her credit for. And how the hell had she known to go for the water? Unless, of course, she was a huntswoman. Why had it never occurred to him that she hunted? Turning his horse about sharply, he urged it into a canter, seeking a cliffside path by which he might reach the shore again.

Finally he found one, and his animal carefully picked its way down the steep incline to the beach. The mid-October sun was already low on the horizon. A chill wind blew off the water, while above him the gulls soared, screeching, diving now and again for their supper. Drawing his mount to a halt, he looked up and down the beach, but he could see no sign of Ellen. And there were no caves in this vicinity in which she might hide. He was puzzled. Where the hell was she? Where could the woman have gone? She had to be somewhere near. *She had to be!*

He rode north up the beach but could find no trace of her. The gusty winds would have blown any trace of her footprints away by now, for it had been several hours since he had released her before his castle. He stared into Solway Firth, but the full-bore tide was high, the waters rough, the currents strong. He could not imagine a petite creature such as the lady of Duffdour swimming her way to freedom, even here at the narrowest point of the Solway. Could she have taken her own life, walking into the cold waters of the firth to drown herself? Nay! She would not have had the courage. Few did. So where was she?

Sir Roger rode back down the beach until he reached the path that led directly up to his lands. He reached the top of the cliff and, turning, viewed the brilliant sunset over the sea. He didn't want to admit it to himself, but it was just possible the laird of Duffdour's wife had escaped him. He swore furiously beneath his breath. He had been a fool to give in to her taunts! An arrogant fool! He had known that she was baiting him, but he was so certain of her helplessness, of his superiority, that he had made his harsh conditions and, when she had agreed, released her. He chided himself for allowing her that extra modicum of time. But because he knew she could not escape him he had been generous, and like the whore, the slut she was, she had taken advantage of him.

His horse clopped across his drawbridge, and, entering his courtyard, he ordered the drawbridge raised for the night. Let the little bitch remain outside his walls in the cold October night. He would ride out again in the morning to find her. Cold, hungry, and probably wet, she would be more than willing to return to the castle. He'd cut a hazel switch, strip her chemise from her, and whip her for her impertinence. He'd put a rope about her delicate neck and trot her naked back to the castle.

Then she would sit unclothed, hungry, and shivering in her tower rooms until he deigned to send for her. There would be no wood for her hearth. No water to drink. And after several days of denying himself the pleasure of her body he would have her brought to him in his hall. He would make her crawl the length of it on her hands and knees to the high board, where she would beg his forgiveness. Then, before all of his men, he would have her, bending her over his table, taking his pleasure of both her orifices while his men cheered. He would break her spirit, punishing her so that never again would she defy him, or any man. He would teach her her place. She was a whore and a slut.

Roger Colby said nothing as he sat alone in his hall eating his supper. His sergeant wisely asked naught of his master. The laird's wife had escaped, and Rafe was silently glad and relieved. He knew the woman's success was a great blow to his master's pride, but Rafe also knew that if Sir Roger were to regain King Henry's respect and his favor, he had to concentrate on the task at hand, and not on a woman.

He was not surprised, however, when Sir Roger rode out again the following day. His lord would need to come to terms with having been bested by a mere slip of a female. Of course, that would never really happen, Rafe knew, but he would help to eliminate the sting of the loss when he could. He gave Ian Johnston some whiskey, and told him that Sir Roger had more important business to attend to this day, and would see him on the morrow, or if not then the day after.

Roger Colby spent most of his day searching the countryside for Ellen. It began to rain in early afternoon as he sat a-horse looking out over Solway Firth, and knew in his heart that he had been bested by a woman. He shrugged briefly, defeated with the thought. But then he squared his shoulders and straightened his spine. He had wasted too much time on the little Scots slut. He was behaving like the fool she had played him for by wanting her. One juicy cunt was just as satisfactory as another. She was more than likely dead in some ditch. *Good riddance!*

As for the laird of Duffdour, Roger Colby decided that he mattered not at all. Armstrong hadn't been able to find his wife and free her. And while Sir Roger would have enjoyed taunting the man about his lady, and how he had pleasured himself with her while he held her captive, her death in a sense was a sort of revenge. It had been known throughout the borders that Duncan Armstrong loved his wife. Let him mourn her now. Let his heart be broken. Roger Colby had other matters to attend to, and while he was disappointed that he had not been able to satisfy his lust entirely upon Ellen's body, it was time for him to turn his thoughts to other matters, he realized as he rode back to his castle.

"Where is the Scots bastard?" he asked his sergeant as he entered his hall.

"I've kept him in the barracks as you requested, my lord." The sergeant did not ask about the woman.

"Tell him I'll speak with him in the morning," Sir Roger said. "I did not find the laird's wife. She is either dead or has actually managed to elude me. I did not think her so clever, but then of late I have not used my best judgment. She's gone, and it's done with. I have plans to make if I am to regain King Henry's favor. Tonight, however, I want a woman in my bed. The Scots whore roused my lusts, and I need to release them or I shall be ill. Is there anyone new in the kitchens I could use?"

Rafe hesitated just long enough to pique his master's curiosity.

"There is!" Sir Roger said, his eyes lighting up with anticipation.

"I hesitate to suggest her, my lord. She is Farmer John's youngest daughter," Rafe murmured slyly. The girl was Eve's sister.

"Is she as beautiful as my unfaithful whore was?" his lord wanted to know.

Rafe nodded. "More so, if that is possible, my lord."

"Bring her to me. If she pleases me I'll free her from the kitchens, but if I do she will live in the tower, and I will hold the only key to her rooms," Sir Roger said. "This slut will not fuck my captain as did the other."

"You have no captain," Rafe boldly reminded his master.

"Nay, I do not, do I?" Roger Colby said. "Nor will I ever again. And I have no bitch of a mother to tempt my retainers so she could scratch that undying itch of hers."

"No, my lord, you do not," the sergeant replied.

"You would not betray me, Rafe, would you?" He looked at his companion.

"Nay, my lord, I will never betray you," the sergeant responded.

"What is her name? The farmer's slut?"

"Clothilde," Rafe answered.

"Such elegant names for two little peasant girls," Sir Roger mused. "Fetch her to me now." He sat down by the fireplace. "Have her washed first. Between the farm-yard and the kitchens she will be ripe."

"Yes, my lord," the sergeant said, and he moved from the hall to do his master's bidding. It had been providence that he had been in the kitchens when the girl's father had come yesterday while Sir Roger rode out on his futile mission. The girl had been with him, bringing eggs in a basket to the cook. Her father said she was sixteen. He had told the cook to offer the girl a position, and the old farmer, always eager for coin, had left his daughter with them. Sooner than later his master would need to be diverted from the fact that the Scotswoman had escaped.

Rafe had known immediately when Sir Roger had refused to listen to the dogs upon the beach that the laird's wife would elude his master. With luck she would have made it across the mudflats of the Solway before the tide returned, but his master would not have thought of that. And if she did not then she was indeed dead. Either way she was no longer a candidate for his lord's lust. He could not help but wonder, however, if she had reached Scotland. He hoped so. He had more often than not heard the sounds of her weeping as he approached her door, although when he put the key in the lock her keening had ceased, and she was composed when she faced him. And she had always been polite, never cursing at him for her plight like many another would have done. Aye, he did hope she was not dead and had managed to reach safety. Like Sir Roger, he knew the stories of how much the laird of Duffdour loved and cherished his wife. Rafe smiled, imagining the man's joy at being reunited with her.

He didn't want to let her go. He held her tightly against him until finally Ellen protested.

"I cannot breathe, Duncan. You are holding me too fast." But her voice was happy even as she said it.

"I'm afraid if I let you go I will lose you again," he replied. "I've sent that little bitch Evina to Maggie's convent to have the devil beaten out of her, and to teach her some manners. Machara told me how Sir Roger kidnapped you."

"Why did you not come after me, Duncan?" Ellen asked. Best to put him on the defensive right away, she thought to herself regretfully.

"But I did! We rode immediately to Devil's Glen, but the house was shut up, and there was no one we could find who knew where Sir Roger might have gone," he said.

"His family's small castle sits near the mouth of the Solway on the English side," Ellen told her husband. "Could you find no one who knew that?"

"Little was known of him but that he came into the borders with the authority of King Henry to unite the men there and use them to harry us on our side of the border," Duncan explained. "Everyone we questioned believed that Devil's Glen was his house. He had a group of about two dozen men who had come with him, and a sergeant."

"Rafe," Ellen said. "The sergeant's name is Rafe. He

is not a bad man, Duncan, although I cannot say the same for Sir Roger."

"Why did he take you? He never asked for ransom," the laird responded.

"He stole me to punish you. He believes that since you led the borderers who destroyed the English villages, and stole their stock, you are to be held solely responsible for costing him King Henry's favor," Ellen explained. "The royal favor was all that Sir Roger had, Duncan. It gave him great pain to lose it. And so he decided he would steal from you the thing that meant the most to you, the thing that it would give you pain to lose. He decided that thing was me."

"He was right, wife," Duncan said softly. "Did he hurt you, Ellen?"

She knew what he was asking, and, looking up into his face, she answered him. "Nay. He did not harm me," she said as softly. And to her surprise the lie did not trouble her. "I was brought to Colby Castle, and imprisoned in a dungeon cell. There I languished for well over a month. I saw no one. Spoke to no one. What little food I was given was brought to me by a taciturn jailer who rarely spoke. I was so lonely for the sound of a human voice that I talked aloud to myself. And I made friends with a young rat. I would speak with him. He listened politely, for he knew I would share a bit of my food with him," she told Duncan with a mischievous smile.

They had greeted each other outside. Now together they walked hand in hand back into the hall at Cleit, where Conal and Adair waited to welcome the laird of Duffdour. And when they had they discreetly absented themselves so the reunited couple might speak together. Ellen took up her story again.

"I thought surely you would find me, husband. I waited and I waited, but you never came. I know now it is because no one realized that Sir Roger had this home. His family must have once been of importance, for Colby Castle is sturdily built, and obviously in a place of strategic import, for it has fine views of the Solway and the sea. That first day I was housed in the tower I thought it was the sea itself," she told him.

"And Sir Roger conducted himself as a gentleman at all times?" he pressed again.

"Husband, say what it is you wish to say. Did he mount and fuck me? Nay, he did not," Ellen said testily, and it was the truth, she reasoned with herself. "But he did fondle and kiss me several times in preparation for doing so. He was quite plain in his intent, but he has a vile opinion of women. He calls us all whores and sluts. He thought I could be seduced if he isolated me from the world without the comforts of company, and when he saw that I couldn't he determined he would force me to his will. Almost a week ago he brought me into his hall and told me so.

"And it was then that I learned that Ian Johnston was also in Sir Roger's clutches. He had been languishing in the castle dungeons for almost five months. My *host* had him brought up from that foul place. I was shocked by what I saw. The creature was bearded, with long hair, and he stank to high heaven. Sir Roger told him he might regain his good graces if he aided him in an endeavor he was about to undertake. Of course, Johnston immediately agreed, as would any if it meant escaping those dungeons."

"What new mischief is that English devil up to now?" Duncan asked his wife.

"Sir Roger had been briefly visited by someone from King Henry himself. He brought Colby a message. It was a riddle. The king sent to say to Sir Roger that there was a thorn in the paw of the lion, and he wished it removed."

"The lion is England, the thorn James Stewart," the laird of Duffdour said.

Ellen nodded. "Precisely. When Colby told me this riddle he was confused, and I foolishly burst forth that the lion was Henry Tudor. Sir Roger figured out the rest, and plans to attempt to assassinate our king in order to regain his king's approval."

Duncan nodded. "Go on, wife. Tell me of your escape."

"That morning in the hall after the castle sergeant had taken Johnston off to be cleaned up, Sir Roger told me that that night he would have me in his bed. Since I had always been confined closely, I knew there was no way I could escape if I were put back in my tower to await this fate. Oh, I might have jumped from the windows, but frankly I am a coward, husband. Besides, as I stood there in the hall I realized I had but once chance to evade Sir Roger's lustful intentions. And so I taunted him."

"You what?" Duncan looked puzzled.

"I taunted him and cut at his pride. I told him he was a coward to force me to his will when I did not want such a thing. He mocked me, saying as he so often did that all women were whores and sluts, and that I would give in to him. I continued to deride him, saying he had not the courage to let me loose to run. I challenged him to give me an hour, and then come after me like a hunter hunting a roe deer. He was fully aware that I was baiting him, and yet his pride could not withstand my ridicule. He agreed on the condition that when I was caught I would become his willing mistress, and remain with him until he tired of me. And he further insisted that I run barefoot and in my chemise."

"The swine!" the laird burst forth, his outrage jostling the settle where they sat.

The outburst made Ellen laugh. "Nay, Duncan, it was actually better. I had no heavy skirts to weigh me down, and I spent most of my life in the Highlands barefoot. He did me a favor, although he knew it not."

"You took a terrible chance, sweeting," her husband said. "He should have caught you. What miracle prevented him from doing so?"

Ellen then told him the story of her grandfather and the great buck. She explained how she had followed the wisdom of the noble creature by taking to the water. He was amazed that she had had the knowledge to back across the narrow beach, sweeping her footsteps away so no trace of her could be easily found.

"I did think I heard the dogs briefly, but then I did not," Ellen said. "When I thought it safe I left the water and ran along the sand until I came to its end. The waters were gone in that area of the firth, and Scotland was just a little distance away. I began to pick my way as quickly as possible across the mudflats. I was almost to the other side when I saw a group of men gesturing to me. I was near enough to see that they were monks. At that moment I heard a mighty roar and, turning my head, saw a wall of water rushing up the firth toward me. One of the men broke from the others, pulled up his robes, and, running out to meet me, grabbed my hand and told me to hurry.

"We ran but the waters finally overcame us. Brother Griogair began to swim, pulling me along as he did, and I swam with him, for I learned to swim as a child. It was but a moment, although it felt longer; then our feet touched the bottom again. The monks took me to the monastery, and the next morning Brother Griogair took me to his cousin, Robert Ferguson, the laird of Aldclune. Robert Ferguson took me to his cousin David, and together they brought me to safety at Cleit."

"I owe the Fergusons more than I can ever repay them," Duncan Armstrong said, and he pulled her into his lap, his arms tightening about her.

"Conal has promised them that they may ride with us when we kill Colby," Ellen said. "And I would make a small gift of some sort to St. Andrews. Perhaps one of the gold coins from my dower? They did save my life, and then saw that I was brought back to you, husband. I think that is worth a gold coin, even though we have not many." She laid her head on his shoulder.

"I agree," the laird said, turning his own head to give her a quick kiss. Then he grew serious. "But what of this plot against the king?"

"I only know that Sir Roger will make an attempt on the king's life. I know nothing more, and I did not think it behooved me to wait about, given Sir Roger's plans for me, husband," Ellen said with some small humor. "We have the advantage of knowing that he plans such an attempt, and that Ian Johnston will be somehow involved in it. That I have this knowledge will not deter him, for he thinks little of the female intellect or honor. And more than likely he will think me dead, as he could not find me. It would never occur to him that I actually could have outwitted him and escaped him. Such a thought would be too painful to his great pride."

"You seem to know your captor well," Duncan said, his tone sharp.

Ellen heard it, but she never moved in his arms, saying instead, "He was not a particularly complex man, husband. It was apparent from the moment he stole me away that his pride rules him in every decision he makes. Having lived at court, I am capable of taking the measure of a man very quickly, for the wrong friend can cost you more than royal favor. To survive at court you must live on instinct and your wits."

"Sometimes you amaze me," the laird told her candidly. "I keep thinking you are this innocent little Highland girl, but you are not, are you, wife?"

"Not since my first week in Lady Margaret's household," Ellen replied with a chuckle. "I quickly learned to blend in lest I be singled out, and to keep my thoughts to myself, and never to share my private thoughts with anyone. At court, when you have no great family name or powerful protector, it is best to be discreet," she told him.

Now it was he who chuckled. "You are a wise woman, Ellen, my wife," he told her. "A very wise woman."

"How is the bairn?" she asked him now that she had told him her tale and he had seemed to accept it. "Is my son well?"

"Peigi, bless her, found a wet nurse that same day

you disappeared," Duncan told her. "There were several nursing mothers in the village, including Machara. Peigi found her the healthiest, saw how her infant was thriving and that she had very big breasts laden with milk. Her own bairn could not take it all. It allowed me to move her and her bairns into the house. Her oldest boy was apprenticing with his father, who was my fletcher. Now that task is his. The arrows he makes are sturdy and fly true. I put Farlan, for that is his name, with the man who was Duffdour's fletcher before his father. The old man was recently widowed, and, while frail, he is still capable of overseeing a young fletcher. Farlan gets on well with him. Evina proved difficult. I found her one night naked in my bed awaiting me. Artair told me she had been causing difficulties among the men, who were stealing from one another in order to pay to fuck her."

"*What?*" Ellen stiffened in his arms.

He heard the jealousy in her voice, and grinned. "I took her back to her Machara, who beat her soundly. The next day I sent her to Maggie's convent with instructions for Mother Mary Andrew to teach Evina how to be respectable so we could marry her off. She ran away after a week, and hasn't been heard from since. She's undoubtedly found her way to some brothel, where she can ply her trade with impunity."

"Good riddance!" Ellen snapped. "Now you have told me everything except how our wee Willie is. You say he is well? Laria, the nursemaid Peigi chose, does well with him? He thrives?"

"Laria was at first jealous of Machara, but when she saw that the woman's only function was to feed the bairn she grew content. And aye, Willie thrives. He knows us all when he sees us, and his bright eyes light up."

"He does not know me," Ellen said sadly.

"Ahh, sweeting, he will after a few days, and he'll never know that you were gone from him these months," Duncan comforted her. "While he has my eyes, the hair he had at birth, the little of it there was, has fallen out, and 'tis growing back as red as yours again."

"Oh, dear!" Ellen said nervously. "Red-haired men are troublesome, I fear. My grandsire had red hair in his youth, although I certainly never knew him then, but he always said redheaded men were difficult, and he certainly proved it himself."

Duncan Armstrong chuckled. "Willie will have two strong parents to raise him and teach him what is right," he said. "Are you well enough for us to go home tomorrow?" he wondered solicitously.

"Aye, I want to go home," Ellen told him. "When will we take our revenge upon Roger Colby? I am going with you, for I wish to see him die."

The laird of Duffdour was surprised by his wife's declaration. *I am going with you*, she had said. Not *I want to go with you*, or, *Will you take me with you?*; nay, she had said she was going with him. "I cannot forbid you," he heard himself saying. Now, why the hell would he want to put her in danger from the English again?

"Thank you, husband," Ellen replied. "I am grateful you understand my desire to see punished this man who has robbed us of precious time and each other's company."

"I cannot help but feel your passion for revenge is fierce, wife," Duncan noted. "I would have thought you would never want to see him again." Was she hiding something, he wondered silently?

"Do you not understand the cruelty I suffered at the hands of this man?" Ellen cried softly. "For weeks I lived in a damp, dark cell with no human company! I would still be there had my jailer not noticed that I was ill, and feared for his own safety should I die in his custody. Taken from all I loved, I was forced to watch my milk dry up while I lived with the knowledge that my son might die without me. I lived with the stink of my own milk souring and drying on my only garments. I was flea-bitten. My breasts ached.

"And then I lived in a tower where, while I had light and sun and watched the phases of the moon, I was again left to myself but for the sergeant and the old servant who brought me food each day. But no one spoke to me, or with me. It was if I were invisible. Then one day Roger Colby came to my tower. We played chess. Then he touched me, and I resisted his touches. To my relief I did not see him for many days. But then he would have me brought to the hall, where we would eat at the high board as if naught were amiss. And he would force his kisses and his touches upon me while I lived in fear of being so eager for human companionship that I would begin to like his kisses, his touches. Have you any idea, husband, how guilty I felt about thoughts like those?

"But I forced back my own needs because I knew that you would come to rescue me. But you did not come, Duncan. Oh, you rode the border on both sides, I know. But did you never think to seek beyond the border? Did you question every man who had ridden with Sir Roger Colby? Certainly one of them had to know about Colby Castle. If I had not managed to escape, husband, what would you have done? Would you have given me up for lost? Left me to an undeserved fate?"

"We sought high and low for you," he protested.

"You did not seek far enough!" Ellen snapped. "And now you are surprised that I would see the man who stole my life from me, and would have violated me had fate not reached out to help me, dead with my own eyes?"

"I said you could go," he answered her helplessly.

"Aye, and in your mind you questioned why I felt so strongly about it," Ellen shot back and, seeing him flush guiltily, felt pleased.

"Yet you did not feel so strongly about Balgair Mac-Arthur," he said.

"I thought I had killed him," Ellen replied, "and when I found I hadn't I almost died of fright. I shall never be able to visit the Highlands without fearing his enmity reaching out to touch me, to wreak his vengeance upon me. But Balgair is not likely to come down from his Highlands after me, husband. Sir Roger Colby is nearer, however, and surely he has proved to you that what he wants he can take, and that he has no respect for you, or for your lands, or your wife. I have delivered a mighty blow to his pride, Duncan. He never thought to have me outwit him. A woman. A whore and a slut."

"He has greater matters to consider right now than just the hurt you did his pride," the laird of Duffdour said.

"Aye, he does," Ellen agreed. "But if you do not seek him out and slay him now, he will go to ground again while he hatches his plot against our king. It will be more difficult to find him then, or to prevent his mischief."

The laird of Duffdour thought for several long minutes. She was right, of course. They could not waste any more time. "You should go home to Duffdour, and leave this to my brother and to me," he told her.

"Nay, I will ride with you. Until I have seen Sir Roger dead with my own eyes I will not feel safe at Duffdour. Our son has lived—thrived, according to you—these last months without me. Knowing that, my own heart is at ease, but I will not be unless we ride for Colby Castle tomorrow," Ellen said stubbornly.

Duncan Armstrong laughed. It was obvious that he couldn't argue with her. "We ride tomorrow, wife," he said.

Ellen looked up at him. "Thank you," she said simply, and, leaning forward, she kissed his mouth. "You would not want some weak-as-water wife, now, would you, husband mine?" she teased him gently.

"I do not think I ever want to make an enemy of you, wife," he told her.

She slept that night within the comfort of his arms, but he wisely asked nothing more of her, and Ellen was relieved, for she was not yet ready to give herself to him. Still, had he asked she would have acquiesced, for she

loved him. That he was perceptive enough to understand
her pleased her more than she could say.

The lairds of Cleit and Duffdour rode out the next morning, Ellen riding between them, with their men prepared
to do battle. They went the way Ellen had come, riding
to David Ferguson's home first, and on the following
morning to meet up with the laird of Aldclune. At St.
Andrews monastery they waited out the tide, and then
crossed the mudflats of the Solway into England, following the several miles along the beach to Colby Castle. Once there they discovered that Sir Roger and Ian
Johnston had already gone, but Ellen begged mercy for
the sergeant and his men, saving their lives.

"This man was kind to me," she said quietly. "For that
alone, spare him, my lords. He did not ride into Scotland
to harry our people. His place has always been here at
Colby. And if he says he does not know where his master
has gone then he does not lie. While he is loyal to Sir
Roger, I do not believe he is a fool."

"Does my wife speak truth, man?" the laird of Duffdour asked.

"Aye, my lord, she does. I can tell you only that I suspect
my lord has crossed over into Scotland, for he took the
Scot with him and they rode northeast," Rafe replied.

"We cannot fire the castle, for we have not the means,"
Conal Bruce lamented.

"We'll come back," the laird of Aldclune said with a
grin.

"What the hell do we do now?" Conal Bruce asked
his brother as he and their men rode away from Colby
Castle. The Fergusons had elected to return home across
the Solway, for it was closer and easier for them.

"We have to find Jamie and tell him what is happening," Duncan Armstrong said.

"He'll be hunting at this time of year," Ellen told
them, "but where he is hunting is, of course, another
matter. He could be in the borders, or he could be with

Huntley in the Highlands. Wherever he is, we must find him quickly. Our only advantage is that Colby doesn't know where he is either."

"I should take you home," Duncan Armstrong said to his wife.

"There is no time," Ellen replied, "and I won't go. I owe the king a great favor for saving me from Balgair MacArthur and giving me a good husband who loves me."

"She's right," Conal Bruce said. "Time is of the essence."

And so they rode hard for Hailes, for they knew that Patrick Hepburn would know where the king was, and if Patrick was with the king, his brother, Hercules, would know.

The king, they learned, was hunting near Sterling. Hercules Hepburn promised them that he would personally ride to James, and advise him of what little Ellen knew. Even the merest rumor of an attempt on James Stewart's life needed to be noted.

"I can tell the king, and Patrick will certainly back me up in this matter, of how dangerous a man Colby is," Hercules said. "The king has been spending too much time on the matter of the young English king who is under his protection. We'll all be marching down into England sooner than later to support his cause, I have not a doubt."

Ellen could but imagine what Adair would say to that. She was still angry at the king for supporting the pretender, especially when James Stewart knew the truth. Still, Ellen thought, it had nothing to do with her. She was at long last returning home to Duffdour, but she was not content that Sir Roger yet roamed free. She knew she could not feel secure in her own home until she saw him dead. But the autumn was ending, and the winter was settling into the borders. She had to take up her life again no matter her fears, and she longed to hold her bairn in her arms once more.

Chapter 15

"You've surely gotten value for your coin by now, my lord," the Earl of Bothwell said to his king as he stood by his side in the great hall at Sterling. "It should soon be time to end this charade."

"Aye," James Stewart murmured as he sat watching the pretty boy who called himself England's true king graciously holding what amounted to his own royal court within the Scots court of James Stewart. "I wonder if the cost of irritating and frightening Henry Tudor has actually been worth all the good coin I have laid out."

"The fact that King Ferdinand and Queen Isabella attempt to interfere is certainly proof that you have made your point, my lord," the earl said.

James Stewart chuckled softly. "I was determined to dislike the ambassador they sent me, but damn, I do like Pedro de Ayala. He has a way about him that reminds me of one of my island chieftains, but there is also that hawkish look of a Moor about him as well."

"Aye, he's a good man," Patrick Hepburn agreed. "Honest to a fault, which I find interesting, given his master. Is there a slyer man in all the world than King Ferdinand? Yet I believe every word that comes from de Ayala's mouth. There is, it would seem, no chicanery in him."

"I like the way his eyebrows and mouth quirk when he must deliver a message from Spain," the king said. "Especially one he doesn't believe himself. When he said that a marriage between me and one of the *infantas* was a consideration, I knew that he didn't believe it for a moment."

"Sooner or later," the Earl of Bothwell said, "you will have to take a wife, Jamie."

"Later," the king replied with a smile. "Spain will not give me one of their daughters, for they consider Scotland too barbaric a place for one of their pampered princesses. There are no available princesses in France, and my dear friend King Henry of England has turned me down. Besides, his lasses are too young."

"For now," Patrick Hepburn said softly.

"Ah, Patrick, the only value in an English princess would be the peace between our two lands. I am content for now with a complaisant mistress."

Hercules Hepburn now came to join them, bowing to the king, murmuring low in his brother's ear. Both men were surprised to see him, for Hercules was not particularly a man for the court.

"Tell the king," the earl finally said as his brother finished speaking.

"My lord, you are aware that the wife of the laird of Duffdour was kidnapped by the English several months ago. Just over a week ago she managed to escape her captivity. She brought news of a very dire nature. Her captor, Sir Roger Colby, had a visitor from King Henry. Sir Roger has been much out of favor with his king since our borderers put a stop to his raids and inflicted serious damage on the English late last spring. But he can regain his king's favor, a messenger from King Henry told him, by removing the thorn from the paw of the lion. Sir Roger took that to mean that King Henry wanted him to assassinate you, and he means to do it. He has enlisted the aid of the traitor Ian Johnston. The lady of Duffdour did not know when or where such an attempt would be made, but she did want you to know," Hercules Hepburn finished.

"How did she escape Colby?" the king wanted to know. "And where was he hiding her? For I know Duncan Armstrong could find no trace of her."

"Colby, it seems, has a small castle in northwestern Cumbria on the sea near the Solway. The lady escaped by taunting him into releasing her and trying to hunt her down like an animal. She managed to elude him, and crossed the mudflats of the Solway just before the tide turned. The monks at St. Andrews monastery took her in and brought her to Robert Ferguson, the laird of Aldclune. He shepherded her to safety at Cleit, which was nearer to him than Duffdour. Armstrong met up with her there. They then rode back into England with a troop of Bruces, Armstrongs, and Fergusons to hunt down Sir Roger. But he was not at Colby Castle, and neither was the traitor, Johnston. We believe he has already crossed over into Scotland with his companion, and is even now finalizing his wicked plans. I sent them home, promising to come to you, my lord, and warn you."

"Do any of you know Sir Roger Colby?" the king asked. "Could you recognize him if you saw him?"

Both the earl and his brother shook their heads in the negative.

"Then, Hercules, you must ride to Duffdour, and as Armstrong has not already killed this Englishman, Ellen MacArthur must return with you to court, for she will be able to identify the assassin easily," the king said.

Hercules Hepburn looked uncomfortable at the king's request. "My lord, the lady has not been home in several months. She has a young bairn."

"Aye, my bonny will not be pleased that I take her from her border nest, but she will come, Hercules. She is like a sister to me, and she will not see me harmed if she can help. When she protests—and she will—tell her that I need her as she once needed me," James Stewart said. Then he smiled to himself. Ellen would be irritated by those words, for he knew better than any that she did not need to be reminded of her debt to him and would gladly pay it a hundred times over. Still, those words would save his Hepburn friend from a long and futile outburst.

And they did when Hercules Hepburn uttered them to an angry Ellen at Duffdour several days later.

"He said *that*?" she demanded to know from the unhappy messenger. "He actually said just those words, Hercules?" Her look was grim.

"Aye, lady, he did," the big man replied nervously. This wee lass was actually making him very nervous as she paced up and down before her hearth, her skirts swaying and swirling about her ankles. "The king said it. I am to wait and escort you to Sterling."

"This will be the last time," Ellen said darkly. "The debt will now be paid in full," she muttered almost to herself. "I am tired of being dragged from pillar to post by men playing games! Gunna!" she shouted. "Pack a trunk. We are going to court."

"Now, dinna ye fret, my dearie," old Peigi said. "We'll look after the bairn."

"William is coming with me," Ellen said in a fiercely determined voice. "I am barely home to a bairn who doesn't know who the hell I am. I will not leave my son again. If the king will have me at court, then he will have my bairn too! Have Laria pack what she will need for herself and for Willie."

Duncan Armstrong hid a small smile. "I'll come too," he said quietly.

"You most certainly will," Ellen told her husband. "I'll not be left without your good company and your protection, my lord. Settle yourself down, Hercules Hepburn, for it will be at least two days before I am ready to travel." Ellen turned to her husband. "Send a message to the king at Sterling that we are coming *en famille*, and I will expect that we are given accommodations that suit. I do not care that we are not a great name, or important. We are important to James Stewart's safety, and until that is assured I will expect to be housed comfortably."

Now Hercules Hepburn began to grin. He was more than aware of how tight housing was at court, and especially now, with Katherine Gordon and her *royal* husband taking up space. He wondered who would be pushed out to make room for the Armstrongs of Duffdour, *en famille*. But he said nothing, instead settling in to enjoy the warm hospitality of Duffdour. And while he did he told the hall of what the king had been up to these last months, for news was slow in coming to Duffdour.

In the early autumn after the harvest had been gathered, King James, in the company of his earls and the young man who claimed to be King Richard IV, crossed the Tweed into England from the eastern borders. The *true* king had been assured by the Yorkists in exile that the English would flock out to his banner to greet him, to welcome him. Together they would then march south to displace the Tudor usurper.

But the invaders found an empty countryside, Hercules told them. The populace had fled to the stone towers built by their local lords to shelter everyone during such an attack. People and animals, the local harvest, the hay—all had been sheltered. Under ordinary circumstances the towers would have sufficed. But this Scots army brought with them siege guns, which, when fired, brought the towers tumbling down, and the people and animals streaming out in terror. The stock was driven off, the defenders slaughtered. It was at that point that England's *true* king protested the killing of *his* people, and decamped with his followers back to Edinburgh to rejoin his wife. The listeners in the hall hissed with their disapproval.

"And so our attempt to put a friendly Englishman on England's throne became nothing more than a large-scale border raid," Hercules Hepburn said. "And, of course, I fear we disappointed the *true* king very much by taking whatever we could lay our hands on in stock, hay, and grain and decamping back to our own homes. But what did he expect? 'Tis the way of the borderers in both camps, though, isn't it?"

There was much nodding and agreeing in the hall.

"And while your good lord was seeking his wife, the king and his friend, the Spanish ambassador, came into the borders once again to make certain we were all fortified, for certainly King Henry will eventually retaliate for this incursion into his lands. But the worst was yet to come for our poor king." Hercules chuckled. "He has been forced since his return to listen to the nattering of Katherine Gordon extolling the virtues of her husband's compassion for *his* subjects."

The listeners in the hall laughed along with the big man at this.

"Katherine Gordon is overproud for my taste," Ellen noted. "She always put herself above the other girls in the lady Margaret's household. I cannot say I particularly liked her. Although we are both of the Highlands, she spoke of those of us in the more western regions as if we were savages. Thinking that she is queen of England cannot have made her any better."

Hercules Hepburn grinned. "Aye, she is prouder now than before, believing her rank improved. Well, you need have nothing to do with her if you choose. I'm sure the king's aunt will be happy to see you again. She's a grand lady. And she will certainly make certain that you have a comfortable place to lay your heads," he assured Ellen.

And when they arrived at court a week later Hercules learned that his brother, Patrick Hepburn, the Earl of Bothwell, had made the sacrifice, giving up his own apartment to the Armstrongs. And the king was almost meek when Ellen found him in his privy chamber shortly after settling her family upon their arrival. He had warned his personal guard that she would seek him out, and they gave way as the petite whirlwind stormed past them into the royal presence.

"My bonny," he greeted her warmly. "I have looked forward to your arrival."

"Do not 'my bonny' me, Jamie Stewart!" Ellen replied, not in the least mollified by his familiar term of endearment.

"Your apartment is satisfactory?" the king continued, ignoring her outrage.

"Was there no one else in all the world but me to identify Roger Colby?" she demanded. "I was held by him for over three months, and only a miracle led to my escape. I was but barely home, and my bairn wailing at the sight of me, for I am a stranger to him. Now you must call me to court?" She was flushed and breathless with her ire.

The king thought her extremely pretty in her anger. "Sit down, my bonny, and we will speak on it. You have brought the bairn with you, have you not? He'll know you soon enough, and will love you as we all do."

"My lord, do you really think me such a fool as to be cozened by your words?" Ellen sat down in a high-backed tapestry chair by the blazing hearth, holding her hands to the flame, for they were cold. She could hear the wind rising outside of the windows.

"Ellen MacArthur, my sweet sister—for I do think of you as such," the king began, and his voice was sincere, "we all know Sir Roger's reputation, but only you have had a long acquaintance with him, can pick him out of a crowd, can cry, 'There's the assassin!' "

"The border lords all know Johnston," she countered.

"And because they do it is unlikely Johnston will be with him when he attempts his assault on my person," the king replied. "Only you know Roger Colby's face."

Ellen sighed. "Aye, I do. I will never forget it," she

said. "But surely this Englishman cannot just boldly come into your court, my lord."

"He will come disguised, of course, and not as an Englishman," the king responded. "He could gain entry with some young lordling who has lost to him dicing, and allows him to accompany him as a means of repaying the debt. There are some, my bonny, who consider coming to my court to be a treat." The king grinned engagingly at her, and Ellen was forced to laugh. It pleased him to see her mood lightening.

"He might even come as someone of lowly stature," Ellen said thoughtfully. "I know that is what I would do. You do not pay a great deal of attention to your servants, my lord. I will wager you do not even know most of their names."

"I do know the faces of those who serve me," the king answered her, "but you are correct, my bonny. I must speak with my household steward and have him be extra vigilant of any new varlets he might employ. The castle will be filled to capacity during the Twelve Days of Christmas."

"This is a very dangerous man, my lord," Ellen said. "He wants only to be in King Henry's favor again. He will do whatever he must to attain that goal. I beg that you not underestimate Sir Roger, nor allow those about you to do so."

"Did he harm you?" James Stewart asked her.

"Nay," Ellen said.

She replied perhaps a bit too quickly, the king thought to himself, but he did not press her. He had not the right, and whatever she had said to her husband, it had not changed Duncan Armstrong's devotion to Ellen MacArthur, the king saw in the days that followed. The border lord loved his wife unquestioningly and with all his heart.

December brought a host of feast days all leading up to Christmas Day itself. While she truly wished she were back at Duffdour, Ellen had to admit that Christmastide at Sterling was quite enjoyable. As long as the weather was good they hunted during the day. In bad weather the great hall of Sterling Castle was filled with the king's guests, all gossiping, playing games, and eating. Most evenings there was feasting and dancing in the great hall. It was a beautiful chamber, Ellen thought.

It had been the much maligned king, James III, the present king's father, who had seen to the building of the hall. It had five great fireplaces. The walls, in an opulent rich lime yellow known as King's Gold, were much admired by all who came to Sterling. The graceful tall stained-glass windows were decorated; the sun shining through them on an early winter's afternoon reflected their colors on the floors. There was a large hearth behind the high board with a great Yule log burning merrily. The other four hearths burned brightly too. James IV was sending out ambassadors to various countries. His court was also receiving ambassadors. Many languages could be heard being spoken in Sterling Castle's great hall on any night. French. German. Italian. Spanish. Gaelic. Latin.

The gossip was rife this Christmastide, for the laird of Duffdour's wife seemed always to be near the king. Lady Margaret Stewart, the king's aunt, told anyone who would listen that her nephew was very fond of Mistress Ellen. "She is like a sister to him," the princess said. "Do you not remember before her marriage how she was his favorite chess partner?" Margaret Stewart reminded them. "And 'tis he who matched her with Duffdour. The poor lass was held captive by the English recently, and the king rewards her bravery by bringing her to court for a visit."

The court listened to the princess's explanation, and then could not decide what to think. There seemed to be nothing more than genuine familial affection between the king and Ellen MacArthur. Her husband was always in sight, as was the king's current mistress, the adorable Meg Drummond. And yet . . . perhaps the king was tiring of the Drummond girl, some thought meanly. Nay, others said. Meg Drummond was with child, and it was obvious that the king loved her. There was even talk of making her his queen, and why not? Two Drummond women had been queens of Scotland in the past. Why not a third? Surely a good Scotswoman as opposed to some foreigner.

On Twelfth Night the king was to hold a costume gala in Sterling's great hall.

"A costume gala?" Ellen said despairingly. "Our own clothing is poor stuff compared to what other folk wear. What are we to do? Since I must be there I shall have to wear a costume, Duncan."

"Go and speak with the king's aunt," her husband advised.

"Aye," Ellen agreed. "Lady Margaret will know what we should do."

The king's aunt suggested that the Armstrongs of Duffdour go as ancient Greeks. "White material," she said. "Simple. No fuss. My maids and I shall help you make the costumes. Duncan shall wear a short tunic, for he does have fine legs," the princess noted, and her maids giggled. "And you shall wear a Doric chiton. Come along," Lady Margaret said briskly, standing up. "We shall take this opportunity to raid the storerooms." And with her maids and Ellen hurrying after her, she moved off.

In the storerooms at Sterling Castle they found exactly what they were looking for, and quickly snatched the fabric up, carrying it off back to the Lady Margaret's apartments. It was a fine light white wool. After measuring Ellen, the princess sent her off, for she was one of the few people who knew why the laird of Duffdour's wife was at court. When Ellen had gone, she sent for the laird so he might be measured.

On Twelfth Night the laird of Duffdour and his lady

entered the great hall at Sterling to find themselves surrounded by all manner of folk in all manner of garb. Duncan Armstrong wore a short-sleeved white wool tunic
that came to just above his knees. Its neckline was round
and decorated with a black-and-white dentil band that
was repeated down the shoulder and around the sleeve,
as well as at the hem of the tunic. A silver ribbon was
tied about his dark head. On his feet he wore sandals,
a great inconvenience, as a draft ran across the floor of
the hall, chilling his legs and his feet. Ellen was dressed
in a Doric chiton; the upper part of the garment, which
was bloused, was called a kolpos. The chiton fastened
at the shoulders with ribbon ties, and was decorated at
the bustline, the edge of the kolpos, and the hem of the
chiton with a delicate design of tiny purple spheres. Her
red-gold hair was caught up in a gold caul, and she wore
gold sandals upon her feet. Their costumes were simple
compared to those about them.

The king was dressed like one of his ancestors, with
a rough wool plaid about his loins, a bare chest, a round
leather shield studded with brass nails, and an ash wood
spear with an iron spear point. The Spanish ambassador, Don Pedro de Ayala, stood next to him, dressed as
a Moorish lord in a long, colorful striped silk robe and a
gold turban with a great red jewel in its center.

"Surely it isn't real." Ellen gasped when she saw it,
but the gem did sparkle brightly as Don Pedro turned
his head to smile at her.

" 'Tis paste, lady," he told her, and he again smiled his
charming smile.

Ellen looked out over the hall at all the excitement
and color the gala was producing. " 'Tis amazing, my
lord. Beautiful, wicked, and perhaps a little dangerous."

"For some, my bonny, it will be dangerous," he said.

"This would be a perfect night for the attempt," the
Earl of Bothwell murmured. He had dressed himself in
a long dark-colored gown decorated with stars, comets,

and moons. "I am Merlin, the sorcerer," he told them. "It is my duty to keep the king safe."

They sat down to a great feast that night. Sides of beef had been packed in rock salt and roasted over open pits until their sizzling juices caused the red coals to leap with every drop escaping from the meat. There were great barrels of oysters packed in ice and snow that had come from the coast. There was venison, and ducks toasted black on platters and swimming in a sweet sauce of plums and cinnamon. Whole salmon and trout, mussels and sea scallops were presented. There were chargers holding artichokes steamed in wine. Bowls of vegetable pottage. Capons, and pies filled with rabbit and small birds. There had been baked great round loaves of bread to be placed upon each table, and at each place there were good-size bread trenchers to hold generous amounts of food. Large wheels of cheese, both hard and soft, were put out. Crocks of butter and small dishes of salt were placed in the center of each table below the high board. There was ale and wine readily available. Ellen and her husband were seated at the far end of the high board, as they were the king's personal guests.

As the meal was coming to an end, sugared wafers and a carafe of a sweet Spanish wine Don Pedro had brought for the enjoyment of the king and his guests at the high board were brought forth by one of the ambassador's servants, who was garbed as a dark-skinned Moor. As he bent to pour the liquid into Ellen's cup she caught his eye. The man stiffened, but continued pouring. When he had finished he stepped back. Don Pedro arose to make a toast.

"No!" Ellen cried, jumping to her feet. "Wait!" She picked up her cup and, handing it to the servant who had poured the liquid said, "Drink!"

The fellow shook his head, but said nothing.

"Drink it!" Ellen commanded.

"Señora," the man said, and then he shrugged.

"My servants do not speak your tongue," Don Pedro said. "What is wrong, my lady? How has my servant offended you?"

"He is not your servant, my lord ambassador," Ellen said. "He is Ian Johnston, and the wine he has poured I believe is poisoned. He would have killed all at the high board in order to kill the king. Where is your master, you traitorous coward?"

"Seize him!" the king called as the man made to bolt.

Several men caught hold of Ian Johnston as he sought to jump from the dais.

Don Pedro Ayala went over to the man and looked at him closely. He ran a finger down his face, looking at the brown stain it gathered. "He is not one of my servants, but where, then, is my servant?"

Duncan Armstrong arose and stood before Ian Johnston. "Where is Colby?"

"I'll never tell you! Any of you!" Ian Johnston said. "Why should I? You cast me out. Drove my wife to the grave. Cost me my son! I'll tell you nothing!"

"You're mad, Ian. 'Twas you who betrayed your fellow border lords," the laird of Duffdour said. "You beat your wife to death. And 'twas Colby whose raid caused your wife to miscarry. Yet you aligned yourself with him and betrayed your own country and king. Now you would involve yourself in a plot to kill that king?"

"He had her, you know," Ian Johnston sneered. "Did you know that, Armstrong? Did you? Colby told me himself!"

"You are a liar," Ellen said in a cold, hard voice.

"Am I?" Johnston said, and he smiled at her. "Will you swear on God's name that you returned to your husband as you left him?"

"Aye, I will!" Ellen answered, her voice strong. Duncan would not be hurt by Ian Johnston's words; nor would his name be besmirched by the villain's lies. "Let God and his Blessed Mother bear witness to my words. I was not shamed or used by Sir Roger Colby. The only man I have ever known is my husband, Duncan Armstrong!"

"I think you have shamed the lady," Don Pedro said softly. "I think you must die."

"Aye," the king agreed. "But if you tell us where Sir Roger is perhaps we will spare your life, Ian Johnston."

"Never!" Johnston said, and he spit at the king's feet. *"Never!"*

"Then you have chosen your own fate," James Stewart said. "As I have better things on which to spend my coin, we shall save the cost of the hangman and the rope. Give him one of the goblets to drink. He shall die as he meant me to die."

At that very moment Ian Johnston broke free of his captors and, jumping down from the dais, tried to escape the hall. But the great chamber was crowded with trestles, benches, and courtiers. He had barely begun to push his way through them all when Hercules Hepburn with a roar leaped up from a table below the high board and tackled the man, wrestling him down onto one of the trestles, which was swept clean of its cups and trenchers by the two men.

"Shall I break his neck, my lord?" he called to the king.

"Nay, but secure him, Hercules, for he is about to have his last cup of wine," James Stewart said.

Several men now came forward to hold Ian Johnston down upon the trestle top. They pinioned his arms and his legs so he could not move. The captive spewed curses upon all about him in his terrified rage. Now Don Pedro de Ayala stepped down from the high board, a cup of the poisoned wine in one hand. He walked slowly to where the captive now lay helpless, yet still full of fight.

"I have just been told that my servant has been murdered," he said. "Since you are wearing his costume I must assume 'twas you who killed him. It is therefore my right to have revenge. Hercules Hepburn, if you will pinch his jaws open for me," the Spanish ambassador said in a soft voice.

"Immediately, my lord," came the reply, and Hercules' big hand forced open Ian Johnston's mouth.

Johnston attempted to struggle further against his captors, turning his head this way and that. He fought to close his mouth, but Hepburn's hold on it was strong. Johnston's eyes were filled with fear, and a stench arose from him as he soiled himself.

Don Pedro smiled a slow, cruel smile. Then he crossed himself, and without another word began pouring the contents of the goblet he held into Ian Johnston's mouth. His other hand had reached out to pinch the man's nostrils shut so he had no choice but to gulp down the dark red wine if he were to breathe at all. When the first goblet had been emptied, the Spanish ambassador snapped his fingers, and a servant put a second goblet into his hand. He began to empty that one as well down the helpless man's throat. When he had almost finished, Ian Johnston's body began to convulse.

The men holding him released him, and their victim began to scream in great pain as the poison ate at his guts. He rolled off the trestle and onto the floor, howling. His body curled itself into a fetal position. Those about him backed away in horror from the traitor in his dying throes. And then, with a fierce shudder and a loud cry, Ian Johnston died.

Watching from the high board, Ellen kept her face stony. She shed not a tear, although several women in the hall were now suffering hysterics. What did they know? she thought coldly. Ian Johnston had attempted to destroy her. To destroy her marriage. To destroy Duncan. He was a vicious man who had killed his own wife by beating her to death. He deserved the death he had just suffered. He was every bit as bad as Sir Roger Colby, and she was glad he was dead. She hoped he would rot in hell for eternity.

Don Pedro returned to the high board. "Your honor

is now restored, madam," he told her quietly. He took up her hand and kissed it.

"Thank you, my lord," Ellen told him. "But in truth, honor that has not been lost cannot be impugned, even by a villain."

The Spanish ambassador bowed and smiled his charming smile. "I admire your strength, señora. I can see you are not a woman to be trifled with, and I envy your husband for having such a strong wife."

Ellen gave him a little smile. "You flatter me, my lord." Then she turned to the king. "But we have not yet caught Colby."

"We will another day, my bonny," he told her. "You have saved my life this night. All of our lives at this board. We owe you a great debt of gratitude."

"Oh, yes, we do!" Katherine Gordon cried. "What if you had not recognized the assassin? This is surely a plot by Henry Tudor, that foul usurper, to kill my beloved husband, England's true king. But next year we will march into England and throw him from his hollow throne, won't we, cousin James?"

"Indeed, cousin, we will," the king replied. *If for no other reason than to end this so I do not have to keep supporting you and that coward to whom you're wed,* James Stewart thought. *If we succeed, then I have a friendly English king to the south. If we fail, the king now on the throne will make peace, for he cannot afford a serious war any more than Scotland can. Either way I win. But this time, Richard of England, you will not leave me because you cannot bear the sight of Englishmen being killed. Perhaps if Henry Tudor knew as you have now learned what misery a border war entails, he would be more willing to make a real peace with me. Well, one way or another I shall have that peace by this time next year.* He turned to Ellen. "I would reward you."

"Then let us fortify Duffdour even more," Ellen said. "And let Cleit be fortified, for surely the English will come at us again next spring."

"Agreed," James Stewart said. "And I shall pay for these new fortifications. Now, take that cur's body from the hall and bury it in unhallowed ground. I think we have eaten and drunk and been entertained enough for one evening. This is one Twelfth Night you shall not forget. Go home or find your beds, all of you!" Then, taking his lovely mistress, Meg Drummond, by the hand, the king walked from the hall.

Ellen turned to her husband. "We still can't go home," she said despairingly, reaching for his hand.

"Aye, you must remain, but I cannot stay any longer from Duffdour," Duncan told her. "Thank you for gaining us further fortifications, and the means to build them."

They walked from the hall and to their apartment. Laria, Machara, Willie's wet nurse, and the baby were nowhere in sight. Ellen waved Gunna away as her tiring woman came forward. An icy hand was gripping her heart. "You would leave me?" she asked him quietly.

"I cannot remain with the court," he said. "It's January, and I must begin the business of reinforcing Duffdour's defenses before the spring comes. And I must stop at Cleit to tell Conal he can also build up his defenses. Thanks to that cowardly fraud the king is using to bring King Henry to reason, the borders will be aflame come spring. To whom can I delegate such authority for what must be done? I am no great lord with servants at his beck and call. I am the laird of Duffdour. The responsibility for it, for its people, is all mine," Duncan Armstrong said.

"You would leave me," Ellen repeated bleakly.

He sighed. "I know you cannot come home, wife, until Sir Roger has revealed himself so the king may be safe. But I cannot sit here and wait for the bastard."

"Ian Johnston's words have given you pause for thought," Ellen said candidly. "You were eager enough a few weeks ago to slay Colby yourself. Why suddenly are you no longer interested in such a venture? You think me not worthy of your revenge, Duncan? Perhaps you would prefer I remain at court and not return to Duff-dour at all," she cried. She was suddenly frightened. Was she losing him?

"Nay, that is not so! I want you home, wife, but you must remain with the king until Colby is caught and slain!" He put his arms about her, drawing Ellen close, but she was stiff and cold in his arms. "Come, sweeting, do not be angry at me." He pulled the caul from her head and let her long red-gold hair flow loose as he slid his hand up to cup her head in his palm.

"I don't want you to go, husband," Ellen said, low.

"I have to, and you know I do, wife. The English will come for me, for Duffdour, you may be certain, for it is known that I am the one who broke the back of Sir Roger's troops last spring. If I can get the walls higher we should be safe," he told her.

Ellen began to cry. She knew he spoke truth to her. He had to return to Duffdour.

The laird took his wife's small face between his hands and kissed her tears away. "Don't weep, wife," he pleaded with her, but his gentle words only made her cry all the harder. Finally Duncan Armstrong did what most men madly in love with their wives would do in such a situation: He decided to make love to her.

Taking her hand, he drew her into their bedchamber and down onto the bed. His hands pulled away the top of her simple costume, baring her breasts to him. He caressed them tenderly, and then began to cover them with kisses. Ellen sighed, her sadness easing with his gentle touch. His mouth closed over a nipple, and she sighed again. He tugged on the sentient flesh, and she murmured, low. His teeth delicately grazed the skin, and then he moved to do homage to her other nipple.

"Oh, that is so nice," Ellen whispered. Her fingers began stroking the nape of his neck. His dark hair was shaggy and needed to be cut, she thought as her hand played with it.

He pushed her skirts up, and the dark head began a slow journey down her torso as Ellen drew her breath in sharply. There had hardly been a moment to make love since her return from England, and the truth was, she was yet nervous. Oh, they had coupled several times, but it had been a hurried thing, more for his pleasure than hers. Yet now he was taking his time and truly making love to her. The kissing, the touching she had admitted to Duncan, but he'd never know the pain she still felt, or the fear she had that she might not escape. Some things were better left unsaid.

Ellen pushed her unhappy thoughts from her and concentrated upon the man whose warm lips and tongue were now caressing her skin. "Wait," she said softly, and when he lifted his head she pushed the skirts of her costume off and onto the floor. "Now you, my lord, for while your tunic is short, I prefer the feel of your flesh against mine."

He complied, and then, sliding between her legs, he began to kiss her hungrily, his hands holding her head between them, his lips scorching hers, his tongue dueling with hers within the warm cavern of her mouth. Ellen stretched beneath him, murmuring as her hands smoothed over his shoulders and down his back. The feel of his smooth, warm chest crushing her breasts left her weak with her longing for him.

Duncan felt her trembling beneath him. Was it fear? Was it her natural excitement when they made love? Why did Ian Johnston's wicked words keep echoing in his head? *He had her!* The words burned, and yet Ellen had denied that Colby had raped her. She had admitted to his kisses, his obscene touches, but she had insisted there had been no rape. And he had believed her. Until tonight, when a condemned man had accused her. Did a man facing imminent death lie? He wasn't certain.

"What is it?" Ellen asked him, suddenly aware that his thoughts had turned elsewhere.

"Why did Johnston say Colby raped you?" Duncan

said, knowing even as the words left his mouth that he was making a mistake. He rolled onto his side. Why was he questioning her about this? What the hell was the matter with him?

"Perhaps he said it because he had been caught, and was about to die," Ellen suggested calmly. "Some men, when they face death, confess to their faults, their sins. Others are angry that death has caught up to them, and want to strike out and hurt anyone they can. Ian Johnston was not a man to admit to his faults. He murdered his own wife and then lied about it. He knows we are happy in our marriage, husband. And so he reaches out to hurt us as death claims him. When Sir Roger made plain his intent to make me his mistress, Johnston boldly asked if he would share me. God forgive him for what he said tonight. God forgive you for the doubts regarding my chastity that it has raised in your mind and heart, Duncan."

He gathered her into his arms. "I am sorry," he told her, "but the truth is, his cruel words raised such pictures in my mind that are difficult to get out."

"Make love to me," Ellen said to him.

"What?" He looked surprised.

"Make love to me," she repeated. "Let us wipe away those horrid words, and make dreams for you to dream when we are apart," Ellen tempted him. Leaning over him, she bent and kissed the nipples of his chest. Then she began to lick him. If it took every ounce of her strength she would destroy those evil pictures Ian Johnston had drawn and placed in Duncan's mind and heart. She brushed his lean naked body with her long red-gold hair. It was soft and perfumed, and his eyes closed as he enjoyed the sensation of her budding passion. Her tongue licked over his torso, swirling about his belly with slow, leisurely strokes. He exhaled in a long, soft hiss as her head moved lower, and he felt her press a hot kiss through the thick mat of pubic hair covering his mons.

"Take me in your mouth," he begged her. He had

taught her that delightful diversion right after William had been born. She had been surer of herself then, and had been growing bolder with their lovemaking.

Ellen laughed, low, and, taking his manhood between her thumb and her forefinger, lifted it up as if to inspect it. She then licked his length from tip to root several times. He moaned with his open pleasure, and grew slightly firmer beneath her skillful tongue. But then she took him into her mouth, drawing upon him until she was close to swallowing him. Duncan groaned, and she began to suckle upon him. When his cock had grown hard and throbbed within her mouth, Ellen released it and, climbing upon her husband's body, she sheathed him within her own.

Duncan reached up to fondle her round breasts as Ellen rode him hard. Leaning forward, she kissed him a fiery kiss; then she licked his face and nipped at his ears. Faster and faster she moved upon him, and he howled as he reached his peak, but though he flooded her with his love juices he remained hard within her. Opening his eyes, he let his gaze meet hers.

"You, husband, are the only man whose cock I have entertained," she told him. "If you ever suggest otherwise again I shall leave you, Duncan. Do you understand me?"

In response he rolled her over and began fucking her deep and hard. She had not lost her equilibrium when he first had, but now he made certain that she did. "I understand, wife!" he told her as he reamed her fiercely. And Ellen felt herself soaring in a heaven of pleasure as he brought them both to sweet fulfillment. And afterward they slept entwined in each other's arms. They were sated, and if either of them had any fears, those fears had been calmed, at least for the interim.

When the winter morning came, Duncan Armstrong arose and prepared to leave Sterling for Duffdour. He left two of his men with Ellen for her personal protection, but the rest of his clansmen would ride home with him. An hour after sunrise he bade his wife, their bairn, and their servants farewell. Then, kissing Ellen and swearing his love a final time, he rode out from Sterling Castle, south and west for Duffdour.

After the Mass that morning Ellen spoke with the king in his privy chamber, asking that he forgive the laird for departing without giving his lord a formal farewell.

"Nay, my bonny, I expected last night that he would go quickly. We cannot trust the weather at this time of year, and he has a two-day or longer ride home, and much to do when he gets there. How high are your walls?"

"Ten feet, my lord," Ellen said, "but Duncan says he will raise them to fifteen or more during the winter. There was some stone left over, and the quarry is nearby. The cold will not deter them. Only the snows."

"I am sorry, my bonny, that you could not leave with your man, but as you said last night, Colby is not yet caught," James Stewart replied.

"He will go to ground for a short while, I think," Ellen told the king. "He has lost his ally in their failed attempt to poison you. He is a clever man, and will consider carefully before trying again. But try he will, I fear."

"I know," James Stewart said. "And King Henry will wait to see if his man is successful before he brings his armies into play against us. He would have come last autumn following our debacle into England had not some of his own subjects objected." He chuckled. "It would seem that we kings are much alike, and our subjects too."

"What happened?" Ellen asked.

"The Cornish objected to being taxed to pay for a war on England's northern frontier. You see, they are at the farthest southern end of England. A rather large group of Cornishmen marched all the way up to London, forcing Henry Tudor to do battle with his own subjects instead of mine. I lit many candles to Saint Ninian in thanks, my bonny," the king told her with another chuckle. "But the English king would have a truce of me. He would have me turn over King Richard the Fourth to him, but I have refused. As much as I would enjoy ridding myself of my guest, it would be dishonorable to do such a thing. Now it is suggested that I go to London to negotiate personally with Henry Tudor. I shall not, however, for sooner or later any visit I make to London will be called an act of homage, and I shall be called a vassal of the English. I will not meet any king of England except on our common border, but what am I to do with Katherine Gordon and her husband?"

"Why not offer him an earldom here?" Ellen suggested to the king. "You know what Adair Radcliffe has told you, and you know she does not lie. You have had your use of this Yorkist pretender, whoever he is, my lord. And he has cost you a pretty penny, I have not a doubt. He will never be king of England, whatever he may believe, and we both know it. Give him a Scots title. It would make the Gordons of Huntley happy, for it would mean their daughter would remain in Scotland."

"And I should have to spend the rest of my days listening to her natter about all of her Richard's virtues," the king said with a small smile. "But 'tis a clever solution to a thorny problem, my bonny. You are wise, my little Highland lass. How did you become so skilled as to offer such a good answer to my difficulties? My advisers are not so useful in the matter as you have been."

"You forget, my good lord, that I have lived at court on and off for the last few years. I do not concern myself with gossip, lovers, or fashion, but I do listen. And few, if any, pay attention to me, for most men do not believe women can understand the difficult tasks of politics and government," Ellen told James Stewart, "but I do. And of course, common sense, of which women have far more than men, plays a part in it too."

He laughed. "I do not think Duncan Armstrong knows the wife he has been fortunate enough to gain, my bonny. I think he owes me a great debt for matching you with him." Then the king grew serious. "Did Johnston's words distress him? I saw how pale you grew with them, and how disturbed he became when he heard them."

"Aye, he was harmed by them, to be sure," Ellen admitted. "But he also knows I do not lie. Roger Colby did not rape me, my lord. He kissed me. He fondled me, and indeed he had every intention of having me as his mistress, but he failed in that, because he allowed his pride to get the better of him."

"And you escaped," the king said. "It was said you crossed the mudflats of the Solway when the tide was out."

"I did, but not because I was clever, and I was almost drowned in the attempt," Ellen admitted to him. "I tricked Colby into releasing me in order to hunt me down like some animal. He was so certain he could that he escorted me outside of his castle himself and let me go. What he was not cognizant of was that I hunted with my grandsire as a girl in the Highlands. I knew enough to take to the water so his dogs could not track me. And his sergeant had told me the castle sat not quite on the Irish Sea, but on the Solway. And to my good fortune it was at the far end of the firth. What I did not know was that the tide was about to reenter the firth. Actually, having been raised in the Highlands, I knew nothing about tidal rivers. I reached the narrowest part of it, no more than a mile wide in distance, and, seeing Scotland across the mudflats, I ran across as fast as I could. I was almost to the other side when I heard this mighty roar and saw the waters spilling forth from the sea. A group of monks on the shore observed me, and one of them came to help me. We swam the last yards to the beach, and without Brother Griogair I should have drowned. 'Twas God's own luck, my lord, that I escaped unscathed."

"Amazing!" James Stewart said to her. "I had not heard the entire tale, just that you had managed to get away. I believe it is fate that put you in my hands, Ellen MacArthur. You know I have the eye and often

see things others do not. I now think you were meant
to be captured by Sir Roger so that when the day came
you would be able to identify him and save my life. You
saved it last night when you recognized Ian Johnston beneath that walnut stain he used to impersonate a Moorish slave."

"If it please you, my lord, I should rather Roger Colby
never existed at all," Ellen told the king, "but I will stay
with you until he can be caught and executed. You saved
me from a horrid fate, Jamie Stewart, and I owe you a
debt. But after this we are quits, my lord. Can you understand that?" She looked directly at him.

The king smiled at her. "Aye," he said, "I can, and I
agree, my bonny. After this your debt to me is indeed
paid in full, for you will have saved my life twice."

"Good!" Ellen told him. "For I cannot be the kind of
wife that Duncan Armstrong deserves if I cannot be at
Duffdour. And our son needs to be there, as it will one
day be his to care for and protect."

"You love him very much, don't you, my bonny?"
James Stewart said.

Ellen nodded. "Aye, my lord, I do."

At the end of January they departed Sterling Castle for
Linlithgow, where they would remain the rest of the
winter. Although Ellen found the king's mistress, Meg
Drummond, charming, she preferred the company of
the king's aunt. And then too there was her son, wee
Willie, who now, to her delight, knew his mother well.
His little face would light up as she came into his view,
and he would hold his arms out to her to be picked up,
which Ellen always did. He was looking more like his
father with each passing day, and Ellen missed her husband greatly. Although she wrote to him, he had not the
time to write to her.

But the only thing Duncan Armstrong wanted to
hear was that his wife was coming home soon. Had he
not been busy adding to the walls of Duffdour, he might

have gone hunting for Sir Roger Colby himself. And then in late winter the laird of Duffdour learned that someone had been living at Devil's Glen in the past few weeks. He sent to Linlithgow to inform the king. James Stewart came with all possible haste, and to the laird's delight he brought Ellen with him.

Chapter 16

*E*llen flew into her husband's arms, kissing him, receiving his kisses, and the king laughed heartily. "What, Duffdour, have you missed the wench?" he teased the laird.

His arm about his wife's supple waist, Duncan Armstrong admitted, "Well, perhaps a wee bit, my lord."

"She's a good lass," the king replied. "I hope we'll be able to end this problem so she will not have to return with me to Linlithgow."

"Aye," the laird said. "I would like that. Duffdour is not quite the same without its mistress." He nodded almost imperceptibly to Sim, and the servants brought wine to the king and his small party. And while they were thus diverted Duncan Armstrong turned to his wife. "The bairn?" he asked her.

"At Linlithgow, husband," Ellen told him. "I did not want to take the chance of bringing him, only to have to go back. Machara and Laria will take good care of him. I brought Gunna home with me. If we kill Colby I can send for them. If we don't, and I must return with the king, it is easier on the bairn. Besides, we traveled quickly, and the pace would have been too difficult for him and his nurses."

"I've missed you both," the laird said.

"And I you," Ellen returned. "You should see our son, Duncan! He looks just like you, but he does indeed have my red hair, and a temper to match it." She laughed. "But, oh, he can be so charming when he is getting his own way. Even the princess adores him, as do all the ladies at court. She says he will one day break many hearts. With all his admirers he has become quite spoiled, I fear."

"Coming home to Duffdour will be quite a change for him then," the laird said.

"He'll adjust," Ellen assured her husband. "He is, after all, quite wee, and is actually very good-natured. There will be other things here that will catch his attention, like the dogs in the hall, the cats in the barns, the horses, the sheep and cattle. Willie is a very bright little fellow, husband. He doesn't just look like you. I can see he has your intelligence when he grows quiet, and you can see he is considering something."

"You put a great deal on a young bairn, wife," the laird said. "He will not be a year until the end of this month."

"You do not know him!" Ellen defended her child.

"Nay, I do not, for my wife has been at court these past months, and my son with her," Duncan Armstrong replied tartly.

There it was again, Ellen thought. That suspicious tone in his voice.

"May I remind you that I have not been at court by choice," Ellen answered him spiritedly in equally low tones. "I am not a great name, nor the wife of a man with a great name. I have no wealth. I must live at the mercy of the powerful, little better than a servant, husband. I am barely noticed or even spoken to by the women of important families. Only my small connection with the king and his aunt prevents me from being entirely ignored. Do you think I prefer such a life to being in my own home, where I am mistress of all? Where I am respected?" There were tears in her eyes. Ellen stamped her foot at him angrily, causing the others in the hall to turn curiously.

"What is this, my bonny," the king wanted to know. "You are scarce home, and you are quarreling with the man?"

"My foot fell asleep, my lord," Ellen said. "I was merely stamping it to waken it."

"I see," James Stewart said, and his eyes were twinkling. He turned to the laird. "Now, my lord, tell me when we will ride out to run this English fox to ground."

"As the day is almost done, my lord, and 'tis moondark tonight, I thought we might go foxhunting on the morrow," Duncan Armstrong said.

"Excellent!" the king responded enthusiastically. "I long to meet this man who would kill me in order to regain the favor of his king. Not that Henry Tudor would admit to even suggesting such a thing. Nor would I, were our positions reversed."

While the men spoke Ellen had slipped from the hall and gone down into the kitchens to make certain the meal about to be served would suffice. The king had sent a messenger ahead of them who had arrived several hours before the royal party to warn the laird of their arrival, and how many would need to be fed. Ellen found her kitchen bustling, with fires roaring in the two hearths, pots steaming, and the smell of bread baking. The cook, a tall, thin woman, hurried to greet her mistress, curtsying.

"I can see you have everything well in hand, Lizzie," Ellen said, smiling.

"Welcome home, my lady!" the cook greeted her. "Aye, I think we will manage, though it be early spring and the larder scant. You'll not be shamed at the high board, I promise you, and below the board there will be plenty of good venison stew, bread, cheese, and ale for all. How long will we need to feed this lot?"

"Probably several days," Ellen replied. "Perhaps we can send some of the men fishing to help add to our supplies. And rabbits are always in good supply."

"Aye," the cook agreed. "We will manage, my lady."

"I know I can depend upon you, Lizzie," Ellen told the cook. She looked about the kitchen. "And the rest of you as well. I tell you that at court the servants cannot hold a candle to those of you at Duffdour. Thank you." Then Ellen left the kitchens to return upstairs to the hall and her guests.

"The house will be better for her return, and the laird too," the cook said to her staff, and they all nodded. It had been a long, dark, and dour winter with the laird more days than not silently eating a hot meal alone down in the kitchen at night, or taking something to his chamber. Duffdour had not been a happy house without Ellen.

Pleased to be sitting at her own high board again, Ellen looked out over the hall. The hearths burned brightly. The table and the sideboard gleamed with evidence of their care, and the lady of Duffdour was pleased to see that even though she had been away for several months, her servants had not become complacent or lazy. Below the dais the trestles and benches were filled with the king's men, and the Armstrong clansmen were all eating the venison stew from their bread trenchers while the ale flowed freely.

At the high board a bowl of stew had been placed, along with a fat capon roasted perfectly and stuffed with dried apple, onion, and bread; a small ham; and a platter of freshwater mussels in a sauce of dill and mustard. There were two small wheels of cheese, a hard yellow and a soft creamy one. Butter and fresh bread had been set in the center of the board, where those seated could easily reach them.

"I've sent to Conal Bruce and to Robert Ferguson,"

Duncan told the king. "Conal will be able to catch up to us tomorrow. As for Ferguson it will take him longer."

"How far is this Devil's Glen?" the king wanted to know. "Is it in Scotland, or is it in England?"

"It's a good half day's ride, which is why I want to leave before sunrise," Duncan answered the king. "As to where it is, some say 'tis Scotland, and others that it's England. No one has ever really been certain, but I believe 'tis England, for it is several miles from any landmark I recognize as being Scots."

"There is a house there?"

"Aye, a dark stone house, barns, and pens, for 'twas there that Colby and his raiders kept the cattle, sheep, goats, and other stock they stole on their raids," the laird answered.

"Is the house defended?" the king wanted to know.

Duncan Armstrong shook his head. "Nay. 'Tis just a house. Its safety lies in being at the end of a narrow glen, which makes it difficult to get in and out of because the path is very restricted. A peddler seeking shelter brought us word that he saw horsemen going in and out of the glen recently. I sent men to keep a watch, and indeed there is some small activity. One of my men slipped down the glen under cover of darkness, and the house showed lights. He listened in the shadows of the stables, and heard the men there referring to 'my lord.' It has to be Colby, for the house is his."

"But you cannot be certain," the king noted. "Could he have sold the house?"

"Who would buy it?" the laird wanted to know. "It is small, isolated, difficult to reach. He saw to its building himself, I have learned. Took a wee bit of unclaimed land, and built a house, barns, and pens for the very purpose for which he used it: He assumed he could creep back to Devil's Glen and we would not be the wiser. And we wouldn't have been, my lord, but that the peddler saw the comings and goings. We did not burn it the night we sought out the women Colby had stolen from

Cleit village. But this time we shall burn it to the ground so that the English fox does not have his den to return to if he manages to escape us."

"If we go early," Ellen said quietly, "we shall not have the advantage."

The laird looked briefly puzzled, and then he smiled. "You are thinking of the limited width of the path through the glen," he said.

"Aye," Ellen responded. "If but one or two men can work their way down the track at a time, how can you surprise him? Will he not notice your men coming out of the glen into the open area before his house where the glen widens and ends? And how long will it take all your men to reach the clearing before the house?"

"I had thought that we would gallop down the glen to the house," the laird said.

"Would it not be better to depart earlier so we could get down the trail into the glen before the sun rose?" Ellen asked her husband. "We could slay those sleeping in the barn and the stable quickly and easily, leaving only Colby and whoever is in the house with him to dispose of when we break into it. Galloping is noisy, and they could block the entry to the glen's clearing before all your men got through."

"By God's blood!" the king swore softly. "Your wife is a strategist, Duffdour. And a damned good one, I believe. How, my bonny, did you learn such things, and how can you speak of slaying sleeping men so coolly and easily?"

"My lord, remember where I was raised. In the Highlands we do not waste time or men when we feud. I learned much listening to the men in my grandsire's hall plan raids or speak of raids past. The element of surprise is crucial if one is to keep casualties low, or even nonexistent," Ellen told them.

"And you would slay all those with Sir Roger?" the king asked her quietly.

"If there are no witnesses, my lord, who is to testify

to what happened?" Ellen asked him softly. "Besides, they are not Scots. If you took Colby captive he would, under the right circumstances, betray his own king. Do you think Henry Tudor wants to be accused publicly of causing the murder of another king? Of Scotland's king? What would that do to the reputation he attempts to forge among his fellow kings?"

"Most of whom have undoubtedly done murder for hire themselves," James Stewart said dryly. "You are a fierce woman, my bonny, which surprises me, for I have known you only as a wee lass and friend whom I sheltered and then rescued."

"Do you really want that pretender you shelter on England's throne, my lord? And if you put him there, how long do you think he would remain? Would you be obliged to go to his defense if he faltered? Of course you would, having put him there. Has this fellow not cost your treasury enough as it is? His upkeep still costs you. And then too, there are other Yorkist contenders for England's throne with even better claims than any of King Edward's sons would have had were they alive."

James Stewart laughed softly. "So you believe Adair, my bonny, do you?"

"Why would Adair lie, my lord? There is no gain in it for her. She is far too proud of her own blood to allow a fraud upon England's throne, or even to displace her half sister, no matter the hurt that one gave her," Ellen said. "You know she tells the truth, for you are a man who understands people well."

The king smiled at her. "Aye, my cousin Adair speaks true," he said, "but you know why I do what I do, my bonny."

Ellen nodded. "Perhaps one day you will tell me the whole truth of the matter, for I will admit to being frankly curious as to who this pretender really is, my lord."

The young king looked thoughtful for several long moments, and then, reaching out, he took Ellen's hand in his. "Aye, I will tell you, my bonny. I will tell you to relieve my scruples, and so that I need not confess it to the priests, for I have enough on my conscience, I fear. But not today," he said. Then he turned to the laird of Duffdour. "Let us not go tomorrow, but tomorrow night," he said. "The horses and the men will be better rested for the delay, and I like your wife's idea of entering the glen under cover of darkness, dispatching those we can find, and then waiting till dawn to bring Colby to the justice that he deserves."

"It will be as Your Majesty decides," Duncan Armstrong said.

Duffdour had its own harper, an elderly man with a sweet voice. When the meal had been concluded the harper played and sang for them. Sim saw that the clansmen were bedded down comfortably in the barns and stable, while Ellen saw that Hercules Hepburn was given a bed space in the hall, and the king was settled in a small guest chamber. Knowing his appetites, Ellen sent him a pretty serving girl she knew was not a virgin. In the morning the girl was filled with praise for the monarch, and proudly displayed the silver penny he had given her.

"Not one of his da's useless old black pennies," the girl said, "but true silver!"

"How shall you spend it?" Lizzie, the cook, asked her.

"Spend it? Never!" the girl declared. "I'll drill a hole in it and put it on a ribbon about my neck for all to see, and when they ask about it I will tell them proudly that the king gave it to me, for he said I futtered him nicely."

"You'll more than likely have it stolen," the cook said tartly, turning back to her pots, which were already bubbling with the main meal of the day. "Get into the pantry now, lass, for there is work there for you to do."

"I thought I could serve in the hall," the girl said.

"You've done all the serving you'll do today," the cook replied, and the other serving girls scattered about the kitchen giggled. "Get along with you now, lass. There is a pile of rabbits in need of skinning."

The day was yet cold, but clear. There was a sense of spring despite the patches of snow still visible on the far hills. The men in the hall were quiet and took their ease, playing at dice and talking in low tones. They could not be certain what tomorrow would bring, or if they would survive it. The Duffdour cook had seen that they ate well the day long. Come early evening most of the men had returned to the stable and barns to sleep.

The previous night Ellen had slept with her husband, but she had undressed quickly and gotten into bed, turning her back to him in a way that told him she was not to be trifled with by her husband. He was disappointed, but considered that she had spent several days riding down into the border from Linlithgow. This night, however, he was in no mood to be denied his wife's company, and Ellen sensed the change in his attitude.

"You should not wear yourself out, husband," she advised him as, seated upon the edge of their bed, she brushed her long red-gold hair.

He took the brush from her and, seating himself next to her, slowly ran it through her silken locks. "I have always thought that you have the most beautiful hair, wife," he said. He skimmed the brush down the thick, heavy swath of her tresses. "I have missed seeing it, feeling the softness of it." He took a single strand and brought it to his lips. "But most of all, Ellen, my wife, I have missed you." He laid the brush aside and, pushing her hair from the nape of her neck, placed a kiss upon the bared flesh.

Ellen sighed. She hadn't meant to do so, for she was still half-angry with him.

"Did you miss me?" the laird asked, and then his tongue traced the outline of her ear as his supple fingers unlaced her chemise.

Ellen leaned back against him, knowing she was

helpless to deny him. "Aye," she admitted softly. "I had grown used to you next to me in our bed."

He pushed the chemise from her shoulders, and it puddled about her waist as his hands cupped her two round breasts. The soft yet firm globes fit within his open palms perfectly. Gently his fingers squeezed the two breasts, leaving faint marks on her milky white skin. "So perfect," he murmured in her ear, and his teeth nipped at the lobe. His thumbs circled the nipples, slowly teasing them. He watched as the nipples puckered like frosted flower buds, growing dark and tight.

He bent to press several small, hot kisses upon her graceful shoulder. Then his tongue licked up the side of her slender neck, and he turned her head just slightly so he might nibble at her sensuous lips. His mouth worked against hers, kissing hungrily, and then his tongue darted past her teeth to take issue with her tongue. She moaned softly against his lips, her initial reluctance evaporating under his skilled attack.

Ellen felt her heart beating a fierce tattoo. It had been so long since she had lain warm and replete in his arms. There had been only hurried couplings since her return from Colby Castle, and then suddenly they were forced to court, and as suddenly Duncan was gone from her again back to Duffdour. He was her husband, and the plain truth was that despite the hurtful suspicions that lingered deep within him regarding her kidnapping and the months that followed, she loved him. And she knew that he loved her. There were no doubts in her mind about that. Would the uncertainty he had felt ever since Ian Johnston's hurtful lies ever disappear? Ellen didn't know the answer to that, but at this moment she didn't care.

Turning in his embrace, she took his head between her two small hands and kissed him again. "I love you, Duncan Armstrong," she said softly. "I will always love you."

His strong arms wrapped about her tightly, and he buried his face in her long hair. "Forgive me," he groaned. "His words haunt me, though I know better. You would not lie to me, wife. Yet I cannot help myself. I keep seeing this shadowy figure ravishing you, and my anger and jealously know no bounds. Since I cannot take my anger out on Colby, I have taken it out on you, Ellen, my love. I am sorry."

Ellen would not allow Colby or the now-damned Ian Johnston to destroy her marriage to Duncan Armstrong. She would not let them break his heart. "Erase such thoughts by ravishing me yourself, husband," Ellen said to him. "Love me as you previously have, and let us create another son for Duffdour." Lying back, she drew him down into her arms. "I love you, Duncan," she told him quietly. "You have no need to be jealous, my lord. I swear on my life that you have not. You are the love of my life. My only love."

"God's blood, I have missed you, wife!" he cried. He kissed her almost frantically, and she kissed him back as eagerly. But then he ceased as suddenly as he had begun looking down into her face. "We must not be greedy, wife," he told her.

Ellen laughed, low. "Nay, husband, we must not. We must go slowly."

"Sweetly," he agreed, and he moved his big body so that he lay on his side, observing her as a man might contemplate a particularly delicious meal that had been set before him. "Hmmmm," he said. "Where to begin? Where to begin?"

"A bit of breast, perhaps, my lord?" Ellen suggested, and she lifted one up to him. "You will find them quite tender and delicious."

"Indeed," he replied, leaning forward to lick at the flesh she was offering him.

"Oh! That is quite nice," Ellen told him.

"I want more," he said, pushing her flat onto her back, his dark head lowering, his mouth closing over a nipple. He tugged upon the sentient nub. Then he tugged harder.

"And that is nicer," Ellen said with a gusty sigh. "Oh, God, Duncan, your mouth on my breast is sheer heaven!"

The taste of her and the clean fragrance that emanated from her skin were powerful spurs to his senses. It had been months since they had enjoyed each other in this manner. His lust was fully engaged. His cock was hard and ready for her, but he was not quite yet of a mind to couple their bodies. He slowly sucked upon each of her breasts, enjoying the firm but tender flesh. Then his kisses began a deliberate and tortuous journey down her torso. Her skin was soft. He lingered awhile in the deep valley between her breasts, his mouth warm over her beating heart. He used his lips and his tongue on her quivering body, and enjoyed the wonder of her slow but steady arousal.

Ellen had closed her eyes to better revel in the sensations that his lovemaking was engendering within her. Briefly, for she quickly dismissed the unpleasant thoughts, she remembered Roger Colby's mouth and hands on her. How different it was to be loved by a man who loved her, not defiled by a man bent on revenge. The dishonor of what the Englishman had done to her began to evaporate with the joy she felt in her husband's passion.

His mouth now reached her belly, and he licked it slowly, all the while kneading it with a gentle hand, but it was the red curls below that tempted him onward. He pressed his palm flat against them, and Ellen gasped at the bolt of sensation that imploded within her. His long fingers played among the tight curls until a single digit was tracing a torturous path down her shadowed slit. He moved his big body so that he might lower his head, which he then buried within that fiery bush.

She felt his tongue imitating the finger that had gone before it, the tip of it pushing through her nether lips, his fingers now spreading her open; finding her most sensitive core, encircling it in leisurely fashion as she tingled with pure delight. "Oh, Duncan, yes!" she encouraged him, and when his mouth closed over that tiny tender nub to suck upon it, Ellen screamed softly, and her senses reeled.

He was dizzy with the scent of her, the taste of her, his face buried within her most secret place. He sucked. He licked. He lapped at her juices, which were beginning to flow, while she writhed and encouraged him with little cries of pure delight. His heart was hammering furiously and threatening to burst through his chest. He was like a drunken man. And then he realized the throbbing ache of his manhood. He needed to be inside of her. Reluctantly he drew away from her moist sex and, quickly mounting her, drove hard into her sweet sheath. It closed tightly about him, squeezing him, loving him.

"Oh, yesss!" Ellen hissed. "Oh, yes!"

"Witch!" he accused. "I adore you!" And he thrust harder and faster until they were both breathless.

Ellen clung to her husband, her legs wrapped tightly about his firm body. Her nails raked down his long back, furthering his efforts to pleasure them. "Give me a bairn!" she demanded of him.

"Do you love me?" he countered, breathing heavily as he rested a moment.

"More than life itself, Duncan Armstrong!" she declared. "And don't stop fucking me until I am full of your juices, and your great cock is well satisfied."

He laughed aloud at her words, and began once again to pump himself into her. *Slowly. Slowly. Faster! Deeper!* Until the woman beneath him was weeping with the pleasure he was giving her, and he was on fire with the pleasure she gave him in return. And then their passions shattered in an explosion of lust fulfilled. Duncan howled with his relief as his juices burst forth to flood her secret garden. Ellen screamed with satisfaction as she soared, filled with delight and love for this man who was her husband. Her legs fell away from his body as he rolled off of her.

But then, reaching out, he pulled her into his arms, holding her close. His big hand smoothed the long hair now tangled by their lovemaking. He kissed the top of her head, and felt her lips warm on his chest. Then together they slept until Gunna came to awaken them a short while after midnight. She brought water for them to bathe, and had already laid out fresh garments for them while they had slept.

"Is anyone else awake yet?" the laird asked the serving girl.

"They are just now beginning to stir in the hall, my lord. Sim has awakened the king and the Hepburn's man, and sent a man to the stable and barns to rouse the men. Cook has newly baked oatcakes and dried meat for the journey."

"Good. Tell Sim I'll be down shortly," Duncan told her, and when Gunna had gone he said to Ellen, "I don't want you going, wife."

"Put it from your mind, my lord," Ellen said, her voice determined. "It is my right to see Sir Roger Colby punished, husband. I will not remain behind."

The laird nodded. "Very well, then, let us get the stink of our coupling off of us or our passion will be ascertained by all." He would not argue with her. It *was* her right, but he had hoped that by offering her the opportunity to remain at Duffdour she would have taken it and been kept safe. But then, his Highland wife, his border bride, was not a weak woman to be wrapped in a sheepskin and protected, for all her petite stature.

The water in the pitcher was hot, and there was enough for two full basins. They washed themselves and dressed for hard travel. Ellen would not ride sidesaddle, and so, having put on a clean camise lined in rabbit fur and a natural-colored linen shirt, she pulled on a pair of dark green woolen breeks that came to her knee, woolen stockings, and her brown leather boots. Finally Ellen drew on her worn leather jerkin with its staghorn buttons. It was a garment her grandsire had given her the year before she had been sent to court. Then, dressed, she sat down, brushed out her hair, and plaited it into a single thick braid, which she tucked beneath one of her husband's laird's bonnets, with its silver clan badge. The badge showed a raised arm in its center, and its rim was inscribed about the edge with the Latin words *Invictus maneo*, which translated into "I remain unvanquished."

"Why does your bonnet have an eagle's feather, and mine does not?" Ellen asked him.

"Because I am the laird," he told her with a small smile as he fitted a dirk into his boot. Then he kissed her little nose. "And you are but the laird's wife, Ellen, my love."

"Well," she allowed, "I suppose that's fair. And you make a much better target that way, my lord husband. My father's cap had the eagle feather. I used to wear it."

He laughed aloud. "With God's good luck you'll not be a widow too soon."

"I would hope not," Ellen declared. "I want another night like tonight." And she laughed when he flushed. "I'm certain we made a strong son, Duncan."

"Or a very headstrong daughter," he replied, grinning. "You blooded me, wench."

"We had best hurry down to the hall before everyone else is there and ready to ride. It will be difficult going without the moon," Ellen noted.

"The night is clear, and there will be a sliver of moon, enough to keep us from having to carry torches. And the horses' hooves will be muffled, so our passing will barely be noticed unless someone is up and awake, which is unlikely," the laird said.

"I remember the countryside being desolate," Ellen told him.

"It is, mostly," he agreed as they descended into the hall.

There they found the king and Hercules Hepburn commiserating with each other about the early hour. Together they went outside to the front of the house, where the horses and the men were milling about. Sim and several servants were passing out the oatcakes and dried beef to the group to be put into the pouches they all carried. Water bottles were filled, some with wine. Finally the raiding party was ready.

The king and the laird of Duffdour at their head, Hercules Hepburn and the lady Ellen behind them, they moved across the open area between the house and the walls, through the gates, and out onto the moor. The sky above them was as black as onyx stone, and filled with bright stars and the barest sliver of a waning moon. To Ellen's surprise there was just enough light for them to ride freely. And there was no wind. The air was April cold, but one could sense the milder weather to come.

After they had ridden for several hours, and a false dawn was just beginning to brighten the horizon, Ellen heard the sound of horses other than their own. She looked about nervously, but Hercules Hepburn reached over, patting her arm, and nodded that it was all right. And then Ellen saw coming to join them Conal Bruce and his clansmen in the company of Robert Ferguson, the laird of Aldclune, and his clansmen. They had been a large party riding out from Duffdour. Now they were a very large party, and Ellen suddenly realized it didn't matter how many men were at Devil's Glen. Sir Roger Colby was already a beaten man.

They stopped briefly to rest the horses, to eat oatcakes and chew on the dried meat, to drink from their flasks. Ellen watched proudly as her husband and the king went to thank the Bruce and the Ferguson clansmen for joining with them. Soon it would be over. Soon Sir Roger Colby would be punished for his presumption in kidnapping and holding the laird of Duffdour's wife, and for daring to attempt a plot on James Stewart's life. And then she would be free, Ellen thought. Free to be the lady of Duffdour. To mother her son, to nurture the bairn she was certain she and Duncan had created but a few hours back. She breathed deeply of the cool air surrounding her. This was what freedom smelled like, Ellen considered, and she smiled.

They continued on after their brief stop, reaching Devil's Glen as the false dawn waned away. Hercules Hepburn volunteered to ride down the narrow access to the glen so they might know what awaited them. He was gone close to an hour, and then he returned to make his report to the king and the laird of Duffdour.

"He's there, or someone is there in the house," he told them. "He has few men that I can see. There are perhaps a dozen of them sleeping in the barn."

"You went in?" Ellen was horrified.

"Aye, how else were we to know?" the big man said. "I was quiet, and not a one stirred. They're undoubtedly drunk and bored, having little to do. A right nasty-looking lot, if I do say so, my lords. I could not say how many are in the house, however."

"You didn't go in?" Ellen teased him.

Hercules Hepburn grinned. "Nay, lady, I fear that there I bowed to discretion." Then he turned to the king. "But the door is nothing more than a door. The man either has no fear of being attacked or is a fool."

"What say you, Duffdour? Should we enter the glen now, or wait?" the king said.

"Now, while none are stirring," Duncan Armstrong said.

"We should leave some men here to guard the mouth of the glen, just on the chance that Colby has adherents coming to join him," Conal Bruce suggested.

"Aye, that way we'll be warned, and cannot be attacked from two sides," his half brother agreed. "And Ellen must remain here too."

"Nay," Ellen said.

"I don't want you caught up in the fighting," her husband retorted.

"Nay, I would be there when the light fades from Roger Colby's eyes," Ellen replied stubbornly. "If one of you kills him, then I miss my opportunity to watch him die. And he does not know that I am partly responsible for his downfall." She turned to the king. "My lord, at no other time would I go against my husband's wishes, but it is my right to see Colby meet his fate. This man kidnapped me, imprisoned me, abused me, and called me a whore and a slut. He said all women were. Let me come with you!"

James Stewart considered. The young woman he had known as an innocent girl, whom he called "my bonny," was, he was surprised to realize, his friend. Kings, he knew, by virtue of their exalted positions, had no friends, yet Ellen MacArthur was his friend. Still, he did not wish to make an enemy of even as unimportant a man as Duncan Armstrong. His border lords were invaluable to Scotland. "Let the main party go ahead first," he said to Ellen, "and when we have gained the glen I will send a man back for you. By the time you reach us the others will be slain, and we will be ready to assault Sir Roger's house." He took her small gloved hand up in his hand and kissed it. "I believe that will relieve your good husband's fears, my bonny. And it should suit you. Does it not?"

Ellen nodded. "Thank you, my lord," she said, and looked to Duncan, who nodded his agreement.

"Then it is time," James Stewart said.

The laird of Duffdour ordered six of his men to stay behind with his wife, and they secreted their horses behind some trees. Then together he and the king led the raiding party into the access to Devil's Glen. The trail was narrow, and it would take them some minutes, moving slowly, to maintain the element of surprise before they reached the glen's clearing. Above them the sky was beginning to grow light with the coming dawn. The birds in the bare trees called back and forth and sang their morning songs. They moved carefully in order to preserve the peace of the place. And finally they came out from their limited access. Before them stood the dark stone house, and about it two barns and several empty pens.

"The men are in the barn farthest from the house," Hercules Hepburn said.

"See to it," the king ordered him.

The big man gathered a group about him, murmuring his instructions. Then Hercules and his party moved across the open space and entered the barn where Colby's men were sleeping. They heard not a sound as the barn's inhabitants were quickly slain. And when the deed had been done, Hercules himself returned down the narrow track to fetch Ellen back.

When he reached her he told the others with her that they were to remain watchful, and send one of their own if anyone approached the entry to Devil's Glen. Disappointed, the Armstrong clansmen watched as their lady and her escort went back down the slender access to Devil's Glen. They moved slowly, for they went single-file. Hercules Hepburn, being a big man with a large horse, took up so much of the path they traveled that it was necessary for Ellen to come behind him.

She looked about her as their horses walked along. On either side of her rose up sharp hillsides, almost cliffs, of rock and earth, small trees, and brush somehow managing to cling to them. It would be a very dark trail in summer when the leaves were on the trees. And, looking up, she could see but a thin strip of sky. It was difficult to tell exactly what time of day it was, the bit of sky was so scant. She now had a greater appreciation for the care that was necessary to get through into the deep heart of the glen itself. And Ellen suddenly understood how the glen had gained its name. It seemed it was a devil of a place to reach.

She must face Roger Colby a final time. Had she been mad to come? But if she had not come, how was she to know what would be said? How could she defend herself, her reputation, if she were not there? *Oh, holy Mother*, Ellen prayed silently as she rode along, *prevent Sir Roger from hurting Duncan! From harming us.*

"We're almost to the end of it," Hercules Hepburn said. "It's a wicked path, isn't it? And a fine den the English fox had to go to ground when he led his raiders last year."

"Aye," Ellen agreed. "The entrance to the glen is well hidden, and getting here is not easy. 'Tis a well-protected place. I am surprised Sir Roger had no one guarding the entry, but then, I suppose unless you knew it was there you wouldn't find it but by accident. The English felt safe here. Is it England or Scotland?"

" 'Tis one of those places in dispute, but your husband says 'tis England, for any landmarks he recognizes are several miles to the north," Hercules answered her.

Ahead Ellen could see the path widening, and after a short while they entered the main area of the den itself. At first she did not spy the king and the others, but then she saw them in the shadows of the barns, and she realized that it was light enough now for anyone looking from a window to see the visitors. They joined the others.

"We are discussing how to approach this with the least loss of life," the king told Ellen as she rode up to him.

"I should post a group of men at the rear of the house, or anywhere else there is likely to be an exit," Ellen said. "Then I would knock upon the front door. It is obvious even to a woman that you cannot make a great assault upon the building. You need to get inside of the house. Actually, I should be the one to knock, for even the most suspicious servant or soldier will not consider a little woman such as myself a threat."

The men about them listening chuckled softly.

"I forbid it!" Duncan Armstrong said.

"My dear lord," Ellen answered him in dulcet tones, "I am the logical choice, for given the preference between a big man and a small woman, would you not open the door to the woman but not the man?"

"I don't want you in any danger," the laird said softly.

"With three clans standing behind me?" Ellen asked him.

"She is determined to be a part of all of this, aren't you, my bonny?" the king intervened between them. "And she is right, my lord. If we batter the door in, which we can do, we alert those inside to our hostile intentions. But if the door is opened we can push through, muffle the doorkeeper, and take the others in the house quickly, possibly even without bloodshed. Because we do not know how many there are in the house, those in the barn had to be slain, for we could not leave any of our party to guard them. It is unlikely these men will have any deep loyalty to Sir Roger. Once we have done what needs doing they can be released. I want no unnecessary deaths on my hands. The lady of Duffdour, having a quarrel to settle with Sir Roger Colby, must be the one to gain us entry to this house," the king concluded.

"It is past the dawn now," Hercules Hepburn noted. "Someone is certain to be stirring within. Now is the time for us to strike, my lord."

The king nodded. "We will take the house, bring Sir Roger to justice, and release any others within. Then we will fire the house so that no other English may shelter in it, and use it as a base from which to raid into Scotland," he said.

There were murmurs of agreement from the other lairds and their captains. Better to return home with all of the men you departed with than to leave widows and orphans. The laird of Duffdour sighed, then, looking at Ellen, took up her hand and kissed it. Words between them were not necessary. He knew she must do what she must do. The clansmen dismounted their horses and, opening the gates to one of the large pens, drove the animals into it for safekeeping. The creatures would not be visible from the house.

Then the men began to move stealthily across the clearing toward the house. The area was still dim with the early hour, but they nonetheless kept to the shadows. They surrounded the house, blocking the two other entrances that they found. The largest group, headed by the king and Duncan Armstrong, hid themselves in the shadows by the front entrance to the house as Ellen stepped forward and knocked loudly. Within, all was silent. She pounded upon the door again, this time crying out loudly for help.

"Let me in! Let me in!"

In the silence that followed she heard a shuffling step approaching the door. Then a voice demanded, "What is it you seek here?"

"Please," Ellen replied. "I was set upon by robbers trying to reach my sick mother. My horse has been stolen, and my purse. I am but a woman alone. Help me, I beg of you, for God's good mercy," Ellen pleaded.

There was a long pause, and then they heard the metallic scraping of a key in a lock, and the iron bolts keeping the large oak door tightly shut being thrown back. The rusty hinges of the door protested loudly as the door was opened to reveal a wizened old woman. She looked at Ellen and said, "Come in then."

Ellen stepped quickly aside, revealing James Stewart and his companions.

"We shall indeed come in, old mother. Do not scream, for there is only one whose blood need be shed this day, and 'tis not yours," the king warned.

Her eyes huge in her head, the doorkeeper backed up to allow them inside. They did not shut the door behind them. "What do you want?" she finally managed to say.

"Where is Sir Roger Colby?" the king asked quietly.

"So at last the devil comes to claim his own," the old woman said. "Well, 'tis not my duty to protect him. I am the housekeeper and the cook here. He's upstairs with his whore, and asleep yet, for he was late in the hall. Then he wanted the wench sent to him to assuage his lust. He beat her first, though, for he had caught her sucking cock in the barn earlier. I heard her yelling, and the sound of the strap." She grinned. "Aye, he gave the little bitch a good hiding."

"How many others in the house?" the king asked.

"Only the two who guard his chamber door," the woman said. "The rest are in the barn. 'Tis not like the old days, when all the local families paid him homage and rode with him through the borders."

"Is the door of Colby's bedchamber the only entrance or exit?" the king wanted to know. "And are the windows large enough for a man to escape through?"

"The door is the only way in or out," the woman said. "The casement windows are too small for a man to get through, and even if he did, the drop is too far. He'd break a leg if he tried. You mean to kill him then. Good! Do the whore too, for she's a bad 'un."

"Which door?" came the next question.

"The last one on the left at the end of the hall," the woman said. "I've helped you. You'll not kill me, will you?"

"Gather your possessions up," the king said in a kindly voice, "and you may have a single animal from the stables. Then go, and do not come back." He turned to a young clansman wearing the Bruce plaid, whom he knew by name. "Tad, go with her. My man will help you and see you safely through the glen," he told the woman. "Tell the others she has been given her life and her freedom by the king."

The woman's eyes grew round again. "You are James Stewart?" she said.

The king nodded, and the woman knelt, grabbing at his hand to kiss it. "There, woman, none of that," he said, raising her up. "Go!"

"God bless you, Jamie Stewart," the woman said fervently. "And thank you!"

"Young or old," Hercules Hepburn said with a chuckle as the old woman hobbled off with Tad, "they all love him."

The king grinned. Then he said, "My lords, let us be about our business here."

Chapter 17

"My men and I will fetch him down here to the hall, my lord," the laird of Duffdour said to James Stewart.

The king nodded and, taking Ellen's hand, said, "Come along, my bonny. We will await the villain together." And he led the way into the hall of the house. It was not a big room, and had but one fireplace. "Your hand is like ice, my bonny. Are you afraid? You need not be."

"I am not fearful," Ellen lied. "I have waited for months to see an end to this, my lord. And too, I do not believe Duncan can be easy until this man is dead. He can never forgive him the harm he did to me, though, praise God and his Blessed Mother, I managed to escape the worst when I fled across the Solway. Surely the holy Mother was with me that day. But I cannot be easy until I see Roger Colby dead with mine own eyes. I can never forget how easily he was able to take me from Duffdour, and I will never again feel completely safe there, or anywhere. That he could trespass on my husband's lands and steal me away! And even the men at arms at the door did not know until it was too late."

"Where were they that they were so lax?" the king asked curiously.

"Entertaining the village whore outside the door," Ellen said. "Obviously a man's brain and his cock are not connected in any way."

James Stewart grinned. "That, my bonny, is a truth known by most," he agreed.

Several clansmen came into the hall now with two men at arms in their custody.

"What shall we do with them, my lord?" one of the captains asked.

The two men looked frankly terrified.

"I have no quarrel with either of you," the king said. "When this business is done with I will see you are released unharmed. You have the word of Scotland's king on that. Will you both remain silent and quiet now?"

The two frightened men nodded simultaneously.

Suddenly from above them came an outraged shriek.

The king smiled. "Ah," he said, "I believe the bedroom has been breached." And he was exactly correct.

The laird and his men had taken the two men at arms quickly and silently, clapping hands over their mouths so they could not cry out as they were hustled downstairs. They waited until the two men were gone, and then, reaching out, Duncan Armstrong's fingers made contact with the handle of the bedchamber door. Slowly, carefully, he opened that door and stepped inside, his men at his back.

Roger Colby lay naked on his bed. He was sprawled upon his belly, one arm over a naked girl who lay on her back, her legs spread wide, her secrets seen by all. The laird of Duffdour recognized the girl, and shook his head. It was Evina, stepdaughter to his son's wet nurse, Machara. He wondered what made a girl like that a born whore.

"Wake them up," he said to his captain, Artair.

Artair nodded to several of his men, and two of them

immediately yanked the sleeping girl up from the bed. Evina shrieked with both surprise and outrage at this treatment of her person, and when she did Roger Colby's eyes flew open to discover the sharp point of Duncan Armstrong's sword just touching the beating hollow in his throat.

"Put some clothing on, you little slut," the laird said angrily. Then, turning to his men, he told them, "Take her downstairs and put her with the others. The king will decide what to do with her." He swiveled his head back to Roger Colby. "I cannot say it is good to see you again, my lord."

"Have you come to kill me then?" Sir Roger asked him.

"I should like to kill you," Duncan admitted, "but that decision must be the king's alone, and not mine. If it were mine I'd run you through right now."

"An act hardly worthy of a gentleman, but then, you are a Scot," Colby said insultingly, with a small curl to his lip.

"I don't want to die! I don't want to die!" Evina screamed hysterically.

"Jesu!" Sir Roger swore. "Will someone please shut the whore up? They are not here to kill you, you stupid slut. They are here to kill me."

The girl had managed to pull on her chemise and her skirts. With a slight nod of his head Duncan Armstrong indicated that she should be removed from the chamber. Two of his clansmen hustled Evina from the room. The laird slowly withdrew the tip of his blade from the Englishman's throat. "Get dressed," he said, and then he stepped back from the side of the bed as his men surrounded it, handing Sir Roger his breeks, a camise, his shirt.

Colby arose, pulled a pot from beneath the bed, peed into it, set it down, and then dressed himself quickly, pulling on his boots at the last. "I'm ready," he finally said. "Where are we going, my lord?"

"Down into your hall," Duncan said. "I did not come

alone, but brought you a most distinguished visitor, my lord."

They exited the bedchamber, the laird of Duffdour leading the way, Sir Roger Colby surrounded by the Armstrong clansmen. When they had gained the hall the Englishman was very surprised to see his former captive among the men there, but he said nothing. He was led to stand before a red-haired young man with startling blue eyes. Instinctively he realized who this young man was. His inbred good manners caused him to offer his best court bow.

"I understand you wish to kill me, Colby," the young man said pleasantly.

"An ugly rumor, my lord," Sir Roger responded.

"Johnston is dead, you know. The poison he carried and put in the Spanish ambassador's gift wine was quite lethal," James Stewart said. "How clever of you to send him to do the deed. If he had succeeded no one would have tied it to your master. The rumor would have been circulated that he was an adherent of my late father, God assoil his good and gentle soul," the king finished, crossing himself piously.

"A man 'tis said that you murdered," came the bold reply, and the clansmen in the hall hissed with their disapproval of the Englishman's words.

"I have never done a deed and not owned up to it," the king answered, "and I did not slay my sire; nor was I responsible for his death. You, however, are not as honest as I am. And with Ian Johnston gone, Sir Roger, you have lost your cat's-paw. If you dare to kill me yourself, your king cannot possibly restore you to his good graces, I fear. Henry Tudor is hardly secure upon his own throne, and to be found guilty of ordering the assassination of another duly anointed king would surely destroy what small credibility he has managed to earn with his fellow kings. You have lost your opportunity to regain his favor, and he will not have you back at court. What is left for you, my lord?

"As for me, my lord, I take it quite badly that you would seek my life. We have no other choice, I fear, but to settle this matter between us here and now. Give him a weapon," James Stewart ordered to no one in particular.

"My lord!" Hercules Hepburn burst forth, "you cannot fight this man yourself! You are Scotland's king. You have no legitimate heir to follow you."

"Hepburn is right, my lord," Conal Bruce said. "Any one of us would be happy to take on this small task for you."

"If anyone is going to fight this bastard, it will be me!" Duncan Armstrong declared. "He stole my wife, held her captive for weeks, abused her. It is my right, my lord, to have satisfaction of this Englishman."

"My lords, I thank you," the king told them. "But this man would kill me. I think 'tis my right that is the greater. Give him a sword," James Stewart repeated.

Ellen stood frozen with shock as Sir Roger was handed a sword. What if the dastard killed the king? She wanted to scream her protest, but no sound would issue forth from her throat. Next to her Evina whimpered, genuinely frightened by what was happening about them. Ellen turned on her furiously. "Shut your mouth!" she hissed.

Sir Roger Colby was handed a sword. The clansmen formed a large circle about the two men, who slowly began to circle each other, their weapons clutched in both hands above their heads. Colby struck first, but the king was younger, more agile. He dodged the blow, laughing, and swung his own broadsword to deliver a deep cut to Sir Roger's right arm.

"You need to be quicker, Colby," he said as his weapon cut his opponent a second time on the left arm, in almost the exact same place. "As you see, my lords, I have wounded both of his arms, now rendering them weaker. And given the at least fifteen years he has on me, this dispute shouldn't last long." The king dodged a blow aimed at his shoulder. "You must be quicker, Colby," he taunted the man.

"And you not so arrogant," the Englishman replied as his weapon made contact with the king's. "God's blood!" Colby swore angrily when the king's blade blocked him. Then he said, "If I kill you, your men will certainly slay me. This is not a fair fight to begin with, is it?"

"Of course, you will die this day one way or another," the king replied pleasantly. "Is not that why we are here? To kill you so you do not kill me."

The men forming the circle, their arms stretched out wide to hold their formation, swayed back and forth with each move that the two combatants made. Metal clanged loudly against metal. At one point sparks actually flew off the blades as the king and his opponent delivered blow after blow against each other. They were very well matched.

"Not as easy as you thought, done fairly," the king remarked. "Poison is a woman's weapon," he said scornfully. "Or a Florentine's."

"I'll wager Johnston did not die well," Colby returned. He was becoming winded.

"He did not," the king agreed. He was just feeling warmed up.

"Will you?" Sir Roger asked mockingly, dancing about, his sword making circles above his head as he rotated it threateningly.

" 'Tis not my time," James Stewart said as he began to move closer to his quarry.

"And how do you know that?" Colby demanded with a sneer.

"Because I have the eye," James Stewart responded. "Everyone knows that I have the eye." Then he swung his sword, cutting deeply and cruelly across Sir Roger's torso, thrusting his blade up hard, withdrawing it swiftly.

They all watched silently as the line of the slice blossomed with scarlet, and Sir Roger's shirt was stained with his blood quickly bubbling up and dripping upon the stone floor of the hall.

The Englishman's sword fell from his hands as he dropped to his knees. Some of his guts were beginning to ooze forth from the mortal wound the king had given him. His hands clutched at his middle, attempting to push his innards back into his injured body, but they did not seem to want to go. Sir Roger fell over onto his side, and then slowly rolled onto his back. "At least I die with honor. 'Tis better than I deserve, I think," he said self-deprecatingly. Then he coughed, and a trickle of blood drizzled from the side of his mouth. His eyes were half closed, his breath labored and harsh.

The king had lowered his weapon now. The hall was quiet but for the harsh breathing of the dying man, the frightened whimpering of the whore. Ellen, who had been part of the circle surrounding the combatants, stood quietly, watching the life drain from Sir Roger Colby. Oddly, she felt nothing. Not the relief she had expected. Not satisfaction. Not sadness. It was as if she stood completely apart from everything that was happening.

And then Duncan Armstrong came and knelt by the Englishman. "Did you," he asked in a voice heard by all in the hall, "fuck my wife?"

Ellen gasped and grew pale with her shock.

The Englishman forced his eyes open to meet the fierce look of the laird of Duffdour. No one in the hall made a sound as they strained to hear the dying man's answer. "Nay," Sir Roger Colby said in a firm, hard voice, marshaling the very last of his strength. "The damned vixen outwitted me, I am ashamed to say." With great effort he turned his head to find Ellen again, and when he did his gaze met hers mockingly, and he smiled the cruel smile she well remembered. "Did you not, madam?" And then his body was racked by a great shudder, his head fell to one side, and he died.

The hall was now enveloped in a deep silence. The

laird of Duffdour arose and went to his wife's side. "Wife," he began.

"Do not dare to address me," Ellen said, her voice shaking as she struggled to control her anger. "How dare you hold me up to public shame, Duncan Armstrong! I told you what happened while I was held captive by Sir Roger Colby. You said you believed me, but you did not, did you? You did not trust me! How can I ever forgive you for this?"

"He had to ask, my bonny," the king said. "Any man would have."

Ellen rounded on James Stewart. "Nay, he did not have to ask! I told him what had happened while I was in Colby's custody. But from the moment Ian Johnston spewed his evil lies there was doubt in my husband's mind. Another man, a stranger, was to be believed before a woman, his wife, was to be believed." She turned to Duncan. "Did I ask you about the women you fucked before we were wed, my lord? Was I not a virgin on our wedding night? Have I ever given you any reason to believe that I would be unfaithful to you, or you to me? Did I ever ask you if you fucked this little slut?" Ellen pointed to Evina.

"I offered, but he wouldn't have me," Evina said matter-of-factly.

A ripple of laughter greeted Evina's words.

Ellen glared at them all. Then she pointed a finger at Hercules Hepburn. "*You,*" she said, "will escort me back out of the glen to where my husband's six men wait. And they will escort me home." Then she stalked from the hall without another word, and at a nod from the king, Hercules Hepburn quickly followed her.

Duncan Armstrong moved to go after his wife, but the king said, "Let her ride off her temper, my lord. You will have plenty of time to work out this thorny problem you have created for yourself. What in the name of all that is holy made you ask Colby such a question? What if he had confirmed Ian Johnston's words? Sometimes it is better to accept what we are told, and ignore the rest."

"I could not help myself," the laird said, low. "Even as I spoke the words I knew I could destroy my marriage, but I had to know from Colby himself. I did believe Ellen, but then Johnston's words put the seed of doubt within me, and that doubt grew even though my common sense told me I was mad even to consider such a thing."

"Aye, you're mad. Mad with love for the little red-haired wench," James Stewart said. "And you're a fool, Duncan Armstrong. If you love a woman, you must believe what she tells you, especially if she has never given you any reason to doubt her."

"I know! I know!" the laird said brokenly. "Now what am I to do? She will never forgive me, I fear."

"Aye, she'll forgive you." The king chuckled. "But not for some time, I suspect. She will want to make certain you have learned your lesson before she does. But for now we have other things to do." He turned to the clansmen. "Fire the house," he said.

"What about the body of the Englishman?" Conal Bruce of Cleit asked the king.

"Let it burn with the house," the king replied. "And we'll remain until the fire is out, and we'll rake the ashes cold. No one will use this house again."

"My lord, you sustained a slight wound," a clansman said to the king. "It should be treated and bound up."

"It's naught but a scratch," James Stewart replied. "I'll have it tended to when we return to Duffdour."

"What about *them*?" Conal Bruce said, his head jerking to indicate the two men at arms who had been in the house when they took it.

"Give them a horse apiece, and send them on their way," the king said.

"And the whore?" Conal Bruce asked, looking to Evina.

The king turned his head toward the girl. She made

a feeble attempt to flirt with him from the corner where she stood. "By the time we've burned the house and the barns, and made certain not to set the moor afire, 'twill be day's end," the king said thoughtfully. "We'll camp here until the morrow. I have no wish to travel again in the darkness. We'll go back to Duffdour in the daylight. Let the girl stay, earn a few coins, and amuse the men. Tomorrow when we leave she can be sent on her way. We'll give her a horse for her troubles. And as for you, Duncan Armstrong, you are better letting your wife get over her pique before you go home again." The king laughed.

James Stewart's orders were carried out. The livestock belonging to the house, which consisted of horses, two cows, several chickens, and geese, were removed from their enclosures and penned outside. The barns and the house were set ablaze. The two men at arms who had been spared by the king were more than aware of their good fortune when they were taken into the barn to get their promised horses. They looked nervously at their dead companions, and hurriedly saddled their animals, leading them quickly out of the barn to mount up and ride away without ever turning about. Both men knew without even voicing it that only chance had saved them when Sir Roger had chosen them to guard his door last night. They rode for Colby Castle to tell Rafe, their sergeant, that the last of the Colbys was now dead and in hell.

Behind them the barns that had once held the pilfered livestock belonging to the Scots borderers began to burn. The king had allowed the clansmen to pillage whatever they could carry from the house. There had been little, for the house had been nothing more than a hidey-hole for Sir Roger and the English borderers. Duncan Armstrong was given the two milk cows, for Duffdour was the closest of their homes, and milk cows did not travel great distances well. The hens and the geese were killed and roasted for the clansmen's supper. The horses would be divided among Conal Bruce, Robert Ferguson, and Hercules Hepburn. It was hardly booty worthy of a successful raiding party, but Sir Roger Colby was dead, and that had been, after all, why they had come. The king was no longer in danger from this particular Englishman.

By day's end the structures that had stood in Devil's Glen were gone, burned to a pile of gray ashes. There was no evidence of bodies remaining, as they had been incinerated along with the buildings. Although they remained the night, their campfires burning brightly, hardly any of the men slept well. This was surely a haunted place now, but they had been safer in this hidden dale than they would have been out on the open moor. It was nonetheless with relief that they rode out at the first sign of light the following day. Halfway through the morning, Robert Ferguson and his men bade the king farewell, riding off in another direction. And at midday Conal Bruce and his clansmen left them, riding for Cleit. Afterward they saw several small parties of riders as they rode along, but as no one seemed to be of a mind to stop, they could not tell if they were English borderers or Scots. But so much daylight activity caused the king to comment that he suspected that the spring would be very active here in the borderlands, and Duncan Armstrong agreed. Finally in late afternoon they reached Duffdour. Its gates were closed, as they should be, and only when the laird was identified did they slowly swing open to allow him and his party admittance.

They dismounted and entered the house, going directly to the hall, where a domestic and calm scene greeted them. Ellen sat by her tapestry frame, working diligently. Little Willie toddled about the chamber under the watchful eye of his nursemaid, Laria. The servants were setting the high board for the evening meal.

Ellen arose and came forward to greet them. "Welcome back to Duffdour, my lord," she said to the king. "If you are up to a game of chess after the meal I shall be delighted to oblige you." She smiled mischievously. Then she glanced at the laird.

"Sir," was all she said, and her voice had taken on a chill.

The meal was served: a lovely hot pottage of vegetables, roasted rabbit, trout with a dill sauce, bread, and cheese. And afterward the last of the autumn apples was brought forth, baked with cinnamon and honey, to be served with heavy cream. Knowing the young king had a sweet tooth, Ellen had seen to this special treat. The hall emptied early, for the laird's men were tired, as were the Hepburn clansmen. At Ellen's request Sim brought forth the small gaming table, setting it before one of the hearths so they would be comfortable. Ellen fetched the chess set and placed the pieces neatly upon the game board. Then she and the king sat down to play.

The laird amused himself playing with his son, who was now a year old. It was like looking into a mirror, he thought. The lad did look like him but for Ellen's red-gold hair. He wanted more bairns, and wondered if that passionate night they had recently spent together had proved fruitful. If not, he could tell it would be a while before he got another chance to father a bairn on his wife, for it was obvious she was still very angry at him, and he didn't blame her. What devil had tempted him to kneel next to the dying Englishman and ask him whether he had fucked Ellen? She had said it hadn't happened. Why hadn't he believed her? She had never proven untrustworthy.

Why, when Johnston had, with his dying breath, accused her of whoring with Sir Roger, had Duncan Armstrong believed him? Because he was dying, and presumably would not go to God with a foul lie on his conscience? Why had he believed a man who had turned traitor to his country? A man who had beaten his wife to death, and then lied about it? A man who had tried to murder his king? The laird of Duffdour had taken the word of a creature like that over the sweetest and truest woman he had ever known. A woman he adored. He deserved Ellen's scorn. What he didn't know was how he was ever going to get her to forgive him for being a jealous fool. Quietly he departed the hall for his bed.

Ellen played badly, for she was still angry, and when the king beat her three games in a row she sighed. "I cannot concentrate upon the game tonight, my lord. Forgive me for being such a bad partner."

James Stewart reached out and took her hand in his. "He feels worse than you do, my bonny. Jealousy is what caused him to behave the way he did. We men are ever fools over the women we love."

"I know," Ellen responded, "but to have asked the man such a question as he lay dying. And before a hall full of strangers too! I have never given Duncan Armstrong any reason to mistrust me, my good lord. I would have killed myself before I allowed any man to dishonor me and my husband's name. But Duncan did not trust me. A good marriage must be based upon trust, my lord. Love, passion—these change. But trust stays firm." Her eyes filled with tears. "And I love him. I shall never love another."

"Then you must forgive him, my bonny," the king advised.

"My lord, you are yet young, and know little of women except how pleasant they can be when you kiss them or bed them. A woman must be trusted by the man she loves. Without trust all else fades away. It will be a while before I can forgive Duncan. He will have to earn both my love and my trust all over again," Ellen said sadly.

"Let me divert you briefly from your sorrows, then, my bonny," the king said to her. "Remember I promised you that I should tell you all I know of the *true* king of England? Would it please you to hear the tale now? And when you see her you may tell Adair Radcliffe this story if you would. Or not."

"Aye, I should like to hear what you have learned," Ellen said eagerly. She had to admit that she was very curious about the young man who had caused such a stir at court, was causing her own king such expense, and was causing King Henry great distress. And she did need to be turned from her own troubles. "Who is he really?"

"My spies have been out and about in Flanders, France, and Burgundy, ferreting out all the information that they could," James Stewart began. "It is a most interesting tale. I have not a doubt that at this point in his existence the *true* king actually believes this fabricated legend that has been woven about him."

"Wait," Ellen said. She removed the game pieces from the board and put them back into their carved box. Then, rising, she went to the sideboard, returning with a small carafe of her husband's own whiskey. She poured a generous dram into the king's empty goblet. Even Ellen knew that a man with a good tale to tell told it better with a well-lubricated throat.

The king grinned appreciatively, and drank some of the whiskey down.

"Now, begin," his pretty hostess said.

"It is highly possible there is Plantagenet blood running in his veins," James Stewart said. "But where that blood comes into the picture is a moot point. His resemblance to the last of the Yorkist kings and their family is so strong that it was first thought he was a son of King Edward's younger brother, George, Duke of Clarence, or a bastard of King Richard the Third. As there was a lot of back-and-forth between England, France, and the low countries during their dynastic struggles, it is highly possible that several bastards were fathered by that family. We shall never really know, my bonny.

"Our *true* king was born in the town of Tournai in Flanders. His father is listed in the town records as one Jehan de Werbecque, a man of good blood, but no means. He toiled as a civil servant. Our *true* king's mother was one Katherine de Faro. Her son was baptized Perkin de Werbecque. He was sent away with a wet nurse to the house of a cousin in Antwerp, one Jehan Stienbecks,

when he was barely a year. This leads me to believe that
while he bears Jehan de Werbecque's name, he is not
his natural-born son. De Werbecque may have married
her as a favor to someone to save her reputation, or it
is possible she was already his wife in fact, or at least
betrothed to him. It seems odd to me that a man would
send his firstborn son away as a wee bairn."

"If the child was not his," Ellen suggested, "perhaps
he could not bear the sight of him. After all, he gave
the lad his name, saving him from ignominy, but having his wife's dishonorable behavior before him daily
may have proved too much. Would not most men continue to wonder about a wife's faithfulness under such
circumstances?"

"Aye," the king agreed, "it would be difficult, particularly if she had already been his wife. She is fortunate he
didn't kill her."

"So Perkin was raised in Antwerp," Ellen said, now
using the pretender's real name.

"He was, and put to work by the time he was six years
of age as a boy servant, and we have traced several of
his employers. He served in the household of one John
Strewe, a fairly successful English merchant. It is in that
employ that he probably learned his English. This allowed him to gain a position in the household of Lady
Brampton, the widow of a known Yorkist sympathizer.
He went with her to Portugal. In Portugal he left Lady
Brampton. Her funds were limited, and she could probably not afford to keep a large staff. A boy servant
would, of course, been dispensable and let go. But she
may have seen to him by first finding our *true* king em-
ployment with a Portuguese knight, one Vaz da Cunha.
But obviously the man did not suit him, for he is next
found in Cork, in Ireland, employed by a silk merchant,
Pierre Jean Meno."

"He has certainly lived a most interesting and var-
ied life," Ellen noted, "yet I cannot help but feel sorry

for him. He has known no love, only servitude and pretense."

"Katherine Gordon loves him," the king noted dryly.

"Forgive me, my dear lord, but Katherine Gordon loves the idea of being queen of England," Ellen responded. "She is a proud woman, as I well remember from my time in your good aunt's household. On the rare occasions she had to speak with me she would not even look at me. Still, she has my sympathy, for this will end badly for her, I fear."

James Stewart had the good grace to look uncomfortable at Ellen's words, although he knew she had not been taxing his behavior in the matter.

"Will you continue on with this most fascinating tale?" Ellen asked him, and she added another dram of whiskey to the king's cup.

"The Irish, for whatever reason, have always had a deep loyalty to the House of York," the king began again. "And they have no love for the Tudors. The place is a hotbed of intrigue most of the time. Our *true* king, a pretty fellow with a fine figure, was used to advance his master's wares. He was dressed in the best silks in the latest fashions, and paraded about the town. He was about seventeen then, and his resemblance to the lords of the House of York was suddenly very apparent in his fine garments.

"Two of the most powerful and important men in Ireland, the Earl of Kildare and the Earl of Desmond, heard the tale of the young man who looked so like the dead or slain kings of the House of York. They came to observe Perkin Warbeck, as he was now known. And as they had known the last of these unfortunate kings well, they did indeed agree that the resemblance to the men of York was remarkable. So, wishing to cause Henry Tudor as much unhappiness as possible, they convinced the lad that he was not Perkin Warbeck, but Richard of York, England's rightful king."

"How can you know this, my lord?" Ellen wondered.

James Stewart chuckled. "After Adair Radcliffe was so insistent that Warbeck was not her half brother, and I had seen with my own eyes that he did not recognize her at all, I began to make inquiries. You see, my bonny, the perpetrators of this charade would not have necessarily known about Adair, for often children other than royal were raised in the king's nurseries for a variety of reasons. And, not being intimately acquainted with the workings of King Edward's nursery, they were unlikely to know that Adair was a king's brat, his bastard. Because she was of little importance, and Elizabeth Woodville was not pleased to have her there, little attention would have been made of her. And neither Kildare or Desmond could have ever known that Edward the Fourth's bastard daughter, even if they were aware of her existence—a woman who knew her half brothers well—was in Scotland, and had access to the court of King James."

"So you would not have ferreted out the truth were it not for Adair," Ellen said.

"Oh, I had my suspicions prior, which is why I sent for Adair," the king admitted. "It was all too convenient, and I well know the hatred the Irish hold for Henry Tudor. Either way, my bonny, I knew I could use Master Warbeck for my own means."

"How did the Duchess of Burgundy become involved?" Ellen inquired.

"Ahh, now, that lady is not quite as honest as she would have all believe." James Stewart chuckled. "You see, part of her dower portion had not ever been paid. Indeed, it was long overdue. Her brother Edward was holding on to it as long as he could, but then he died suddenly. And King Richard, her other brother, was beset from the start of his reign by his sister-in-law's attempts to put her eldest son into his rightful place on the throne, and the threat of a civil war. And then his own wife and son died. And then Margaret Beaufort and Edward's widow, Elizabeth Woodville, arranged a marriage between Adair's half sister, Bess, and Margaret Beaufort's son, Henry Tudor, which led to Henry's invasion of England and subsequent victory over King Richard at Market Bosworth several years ago.

"Henry Tudor has no intention of paying the remainder of the Duchess of Burgundy's dower portion. Indeed, I have been told he is a man who is quite close with a penny." The king chuckled. " 'Tis his Welsh blood, I fear. The Welsh do have the reputation of holding tight to whatever they lay their hands on," James Stewart noted. "So the duchess is irritated, and wishes to do harm to England's king for that and, I am told, for other personal reasons. Four years ago Henry Tudor's government began hearing rumors about this Yorkist prince in Ireland. And they were frankly concerned. At the same time Margaret of Burgundy learned of our pretender as well."

"Why didn't the English take him from Ireland?" Ellen asked. "That would have surely been the wise thing to do."

"While England technically holds Ireland, they have powerful enemies there in the person of the earls of Kildare and Desmond, who can raise armies to fight the English easily. Henry Tudor did not wish to start a war over a rumor. A war that would cost him gold, as well as good English lives. So while he and his council debated the matter, Margaret of Burgundy acted. She sent for Perkin Warbeck to come and meet with her in Flanders. At that point Kildare and Desmond had him convinced that he was the young Richard, Duke of York, who had been smuggled from England after his brother had been murdered in the Tower of London."

"But Adair said her brothers were killed at Middlesham Castle," Ellen said.

"Aye, and I believe her," James Stewart answered, "but the Tudor adherents had put it out when their man seized power that King Richard had murdered his nephews in the tower. This is the tale that was bruited all about Europe in the Tudor effort to discredit King Richard the Third, and make their man Henry Tudor's usurping of England's throne legitimate. Yet Edward the Fourth's brother, George, Duke of Clarence, has a son with a far stronger claim to England's throne as a male heir of the House of York. Only Henry Tudor's marriage to Edward the Fourth's daughter, Elizabeth, gives him any legitimacy. That and the fact that Edward, Earl of Warwick, Clarence's son, is in the Tower.

"Adair has always spoken of her uncle Dickon's great love for children, and how kind he was to her in particular. The look on her face when Warbeck, in keeping with the Tudor rumor, said that Richard was not kind was an amazing one to behold. Only her upbringing in the royal nurseries kept her from smacking him, I am certain," the king said with a small chuckle. "She loved her uncle dearly."

"Certainly Warbeck would not have repeated such rumors to the Duchess of Burgundy," Ellen said. "How could she sponsor him under those circumstances?"

"Of course she would have defended her brother Richard, and laid the alleged murders at the hands of others unknown. And he, carefully tutored by the Irish, who believed the same, would have gone along with the deception. And it suited Margaret of Burgundy to say he was her nephew Richard. If she could not have the remainder of her dower portion she would have revenge upon the Tudor usurper. And she was not alone. It suited other monarchs in Europe to take up the cause of this displaced *prince*.

"My French ally, King Charles the Eighth of France, the counselors of the young Duke of Burgundy, Maximillian, king of the Romans, were all actively involved to one extent or another in this deception. It suited their purposes, as it has mine, to attempt to destabilize Henry Tudor's throne. Warbeck was welcomed into France and entertained royally. King Maximillian took him to the funeral of the Holy Roman Emperor, Frederick the Third. He was welcomed into Vienna and treated as if he were indeed the rightful and legitimate king of England.

"At this point the English were becoming quite frantic at Warbeck's existence. They made attempts to seize him, but he was well protected by those about him. However, those shielding him entered into negotiations with the English to determine which was more to their advantage: retaining him, or accepting a large bounty for his person. Isabella, the queen of Spain, was petitioned for aid, but she is a careful woman. I suspect she knew the truth, as did the rest of them, but was more honorable. She ignored the plea for aid."

"This Warbeck fellow has lived a great deal in so short a time," Ellen noted. "What happened next, and how did he end up here in Scotland?"

"Well," the king continued, "Maximillian, who succeeded Frederick the Third as Holy Roman Emperor, decided the best thing was to get the pretender out of all their kingdoms, as he had now served his purpose. But he did not wish to make this apparent publicly. So he mounted a small expedition of ships and men and sent Warbeck off to invade England. The little fleet sailed to stand off the coast of Kent, but strangely there was no popular uprising in the pretender's favor, and his few followers who landed were cut off by the local authorities.

"Discouraged, for he had been assured by those around him that England would rise to welcome him, he sailed for Ireland, where he met up with the Earl of Desmond in Munster. They attacked Waterford, but the attack failed. It was then that the *true* king fled to Scotland, and I took my turn using him to keep Henry Tudor agitated," James Stewart concluded with a small smile. "And it has cost me a pretty penny, my bonny."

"You should not have wed him to Katherine Gordon," Ellen said.

"I needed Huntley back in my camp," the king replied. "George Gordon is a good man, a fine soldier, but,

God's blood, he is naive in many ways. How could he not know this was a fraud? Yet he was willing to take the chance that this man who claimed to be a king was indeed a king, and if he gave his daughter in marriage to him, that she would be queen of England one day," the king said, shaking his head. "But my first concern must be for Scotland, my bonny. Gordon and his adherents were keeping me from bringing my kingdom together. I did what I did to prevent further chaos. The Earl of Huntley did not have to give his permission for his daughter to wed Perkin Warbeck, but he did."

"George Gordon gave his permission for his daughter, Katherine, to be wed to Richard, Duke of York, England's *true* king, not Perkin Warbeck," Ellen reminded the king in a soft voice. "You took advantage of his pride, my lord."

"I did indeed," James Stewart admitted.

"I remember when we came to court almost two years back to meet this man being touted as England's king. You told me but part of the story then, and I thought you ruthless," Ellen said.

"You called me ruthless," he corrected her with a small grin. "And at that point in time I did not know all that I have told you this night. It was after we spoke that night, after Adair was so positive that Warbeck was not her half brother Dickie, that I sent out my spies and sought for the truth of the matter."

"Aye, I did call you ruthless," she remarked. "And you said you were a Stewart king, and Stewart kings were ruthless by nature. Then you told me the tale of the first James, who had betrayed a Gordon friend by sending the woman he loved and planned to wed into the arms of another man." Ellen shook her head. "I thought it so sad. You told me then that kings are either loved or feared, but that you intended to be both. You are already well loved by your people, my dear lord. And in time, as they come to know you better, to know you as I do, I believe that you will be feared too. And that makes me sad as well, for you are a good man, Jamie Stewart."

The king reached out and took her two hands in his. "Never be afraid of me, Ellen MacArthur," he said, and he kissed those two little hands. "I have counselors who advise me. I have servants, a confessor, and a mistress I love. I have siblings and dozens of relatives. There are those who call me friend, but I am no fool. They call me friend because they have gained lands or other honors from me. They enjoy power and all it offers them through me. I have only one friend, my bonny, and I am holding her hands in mine now." He kissed her hands again and smiled. "But never shall anyone but you hear me admit to such a thing, Ellen MacArthur."

Ellen's fingers closed about the king's. She drew his hands to her and kissed them in return. Looking into his blue eyes, she said, "It is nae easy being a king, Jamie, is it?" And, taking her hands back, she smiled at him.

"Nay, 'tis not, my bonny," he told her. "And few realize it."

"What will you do now with Perkin Warbeck?" Ellen asked him.

"I will mount a final expedition into England in a few months' time. Perhaps the north will rise for this alleged son of York, and if it does then King Henry will be kept too busy to trouble with Scotland for a time," James Stewart said.

"And if the north of England does not rise for him?" Ellen pressed.

"I have put my private secretary to seeking out defunct titles that once belonged to the Crown. I will choose one, revive it, and offer it to Warbeck with suitable lands and a modest income. That will please the Gordons, and keep their daughter near."

"Now, there is the James Stewart I know and love," Ellen told him.

"You do not like the ruthless fellow?" he teased her.

"I do not dislike him," Ellen countered, "but I prefer

the kindly man I came to know when I arrived at court from my Highland home."

The king chuckled. Then he said, "Will you tell Adair what I have told you?"

"I think not," Ellen said. "She loved her uncle and her siblings. She still feels the anguish of her half sister's betrayal, and King Henry's severe actions toward her and his permitting King Richard's memory to be sullied when he knew the accusations were not true. To learn that you have been so deliberate and calculating in your behavior and your actions with this fraudulent Warbeck would destroy what small faith she retains in you. And she would be very angry at first should she learn all you have told me, my dear lord. It could cause a breach between Adair and her husband, Conal Bruce. Conal is your loyal man, but if his wife gained this knowledge he would find himself caught between her anger and his king. He loves Adair, but he is an honorable man. Forced to choose he would pick his king," Ellen said quietly.

"An honorable man," the king repeated. "Much like his older brother of Duffdour, my bonny."

"I need time, my good lord," Ellen said. "I cannot say I forgive Duncan Armstrong until I am truly ready to forgive him. And he would not want me to, for he knows that I, too, have my honor."

"So what is to happen then?" James Stewart asked her.

"We will live side by side each day. I will show my husband no disrespect, for he is laird of Duffdour, and is entitled to even my good regard as such. But I will not share myself with him until I am satisfied he has learned to hold me in as high esteem as I hold him," Ellen said. "Women, my lord, have their honor too, and Duncan besmirched mine when he knelt by Roger Colby and asked that infamous question of the dying man."

"Be as generous of spirit, Ellen MacArthur, as I know that you can be," the king said to her. "Do not keep him twisting at the end of your rope too long."

"It is Duncan who shall make that decision," Ellen replied serenely.

James Stewart arose from his chair. "I am for bed, my bonny. I shall depart on the morrow for Linlithgow."

"Sleep well, my lord," Ellen said, and watched as he walked from the hall. Turning, she looked into the fireplace, where the flames were now burning low. The days ahead, she knew, would not be easy ones. With a sigh she stood up and climbed the stairs to her own bedchamber.

Her husband lay already sleeping in their bed. She was grateful he had not lain awake in an effort to speak with her. She could not have remained calm yet. Stripping off her gown, she washed her face and hands, scrubbed her teeth, and got into the bed, turning her back to him. She would be awake before him, and down into the hall to see to the comfort of the king before he left Duffdour.

Duncan had not been asleep when she had come into the chamber, but he instinctively knew that she could not be reached by either reason or passion right now. He had seen her anger tonight, and although he had always heard that red-haired folk had fierce tempers, he had never until this day seen it in his little wife, with her sweet nature. Then he remembered the girl who had taken a knife and carved Balgair MacArthur's handsome face into a mask of horror. The laird of Duffdour realized that it was going to take a certain amount of time to regain his wife's love and respect. But he would do what he had to do, because he loved her. He smiled softly to himself in the darkness. And he knew that she loved him. It would take time. But she would eventually forgive him. Of that, Duncan Armstrong, laird of Duffdour, was certain. Closing his eyes, he slept.

Chapter 18

$\mathcal{E}$llen awoke at the first bird twitter outside of the bedchamber windows. Rising, she washed, dressed, and hurried down into the kitchens, where Lizzie and her helpers were already taking freshly baked loaves from the oven. At the table sat a young boy and a young girl. The lad was carefully slicing the tops off of the round bread trenchers that had been baked yesterday morning and left in the pantry since then to harden. The lass seated across from him was carefully scooping the soft bread from the insides of the hard shells, leaving just enough to make the trencher leakproof, while opening the round loaf wide enough to contain the meal. The bread scooped out would be put into the stew cooked that day. Lizzie was a frugal woman and would see nothing wasted, for like all the others in her kitchen at Duffdour, she had known times of hunger.

"Good morning, mistress," she greeted Ellen.

"The king and his party are leaving this morning," Ellen reminded all within hearing. "Everything has been prepared?"

"Indeed, mistress, everything is in good order," Lizzie reported proudly. "The oatcakes were baked yesterday

so they would be firm today and not crumble in the
men's pouches. I've roasted a nice plump rabbit for
the king to dine on when they stop to rest the horses.
The oat porridge is cooking now for breakfast. There
will be hard-boiled eggs, fresh bread, butter, and cheese
for the men. I'll have ham, and lovely eggs poached in
cream with nutmeg for the high board, along with bread,
butter, and cheese."

"Thank you, Lizzie," Ellen told the cook. "It is good
to know I can count upon you and your helpers. Be certain there is both ale and cider for the trestles." Then
she hurried from the warm kitchens and up into the hall,
where the servants were already setting up the trestles
needed, along with the benches. The fires in the hearths
were burning high, taking the night chill from the room.

The men began streaming into the hall just as it appeared the sun was about to rise. The servants began
coming up from the kitchens with the trenchers of hot
oat porridge, placing them before each man. The bread,
butter, and cheese were set out. Two serving girls with
pitchers filled the wooden cups. A servant came to tell
Ellen that the king would be arriving at any moment.
Ellen sent the man to the kitchens to see that the food for
the high board was brought up immediately, and then to
the stables with instructions to see that the horses were
saddled and ready for the king's departure.

"Good morning, wife," Duncan Armstrong said to
Ellen. He smiled down at her, thinking she was the most
adorable of females, even when she was angry at him.
I am besotted, he considered. *A fool enamored of his
wife.*

Ellen turned. "Good morning, my lord," she greeted
him. But she did not smile.

"You slept well?" he inquired politely. Of course she
had, and he knew it, for he had wakened on and off
the night long, unable to find peace, while Ellen slept
deeply.

"Actually I did. My conscience, you see, is a clear

one," Ellen answered him pertly. "Now, excuse me, for I must greet the king, who has just entered the hall." She turned away from him and, going to James Stewart, curtsied. "Good morning, my lord. I hope your night was a restful one. The meal is ready, and the horses are being saddled as I speak. I have some small provisions for you and your men for your day's ride."

"Good morning, my bonny!" the king said jovially. "Aye, we'll make for Hailes today. My Meg will be awaiting us, and right glad will I be to see her."

The king, the laird, and his wife sat themselves at the high board with Hercules Hepburn, who had joined them.

"Poached eggs in cream sauce!" the king enthused. "Meg's sister's cook adds marsala wine to hers." He helped himself to a generous portion.

"I regret we have no marsala," Ellen said, "but the sauce is dusted with freshly ground nutmeg. Ours is but a simple kitchen, my lord."

"I shall see that you are sent a cask of marsala," the king replied. "I know you have tasted it, for my aunt has a taste for marsala wine." He chuckled.

"I remember," Ellen responded, dimpling. "She said it helped her sleep."

The king turned to the laird. "Your border hospitality, my lord, is always most welcoming. And I am relieved to see you are well prepared for any English incursion."

"We here in the west will see some fighting," the laird said, "but we border on Cumbria, a region as wild as our own. 'Tis the eastern borders that will suffer the worst."

The king nodded, as did Hercules Hepburn. "I will make one more incursion on behalf of Katherine Gordon's husband," he told the laird. "I know when I call that I can count upon you and your clansmen to join me."

"We will be there, my lord," the laird said.

When the king had finished his meal he was escorted by his host and hostess outside, where the horses were waiting. His men were already mounted and ready to go. Hercules Hepburn thanked Ellen and the laird for their kind hospitality. James Stewart shook the laird of Duffdour's hand in friendship. He kissed Ellen on both of her cheeks. Then, mounting his horse, he led his men from Duffdour's courtyard and through its gates.

The laird and his wife watched until their guests were well onto the border track that they would follow. It was then that Ellen rounded on her husband furiously.

"What do you mean, you will join the king on another of his futile incursions into England for that fraud with whom he has been torturing the English king?"

"Is he truly a fraud?" Duncan asked her. "And keep your voice down, woman!"

"Aye, he is, and James Stewart knows it," Ellen said.

"If the king calls I must go," the laird told his wife. "You know I must go."

"It was not fair of him to ask you, given his knowledge, and mine," Ellen replied.

"I could not stay behind if the king rouses the borders."

"You could be ill when he calls, couldn't you?" she asked.

"I am neither a coward nor a liar like Ian Johnston," the laird responded testily.

"Ahh, now you admit the man is a liar!" Ellen said, outraged. "You were not so certain in the recent past, my lord, were you?"

"My children, my children, why are you quarreling?" Father Iver, Duffdour's elderly priest, had come upon them.

"The laird is a fool!" Ellen said, and then she hurried into the house.

"You have obviously given your good wife great offense that the temper so common to most red-haired folk has exhibited itself, my son," Father Iver said mildly. "I do not believe I have ever seen the lady so outraged. Do you need to confess to me?"

"My wife speaks the truth, good Father," the laird told the priest. "I am a fool."

"Come into my cottage," Father Iver invited, "and tell me what has set you at odds with the lady. Perhaps I may help to reconcile you."

There was still a bit more work to do on the inner walls about the house, but it was early yet, and the laird considered that the elderly priest might indeed have a suggestion to help him. He certainly didn't know what to do. He followed the frail old man into the small one-room cottage and sat down upon a stool to speak with the priest, who was seated in the single chair in the room.

"What has happened between you, my lord?" the priest asked. "Have you perhaps been unfaithful to your wife, and she learned of it?"

"Nay, I have not been unfaithful, good Father. But I have accused my wife wrongly of that sin," Duncan began. Then he went on to explain to the elderly priest what had happened at Devil's Glen. "She had confessed to me that he had forced his kisses and caresses upon her while he held her in his custody. But she swore nothing worse had happened, and I thought I believed her— until Ian Johnston accused her as he lay dying." The laird ran an impatient hand through his dark hair. "Father, I thought that a man about to face God's judgment could not lie. But Johnston did, and suspicion raked me, though I told Ellen I did not believe him."

"Until the moment Sir Roger lay dying," the priest said, nodding. "The temptation was simply too great for you, my son. You love your wife, and could not imagine how this villain resisted her even as you tried to believe her. Your faith in her was shaken, and you saw in the dying Sir Roger your last opportunity to be certain." Father Iver shook his white head. "Aye, my son, as a man I understand. Women are weak, as we know, and prone to lying to cover a host of their sins. But men are weak too, and prone to jealousy where their women are concerned. But you had never had reason prior to the lady's kidnapping to doubt her. And she did tell you that he forced kisses and caresses upon her that she resisted. Was it Ian Johnston's words alone that roused you?"

"Aye! He was dying, good Father. Why would he tell such a lie when he lay dying? Did he not fear for his immortal soul at that moment?" the laird asked.

"There are many reasons he said what he said," the priest considered thoughtfully. "Perhaps he *assumed* Sir Roger had violated your wife. Perhaps Sir Roger *intimated* it to appear more dangerous than he was. Or perhaps Ian Johnston was jealous of you, my son. You are a respected man here in the borders. He was not. You have a wife you love. He did not love his wife. Your wife gave you a healthy son and heir within a year of your marriage. His woman, poor lass, could manage only stillbirths and miscarriages. Did it not occur to you that Ian Johnston hated you for your good fortune, Duncan, my son? Hated you enough to spew forth a lie he knew would eat at your pride, your soul, and perhaps even destroy your marriage as he destroyed his? It is hard to imagine such wickedness, but it does exist," Father Iver concluded, fingering the beads at his waist.

Duncan Armstrong nodded slowly. "Aye, I believe Johnston did hate me. Still, like you it is difficult for me to conceive of such evil in one man."

"The corruption in him is what drew Sir Roger to him," the priest responded. "Being the most depraved of men himself, he recognized a similar but weaker soul, and used him to his own ends. But these matters are past. Now you must restore your wife's faith and trust in you again, my son. It will not be easy."

"She hates me," Duncan said despairingly.

The priest chuckled. "Nay, Duncan, my son, she does not hate you. She loves you, and I suspect you well know it. However, you have tested her love by being all too human. You will, I fear, have to do the one thing that is

most difficult for men to do: You will have to apologize
to your wife, and admit to your faults."

"Apologize?" The laird of Duffdour looked surprised.
"For what need I apologize? I was jealous. Any husband
would have been jealous. Would Ellen have preferred I
not be jealous of a man who held her captive for many
weeks, and who she has admitted kissed and fondled
her?"

"You must apologize for not trusting her, not trusting her word," the priest said. "Normally I should not
even consider such a thing, my son. But you have hurt
a woman who never gave you any reason to doubt her,
and only by telling her that you are sorry can you give
her the opportunity to forgive you. And she must, for
the sake of her own soul."

The laird stood up. "I will think on it," he told Father
Iver.

"Do not wait too long to make your peace with her,
my son," the priest advised. "The longer you wait, the
wider this breach will grow, and 'twill be harder to close
it, to heal the wounds you have both inflicted upon each
other." He watched as the laird walked off, going to a
group of workmen now reinforcing the little wall about
the house. Father Iver shook his head. Duncan Armstrong was an intelligent man, but he was also a stubborn one. He decided he would speak with Ellen.

He found her in the kitchen gardens transplanting
seedlings into the freshly turned soil. "I would speak
with you, my daughter," he began.

Ellen looked up. There was a smudge of dirt on her
right cheek. "Do you mind if I work while we speak, Father
Iver?" she asked him hopefully. "Old Malcolm says the
rains will come tonight for at least two days. I need these
seedlings planted today or I shall not be able to plant again
for a good week. There are peas, and many of the herbs I
used in my apothecary. Our growing season is not as long
as I might wish."

"Of course, my child," the priest said, lowering himself to the small wooden bench by the low garden wall. "I have spoken," he began, "with the laird. He is quite devastated by the troubles between you, poor lad."

"Father, you waste your breath on me. If Duncan will come and tell me he is sorry for doubting me, then all will be well between us. I will put from my heart and mind the picture I retain of his kneeling by Roger Colby as he lay dying, and asking for all there to hear, 'Did you fuck my wife?' My own husband doubted me and shamed me before the king, before all who were there. I am his wife until death, good Father. I will keep his house and entertain his guests. I will care for our bairn, but there will be no more bairns of my body until Duncan Armstrong can apologize for those words, for his doubt. And there is nothing more to say on the subject. I thank you for your caring."

The priest arose slowly. He was a man who knew how to retreat, and when. "I would have you know, my daughter, that I am in full concord with you. The laird treated you shamefully, for you are—have been—a good and loyal wife to him." Then he ambled off, pleased to have planted the idea in her head that he was on her side. She would not shut him out, and he would be able to help the laird and his wife mend their breach, for now each of them believed the priest was on their side.

Ellen continued planting, her hands scooping out holes in the earth, transplanting the seedlings she had been growing for the last month in her apothecary. Her conscience still tweaked at her slightly, but she would have to live with it. She had admitted to kisses and caresses. She had not told her husband of the night Colby had used her with his fingers, with that horrible thing he called a phallus. She would never tell him. She had done the right thing in keeping it to herself, although the memory of it still hurt her.

But look what trouble the dying Ian Johnston's words had caused her. Duncan had a picture in his head of Colby futtering her, and until Colby himself had dis-

abused her husband the notion on his own deathbed,
Duncan had doubted her. If Colby had denied fucking
her, then what he had done certainly could not be called
by the same name. But why had he denied it? He could
have added to Duncan's misery and destroyed her world
entirely, by saying he had, or by remaining silent. Yet he
had denied it, and she would pray for his soul her life
through because he had.

She had suspected that despite his claim that all
women were whores and sluts, Roger Colby had come
to admire her determination. Admire her. Believe just
a little bit that perhaps there were good women in the
world. She wondered if perhaps he had even hoped in
the deepest part of his soul that she would escape him
that day. They had both known she was taunting him
deliberately that morning in his hall, but he had acquiesced to her challenge and given her a chance to escape
him. She had no doubt what would have happened had
he caught her. Whatever small admiration he might
have had for her would have disappeared as he took her
where he caught her. Ellen shivered. Certainly God and
his blessed Mother had been with her that day.

But now she had a worse difficulty to face, to manage.
Duncan had hurt her, embarrassed her publicly. Until he
made his peace with her she could not forgive him. She
wished she were a greater soul and could forgive him
the jealousy that caused him to doubt her, for that was
really all it had been. But she could not. If he could not
apologize to her then he had no respect for her, and she
was little better than a servant in his house.

Duncan wanted to apologize, but somehow he could not
gather the courage up that he needed to say the words.
He gave Ellen credit, for she showed him no disrespect,
nor berated him before others. She was coolly diffident
toward him, speaking in pleasant if reserved tones when
they were in public. In private, however, she spoke little
to him, and he knew that he dared not force her to his

will in their bed, lest he lose her forever. If he attempted to cuddle her, she pulled away if she could, and if she couldn't she lay stone cold and still in his embrace. The warmth had left her entirely.

It occurred to him that he was no better than his brother Conal, who had been unable to tell his wife, Adair, that he loved her until it became apparent that he would lose her unless he did. Duncan recalled berating Conal for his stubbornness in the matter, but now it would appear he was no better. What the hell was the matter with him? He was a proud man, he knew, but he had never before allowed his pride to ride him so hard. And even the servants were beginning to notice that the laird and his lady were not as they had once been, laughing and full of open love for each other.

And then in midsummer little Willie had an accident. The bairn, now walking all over, had somehow evaded his nursemaid, Laria, and escaped the hall. He wandered out into the small courtyard surrounding the house. The new wall about Duffdour was just about finished, but there were building stones still there, stacked up three and four high. Adventurous, the bairn clambered up to the top of one of the piles. Delighted with his success he crowed triumphantly, and it was then that he lost his balance, falling from atop the pile of stones to the ground below. It was not a precipitous drop, no more than two feet, but Willie was small and had not the balance an older child would have had. He hit his head on a single stone that lay in the dirt as he fell to the ground, and a gash opened in the back of his little head, pouring forth bright red blood. He lay still and silent and very small in the dirt, making not so much as a whimper.

Laria, coming out to seek her little lad, saw him as he fell, and ran shrieking to gather up her charge. She carried the bleeding child back into the hall, calling loudly for help as she came. And she was sobbing wildly as she ran.

Sim heard her even before she entered the hall. Then,

seeing the girl with her burden, he crossed himself, saying, "Holy Mother of God, lass! What has happened?" Then he shouted to another servant, "Fetch the mistress quickly! She'll be in the gardens. Then find the laird! Hurry! *Hurry!*" He turned back to Laria. "Stop your howling, lass. Put the lad there on the high board. What happened?"

Willie was laid down upon the table. Laria continued to weep. "I looked away for just a moment," she sobbed, "and he was gone. I went right outside, for I know how he loves the out-of-doors. *Ohhhhh*," she wailed. "The laird will have my life for this!"

Ellen ran into the hall and, seeing her son upon the high board, hurried over to him. "What happened?" she demanded of Laria.

Laria wept louder.

"The bairn got away from her and out into the courtyard," Sim said.

Ellen slapped the hysterical girl hard across her cheek. *"What happened?"*

Laria gasped with surprise, but then she said, "He climbed a pile of stones left over from the wall, mistress. Before I could get to him, he fell and cracked his head open." She sniffled, the tears coming again. "I tried to reach him."

Ellen nodded. "Go to my apothecary," she said to Laria. "You will find Gunna there helping me make winter syrups. Tell her that Willie's head is cracked open, and to come with what I need to dress the bairn's wound. Hurry now!"

"Yes, mistress," Laria said, and ran from the hall.

"Get me some water and clean rags, Sim. I'll want to clean the wound," Ellen told him. Her voice was calm, but her heart was hammering in her chest. Willie was her bairn. He lay so still and pale, but she could see he was breathing, his little chest rising and falling with even breaths. She took a rag and dipped it into the water that Sim had so quickly brought. Then Ellen lifted her son, holding him carefully as she began to clean the congealing blood from his wound. He began to whimper.

"Let me, mistress," Sim said, taking the child carefully. "You'll work better with your two hands than just the one."

"Thank you," Ellen said as the blood washed away, revealing the extent of the child's wound. The gash was long, but it was not deep. There was no dirt in it.

Laria came back into the hall. "Gunna's coming, mistress," she said.

"Pour a dram of the laird's whiskey," Ellen told the girl, "and bring it to me." When Laria had complied, Ellen drizzled the dram cup over the wound in Willie's head. The child whimpered again, and his mother smiled. "Good! You'll live," she said.

Gunna ran in carrying a small basket. "Does it need to be sewn?" she asked.

"Nay," Ellen answered her. "I think a poultice and a plaster will suffice."

"Mama!" Willie cried, his eyes suddenly flying open. "Maaaama!"

"Mama is here, Willie. You are a very naughty laddie, running away from Laria, and now you have cracked your head. But Mama will fix it."

"Mama, Mama, Mama!" the bairn wailed.

"Where is Machara?" Ellen wanted to know. "Laria, go and find her. I cannot treat my son's wound while he sobs and struggles." She put her arms about the little lad, cuddling him close and careful not to touch the wound. "There, my bairn, there. It's all right. It's all right."

Duncan Armstrong ran into the hall. "Is the lad alive?" he demanded to know. "And how the hell did he get away from Laria? I'll have her hide for this!"

"Calm yourself, my lord," Ellen advised him. "He is your son, and already adventurous. It might have been more harmful, but it wasn't, praise the Blessed Mother. He'll live to do worse, I fear."

The laird came up on the dais and looked at his son.

"Da!" Willie said, and he smiled. "My da!"

The laird took his son into his arms, holding him close.

"If you hold him like that," Ellen said quietly, "I can probably get the poultice on. The cut is shallow and will not need stitching."

"I've got him," Duncan said. "Do what you must, wife."

His blue eyes met her gray-blue ones, and then he said, "I'm sorry. I really am."

"I know," she answered him softly, and her heart felt suddenly lighter. "We need not speak on it again, my lord," Ellen told him. And then she went to work doctoring their son's wound. Gunna had already mixed a poultice of warm barley flour and a paste of dried figs. Ellen cut away the hair about the bairn's wound. Now, his father holding him, she dressed the gash with the poultice, sealing it with a small piece of clean cloth she cut to fit just beyond the ends of the wound.

Machara came into the hall. She had already learned from Laria what had happened. "Give him to me, my lord," she said to the laird. "He's almost done nursing, but at fifteen months he will still be comforted by my breast." She took Willie from his father and, settling herself in a chair by the hearth, she gave the bairn her plump breast, and he began to suckle her, murmuring contentedly as he did so.

The crisis was over. A servant cleaned the high board where little Willie had lain. Gunna gathered up the basket of items from the apothecary and left the hall. Another servant took away the basin and bloody clothes Ellen had used to clean the wound. And the laird took his wife by the hand. They walked out of the house, and the laird instructed one of his men to remove the loose stones that remained in the court, shaking his head slightly at the bloody stone where his son's head had hit.

"I want a man at the front door until the door is locked for the night," Ellen said. "We were fortunate that he only cracked his little pate. He might have fallen into the moat and drowned as he ran across the drawbridge. And who would have been there to see or hear him? 'Tis true the drawbridge is small and the moat not very deep, but still."

"I'll speak with Artair and have a man posted as you wish," the laird said.

"Thank you," Ellen said, and then she began to cry. She wept great, gulping sobs, and Duncan gathered her into her arms. "We could have lost him," she said.

"But we didn't," he reassured her.

"You hurt me," she told him.

"Did you not just tell me we would speak on this no more?" he gently teased.

"But why did you doubt me?" she asked him.

Duncan Armstrong shook his head. "I didn't really, but I am a fool, Ellen. My jealousy overcame my common sense. When Ian Johnston spoke those terrible words, and his eyes glittered with malice as he died, something possessed me, ate into me. Terrible pictures came into my head. It was as if I were bewitched." His arms tightened about her. "I love you, Ellen MacArthur. I could not bear the thought of another man having you. I knew you were faithful, but those wicked words bedeviled me to the point of madness."

Ellen nodded slowly, then said, "Still, husband, we must settle something between us. I will never be unfaithful to you, and I will always speak in your best interests. You must swear to trust me above everyone else, Duncan. If it is to be good between us once again, my lord, you must promise me that."

"I do!" the laird said fervently.

"Then we are reconciled, husband," Ellen told him with a small smile, her tears now gone. "Will you give me the kiss of peace?" She lifted her small face to his.

He bent his dark head to hers, and his lips brushed softly, sweetly over hers. "We are reconciled, wife," he told her. "I do not ever want us to fight again."

"Do not be silly, my lord," Ellen said. "Of course we will fight again. But never do I want any breach between us. We will settle our arguments before we sleep."

"Agreed!" he told her with a happy smile. "I don't suppose you would like to *sleep* now?" he said mischievously.

Ellen giggled, but shook her head in the negative. "The night will come soon enough, husband."

And when it did the laird and his wife departed the hall early, while behind them Sim and the servants nodded, smiling. Whatever had been causing trouble between their master and their mistress, their son's accident had corrected. No one had any doubt that there would be another bairn at Duffdour within the year ahead.

In the laird's bedchamber the fire burned high, warming the room. Slowly, carefully, Duncan removed her simple garments, gently kissing each section of her body as he exposed it. When she stood naked before him, Ellen began to mimic his actions, stripping away the few pieces of clothing he had worn that day. Reaching up, she unlaced his shirt, opening it wide. He wore no camise beneath it, for the day had been warm. Her hands smoothed across his broad chest, and she pressed little kisses upon the warm, furred flesh. Pulling the shirt from him, she raised her face up for a kiss.

His mouth descended, taking hers tenderly. He reveled in the sweetness of her parted lips, his tongue plunging between those lips to seek out her tongue. Ellen murmured softly as their tongues found each other and entwined in a sensuous dance. Kiss blended into kiss until her nipples were tight with longing, and his cock strained against the fabric of his breeks as her fingers struggled to open them.

"My boots!" he groaned. "I've got to get them off."

"Nay, I don't want to wait!" Ellen said fiercely, and she pushed him back so that he fell upon the bed, his legs dangling over the edge. Standing between his splayed legs, she yanked his breeks down, freeing his swollen manhood. Her fingers caressed him, wrapping about the turgid length, tightening gently until he groaned. Ellen bent over him, her tongue skimming up and down his cock with a teasing touch. Then she took him into her mouth and drew upon him, tenderly at first, the pull of her lips growing stronger until he cried out with the pure pleasure her actions engendered.

Ellen raised her head, her eyes limpid. She gazed upon him and, leaning forward, licked him from belly to throat. Her tongue tickled his nipples. She nipped sharply at them. Without a word she mounted him, letting his hungry manhood fill her hot, wet sheath. Then she rode him, slowly at first, then harder and harder. She cried out as his big hands took her breasts, crushing them, leaving the marks of his fingers upon her fair white flesh. Then his hands cupped her buttocks and squeezed them hard.

And as suddenly as she had bestridden him, he swiftly rose slightly, clutching Ellen in his arms, and put her upon her back. He took her legs and pushed them back. Then he began to fuck her strongly. *Harder. Harder! Faster! Faster! Deeper and deeper.*

She clawed at him wildly, keening softly until it became a scream. Her head was spinning, and she could scarce get her breath. Higher and higher he drove her, until she felt faint with the incredible pleasure he was giving her. "Duncan!" she sobbed his name, but he did not answer. Half opening her eyes, she saw his face. It was intense, fierce, concentrated upon the passion between them. And then from deep within her Ellen felt the tremors. Felt them more strongly than she had ever felt them. *I am going to die*, she thought, but she didn't care. And as she slipped over the edge he gave a great shout, and she felt his creamy love juices pouring forth to flood her and create another bairn.

When Ellen finally came to herself again she found she was firmly cradled in her husband's strong arms and beneath the down coverlet. He was fully naked next to her and, turning her head slightly, she saw that his boots lay upon the floor. "Are you awake?" she asked him softly, and heard him chuckle.

"I have been but waiting for you, wife," he told her.

"Did I sleep?" she said, slightly confused.

"You swooned as we reached the peak together, sweetheart," he told her.

"*Oh*," she answered, not certain whether she should be embarrassed. There had been passion between them from the start, but never quite like what had just happened. It had been extremely intense. She felt herself blushing.

"I like you bold," he whispered in her ear. "And you seem to grow bolder each time we make love, wife." There was a hint of amusement as well as pride in his voice.

"I missed you," she excused herself.

He chuckled. "We made another bairn this night," he said.

"I know," she replied, and her voice was filled with happiness.

"Never quarrel with me so fiercely again, wife," he said to her.

"Never give me cause, husband," Ellen replied pertly. She snuggled harder against him. "But perhaps when my anger dissolved, the fierceness of it was channeled into my passion for you, Duncan Armstrong. I love you with all my heart."

"And I you," he responded. "And you must keep that fierceness, even if I do not anger you, Ellen MacArthur, for I do not believe either of us has ever experienced such pleasure as we have this night. Now go to sleep, my darling wife. Before the dawn I will want to bury myself in your sweetness and enjoy our passion again."

"Now, here is something we may both agree upon," Ellen told him happily.

And their happiness was complete once more. Little Willie's head healed, and he seemed none the worse for wear. And Ellen found she was indeed with child this time. The border raids that late summer and early autumn seemed to concentrate themselves more to the east of them, and Duffdour's walls and defenses were not tested. Hercules Hepburn came often to bring them the news of what was happening, and so they were well-informed, sharing their news with Conal Bruce at Cleit.

In midautumn the king came into the borders, not to hunt grouse, but to reconnoiter for another invasion of England, for King Henry was again demanding that he turn over the pretender. As the young man was worth more to James Stewart alive than dead, this he refused to do. The Spanish ambassador, Pedro de Ayala, was attempting to broker a firmer truce between England and Scotland. King Ferdinand, his master, did not like the idea of an England caught between two enemies, France and Scotland. A war among them all could force him to choose sides, which sly Ferdinand did not want to do, preferring to be everyone's supposed friend while actually seeing only to his own interests. And then fires appeared on the border hillsides, calling the clans to war again.

"All this fuss over a man who isn't really who he says he is," grumbled Ellen to her sister-in-law, Adair. She had invited the lady of Cleit and her children to stay at Duffdour while their men were with the king over the border. Cleit had not yet been fully fortified, and Duffdour was safer. Adair, her children, and their personal servants had come gladly. And Ellen was happy for the company, especially as she was with child.

"When will the bairn be born?" Adair wanted to know.

"Probably at the end of May, the beginning of June," Ellen said. "I hope the men are back before then."

"The clans will be back by winter," Adair said. "Neither my cousin James nor the English wish to be encamped in the open come the snows. They prefer to fight their wars in comfort, which is why it is generally peaceable in the borders come winter. I just want them both back safe and uninjured. At least Murdoc is safe in his monastery."

Bits of news filtered into Duffdour. The Scots had bypassed the tower houses and small forts where the local farmers and their animals usually took shelter during a border war. They instead made directly for Norham Castle near Berwick and laid siege to it. Before this could be fully accomplished, the Earl of Surrey came north with a vast army. The Scots were forced to move quickly back over the border, lest they be caught. Basing themselves in the disputed town of Berwick, Surrey's forces began a series of raids in the eastern border, razing Ayton Castle as the Scots, far fewer in number, were forced to stand by helplessly. Both women at Duffdour knew the king would be furious.

And James was. It was the same old thing all over again: a border war that cost Scots lives as well as loss of property and livestock. It was vicious and bloody and useless, as it always was.

"It has to stop," the king said. "We cannot go on like this forever. Every time England and Scotland disagree the border erupts. Our people suffer." And then James Stewart sent his personal herald to the Earl of Surrey, challenging him to personal combat. The winner would take Berwick, and this current war would end. Delighted with the idea, the Earl of Surrey accepted the king of Scotland's offer.

"Are you mad?" Patrick Hepburn shouted at the king when he learned of the challenge. "Surrey is famed for his skill with the sword. No one has ever beaten him."

"I'm younger, and even more skilled," the king defended his decision. "Besides, I sense that my luck is strong, and it tells me I will not be killed by this man."

"You'll not be killed because you can't do it," Lord Home said quietly.

"Aye, we'll not let you," the Earl of Angus said.

But James Stewart was so adamant that he would

fight the Earl of Surrey in a single combat that his lords, not knowing what else to do, sent for the Spanish ambassador, who, learning of the king's proposal, came with all possible speed. Although many of the earls disliked Ayala and were jealous of his friendship and influence with their young king, they realized that if they could not convince James Stewart to withdraw the challenge, perhaps—just perhaps—Ayala could.

Pedro de Ayala had been horrified to learn of what the young king had done, but he also realized that a king's pride was involved. It would take the utmost skill and diplomacy to convince James Stewart to amend his plans.

The king was quite surprised to see his friend. He had left de Ayala behind this time because he did not want to divide his friend's loyalties. De Ayala would have reported the Scots battle plans to King Ferdinand, who would probably have sent the information to King Henry in an effort to show his friendship for England. But now here stood de Ayala before him in his tent.

"So, Pedro, they have sent for you in an attempt to dissuade me," the king said.

"Aye, they have," de Ayala said. "I think you are the noblest of kings to have suggested such a brave yet simple solution to the problem facing you. But one thing concerns me greatly, Jamie."

"And what is that?" the king wanted to know. He would listen to de Ayala because the man had always been candid with him.

"Suffolk has a wife, children, heirs. If you kill him his eldest son will step into his place, and there will be another Earl of Suffolk. But if by the merest chance your foot slips, or, flush with your success, you let your guard down and Suffolk kills you, what will happen to Scotland? It would have no king, for you have no legitimate heirs, no wife. Civil war would ensue in the battle to succeed you, Jamie. And while your clans battled against one another, the English would march into Scotland and annex it.

"I have traveled all over our world, and nowhere but here are the rights of the common man so protected. Not in England, nor my España, nor France, nor in the German or Italian states. Every king before you has built on those rights. You follow in their footsteps, and the common folk adore you. Your earls and the lords love you. You will marry one day, and when you do your son will follow in your path, and that of the kings of Scotland before him, because you will teach him to do so. But there will be no king of Scotland if the Earl of Surrey should have the luck to kill you.

"You cannot do this, Jamie. I understand the desire you have to stop all of this chaos in the borders. A desire so strong that you would risk your own life, and the future of your country. But you cannot allow yourself to do such a thing. First you and King Henry must establish a true rule of law in your borders. As it is now, the lairds rule, and while they are loyal to you, they think nothing on a fine summer's night with the moon high in the sky of raiding into England or settling a feud with one another. And the English are the same. But once you and King Henry bring your laws firmly into the borders and enforce them, disputes between the Scots and the English can be settled in the Warden's Court. But if you are to live to see that you must withdraw your challenge to the Earl of Surrey, Jamie. Your responsibilities are too great."

"I will be dishonored, and the laughingstock of Europe," James Stewart protested. "Besides, you know I have the eye, and it tells me I will not be killed."

Pedro de Ayala nodded. "I respect this strange instinct you seem to have, my friend, but you cannot allow it to lead you astray. What if this instinct is some small devil that wishes to bring chaos to Scotland by causing you to believe you are invincible?"

"I trust those instincts, Pedro. They have guided me my whole life," the king said.

"I will not argue their value to you, but you must still

withdraw the challenge you made to the Earl of Surrey," the Spanish ambassador said quietly.

"How, without bringing shame on myself, on Scotland?" the king demanded.

"It will be difficult, 'tis true," de Ayala conceded, "but it can be done. With your permission I will dictate the letter to the English. You will stand by my side and hear it as it is written. You may perchance wish to change a phrase or a word as you listen."

Reluctantly, but knowing that his friend was right, James Stewart called in his personal secretary. "You will take down what the ambassador says," he told him.

De Ayala began: "To his gracious lordship, Edward, Earl of Surrey, greetings from His Majesty James Stewart, God's own anointed king of Scotland. It is with great reluctance that I now withdraw my honorable challenge to you for single combat. It has been pointed out to me that for a Scots king to do battle with an English earl would be considered an unequal combat. An earl may die and leave his master's kingdom little changed, for the monarch would still rule. But the death of this king would be a disaster to my kingdom, my lords, and especially to my people." De Ayala looked to James.

The king nodded. "Go on," he said.

"I tender you my apologies for rescinding this challenge, which you have honorably accepted," de Ayala concluded. "Does it meet with Your Majesty's approval?"

"I wish to add something to it," the king said, and looked to his secretary. "I promise you, my lord, that upon another day, in a distant year, when I have sired a legitimate heir for my kingdom, I will, if you are agreeable, renew my challenge."

"Most gracious," de Ayala said, although he really thought the king's words quite unnecessary. He realized, however, that James Stewart was merely soothing his pride, and the truth was that there was no real harm in it.

When the letter had been copied, signed, sealed, and sent off, the king asked to be alone. His earls and his lords were so relieved that they did not argue with him. De Ayala understood that James Stewart felt embarrassed, and depressed by what he had had to do. His instincts which had never failed him, had told him that he should have gone after Surrey on this day, for he would have slain him without a doubt. And having avoided the issue, James Stewart knew that one day he would have to deal with Surrey again, and the next time it would be to his detriment. The king dismissed his border lords and went back to Edinburgh with his earls and his small army.

Duncan Armstrong and his half brother Conal Bruce returned to Duffdour with their men, and their wives welcomed them warmly. The English did not come over the border after the Scots. Winter was upon them, and Surrey had not provisioned his army well. They deserted in droves, returning to their own homes. Hercules Hepburn came to Duffdour to tell them that a truce with the English had been signed at Ayton Castle. It would last seven years. The king had not regained the disputed Berwick, but the treaty listed in most careful detail the functions to be held by the Warden's Court for both sides of the border. There were even rules regarding the surrender of wanted men by either side to the other. Both kings were going to try to bring order to the borders.

"And," Hercules Hepburn said, "the king has agreed to cease all activity on behalf of the pretender. From henceforth he will no longer be called King Richard the Fourth. But he will be addressed as the Duke of York. And we won't surrender him to King Henry or any other. That has made Huntley and his Gordons happy, I can tell you."

"My cousin does everything but admit his wrong," Adair said archly.

"Give over, woman," Conal Bruce told his wife.

"There is more, isn't there?" Ellen asked. She was sitting comfortably in her husband's lap.

"Aye," Hercules Hepburn said. "The king has offered the duke a Scots earldom, with some small lands and an income, if he will renounce his claim to England's throne and any English titles. The fool, of course, is resisting such a solution with all his might, but the Gordons are attempting to convince him to accept for their daughter's sake. She is again with child by her husband, and the first bairn is not strong."

"Poor lass," Ellen said.

Adair arched an eyebrow. "You pity her after the way she's treated you?"

"Aye, I pity her," Ellen said. "She has nothing, and I have everything."

"She's an earl's daughter, and she can be an earl's wife if her husband is not a fool, which he is," Adair said. "You are but an unimportant little Highland lass married to an unimportant bonnet laird."

"And you are an unimportant king's brat married to an unimportant bonnet laird," Ellen countered wickedly with a grin. "But you are happy, and so am I. We love the men to whom we are wed. Our children are bonny. Katherine Gordon is married to a pompous fraud, and now, unless her husband accepts King James's offer, she is homeless. And her bairn is not well, and she is to have another. You can't possibly envy her, Adair. And if you do not envy her, then you must pity her."

"Your heart is too good," Adair said with a small smile. Duncan's wife was just perfect for him. She had just enough backbone, and a warm nature.

The Bruces, along with Hercules Hepburn, departed Duffdour just before Twelfth Night, leaving Ellen and Duncan alone and to themselves. The winter set in, to be followed by the spring. Ellen's second son, to be called Ewan, after her beloved grandfather, was born on the first day of June. Like his older sibling he was a sturdy bairn, but he had his father's dark hair, unlike the red-haired Willie.

The summer was a pleasant one, with no raids in their vicinity. The lairds were following the king's law, and the Warden's Court was operating smoothly. In October, when Hercules Hepburn came to hunt grouse in the heather with Duncan Armstrong and Conal Bruce, he brought with him news of what had happened to the Duke of York. Hercules told the tale that first evening in the hall after supper.

"No one could convince this fellow married to the Gordon lass to take a Scots title," Hercules related, "neither the king, nor his own wife, nor George Gordon himself. Poor Katherine gave birth this summer to another weak bairn. And then, leaving her children behind for their own safety, she set sail with her husband. They went to Ireland first, but even Kildare and Desmond would not help him this time. So they foolishly sailed for England, landing in Cornwall, where the duke raised a rebellion among those country folk who were still not happy with King Henry's latest taxes. He advanced as far as Exeter, but could not gain the town, and when royal troops approached he broke and ran, as we have seen him do before. He took refuge at Beaulieu Abbey in Hampshire, and it was there that he surrendered to King Henry. He's in the Tower."

"What happened to Katherine Gordon?" Ellen asked Hercules.

"They say the queen has taken her into her household, and treats her kindly," he answered Ellen.

Ellen nodded. "Poor lass," she said as she had said before, and she meant it. She wondered if Katherine Gordon would ever see her family or her bairns again. Even Adair would see the tragedy in that when she was told.

Ellen snuggled closer to her husband later that night as he lay snoring by her side. She was not a woman of any great worth, she considered. And Duncan was not a man of any significance. But they had a good home, beautiful bairns, and the favor of Scotland's king. Their granaries were full and their livestock fat. *And I would change nothing*, Ellen thought. She reminisced briefly in her memories of Lochearn, but as the years had passed the clarity of those memories had faded away. Duffdour was her home, and it suited her.

"You're awake." Her husband's voice interrupted her thoughts. "Of what are you thinking?" he asked, and he turned so they might face each other.

"That I love you, and that I could not be happier," Ellen answered him, smiling.

The laird kissed her a long, sweet, and lingering kiss. "Go to sleep, wife," he said softly, and he smiled back at her as he wrapped his arms about her.

"Yes, husband," Ellen answered him, and, safe in his embrace, she closed her eyes to dream of more sons, a red-haired daughter, and of even happier days to come.

Afterword

On the twenty-third of November in the year 1499, Perkin Warbeck was hanged on the charge of attempting to escape from the Tower of London with the last true Yorkist claimant to England's throne, the young Earl of Warwick, who had been imprisoned there for many years.

King James IV of Scotland married King Henry VII's daughter, Margaret Tudor, who gave him his heir. And the second sight he was known to possess, called in his time the eye, never failed him. He died in the summer of 1513 at the Battle of Flodden, perishing along with most of his nobility as they once more fought the English, again led by the Earl of Surrey.

Ninety years later, Scotland overcame its longtime rivals when Henry VII's granddaughter, Elizabeth Tudor, England's queen for over forty years, died, leaving England to James IV's great-grandson, James VI, who became James I of England. But even then there was no real peace in the borders.

Read on for an excerpt from

The Captive Heart,

the next thrilling and passionate
tale in Bertrice Small's Border Chronicles.

Available at penguin.com or
wherever books are sold

The queen knew all was lost. At least for now. Perhaps forever, but no! Not while there was breath in their bodies and their son remained healthy and strong. *They* would not steal Edward Plantagenet's inheritance from him. Not while she lived. No! It was unthinkable that Edward of York would supplant them.

"Madame, we must go now," Sir Udolf Watteson said to the queen.

Margaret of Anjou nodded. *"Oui"* was all she said. She did not look about her. The others would be ready because it was their duty to anticipate what was to come. It would not do to be caught now, and besides, if they were, what was to become of their few remaining retainers? Their loyalty to her deserved better than to be caught and murdered by a pack of Yorkist traitors. The queen drew her heavy fur-lined cloak about her and pulled up its hood. *"Allez!"* she said as she stepped through the farmhouse door.

It was still snowing steadily. Fifteen-year-old Alix Givet followed her mistress, her arm about her physician father. "Are you certain you are warm enough, Papa?" she asked him softly, her hazel eyes concerned.

"I am fine, *mignon*," he told her. "You worry too much."

"You are all I have left, Papa," Alix said as a man-at-arms helped first her father to mount his horse and then boosted her into her saddle. The girl rode astride, for it was easier for her in their flight.

"We will have at least several days of rest before we must move on again," Alexander Givet replied. "I just need a little time to be dry and warm to recover, *ma petite*. This ride will be the worst of it, I promise."

"Where will we go then, Papa?" Alix asked him as she gathered her reins into her gloved hands. "We are being driven from England."

"The queen will ask sanctuary from her distant relation Marie of Gueldres, who is Scotland's queen. It will be granted, and then we shall probably take flight for France. You will finally see Anjou, *ma petite*," he told her. "We still have family there, and I shall make a good match for you, Alix, so you will be safe after I am gone."

"I do not want to marry, Papa. I want to remain with you," the girl told him.

The physician chuckled as they began to move north into the storm. "It is your duty to marry, *mignon*, so your papa may have a warm place by the hearth in his old age," he teased her. "Unless, of course, you wish to enter a convent."

"Nay, Papa, I am not meant for the church," Alix assured him.

"Then we must find you a good and generous husband who will take us both in," Alexander Givet said. "Or perhaps I could find a nice wealthy widow who would have us. But two women in a household is rarely a good thing. And besides, I could never marry again after all my years with your mama."

"Oh, Papa," the girl responded, "why did Mama have to die?"

"Her heart was not strong in these last years," the physician told his daughter. "The strain and the tension surrounding the royal couple over the past months were finally too much for her, Alix. I would have taken her home to Anjou, but she would not hear of it. She loved her mistress, and they had been friends since they were girls. Loyalty to each other was something that both the queen and your mother possessed in abundance." He sighed gustily. "I miss her greatly, *mignon*. Blanche de Fleury was the only woman for me." The tone of his voice was sad, and trembled just slightly as he remembered.

Alexander Givet had met Blanche de Fleury at the court of the Count of Anjou. It was a busy court forever on the move, for Rene, the count, who was also the titular king of Naples and Sicily, and his first wife, Isabelle, the Duchess of Lorraine, were sovereigns without a real throne. The youngest son of minor Anjou nobility, Alexander had become a physician. Brought to the court by his father to gain a place among the count's retainers, he quickly found himself assigned to the household of Yolande of Aragon, the count's mother, who was raising his second daughter, Margaret. He was twenty-two at the time.

Negotiations were already underway for Margaret of Anjou to marry the young king of England. Blanche de Fleury was one of the young girls who had grown up with Margaret of Anjou. She had been brought to the Count of Anjou's court at the age of six. Her mother was dead, her father remarrying, and if the truth be known, she had been considered an encumbrance by her surviving parent. She was three years older than Margaret, but the duchess thought that Blanche de Fleury had beautiful manners and would make a suitable companion for her daughter, Margaret.

At first Blanche was like an older sister to Margaret. But as the young girl grew, the two became friends. When Margaret was sent at the age of twelve to her paternal grandmother to be trained to be a queen, Blanche went with her, as did the young physician, Alexander Givet. But before they departed for Yolande of Aragon's household, it was decided that the young physician should be wed. The count's mother looked among her granddaughter's companions and concluded that the fifteen-year-old Blanche de Fleury was a sensible choice. She sent to the girl's father for his permission, although it was actually no more than a formality since the count approved the match his mother was proposing. It was, Alix's mother later told her, a fortunate match. She was acquainted with the young physician, and like most of the girls in Margaret's circle, Blanche thought Alexander Givet handsome. She was not unhappy to find herself his wife.

Her new husband was, at twenty-five, ten years her senior. And to her surprise, he was interested in what she thought and what she wanted. And Blanche did indeed know what she wanted. She wanted to remain with Margaret of Anjou. In this her husband concurred, for to go to England among the household retainers of its new queen was quite an honor. So Blanche took the potion her husband fed her each morning to prevent any children from being born, and she told no one, not even her confessor. And if the wise Yolande of Aragon suspected, she said nothing. Blanche de Fleury was an excellent influence on her granddaughter, and it was Yolande who made the decision that the physician Givet and his wife would be among those accompanying Margaret to England.

But once in England Alexander and his wife began to long for a child. Perhaps a son who would grow up with their queen's children. But their only child, a daughter, was born to them in April of 1446 while Margaret of Anjou remained childless until 1453. The English king was devout and shy of his young bride, who was acknowledged to be a beauty. Intelligent and vital, the young queen realized her husband's weaknesses at once. Henry was not suited to rule. Still, she became fond of him, and allied herself with the Beaufort-Suffolk faction at court to see her husband's position was protected by his competent relations while he pursued his religious and scholastic leanings, founding Eton College and King's College in Cambridge.

But Henry Plantagenet's weaknesses finally proved too much. His first bout with insanity occurred shortly after the birth of his only son, Prince Edward. In the year that followed, the next man in line for the throne following the king and his infant son, the Duke of York, reigned as Protector. Upon the king's recovery a year later, the queen and Edmund Beaufort, the Duke of Somerset, grew all-powerful. Almost immediately, rivalries between the Lancaster and York factions broke out. Edmund Beaufort was killed at the first battle of St. Albans in May of 1455.

A rough peace of sorts was made, but four years later the hostilities broke out once again. King Henry was captured at Northampton in the summer of 1460, and forced to accept the Duke of York as his heir, eliminating his own son, little Edward Plantagenet. Furious at this attempt to exclude her child from the succession, Queen Margaret rallied the Lancastrian forces and five months later won a victory at Wakefield, where the Duke of York was slain. Two months later the queen's forces won the second battle of St. Albans, freeing the king, who had been held captive by the Yorkists since the previous July.

But the king's victory over his rivals was brief. The Duke of York's heir was crowned King Edward IV two weeks later in London, formally deposing Henry Plantagenet. The new king then went on to drive the old king and his family up the length of England until they reached Towton, where the final battle had taken place. Now Henry Plantagenet, his wife, his son, and their few remaining followers rode north into the borders as the early spring snows swirled about them.

They were relying upon the hospitality of Sir Udolf Watteson, a Northumbrian baron of minor family and no court connections at all. Their brief presence in his home was unlikely to ever be noted by the powers that be because Sir Udolf was one of those unknown factors, being an unimportant man who, until the battle of Towton, had never even laid eyes on King Henry. He had little but his lands, which were rugged and not particularly arable, a stone house of no distinction, and nothing of value that would appeal to anyone. How did you punish a man like that even if those now in power down in London learned of his part in sheltering Henry Plantagenet? But it was unlikely King Edward would ever learn of Sir Udolf Watteson or that he sheltered the former king and his family. In the important scheme of things, the unknown baron didn't matter at all.

The snow fell steadily as horse followed horse. Nose to tail was the only way they were able to keep from getting lost in the storm. At their head, Sir Udolf led them onward until, finally, after almost two hours in the bitter cold and freezing winds, they saw the faint outline of a house ahead of them. Coming to a stop, they waited briefly, but Sir Udolf jumped from his mount and pounded upon the door of the dwelling. It opened, and the faint light of the interior beckoned to them.

"Come in! Come in!" the baron called to them.

And then there were several boys coming to take their horses to the safety of the barns. Alix Givet dismounted from her small mare, patting the beast to comfort it. Its dark mane was frozen stiff. She went to her father's side. He was being helped down from his own gelding and could barely stand. "Lean on me, Papa," she said softly.

"I am rigid with the cold," he murmured quietly, and then came the ominous cough that had been worrying her these past weeks. He balanced himself a moment, his hand upon her small shoulder as he began to walk toward the house with his daughter.

Once inside, they were brought to the hall, where a hot fire was burning in the large hearth. The queen was already warming her hands over it, the little prince by her side. The king had been seated in a high-backed chair near the warmth, and there was quickly a goblet of wine in his hand. His eyes were closed, and Alix could see he was shaking ever so slightly.

"Welcome to my home!" Sir Udolf said. "I have instructed my servants to prepare a place for you. Your Highness," he addressed the queen. "My house is not grand, but you shall have the best I can offer you. My own apartment is yours."

"*Merci*, Sir Udolf," Margaret of Anjou said softly. "Is there to be food soon? The king needs to eat, and then he must be put to bed to rest. This has been a terrible day for him, and he is not well, as you know."

Seeing the expression of distress upon their host's face, Alix spoke up. "Madame, perhaps it would be best if the king were made comfortable first, and a warm supper brought to him," she suggested quietly.

"Ah, *ma chérie* Alix, that would indeed be best," the queen said, sounding relieved, for she herself had suddenly realized that Sir Udolf's cook would not be ready for guests. Margaret of Anjou went to her husband's side. "Henry," she said, "let us go now to our chambers, and Alix, will you watch over little Edward? I see his nurse has fallen asleep, poor woman. She is too old for all this excitement." The queen helped her husband to stand, and then following Sir Udolf's steward, the royal fugitives walked from the hall.

"This is terrible," Sir Udolf said when they were gone. "That the king should be driven from his lands. He is a good man, and she a good queen. I am glad now more than ever to be a simple man. To have so much power that others would covet it is frightening." And he shook his head, sighing.

"I must agree with you, sir," Alexander Givet said from his place near the fire. "But once King Henry's court was a pleasant place to be. He is a learned man."

"What place had you among it all?" Sir Udolf asked, curious.

"I am the queen's physician. I came with her from Anjou many years back with my late wife, who was one of the queen's ladies. The young girl playing now with the prince is our daughter, Alix. My name is Alexander Givet."

"I, too, am widowed," Sir Udolf replied.

"Have you children?" the physician inquired.

"A son, Hayle. He is twenty. His mother and I were wed several years before he was born. Audrey was not strong. She died when Hayle was four, birthing our daughter, who lived but a day. I married again eight years ago, but she turned out to be a nag. I was not unhappy when she died three years later of a winter ailment. I have a farm wife now, who satisfies my manly urges when I need her. I do not need another wife."

Alexander Givet chuckled. "I am widowed two years now, and I have no need for a wife. My daughter takes good care of me, and we are content in the queen's service."

"Tell me, physician," the baron said, "how am I to house the royal party? My house is not large, but I would not stint on anything or appear inhospitable."

"The king, the queen, and their two remaining servants will share your apartment, Sir Udolf. If there is a chamber for the little prince; Edmee, his nurse; and my daughter, the rest of the party will sleep wherever you have the space for us."

"You must have the bedspace nearest the hearth," Sir Udolf said. "You are not well, physician. I hear the rattle in your chest."

"It has been cold for spring," Alexander Givet said.

"The season can be cruel here in Northumbria," the baron admitted. He waved to a servant, who came to stand by his master's side. "Ask the cook when the dinner will be ready, and bring this gentleman more wine," Sir Udolf said. It was pleasant having another man with whom he could talk. He had had some small education in his youth, but his son could not even write his own name or read. Hayle had not wanted to learn, and could be neither forced nor cosseted into doing it. He was not a man to sit talking of a winter's evening. He preferred the company of his little mistress, Maida.

The servant returned to say, "The meal will be ready within the hour, my lord."

Sir Udolf nodded his acknowledgment. "Go upstairs and tell the queen," he said. Then, turning to the physician, he said, "The meal will be simple compared to what you have at court, I fear."

"The king will be content with a good soup and some bread," the physician surprised his host by saying. "He has never been a man to enjoy a heavy, oversauced meal, Sir Udolf. Sauces often hide spoilage of the meat. The king prefers light meals. Watch what the queen eats when she comes to the high board, and you will see her preferences. She has a delicate belly, and always has."

Sir Udolf nodded and gave the orders to his servant. The queen returned to the hall just as the steward announced that the dinner was served. She and her son joined Sir Udolf at the high board while the others took their places at the trestles below. Edmee and the queen's tiring woman, Fayme, sat with Alix and her father. The physician had more color in his face now that he was warm again.

"The queen was pleased with the food they brought the king," Fayme confided to the others. "A nice thick hot soup, fresh bread, butter, and a baked apple. We were able to get him to eat it all. I did not believe in a place so rough there would be good food."

"We're fortunate to have a place at all tonight to lay our heads," Edmee remarked. "My poor wee princeling being robbed of his rightful place and his heritage. Well, if those Yorkist pretenders believe they can hold on to their stolen goods, they're wrong. You mark my words, the queen will see to it, and we'll be back in London before you know it." She popped a piece of meat pie into her mouth. Edmee was an old woman now, at least sixty. No one knew for certain. A hot meal had restored her spirits.

"I do not think that we will be back in London quite so soon," Alexander Givet said quietly. "I know for a fact that the queen means to send to Queen Marie of Scotland and ask for refuge once the storm has stopped. She means for us to shelter in Scotland. Queen Marie must give her refuge, for their shared blood demands it, but she will be able to do little more than that. Her own child has only recently become king, and he is near our prince in age. It will take time to rebuild our king's forces. She might even send her son to Anjou for his own safety. He and his father will now be hunted down with an eye towards killing them both."

"Mary, Jesu, have mercy!" Edmee cried, and she crossed herself. "They would not kill a child, would they?"

"Every moment Henry and Edward Plantagenet live, they present a danger to King Edward of York," the physician answered. "The father they will kill outright when he is caught. The boy will suffer a tragic accident. It is the way of our world, old woman."

Edmee and Fayme crossed themselves again.

"Papa, do not frighten us," Alix said.

"I do not mean to frighten you," Alexander Givet answered her. "It is the truth."

New York Times bestselling author
BERTRICE SMALL

THE CAPTIVE HEART

THE THIRD PASSIONATE ROMANCE IN THE BORDER CHRONICLES SERIES

The year is 1461, and the winds of war rage across England, uprooting Alix Givet, the daughter of Queen Margaret's physician, and the rest of Henry VI's court. Alix's plight becomes bleaker still when, out of duty to her queen, and to her ill, widowed father, she's locked into a loveless marriage to a cruel Northumbrian. But when her luck changes, Alix has another chance to flee—this time to save herself.

Escaping north over the border into Scotland, she throws herself at the mercy of a dark and brooding laird who might provide the everlasting love of her dreams—if she can warm his cold heart.

Available wherever books are sold or at
penguin.com

New York Times bestselling author

BERTRICE SMALL

A DANGEROUS LOVE

An exhilarating new historical romance series begins.

Adair Radcliffe is only a child when her family perishes in the War of the Roses, so her real father, the womanizing King Edward IV, takes her in, honoring his promise to her mother. Once Adair turns sixteen, the king marries her off without her knowledge in a wedding by proxy.

But when tragedy leaves her a widow twice over, Adair realizes that her already tenuous social position has sunk even lower. Now, all she can do is hope that the Scottish laird to whom she is sold will have mercy on her. But little does master or servant suspect that love knows no rank.

Available wherever books are sold or at
penguin.com

THE LAST HEIRESS

BERTRICE SMALL

The fourth book in the popular Friarsgate Inheritance series

A dazzling tale of passion, intrigue, and
seduction, set against the glorious backdrop of
King Henry's sixteenth-century court,
The Last Heiress stars Elizabeth Meredith,
the youngest Bolton daughter, who will risk
everything to protect her beloved Friarsgate.

New York Times bestselling author

BERTRICE SMALL

PHILIPPA

The eldest child of Rosamund Bolton and heiress to the Friarsgate manor, Philippa Meredith is devastated when she discovers that the man she sought to marry has rebuffed her. But it is this sudden change of fortune that sweeps the spirited beauty back to her place in the court of Queen Katherine of Aragon, and into the arms of Crispin St. Clair, the Earl of Witton. But when Philippa stumbles onto a plot to assassinate King Henry VIII, their very love is tested as they attempt to unmask those who are plotting to tear the royal court asunder.

Available wherever books are sold or at penguin.com